HOW TO TEMPT
THE OFF-LIMITS
BILLIONAIRE

JOSS WOOD

THE ITALIAN'S
BRIDE ON PAPER

KIM LAWRENCE

This book is produced from independently certified FSC™ paper
to ensure responsible forest management.

For more information visit www.harpercollins.co.uk/green

MILLS & BOON

First Published in Great Britain 2021
by Mills & Boon, an imprint of HarperCollins*Publishers* Ltd,
1 London Bridge Street, London, SE1 9GF

www.harpercollins.co.uk

HarperCollins*Publishers*
1st Floor, Watermarque Building,
Ringsend Road, Dublin 4, Ireland

How to Tempt the Off-Limits Billionaire © 2021 Joss Wood

The Italian's Bride on Paper © 2021 Kim Lawrence

ISBN: 978-0-263-28262-7

HOW TO TEMPT THE OFF-LIMITS BILLIONAIRE

JOSS WOOD

MILLS & BOON

CHAPTER ONE

Hey, gorgeous, if you're looking for that pretty pink thong, you left it at my place last night. I'm sitting at my desk, it's in my pocket, and I keep remembering how I slid it down your hips…

ROISIN FROWNED, TRYING to make sense of the words when another message popped up on her screen.

You there? Huh, you must be busy. Anyway, just wanted you to know that I had the best time!

Her fingers hit the keyboard with more force than necessary. I'm so glad you had fun, she typed.

FYI, I'm halfway across the world, you cheating scumbag!

Now, sitting on one of the backless, effortlessly sexy couches in the lobby of The Vane hotel, the luxurious hotel owned by her biological brothers, Roisin O'Keefe scrolled through the text messages she'd exchanged with Kelvin since he'd, inadvertently, let the cat out of the bag.

It was an accident. I didn't mean for it to happen.

Yeah, sure. The "accident" defense was old and tired and didn't work because people weren't prone to randomly falling—naked—into other people's arms, and beds.

We've been together since college. You can't just throw us away, Ro!

No, *he'd* thrown *them* away when he decided to play Remove-Her-Panties with the owner of the pretty pink thong.

Kelvin's infidelity hurt—of course it did, she wasn't a robot—but Ro knew that her heart wasn't completely broken. Maybe just a little battered, slightly bruised?

And, under the occasional prickles of pain, there was relief. A lot of it.

And that was partly because she no longer felt obligated to tell her boyfriend that she'd inherited almost a billion dollars from her biological parents a few months before.

She'd dreaded breaking the life-changing news to Kelvin. As a financial advisor, he would've insisted on taking control of the situation, demanding that she let him act as her business representative. He would've freaked at her insistence on giving most of her windfall away and urged her to buy property, shares, upgrade her house, and her car. And *his* house and *his* car. After six years together, and much prodding, he'd finally proposed and she'd spent the next two years nagging him to set a wedding date. Ro had no doubt that, given her change of fortune, he'd want them marrying right away.

Having access to a billion dollars was a hell of an incentive to marry…

She'd initially felt guilty at her cynical thoughts but now, many weeks after her leaving Los Angeles, she knew her instincts about her long-term partner were right. Kelvin was fundamentally, and sadly, untrustworthy.

Pink thong girl was welcome to him.

Another reason to thank the gods she'd kept her life-changing news to herself—she had yet to tell anyone, not even her adoptive parents, about her inheritance—was she knew that, had she told Kelvin and then broken up with him, he wouldn't have hesitated to sell her story to the highest bidder.

And it was a hell of a story. After birthing three sons and plundering one of Africa's oldest and wealthiest family-owned business, the uber-moneyed and infamous South African powerhouse couple, Gil and Zia Tempest-Vane, found themselves pregnant with baby number four. Uninterested in raising another child—not that they'd given their other three children much attention—they gave her, their only daughter, up for adoption in the USA and immediately returned to their licentious lives jet-setting around the world.

For the best part of the next three decades, they frequently hit the headlines and there wasn't a vice they weren't intimately acquainted with: drugs, orgies, infidelities and bad behavior were routinely covered by the international press. Sadly, not even the death of their son tamped down their pleasure-seeking instincts.

Jack was the oldest of Ro's biological brothers and, from what she'd learned, had been an exceptional young man. Whip-smart, athletic and, according to Radd and Digby, responsible, caring and soul-deep honorable. His death from a brain aneurysm shortly after his twenty-first birthday devastated his brothers. Jack was their guiding light, hero and role model. Their rock throughout their tumultuous childhoods.

Jack's death, and Gil and Zia's lack of grief, were the catalysts for Radd and Digby to emotionally, and permanently, divorce themselves from their parents.

Ro couldn't blame them for that. Gil and Zia's domination of the social pages and gossip columns continued unabated. Their deaths in a horrific car accident in California two years ago left a hole in the news cycle and that hole was partly filled by the incessant speculation of who would inherit their enormous estate.

As far as the world knew, Gil and Zia only brought three boys into the world—Jack, Radd and Digby. Nobody knew about their fourth child as Ro's birth and adoption were well-kept secrets. But when they died, Ro, who'd always known she was adopted, learned that she was *their* child—their sole beneficiary, in fact—and that she had two biological brothers.

Right now, nobody could link Ro O'Keefe, American kindergarten teacher, with Gil and Zia Tempest-Vane. And if the press discovered her connection to them, the internet would explode. She would be front-page news worldwide and hounded wherever she went.

That didn't sound like fun.

Ro flipped her phone from hand to hand, thinking that, at some point, she'd have to tell her adoptive parents about her inheritance, but they had their issues they were currently working through. Issues she was also trying to make sense of…

After a thirty-five-year relationship, one adopted child, and a supposedly rock-solid and indestructible marriage, her parents were talking divorce, telling her that they'd drifted apart and now wanted different things and, maybe—*bleurgh*—different people.

As a result, Ro couldn't help questioning her beliefs about love, commitment and marriage. She'd genuinely believed her parents were perfectly matched, the best of friends who enjoyed a happy, passionate marriage.

No wonder she was confused about love and what it was

supposed to be. Until she could make sense of the concept, she intended to avoid men and relationships.

Ro glanced at her watch, thinking that she had a little time before she was due to meet Radd and Digby on the back lawn of their six-star hotel. In summer, when the bright days slid into light, balmy evenings, the hotel staff served sundowners and cocktails to the guests sitting under the huge oak trees dominating the wide swathe of bright green lawn. The fragrance from the graduated rose garden—white to pink to red blooms—drifted over the prosperous guests lounging in comfortable deck chairs and on outdoor settees, content to listen to a string quartet play the classics while watching the light changing on Table Mountain, the famous Cape Town landmark looming over the hotel.

The Vane had recently been voted one of the best hotels in the world, and Ro was proud of her brothers. They'd worked so hard to make the hundred-year-old hotel—one of the many business enterprises they owned—a destination venue.

It was strange to think that her biological parents had met in this hotel, were married in the chapel on the grounds, had their wedding reception in the opulent ballroom upstairs. It was odd to think of Gil and Zia at all, and she was still wrapping her head around the fact that she carried the genes of the world's most famous decadent couple.

Ro crossed her legs and looked down at the harlequin floor, feeling, as she frequently did, like she was standing in a small bucket on a storm-tossed ocean.

Six months ago, she lived a normal, very middle-class life. She worked as a kindergarten teacher, had an active social life with Kelvin, had lunch dates with her girlfriends and juggled the bills every month. Now, in a foreign country and far away from her support structure, she relied on her brothers and their fiancées for support and friendship.

And, thanks to a bulging portfolio of property, art, cars, stock and cash, she was ridiculously, stupendously, insanely wealthy. With one call to the trust's lawyers, she could have tens of millions of dollars transferred to her account and she could buy anything, anywhere, at any time.

Like many people, she'd dreamed of winning the lottery but, honestly, abruptly acquiring a fortune wasn't nearly as much fun as she'd expected it to be.

It should be simple but it wasn't, especially since she had to keep her identity a secret. On hearing about her parentage and inheritance, she'd traveled to Cape Town and applied for a job at The Vane hotel. She had wanted to learn about her biological brothers before revealing who she was, thinking that if she didn't like them, she was under no obligation, legal or otherwise, to reveal their connection.

Digby, on hearing that she was a kindergarten teacher, hired her to look after Olivia, his interior decorator's niece, so that Bay could renovate certain rooms of this hotel. She'd come to know Digby, then Radd, and on finding them as lovely and honorable as Jack was reputed to be, revealed that she was their sister.

But they were the only people who knew and, as a kindergarten teacher and an ex-employee of this hotel, she couldn't be seen tossing money around like confetti without attracting questions and attention.

"Ro-Ro!"

Ro jerked her head up, a smile hitting her face as she watched one of her favorite people in the world, a two-foot-high fairy, barrel across the lobby toward her, pigtails bouncing.

Livvie threw herself into her arms and Ro caught her, swinging her up onto her knee and returning the little girl's rambunctious hug. Over her sweet-smelling head, Ro scanned the lobby, looking for Bay or Digby, Liv's soon-to-be parents. She didn't see either, but she did see Tall, Dark, Ripped and Handsome—dressed in chino shorts and a white expensive linen shirt—heading in her direction.

Ro's gaze slammed into his, her breath hitched and her stomach was invaded by a colony of squirrels on speed. She felt the heat in her cheeks and her womb, and the world faded as the man, six-four, muscles on muscles, headed her way. Her eyes drifted over him, taking in his designer clothes and the sleek watch on his strong wrist. It might be, she suspected, a limited edition Patek Philippe. Or something else ridiculously expensive and exceedingly rare.

He was a study in black and brown, rich, luscious and lovely...

Warm brown skin, black eyes, high cheekbones and a closely cropped beard. Then his eyes moved to Livvie and blindingly white, even teeth flashed as he smiled.

Ro grabbed the edge of the bench, hoping she wouldn't tumble to the floor. She couldn't—not only was she holding Livvie, but she'd also make a fool of herself in front of some of the world's most discerning guests.

She shouldn't be fascinated by anyone, Ro told herself, her thoughts frantic. She was nursing a battered heart, her life was a mess, she had decisions to make and she did not need the complication of being attracted to a sexy, stunning man.

"You must be Roisin," he said when he stopped a few feet from them. His voice was deep, dark and sinful, and Ro felt her skin prickle.

"It's Ro*sheen*, actually, but I prefer to be called Ro," she corrected him as she stood up. She took a deep breath and held out her hand for him to shake. "And you are?"

"Muzi Miya-Matthews," he said, his huge hand swallowing hers. "I'm a very old friend of Digby's."

Her head swam and she took a deep breath, not wanting him to know how much he affected her.

What had they been talking about? Ah, right. He was the wine entrepreneur and CEO; she'd heard Dig mention him.

"I would've thought we would cross paths before," Muzi said, sliding his hands into the pockets of his chinos, the action pulling his shirt tight across his acre-wide chest, "but life has been a little hectic lately."

Ro stroked Livvie's thigh. He ran, she recalled, one of the oldest premier wine and spirits companies in the country and was regarded as one of the country's best vintners. Muzi Miya-Matthews was a force to be reckoned with in the wine industry, so she had to wonder why he was babysitting Olivia. Especially when Digby and Bay knew that they could call on her, and did, whenever they needed childcare help.

She raised her eyebrows. "You and Livvie?"

Muzi held out his hands and Livvie tumbled from Ro's arms into his, squealing when Muzi pretended to drop her. Actually, it was Ro who squealed. Livvie just laughed.

Muzi looked at her, obviously amused, as he held Livvie like he would a rugby ball, tucked under his arm. "Sorry, it's a game we play, the girl is fearless."

Yep, she knew that. Looking after Livvie required an eagle eye. Or ten. "Bay has only been in Digby's life for a couple of months, but you two seem to have a strong connection?"

Hey, she was a teacher, it was her job to be suspicious.

"Digby is my best friend and I'm tight with his family," Muzi replied, running his big hand over Livvie's head. "Digby has known my grandmother Mimi forever and Bay and Mimi have struck up a friendship. I was inspecting the vineyards next to Mimi's house today and Liv and

Bay were there, lunching with her. Liv walked a part of Mimi's vineyard with me and Mimi's dogs while Bay and my grandmother chatted. Bay needed to see a client on the other side of the city this afternoon, so I offered to hand Liv over to Digby." He rubbed his right ear and grimaced. "She talked nonstop for the hour-long journey back."

Ah, okay. That made sense.

Ro watched as Liv rubbed her eyes and before she could tell Muzi that the little girl was exhausted, he took her and propped her on his hip. Liv immediately rested her head on his chest, eyes fluttering closed. Liv never seemed to run out of energy so seeing her fade was a surprise. "How much walking did she do?" Ro asked.

"A lot," Muzi told her. "She felt morally obligated to keep up with Mimi's dogs."

Muzi adjusted the pink backpack on his shoulder and lifted his chin in the direction of the wide French doors that led onto a wraparound veranda. "Digby messaged me to meet him on the back lawn. I presume you are heading in that direction?"

Ro nodded. "Yes, I'm having afternoon drinks with my—"

Ro stopped abruptly, shocked that she'd almost told this man that Digby and Radd were her brothers. The fact that she was Zia and Gil's natural daughter, and that she'd inherited their extensive estate, was highly classified information. If her identity became public knowledge, her life would become intolerable.

"I know that you are Digby and Radd's sister, Ro."

Ro stared at him, her heart in her throat and dread rolling over her. "How do you know that? Nobody knows that!"

Muzi placed his hand on her lower back and gently pushed her out of the way of a group of Italian women, exquisitely dressed. "Digby and I have been best friends since we were thirteen. He knows all my secrets and I know his."

Ro squeezed her eyes together, tasting panic in her throat. "When did he tell you?"

Muzi frowned as he reached past her to open a French door for her. He gestured her to precede him. "Uh…a while back? When he went on that bender, shortly after he discovered who you were."

Digby had taken a while to come to terms with the fact that his girlfriend's nanny was also his sister and the beneficiary of his estranged parents' large trust.

"You can't tell anybody!" Ro placed her hand on his bare, muscled forearm and tried to ignore the heat of his skin, the sparks of desire burning her. "God, why did he tell you?"

Frost touched Muzi's black eyes. "I have yet to break a friend's confidence and I never will."

It was obvious that her lack of trust in him annoyed him but she'd only met the man ten minutes ago! And if her boyfriend of eight years could betray her, she didn't put much faith in the goodness of strangers. Oh, Digby was going to get an earful from her for running his mouth. He had no right to divulge her secrets.

Ro was aware of the wary glances Muzi sent her as they made their way down the stone pathway that meandered through the extensive grounds of The Vane. A gentle breeze blew strands of her long hair into her face, and now and again she inhaled the scent of fynbos drifting down from the mountain, combined with the sweet scent from the many rosebushes and Muzi's earthy, sexy cologne.

It was a potent combination and one designed to make her head swim. Add a sexy, virile, hot-as-hell man to the mix and she was a jumbled mess of desire, resentment, fear and confusion.

Really, being an heiress shouldn't be this hard.

Approaching the tables under the large oak trees, Ro looked for her brothers and on seeing them, headed in their direction. Radd and Digby stood up as she and Muzi, carrying little Liv, threaded their way through the tables. Like her, Radd and Digby were tall, dark-haired and blue-eyed. When the three of them were together, Ro couldn't help wondering how people didn't notice that she was a feminine version of her big, burly brothers.

Ro accepted their hugs—her brothers were super affectionate—and Radd pulled out a chair for her while Digby took a now sleeping Liv from Muzi's strong arms. He looked down at his soon-to-be daughter, his knuckle sliding over her cheek. Then he looked at Muzi and grinned. "Did you make her train for one of your triathlons? She is only three, Triple M."

Triple M? On seeing her confusion, Digby smiled. "Three M and Triple M are Muzi's nicknames from school, since all his names begin with *M*."

Muzi, Miya, Matthews…right, that made sense.

"I take it you two introduced yourselves?" Digby asked, sitting back down in a comfortable chair, Livvie curled up against his chest.

Muzi dropped into a seat and stretched out his long, long muscled legs. "We did. Although your sister is deeply unhappy that I know she is the Tempest-Vane heir."

Digby caught Ro's eye and winced. "Sorry, Ro, but Muzi, well…he kinda knows everything about me."

That's what Muzi said earlier. It didn't assuage her fears. "All it takes is one slip of the tongue and I will become a media sensation. I do *not* want to become a media sensation."

Digby winced again, looking apologetic. Muzi's face remained impassive and when her eyes hit her older brother's face, she saw sympathy in his dark blue eyes.

"Muzi can be trusted to keep your secret, Ro," Radd assured her. "I trust him, and you know how few people I trust."

Ro nodded, her tension lifting. Radd had massive trust issues and his reassurance of Muzi's integrity dampened some of her fears. She looked at the man in question and narrowed her eyes. "If you let my secret slip, I will disembowel you with a blunt teaspoon. Are we clear?"

Amusement touched his eyes and the corners of his lips lifted in an altogether too sexy smirk. "Perfectly."

"Excellent." Digby released a relieved sigh. He gestured to a waiter and asked Ro what she wanted to drink. She ordered a gin and tonic, the men ordered beers, and Ro dug in her tote bag for her pair of sunglasses. She shoved her glasses onto her face, noticing a scratch in the cheap glass.

Now that she had access to so much cash, she could buy a dozen—even a hundred—pairs of designer sunglasses, shoes, bags and clothes. Ro looked down at her off-the-rack blue-and-white sundress and shrugged. She wasn't a shopper, and never had been, so hitting the Platinum Mile of the Victoria & Alfred Waterfront, one of the city's up-market malls, wasn't high on her list of priorities.

She wasn't sure what was.

Maybe it was time she figured that out.

So this was Roisin O'Keefe, the must-be-kept-secret Tempest-Vane sister.

Muzi slid a pair of designer sunglasses over his eyes and, taking a long sip of his beer—his mouth was suddenly as dry as the Namib Desert—eyed her, knowing his dark lenses would hide his scrutiny.

She was—*crap*—breath-stealingly beautiful.

Her hair was long, a fall of loose curls, and an intense shade of dark brown without a hint of red or gold. It was the perfect complement to her creamy, pale skin and her drop-him-to-the-floor blue eyes.

Blue, it was such an insipid description. They were the color of ancient Chinese vases or old-as-hell Egyptian artifacts. Of ancient tiles in mosques all over the Middle East.

Blue had always been his favorite color.

Pulling his gaze off her face, he allowed himself the immense pleasure of letting it trail down her long and lithe body. Her breasts were perfection, her stomach flat, her legs smooth and slightly tanned. And those pretty pale pink toenails, and the delicate ring on her middle digit, killed him.

Muzi did an internal eye roll at his body's reactions. He was thirty-four, had slept with many beautiful women, and it had been a long time since he'd had this sort of reaction to a woman, any woman.

But there was no denying it, she was as sexy as hell... And solidly off-limits.

She was his best friend's sister. And, since she was now the owner of St. Urban, one the oldest vineyards in the Cape Winelands, Ro was also someone he wanted to do business with. No, he *needed* to do business with her...

He needed her vineyard to neutralize Susan Matthews-Reed.

As it always did when he thought of Susan, his gut roiled. She'd been, without exaggeration, the bane of his life for...well, most of his life.

He'd met Mimi Matthews when his poor, far too young mother sent him to live with his maternal grandmother, Lu, who'd worked as Mimi's long-time housekeeper at La Fontaine, Mimi's Cape Dutch house in the Franschhoek Valley, an hour's drive from Cape Town.

He'd been a fatherless three-year-old—he never knew who sired him—confused by his change of circumstances and missing his mother. He'd left a dirt-poor, rural village for one of the wealthiest areas in the country. But with his grandmother Lu he found stability and comfort. Lu and Mimi showered him with love and affection, and he'd blossomed under their attention.

A few months after his eighth birthday, Mimi's only child, Susan, divorced her husband and she and her two sons, Rafe and Keane, moved into La Fontaine. He'd been thoroughly excited to have boys his age in the house and he and Keane immediately bonded. Rafe, older than him, was cool but Susan…well, she was another story.

His grandmother died when he was ten and, along with feeling grief-stricken, he'd also been terrified, not knowing where he was going to live or who was going to look after him. After Lu's funeral, Mimi sat him down, told him his mother signed away all parental rights to him—as an adult, Muzi suspected money had changed hands—and informed him, and the family, that his place was with her. Mimi went on to adopt him and he became, in all the ways that counted, legal and otherwise, hers.

In the valley, he was regarded to be the luckiest child alive, plucked from poverty and obscurity to become part of a powerful, insanely wealthy and influential family steeped in the history and tradition of Cape wine making.

No one, not one soul, knew that Susan emotionally and verbally abused him whenever and wherever she found him alone.

You're not good enough…
You don't belong here…
You're unlovable…

Leaving for boarding school had been a relief and university, where he studied business and wine making, was the best time of his life. After graduating he joined Clos du Cadieux, Mimi's famous wine and spirits company, and Mimi made it clear that he was to be her successor. Susan once again went on the offensive to rid the company and the family of his presence. As a kid, he'd never understood her hatred of him but as an adult, he realized that he was a threat to her and her sons—or rather to their inheritance—and she wouldn't rest until she kicked him out of Clos du Cadieux and out of Mimi's life.

He was a great winemaker and an excellent CEO, but he didn't carry Matthews blood and that, to Susan, was all that mattered.

Muzi sighed, thinking that the past three years as Clos du Cadieux's CEO had been incredibly hard. Mimi's unexpected announcement of her retirement rattled the industry—she was the wine-making world's doyenne—and his appointment as CEO had made waves, people saying he was too young and inexperienced.

After much discussion, the Clos du Cadieux board approved his appointment, but they also elected Susan as the new chairman and her son Keane as a new board member. Susan immediately began making his life hell: openly questioning his decisions, undermining him to senior management and other board members and generally being a complete pain in the ass.

Her goal was to have complete control of her family's—Mimi's—assets, interests and influence, and he, "the grandson of Mimi's housekeeper, a nobody, for God's sake," stood in her way.

She was smart, ruthless and convincing. And persistent. Worst of all, she'd managed to turn Keane, technically his nephew but emotionally his brother, against him.

As the Tempest-Vane siblings talked, Muzi rubbed his chest, feeling like there was a knife lodged in his heart, reminding him that if you didn't let people in, they couldn't hurt you. And after putting up with Susan's mind games for thirty years, could he be blamed for thinking that being alone was safer? He'd earned the right to fear rejection and never again wanted to experience being emotionally abandoned. Muzi tightened his grip on his beer glass.

He couldn't go there, didn't want to wander down that mental vortex, so he returned his thoughts to business, to what he could control.

Last year the COVID crisis had hit their industry hard, and Susan was using the dip in company profits and turnover as a sword, telling the board that an older and more experienced CEO would've steered the company better through the crisis. Unfortunately, many of the board members were listening.

Muzi knew his ass was on the line.

But he had an idea of how to save it...

Muzi rolled his beer glass between his big hands, acknowledging that, if he wanted to, he could step down from Clos du Cadieux tomorrow and not look back. He had various business interests to keep him occupied and he wasn't short of cash. Actually, that was a huge understatement. When Radd and Digby had sold the innovative internet payment system they developed, and which he'd invested in, he'd become an instant billionaire, so he had enough money to last him several lifetimes.

But Clos du Cadieux was his passion—vineyards and wine the loves of his life. He adored Mimi and knew she was counting on him to continue her legacy of bringing fine wine to the marketplace. He loved the industry, loved his job, enjoyed the combination of science and art, agriculture and sophistication. Clos du Cadieux, the brands and the vineyards it owned, was his life and he refused to be ousted by a petty, insecure, spoiled snob with delusions of grandeur.

If he could add the old St. Urban winery—and assuming he found acres of C'Artegan, a rare, old-world vine on the property—to Clos du Cadieux's portfolio, and develop an exciting, new and stunning wine from those long-forgotten vines, his position within the company would be cemented. He'd be all but untouchable. He'd had his eye on the vineyard for years but Zia Tempest-Vane, who had inherited the vineyard from her mother, refused to sell the property. When she died it became part of the trust she and Gil left behind. With Ro inheriting their assets, he could finally reopen negotiations.

What should be a simple transaction—he was prepared to pay whatever he had to in order to acquire the two-hundred-year-old vineyard, its antiquated cellars and Dutch gable house—could become tricky. Because Ro was extraordinarily beautiful, and he was insanely attracted to her.

She was also his best friend's sister and not even Digby knew he needed her vineyard to cement his position at Clos du Cadieux…

It was all so damn complicated. He'd only ever admit this to himself, but he was terrified of anything that made him feel too much. Emotion and connection, and the losing thereof, led to heartache.

He'd had enough of that in his life, thank you very much.

"How did your meeting with the lawyers go today, Ro?" Radd asked his sister as Muzi pulled his attention back to their conversation.

Ro bit the inside of her lip, looking unsure. Muzi placed his hands on the arms of his chair and started to rise. "I can go if you guys want to have a private conversation."

Ro shook her head. "Since you already know my biggest secret, I don't have a problem with you hearing the details."

Muzi sat back down and Ro looked at Radd, then Digby, and wrinkled her very pretty nose.

"Siya Mabaso, my lawyer, arranged to have Gil and Zia's possessions moved to a warehouse in LA in preparation for the auction. Their house in Carmel has been sold. I've accepted offers for the apartment in New York, the house in the South of France, and the villa on St. Bart's."

Gil and Zia had shown the world how much wealth a couple could acquire when one drained a hundred-plus-year-old company of all its assets, Muzi thought.

"I've been in touch with the representative of Murphy International, and they are going to handle the auction of the art, cars and collectibles. I had a video call with her and she said that Carrick Murphy is personally going to oversee the auction. As I said, if you guys don't want any of their possessions—" Muzi knew that neither of the brothers wanted anything from their parents "—then the proceeds of the sale of the movables and the properties will be donated to the Tempest-Vane Foundation."

"Please don't feel obligated to do that, Ro," Radd quietly stated. "It's a generous offer but you are their heir, it's now your money and you can do whatever you want with it."

"I don't need money, I need answers." Ro stared down at her hands, delicate with long fingers and unvarnished nails. Muzi watched as confusion chased hurt across her face. "I wish I knew why they gave me up for adoption. I mean, it wasn't like they didn't have the money to feed and clothe me, educate me."

Muzi met Digby's eyes and saw the pain within him, the flash of temper and then, devastation. Muzi knew his anger and grief were no longer for him, but for his sister. Ro had no idea—and would never know, if her brothers had their way—that she was tossed aside, given away because she was of no monetary value to them.

Per Digby, a Tempest-Vane grandfather or great-grandfather, noticing that Gil Tempest-Vane was the only male left to carry the T-V name and genes, promised Gil two million dollars—a fortune back then—for every male child he sired. Zia cooperated and they produced three boys for the family tree, boys they went on to ignore and neglect.

But a girl didn't come with a monetary payout, so she was given up for adoption.

Bastards.

Radd and Digby were determined that Ro never learned the truth of why she was given up for adoption. Muzi knew they were trying to protect her, but he thought that if Ro found out after the fact, and from someone else, their brand-new, still fragile ties would fray. He thought the brothers were playing with fire, but this wasn't his family and, because he would never tolerate them shoving their noses into his business, he kept his opinion to himself.

Digby and Radd were just trying to protect Roisin— they were good brothers, good men—and he envied them their close relationship, their friendship. His relationship with the man he'd been raised with, the man he considered to be *his* brother was now, thanks to Susan, broken.

Ro's expression turned troubled. "Siya also told me that he's had quite a few requests from a reporter asking him to comment on rumors that the heir is in the country."

Radd frowned. "They are determined to learn the truth."

"I'm worried that you are not going to be able to hide your identity forever, Ro," Digby told her.

"I'm going to damn well try." Ro lifted her chin, charmingly defiant. "I just need a few more months to get a handle on the business of the trust and then I can return to the States."

Muzi's body tensed at her statement and he felt the urge to protest. What the hell was that about? Why was he reacting like this on hearing about her plans? He'd met her twenty minutes ago, dammit!

"What are you going to do with your South African–based properties?" Muzi asked, keeping his tone casual.

Ro frowned and looked at Radd, then Digby. "I own properties in South Africa?"

"Quite a few, actually," Radd replied, amused. "There's a mansion in Johannesburg, an apartment in Camps Bay and a vineyard, St. Urban, on the outskirts of Franschhoek. Didn't Siya tell you about them?"

Ro rubbed her forehead with the tips of her fingers. "I'm sure he did but I haven't taken it in. I simply told him to put everything on the market."

This was Muzi's opening and he was going to take it. "That's excellent news because I want to buy St. Urban."

CHAPTER TWO

IN DIGBY'S STUNNING converted barn situated right on the edge of The Vane's extensive grounds, Ro curled up into the corner of a plump couch, cradled a glass of red wine to her chest and stared out into the night, the same few thoughts tumbling around her tired brain.

Muzi Miya-Matthews wanted to buy her vineyard, a property she didn't know she owned until yesterday. She couldn't stop thinking about the big, bold, beautiful and built man.

Reporters were still trying to discover the identity of the Tempest-Vane heir.

She was camping out in her brother's house...

She wasn't in Kansas anymore.

Feeling overwhelmed, Ro sipped her wine, reluctantly admitting that she didn't know who she was anymore, what she wanted or how to get there. She wasn't naive enough to believe that, after she'd rid herself of Gil and Zia's properties and possessions, she could go back to living the subdued life of a kindergarten teacher. Even when all the legalities were wrapped up and she'd donated hundreds of millions to charity, bought herself a house, and put enough money away for any future kids' college education and her and her parents' retirement, she'd still be ridiculously, mind-blowingly wealthy.

And how would she explain that to the people she loved and the people who loved her? Her parents, Kelvin, her girlfriends and colleagues?

No, she didn't owe Kelvin any explanations anymore. She could, to an extent, hide her wealth from her friends and coworkers but she would have to explain her change of circumstances to her parents. She couldn't keep the secret from them forever.

But for now, she'd take her lawyer's advice to keep mum.

Loose lips, he'd said, caused problems, and her mother, God bless her, had no filter between her brain and mouth.

But Muzi Miya-Matthews, wholly unconnected to her, knew all about her…and Ro didn't know how to feel about that.

He also wanted to buy her vineyard. The vineyard she knew nothing about.

Ro jumped up and wandered over to the sleek dining table where she'd tossed piles of documents. Siya, her lawyer, had compiled a list of the properties she'd inherited, and Ro scrabbled through the files to find the document containing descriptions and photographs of the trust's assets.

She found the file on the floor, underneath a pile of bank statements. Walking back to the couch, she turned on the side lamp and flipped open the binder, appreciating the color-coded tabs: US Property Holdings, European Property Holdings, African Property Holdings. She flipped to the relevant spot, skimmed over the pictures of the mansion in Sandton, Johannesburg, the flat in Camps Bay, minimalist but with amazing views of the Atlantic seaboard, and finally, right at the end, she came across the description of the St. Urban vineyard.

It was, she read, situated at the foot of the towering

Simonsberg Mountain. It was an "iconic, thatched-roof, whitewashed, historic gabled manor house" constructed in 1799, and now declared a house of historic interest. His brief notes continued... The property included one hundred and twenty-five acres planted with Merlot producing vines. Siya was also currently investigating the state of the house, vineyard and cellars to get an accurate market value.

Ro looked at the photograph of the house, dominated by an imposing, jagged-tooth mountain that looked to be situated just beyond its back door. The vines ran up toward the house and it looked picture-perfect, serene and comfortable. Rich and luxurious.

Why did Muzi want this property? From the little research she'd done since receiving his offer, she understood that, after been hard hit by the pandemic, the wine industry was still in a precarious position. Many vineyards were up for sale, production was down and the market was unstable. And Clos du Cadieux, as per an article she'd read, was cutting costs and streamlining their production.

So what was behind his desire to buy St. Urban? It didn't make sense, business or otherwise. What did Muzi know about St. Urban that she didn't?

Ro heard the beep of an incoming message on her phone, picked it up from the cushion beside her and glanced at the screen.

I messed up, I'm so, so sorry. Please don't throw away nearly eight years because I was an idiot.

Kelvin, again.

Ro rubbed the back of her neck and tasted betrayal in the back of her throat. He'd thrown them away, not her. She dropped back to rest against the arm of her couch and remembered their first date, first kiss and the first time they slept together. Despite her inexperience, she'd always felt completely comfortable with Kelvin.

The truth was that he'd never made her feel half as out of control as Muzi Miya-Matthews did yesterday. Muzi's warm eyes had her quivering and his voice, a deep, sexy baritone, set off fireworks on her skin. He'd only touched her to shake her hand, but his palm had been broad, his grip strong and his effect on her instantaneous. She'd wanted to slap her mouth against his sexy lips, curl her hand around his strong neck, shove her hand under his shirt to see whether he had a six-or eight-pack.

Bite one, or both, his big biceps...

She'd never had such a primal, visceral reaction to a man and, instead of daydreaming about him, she should be concentrating on her topsy-turvy life. She had decisions to make, a life plan to make, a path to construct. She had no plans to return for Thanksgiving but she should be thinking about flying back to the States for Christmas, only six weeks away, and how to broach the subject of her birth and inheritance with her parents. They thought she was taking time to travel before she married. She needed to tell them the truth, discuss their possible divorce and tell them she was never going to marry the man they considered to be a son.

But she wasn't ready to return to LA. Not quite yet.

Ro looked down at the picture of St. Urban and tapped her index finger on the page, still feeling rattled.

She could stay in Digby's house for as long as she wanted—he and Bay had bought a mansion in Constantia and were settling into their spacious, exquisite house—so there was no pressure on her to move. But, with the holiday season approaching, and the country's long summer holidays just around the corner, The Vane would be overrun with tourists.

Radd and Digby sat on the top rung of Cape Town society and constantly invited her to their A-list events, including the ballet, horse races and exclusive balls and cocktail parties. She refused all their entreaties, reminding her new family that Cape Town society would be insanely curious about their new friendship, and who she was, and where she came from. Mostly, they'd want to know why, and how, she came to be close to the famous Tempest-Vane's so quickly.

No, it was better for her to fly under the radar.

She was, she admitted to herself, so very tired. In the last six weeks, she'd gone from being Digby's employee to having siblings, had moved into Digby's fantastic converted barn, had fifty million meetings with her lawyers, discussed the auction to death and had an offer to buy one of her properties from a delicious man with secrets in his eyes.

She was overwhelmed and out of her depth and she needed a break, a time-out, a lot of peace and quiet, and space to think.

She might just find all of that at St. Urban. And while she was there, maybe she could figure out why Muzi Miya-Matthews wanted to buy her vineyard.

Muzi steered his brand-new Lamborghini Urus down the road leading to St. Urban and resisted the urge to place his hand on his heart to keep it inside his chest cavity.

He wasn't faint of heart. He routinely competed in extreme triathlons and had joined Digby on some of his more harebrained adventures—big wave surfing in Hawaii, hiking to the rim of the active Cerro Negro volcano and splashing around in Devil's Pool at the top of Victoria Falls, where a slippery rock was the only barrier between life and a one-hundred-meter plunge. But he was still recovering from an early morning call from Ro inviting him to accompany her to St. Urban and give her a tour of the property.

Would that, she'd politely asked, be something that might interest him?

His answer had been an immediate hell yes! On ending the call with Ro, he'd instructed his PA to reschedule a conference call with an international distributor and to postpone his other meetings, and he left Clos du Cadieux's headquarters to collect her from Digby's old house at the back of The Vane hotel.

"Have you been to St. Urban before?" Ro asked him, half turning in her seat to look at him.

"Once, a long time ago, but only to visit the vineyard. I've never been inside the house," Muzi told her. "It was part of a field trip I did in the second year of my enology and viticulture degree."

Ro winced. "Uh…in English please?"

He smiled. "Enology is the study of wine. Viticulture is the study of grape cultivation."

"As CEO, how much wine making do you do for your company?"

Muzi grimaced. "Not as much as I'd like to." Actually, that wasn't true, he hadn't done any R & D for the past eighteen months. They employed experienced vintners and most of his time was taken up with running the business and trying to outmaneuver Susan. "Making wine is the best part of the job, to be honest."

A faded sign with missing letters indicated the turnoff to St. Urban and Muzi drove onto the dirt road. Ro looked to the left and pointed to the rows and rows of vines. "Are those mine—I mean, the trust's?"

"I'd imagine so," Muzi replied, steering his limited edition, stupidly expensive SUV over a large hump in the road and trying not to think about scratches on his undercarriage.

"I think those are the Merlot vines," Muzi told her, as they approached a large electric gate. God, he hoped it opened—he didn't feel like climbing the gate in his five-hundred-dollar shoes and tailored, designer Italian suit to wrestle with its manual override. He'd do it, he just didn't *want* to.

Muzi parked in front of the gate and rested his wrist on the steering wheel. "Please tell me that you have a remote control for that gate?"

Ro dug in her large tote, pulled out a set of keys and lifted the remote to point it at the gate. Muzi held his breath and after what felt like the longest time, the gate opened with a series of creaks and groans. Good deal, Muzi thought.

He was about to drive on when Ro placed her hand on his thigh. "Hold on a sec... I need to ask you something."

Unless she removed her hand, he wouldn't be able to think of anything but moving her hand a few inches higher. Yep, around her his brain shut down and all he could think about was tasting her wide mouth, exploring her soft, pale skin.

Ro lifted her hand to brush her bangs out of her eyes and Muzi took a slow, deep breath.

She's off-limits, Triple M. Remember that.

"Why do you want this property?"

Muzi frowned, caught off guard. "Sorry?"

Ro's eyes narrowed to slits of deep blue. "You heard me. I looked online and there are many vineyards for sale in this area alone and the reason everyone is selling is because the wine industry is struggling to survive. Most vineyards are cutting back, not expanding so...why do you want this property?"

Muzi ran his hand over his head, silently cursing. He'd underestimated her. Ro was obviously smarter and more insightful than he'd given her credit for. He shouldn't be surprised. After all, her brothers were two of the smartest guys on the planet.

He needed to give her an explanation, one she could believe. If he found C'Artegan vines on this property, he'd be the one to bring wine made from a thought-to-be extinct old-world grape to the market. The Clos du Cadieux board would kiss his damn feet if he achieved that and his position in Mimi's company would be unassailable. He didn't want to lie but he was reluctant to tell her about his quest in case the news leaked and Susan found a way to spike his plans.

"You are obviously looking for an explanation I will buy," Ro told him, her voice frosty. "If you don't want to tell me then just say so."

Okay, then. "I don't want to tell you."

At his blunt statement, hurt flashed across her face. He watched, fascinated, as she sat up straight and primly crossed her legs, staring straight ahead. "Fine."

He was old enough to know that when a woman said fine in that tone of voice, she was anything but. Crap, how could he fix this?

Before he could say anything, Ro turned and handed him a tight smile. "You are the only person, apart from my brothers and their partners, who knows who I am, who knows about my changed circumstances. You know my biggest secret, something my parents don't even know… but, sure, keep your little secret about *my* property."

Dammit. She had him between the tips of a sword and a spear.

Muzi stared out his window, seeing the weeds between the neglected vines. If he told her, and Susan found out, he'd be risking his future Clos du Cadieux plans. But, really, given the huge secret she was keeping about her identity, he doubted she'd let his secret slip.

But trust was hard, it was something that had to be earned. And he made people work harder than most. Sharing information was also difficult; he was a guy who preferred to keep his own counsel. Talking always made him feel like he was standing on a mile-high precipice waiting to fall to a stone slab below.

Ro released an annoyed huff. "Just drive, Muzi."

Instead of obeying her terse command, Muzi jerked his head toward the overgrown vines. "How much do you know about wine and grapes and cultivars?"

Ro half turned in her seat to face him, her expression puzzled. "I know grapes make wine. And that I own a wine farm and that I like wine," she replied. "So, basically, nothing."

He thought as much. "Right. A 'cultivar' is a grape variety that has been selectively cultivated to produce a certain type of wine. The vines beyond that fence produce Merlot."

Ro nodded, interest bubbling in her fabulous eyes.

"Bear with me because I need to give you a quick history lesson. In Languedoc in France, sometime in 1863, a farmer discovered that something was killing his vines. The blight and destruction spread through France and into other countries in Europe and they eventually discovered it was the phylloxera aphid causing the damage. Over fifteen years, the wine industry in Europe was decimated, and France was the hardest hit. Many old and rare cultivars were annihilated."

"That's very interesting but how does it relate to St. Urban?" Ro asked.

"I did my master's thesis on lost cultivars and I tracked down some documentation suggesting that one of your ancestors brought back a cultivar from France before the phylloxera outbreak. A cultivar that was supposedly wiped out in Europe. The cultivar is called C'Artegan."

"And you want to find this cat...cart...cultivar?"

He smiled at her mispronunciation of the word. "Yep. I'm sure St. Urban has C'Artegan vines."

"Surely someone would've discovered it by now?" Ro asked, sounding doubtful. "I mean, can't you just walk the land and see whether there are different types of vines?"

"There are some obvious differences between cultivars, but there are only subtle differences between the Merlot and C'Artegan. Those differences all but disappear when the vines are diseased or have been neglected. Nobody from your family has farmed this land since the 1920s and it's very possible that information on the C'Artegan cultivar was lost and everybody has simply assumed that all the vines are Merlot."

Ro crossed a long slim leg. She wore a short-sleeve minidress in a deep green, covered with tiny flowers, a fun and flirty dress that didn't suit her oh-so-serious face. "And because of a hunch, and some vague documentation, you want to buy this property?"

There was still a lot of skepticism in her voice and Muzi didn't blame her, it sounded like—it *was*—a long shot.

Muzi put his car into gear and accelerated away. "I did a trip to France and researched the cultivar. There wasn't much information but I did find out that C'Artegan grapes produce a soft, intense, marvelous red. It doesn't have a great yield and the vines are as finicky as all hell to grow, which is why few farmers planted the vines. But, when you get it right, the wine is fantastic."

Muzi looked over the Merlot vines with a critical eye, thinking they weren't looking too bad. The vines had been leased to a neighbor for the past thirty years, but Gil and

Zia's death had ended the agreement. It wouldn't take much effort to make them productive again and he'd had a connection in the dried fruit industry who'd buy any grapes Clos Du Cadieux didn't use.

And somewhere within the chaos were, he was convinced, C'Artegan vines.

"If they are so tricky to grow, why do you want them?" Ro asked as he took a turn to the right and caught a glimpse of a large gable peeking through the trees.

"Because I am one of the few winemakers who knows exactly how to handle the vines," Muzi said. "Clos du Cadieux has a couple of hectares of rare cultivars—not C'Artegan though—and the wine I've made from their harvests have not only commanded huge prices but also have won some international awards. If I can make a few cases of red from an old, supposedly eradicated cultivar, I'd cause a splash on the international wine scene and that would be very good publicity for Clos du Cadieux."

And he'd cement his position in the company and be able to shut Susan down for good. The board would never boot a CEO who brought a new, fantastic wine from a rare cultivar to the market. "So, that's the story of why I want to buy your vineyard. Are you going to sell it to me?"

Ro shrugged and smiled. "Can I at least see the property before you wrest it from my grubby hands?"

Muzi heard the note of amusement in her voice and relaxed. She wasn't emotionally attached to the property and she had no reason to keep it. He had a good chance of acquiring the land…

He wished he had as good a chance of getting her into bed.

Best friend's sister. Someone you're doing business with. Keep your focus on what is important, dude.

"Do you know anything about the property?" Ro asked

him, as the road turned away from the house and followed a small stream that ran through the farmland.

"A little," Muzi replied. "From the research I've done, the property has been passed down through the female side of your mother's family."

"Zia Tempest-Vane just carried me, my mother lives in Los Angeles," Ro told him, through gritted teeth.

So she wasn't a fan of her birth parents. Noted. "Zia's family came to this area in the late 1820s and they planted the vines they brought over from the Loire Valley in France. They grew wealthy and at some point built the house, the cellars and a second Cape Dutch gable house on the property. Zia inherited the property when she was quite young, in her early twenties, but from what I can gather, she was never interested in the property. I doubt she even visited St. Urban."

"I find myself admiring her more and more each passing day."

Muzi smiled at her sarcasm. "The house has been closed up since your maternal great-grandmother's death and the land leased to winemakers in the area. That's pretty much all I know."

"It's a good start," Ro replied. "I know quite a bit about the Tempest-Vane history, but I know little about Zia's family."

"And you want to?" Muzi asked.

Ro lifted one feminine shoulder. "Yeah, I think I do, just to get a better handle on who they were and where I came from."

Muzi remembered the pile of bags he'd thrown into his car's trunk earlier. "So, are you planning to stay at St. Urban for a while?" he asked.

"I think so."

Muzi winced. "I don't know if that's a good idea. You

don't know what state the house is in. Hell, I'm not sure if the utilities are connected."

Ro's eyes widened. "Seriously?"

"Did you not hear me when I said that the place has been locked up tight for decades?"

"Great," Ro muttered. "Well, if I can't stay here then I'll find a hotel in town."

Muzi wondered whether he should tell her that there was a popular music, arts and food festival in town this weekend and doubted she'd find a vacancy. He shrugged. If necessary, he'd drive her back to Cape Town. It was only an hour away, or, if she wanted to stay in the area, she could move into one of the many guest rooms at his vineyard on the other side of the valley.

Or into his bed…

Not helpful, Triple M.

Ro fiddled with the clasp of her bag as Muzi turned right to steer the Urus down another narrow, oak-lined road. He caught a flash of white and after another turn and fifty feet, the entire house came into view.

Ro released a surprised squeal and Muzi turned to look at her, expecting to see her dismayed expression. But Ro's eyes were soft with wonder, her generous mouth curved into a wide smile. He felt the power of her smile down to his toes and it took everything he had not to cover her mouth with his.

Damn, keeping his hands off his best friend's sister was going to be a hell of a task.

"I'm seeing a house falling apart so I'm not sure why you are smiling, Ro," he said, bringing the car to a smooth stop.

Ro pointed at the jagged-tooth mountain that loomed up behind the house, sunlight highlighting its many cracks and crevasses. Beyond the mountain, the sky was iris blue, a particularly African, intense shade of blue. It was a beautiful mountain, Muzi admitted, thinking that he was either super jaded, spoiled or ridiculously single-minded if he didn't notice the breathtaking scenery.

Possibly a combination of all three.

"I have to say, its setting is near perfect," Muzi said, resting his forearms on the steering wheel and peering up through the windshield. Two martial eagles were riding the thermal winds high above him and he wished he had a pair of binoculars to get a better look at the majestic birds.

"That's my house?"

Muzi turned his head to look at her profile, taking in her open mouth and wide eyes. Following her gaze, he winced at the once grand, now obviously neglected, house.

It wasn't an exaggeration to say that the house looked a little dismal. The whitewashed walls were gray and dingy, the thatch looked like it needed to be replaced two decades ago, and the once green shutters on the windows were warped and, in one case, falling off.

"Um…well, that looks nothing like the picture the lawyers showed me," Ro said, her voice faint.

Muzi tipped his head to the side. The house looked like a grand old lady who'd fallen on hard times. He looked at Ro. "Do you still want to go in?"

"I suppose I should," she replied, her expression dubious.

Muzi nodded, left his SUV and walked around the hood to open her door. He held out his hand to help her out and electricity crackled between them. His eyes met hers and he saw the sexual interest in her gaze, the heat of desire turning her cheeks pink. Man, it didn't help to know that she was as into him as he was her. God, how the hell was he going to resist her? And he had to. They had business to conduct and Digby would rip his head off if he treated her as he did all his one-night stands and brief flings—with kindness and respect but absolutely no promises, suggestions or hints for the possibility of more.

He didn't need a special person in his life, he was stronger on his own. Because, as he'd learned, if you kept people at a distance they couldn't hurt you.

Muzi dropped Ro's hand abruptly and ignored her look of surprise. Sliding his sunglasses onto the top of his head, he gestured for her to precede him to the front door. The huge door, once the same dark green shade of the windows, looked bent and buckled. Muzi suspected he'd need to use his shoulder to budge it from its frame.

Ten minutes later, after much swearing, his shoulder aching from repeated contact with the old door, they stood in the dank, dark hallway, dust tickling his nose. He looked around, taking in the grimy walls. His big feet hit a carpet and dust flew up his nose, causing him to sneeze. Drop cloths covered various pieces of furniture and Muzi doubted this room had seen fresh air for the best part of forty years.

Whatever plans Ro had for the mansion, she was going to need a hell of a lot of help.

CHAPTER THREE

RIGHT...WELL, THIS wasn't good.

Ro watched Muzi flick up an old light switch and nothing happened. There was a small chance that the light bulb was blown but it was more likely that the house had no electricity.

Completely fabulous. Using the flashlight on her phone to guide her through the shadows, Ro walked toward an open door leading off the hallway and into what she presumed had once been a smart reception room. The wooden floor was covered with dust and big furniture sat under falling-apart drop cloths. Pictures hung on the wall, covered in a thick layer of dust and grime, so much so that she was unable to make out the subjects of the paintings.

Ro slapped her hands on her hips and did a slow circle, her heart in her throat. It was becoming obvious she wouldn't be staying here tonight and, even if she had water and electricity, sleeping in a bed covered in forty years' worth of dust didn't appeal.

She should just sell the place to Muzi and be done with it. It was the simplest, most efficient solution. He could deal with the dilapidated house and the overgrown vineyards. And if he found his elusive cultivar, good for him.

Hearing Muzi behind her, she turned and sent him a tremulous smile. "This isn't what I expected," she said.

Muzi folded his big arms across his chest. "It's a dump," he bluntly told her. He gingerly picked up one corner of a filthy cloth and lifted it to show her the corner of the ten-foot-long credenza pushed up against the far wall. He whistled. "But this, I think, is yellow wood and very old. I suspect that there might be a lot of valuable antique furniture in this place."

Ro walked over to the tall windows and lifted her hand to pull back the faded red velvet curtains. She hesitated. They looked like they might fall apart if she so much as breathed in their direction. But they needed light to see what they were doing, so she took a deep breath, pulled the curtain to the side and found herself smothered by a dust saturated pile of ancient fabric. She screamed and tried to push the fabric away and found herself more tightly entangled in musty velvet.

Sucking in a mouthful of dust, she coughed, desperate for fresh air. What she got was another hit of dirt and she coughed again.

Pinpricks of light danced behind her eyes. She was on the point of passing out when Muzi whipped the fabric off her and she could breathe again.

Ro sucked in a couple of gulps of fresh air and, keeping her hands on her knees, looked up at Muzi. "Thanks."

"Are you okay?" he asked.

Was that a trace of amusement she heard in his voice? Squinting, she saw the quiver of his lips, the warmth in his eyes. "What's so funny?"

"You look like a walking, breathing dust mite," Muzi said, his laughter flowing over her. Oh, yeah, his smile could power the sun. And, beneath his short beard, she saw the hint of two sexy dimples. Dimples were her kryptonite...

"And you have spiderwebs in your hair," Muzi pointed out.

Spiders? *Aargh, no!* Freaking out, Ro lifted her hands

to her head, bent over at the waist and fluffed up her hair, hoping to dispel the webs and, more important, their manufacturers.

"Do you think they're all gone?" Ro asked from behind her curtain of hair.

Ro felt his fingers in her hair, a long curl sliding through his hand. "Yep."

Ro tossed her hair back and met his eyes, dark, deep and oh so intense.

Later on, she asked herself who made the first move, him or her, but in the fraction of a second, his lips were on hers, his hand found her lower back and he pulled her into his big, strong, hard-everywhere body. Her hand curled around the back of his strong neck and his mouth tasted like peppermint and coffee. In his arms, she felt safe and secure, protected.

And yeah, his desire for her, long, thick and hard and pushing against her stomach, was hard to miss.

By their own volition, Ro's hands slid up and tugged his shirt from the band of his pants, then glided under the expensive cotton, and she sighed as they skimmed over his muscled back, the deep dip of his spine. He was so warm, heat poured off him and flowed into her, making her feel like she was walking into a welcoming fire.

His mouth plundered hers and she responded with as much passion, wondering where this need to inhale him, climb inside him, came from. Needing to be closer, she pressed her breasts firmly against his chest, felt the deep groan in his throat and silently rejoiced when he bent his knees to wrap his arm under her butt. He lifted her easily and it felt completely natural to wind her legs around his trim waist. Muzi carried her to the credenza and lowered her to sit on the sideboard, his hands on her thighs, encouraging her to keep her legs wrapped around his waist. Holding her on the edge of the piece of furniture, Ro whimpered when his erection brushed against the thin fabric of her panties, her dress riding up to the top of her thighs.

Muzi stepped back, creating just enough space for him to bracket her face with his strong hands. "You are so damn beautiful," he whispered against her lips.

How could he talk when so much electricity coursed between them, when the air around them, the dust and the dirt, seemed charged with energy?

She was without words, she was simply a big mess of need and want, punch-drunk with desire.

"Just kiss me, Triple M," she murmured, her thumb running down the cord in his neck.

She caught a glimpse of that sexy smirk, saw his head dip to obey her command but then he, without any warning, rapidly spun away from her to release a huge sneeze.

Then another.

Teetering on the edge of the credenza, terrified that she'd tumble off, Ro scooted backward and winced at the feel of dust and dirt against the back of her bare thighs. Thinking that it was more hygienic to jump down, she landed on her feet and...

Muzi sneezed again. And again.

He looked at her with streaming eyes. "I think I have a dust allergy," he croaked.

"I think you're right," Ro agreed, rubbing her hands on the skirt of her dress, wincing at the brown streaks on the fabric. Muzi didn't look much better—his cream shirt showed dusty marks and handprints from her hands running down his wide chest. The back of his shirt would be the same.

Cape Dutch mansion, one. Muzi and Ro? A big, fat zero.

Muzi took her hand and pulled her from the room. "We need fresh air and you need to get the electricity and water reconnected before you set foot in this house again. And when you do, I hope it's after you've had a tetanus shot and you're accompanied by a cleaning company armed with industrial-sized vacuum cleaners."

After crossing the hall, Ro pulled the front door closed behind her and sucked in the brisk fresh air outside. "That sounds like an excellent plan."

Looking down at her grubby hands, she grimaced. "Ugh."

"I have wet wipes in the car," Muzi told her. "Hang tight."

Within minutes he was back with a pack of wipes and two bottles of water. Ro thanked him, yanked out a couple of wipes and attacked her dusty hands. When they were clean, she wiped her face and neck and grimaced. "I'd kill for a shower," she murmured, "but I doubt any hotel in Franschhoek would accept me looking like this."

"You look fine but that's not your biggest problem," Muzi explained, wiping his hands. "There's a festival happening in town this weekend and I doubt there's a vacancy anywhere."

Ro stared at him, her spirits sinking. "You're kidding, right?" He shook his head and she muttered a curse beneath her breath. "Dammit. Then I suppose I'll have to wait until I get back to Cape Town to have a shower."

"There's another option..." Muzi told her. Her head flew up at his comment and her eyebrows lifted in a silent query.

"I own a vineyard across the valley, it's my weekend home." Muzi shrugged. "I have a flat in the city but, after a hectic week working in the corporate world, I come here to unwind and find some peace. Franschhoek is my hometown, where I grew up, and my grandmother Mimi lives across the valley." He grinned at her. "And my house has a shower, Dust Bunny. Quite a few of them, actually."

"I really should get a hotel room," Ro said, thinking that

it was better to be sensible and put some distance between her and the tempting Triple M.

Muzi winced. "Yeah, that's not going to happen. This weekend is a mini replica of their huge Bastille Day festival and while it won't be as crazy as the big festival, the town is packed and I'm pretty sure you won't find a room. Look, I have a huge house that's sitting empty," Muzi added. "At the very least, you can shower there and if you want to go back to Cape Town, I'll drive you."

Muzi lifted his water bottle to his mouth and drained the liquid. She watched his Adam's apple bob up and down and noted the strength of his neck and his raised trapezius muscles. As she'd recently discovered, under his cream button-down shirt was a ladderlike stomach, defined pecs and acres of lovely, lovely skin. A part of Ro—the rebel in her—desperately wanted to go home with him and proceed directly to the nearest shower, *together*.

Wow, pull yourself together, O'Keefe!

She liked him, was ridiculously, stupendously attracted to him, but she'd met him just recently and she wasn't the type to fall into bed with men she'd just met. Oh, she knew she *could*, that woman did exactly that regularly— and more power to them—but Ro wasn't that confident. Her body might be in the mood for some bed-based rock and roll, but mentally and emotionally, she wasn't ready to sleep with him. Or anyone. She wasn't in the right headspace to dive back into the dating pool again.

No, dating was out of the question because the word implied that she was looking for a relationship. She'd rather stab herself with a rusty fork. Relationships meant feelings, possibly even love, and she no longer understood what love was and whether it even existed.

Muzi surprised her by placing his big hand on her shoulder and gently squeezing.

"It's an offer of a shower, Ro, nothing more or less," Muzi told her, his expression understanding and a little tender. Or maybe that was her imagination working overtime.

Ro cursed the heat in her cheeks. "What about the..."

"Kiss we shared?" Muzi completed her sentence. "I'm attracted to you, that kiss should've clued you in, but you're Digby's sister."

She looked at him blankly, not understanding the connection. "So?"

"So Digby would kill me."

"I'm nearly thirty years old, and I fail to see what any of this has to do with him," Ro replied, a tad tartly. Why was she even arguing with him?

"Radd and Digby adore you and they take their recently acquired role as big brothers very seriously. It doesn't matter that I've known them for more than twenty years, if I mess with you, they will rip my head off."

She thought he should take his chances with her brothers and mess with her. It would be worth it. Ro cocked her head to the side. She knew she was playing with fire but, ridiculously, she no longer had a problem with being burned. Not if it meant flying so close to the sun with Muzi. "Would you like to mess with me?"

Muzi touched her cheek with the back of his knuckles. "There is nothing I'd like more but I think it's better to be sensible. One tends to have fewer regrets that way."

Sensible was good. Sensible was clever...

Sensible was also deeply, completely boring.

Muzi nodded to his vehicle. "Let's go get you clean, Dust Bunny." His megawatt smile flashed and her heart bounced off her rib cage and did a couple of flip-flops. "And if you're really lucky, I might even feed you tonight."

Ro sighed. It wasn't the type of lucky she was most interested in but she'd take it.

* * *

Unlike St. Urban, Muzi's house, set in acres of lush vines, looked fresh and lovely and was, as far as Ro could see, dust-free. On reaching his front door, she kicked off her dirty sandals and stepped into the hall, the wooden floor cool beneath her feet. Muzi tossed his keys onto an antique-looking table, exquisitely constructed and horrendously expensive, and placed his hand on her lower back and led her into a large sitting room. The breathtaking lounge—gunpowder gray accent walls and couches in navy and paisley—sported exceptionally high ceilings and an old, massive fireplace. Fantastic, museum-quality art decorated his walls.

Then Ro noticed the bifold doors across the room, opening up to a one-eighty-degree view of the Franschhoek mountains. Ro stared at the view for a good minute, maybe more, before turning to look at Muzi.

"That's one hell of a view, Triple M," she stated.

He smiled at her use of Digby's nickname. "It really is," Muzi replied.

"Is this building old?" Ro asked, her hand on the strap of the tote bag hanging off her shoulder.

"It was originally a mission house but the building burned down in the late '70s. Clos du Cadieux bought the property five years ago but the company didn't want, or need, any of the buildings or the fifty acres to the north. So I bought the building and the land," Muzi told her, gesturing for her to follow him. Ro crossed the room, passing the entrance to a gourmet kitchen featuring marble and top-of-the-range Italian appliances. Turning her head, she sighed at the wide, expansive outdoor entertainment area running the length of the house. A large pool, the same length of the deck, was on a tier below and bright blue water glistened in the midafternoon sun. Beyond the pool, she saw a glorious garden of white roses, swathes of lavender, mature indigenous trees and, of course, the stunning view of the mountains.

Muzi must have an excellent decorator, Ro mused as she followed him down a wide hallway, peeking into rooms where she could. The decor was high-end, unfussy but, in the simple lines and muted shades, there were elements designed to charm. Brightly colored cushions, bespoke art pieces and handpicked fabrics.

Muzi opened a door and stepped back to allow her to enter a room on the right. A queen-size bed, covered with white linen and a pale green blanket on the foot of the bed, dominated the room. The bed was tucked into the corner of the room, next to a half-open French door that led to a private patio and garden. A small couch and tiny desk graced the opposite side of the room. Ro realized that, whether one was lying in bed, or curled up in the corner of the couch, the view of the garden and mountains was never impeded.

And, dear Lord, was that a Paul Cadden sketch on the opposite wall? No way! She stepped forward, convinced it was a print, and her breath caught when she saw the tiny lines by the hyperrealist artist. She placed a hand on her heart… Muzi owned a Paul Cadden sketch, who *was* this guy?

"The bathroom is through there," Muzi said, gesturing her to a wooden sliding door next to the couch. "There's a robe behind the door and use whatever toiletries you need. I'll go and get your bags and Greta, my housekeeper, can unpack if you need her to."

"No need," Ro hastily assured him. "I'm only staying for a night, maybe two. And only until I can book into a hotel in town."

Muzi leaned one shoulder into the wooden door frame. He stared at her, his expression now impassive. "So, are you going to sell St. Urban to me today?"

Beneath his offhand comment was a serious note, a hint of desperation she couldn't easily dismiss. "I could, I suppose."

"But that's not going to happen, is it?"

Ro shook her head. "Sensible me thinks that's a fine plan, but I feel like I want to go back, that I *need* to go back. The house is a mess, but I want to see more of it. I feel like…" Oh, this was going to sound oh-so-stupid. But she'd had a strange feeling from the moment she stepped foot into the house, and it had just increased in intensity since then.

Muzi tipped his head to the side, his expression encouraging her to finish her sentence. "I feel like the house has been waiting for me," Ro told him.

There, she'd said it, and Ro waited for scoffing laughter or a dismissive comment. She got neither and he just kept looking at her with those intense black eyes.

Man, she was still so tempted to step out of her dusty dress and to dirty that all-white bed linen with him. Ro rubbed a hand over her face and stared at the reclaimed wooden planks beneath her feet. She barely recognized who she was around Muzi. She felt like a walking, talking—babbling!—mess of hormones. With Kelvin, sex had been fun, mostly, but not something she thought about that often. They slept together once a week, sometimes twice and it was nice. Mundane. Satisfactory.

She'd never wanted to climb her ex-fiancé and gobble him up like she did Muzi. He made her feel alive, tuned in and turned on and…uncomfortable. Out of control. She had far too much to deal with, to work through. She did not need her inconvenient attraction to a hot, intelligent, sexy African man to complicate her life.

Too late, cupcake.

"Spend some time at the vineyard, but get the power and

water connected at the house first. When you are ready to sell, can you give me the first option to buy?"

It took Ro a few seconds to pull her mind out of fantasyland and back onto the subject. She nodded. "Deal. I'll also get a contractor out there to give me a proper idea of what needs to be done, what state the house is really in. Obviously, nobody has visited the property for a long, long time," Ro continued.

"It boggles the mind."

"It sure does. Why didn't she just sell it instead of letting it deteriorate?" Ro demanded.

"Maybe your brothers can answer that question," Muzi said, "but I wouldn't hold your breath. Radd and Digby didn't have that much more contact with Gil and Zia than you did.

"People should have to take a test to procreate," he added.

"Amen to that," Ro replied. As a teacher who'd encountered far too many less than wonderful parents, she'd campaign for that to happen.

Ro pushed a hand through her hair and dislodged a cloud of dust. Right, priorities, O'Keefe—and hers should be to get clean. While washing the dust off her body, maybe she could flush Muzi from her mind. It was worth a try, she thought.

"I'll meet you on the veranda in thirty minutes," Muzi told her, his intense eyes clashing with hers.

"Are you sure it's okay for me to stay? I don't want to intrude on your solitude or impose on you in any way."

Maybe she was hoping that he'd say that she was, that he'd take her back to Cape Town. Her mind knew they needed distance, emotional as well as physical. Still, she didn't want to be anywhere but here with him.

And that was dangerous.

Muzi took a step, then another to reach her and his knuckles skimmed up and down her bare arm. She sucked in a breath, felt her stomach contract, and that special space between her legs pulsed with want and need. So, that was new...

"If I didn't want you here, I would've driven back to the city. You can trust what I say, Ro."

She managed a small smile and it took all her willpower to step away instead of stepping into his arms. "Thank you." She gestured to the door leading to the en suite bathroom. "I'm going to shower."

Muzi walked away from her and she fought the urge to call him back, to offer him her body. What was it about this man who tempted her to step into his arms, what was with her need to get closer, to discover the secrets lurking in those black, black eyes? She'd better get a grip, Ro told herself, because there was no way she was walking down that road. It was littered with land mines. Her attraction to him was too intense, out of control. Maybe she was over-reacting to him because Kelvin cheated on her and she was looking to get her sexual mojo back.

Whatever the reason, it was imperative to get her attraction to Muzi under control.

Ro walked into the bathroom, thinking that, had she been asked a year or two ago, she would never have imagined that she'd be single as she approached her thirties and that Kelvin would cheat on her.

She would've scoffed at the suggestion of her birth parents leaving her a king's ransom and she would've protested the idea of her parents divorcing.

Her life was far too complicated, and she wasn't good at complicated. Hell, on good days, she could barely handle perplexing. Complicated and convoluted were steps too far.

Take the first step, O'Keefe, focus on the next task in front of you.

And that happened to be getting clean. She'd been bathing on her own since she was a little girl, so she was sure she could manage the task.

It would, however, be *a lot* more fun with Muzi for company.

CHAPTER FOUR

HE LOVED THIS TOWN, Muzi thought later that day, as he placed a hand on Ro's back to direct her to turn right onto a side street of Franschhoek. Galleries and antiques shops filled the tree-lined streets, and vines brought over from France three hundred years ago cascaded down the slopes of the mountains overlooking the town. It was both quaint and sophisticated, laid-back and luxurious.

It was the heart of wine making in the country and the people, passionate about the land, the produce and wine, were warm and welcoming. Because Mimi was the town's most illustrious citizen, he'd been the object of speculation since the day Mimi adopted him. The great and good of Franschhoek were insanely nosy and would be extremely interested to hear that someone, a *female* someone, was staying with him and poking around St. Urban.

That wasn't accurate. Ro was currently *staying* in his house but, unfortunately, not in his bed.

That was where he most wanted her.

Their kiss rocked him to his core and, had he not sneezed, God knows where they might have ended up. Rolling around naked on dust-covered drop cloths? He was embarrassed to admit that it was a distinct possibility.

Ro, like no other woman before, made him forget where he was, hell, *who* he was.

She was beautiful, her deep blue eyes a gorgeous contrast to that deep brown hair, but he wasn't a stranger to beautiful women and had slept with many of them. Nobody but Ro had made him lose his head, forget where he was, too wrapped up in her softness and her scent to care.

She was dangerous, she made him lose control and that was unacceptable.

And that was why, instead of them staying home tonight, he invited her to join him at a restaurant where he always had a standing reservation. Muzi knew that if they'd stayed home, they'd end up burning up the sheets.

And the bed.

And the whole damn house.

He'd feed her, ply her with some extraordinary wine and steer her to the guest bedroom while he locked himself in his master suite. He couldn't, now that he was so close, jeopardize losing his chance to have access to the St. Urban vines for a temporary affair. Digby was his best friend and there was a bro code... *Do not mess with your best friend's sister.*

He was not risking a lifelong friendship, losing one of the very few people he trusted for a roll in the hay.

If he was that desperate, he could scroll through his phone and arrange a hookup for when he returned to the city tomorrow evening.

Muzi released a long sigh, reluctantly accepting that he didn't want sex, he wanted to make love to Ro.

Make love? What was wrong with him? He sounded like a sappy character from a cheesy rom-com.

"This is such a lovely little town," Ro said, breaking the silence between them.

Muzi allowed himself the immense pleasure of looking at her. When she agreed to eat with him in town, she asked about the dress code and looked relieved when he told her that the restaurant was super casual. Her white jeans, gold lace-up sandals and a cute crop top, revealing a few inches of her board-flat stomach, were perfect for a casual dinner.

With her hair twisted into a messy knot, she looked amazing. Sexy. And far too beddable.

Needing to keep his hands off her, Muzi shoved them into the pockets of his gray chino shorts. The restaurant was just down the street and he needed a drink.

No, he needed a few drinks and another very cold shower. And to get his mind out of the bedroom. But as soon as he stopped thinking about Ro, his anxiety about his position at Clos Du Cadieux came roaring back.

If he found the C'Artegan vines, if he could get them to thrive and produce, he had a real shot at securing his position at the company. Hell, even if he only managed to secure the vines, getting them under Clos du Cadieux's control would be a coup. And he was the closest he'd ever been to that happening. He had a good chance of being able to buy St. Urban or, at the very least, he was at the head of the queue.

It was the most progress he'd made in years. Years ago, he'd asked to lease the vineyard from Zia at an above premium rate. But, because she was fully aware of his long friendship with her estranged son Digby, she chose to lease the land to a competitor.

The lease ran out shortly before their deaths and the vines were in a sorry state. When he got his hands on the vines, and he would—hopefully soon—God knew how long it would be until he could expect a decent harvest from the Merlot.

As for the C'Artegan cultivar, there was a chance that the vines had withered and died—the cultivar was finicky and frail—so his offer to buy the farm without inspecting the land was at best, reckless, at worst, completely stupid.

If he bought a farm planted with run-of-the-mill vines, the Clos du Cadieux board, with Susan leading the charge, would come after him with pitchforks and lighted torches. They'd also fire his ass. However, if he discovered a thought-to-be-extinct cultivar and managed to get a small run of wine, he would be considered a wine god and would be pretty much untouchable.

He was taking a hell of a risk, but he was fairly sure that St. Urban still had the C'Artegan cultivar. Tomorrow he'd walk the land, and look for any subtle differences between the vines. If he found vines that looked interesting, he would send samples for analysis…

If they turned out to be the C'Artegan cultivar, he'd pamper and protect them, and in a few years, he'd produce a small vintage of soft, luscious, rare as hell wine. When he released a press release stating that Clos du Cadieux was branching into making C'Artegan wine, their stock would go through the roof.

But if Ro insisted on the sale going through before he had his results back, he would buy the farm himself—he was insanely wealthy and could afford whatever price she demanded—and decide what to do with the property later.

And his position at Clos du Cadieux would be secure…

"Tell me about Franschhoek," Ro said, adjusting the strap of the nude-colored purse on her bare shoulder.

He pulled himself back to the present.

"Before colonization the San and Khoekhoe peoples inhabited this area, but in 1687 Simon van der Stel and twenty-three pioneers arrived in the valley and established farms along the Berg River. A year later, French Huguenots, looking to escape persecution by the Catholic Church, came to the valley and started farming. The residents are very proud of their connection to France and they hold a massive Gallic festival here every year. They claim it's the food and wine capital of South Africa and they aren't wrong," Muzi replied, stopping next to a small whitewashed house. A discreet plaque on the gate told them they'd arrived at Pasco's.

Ro glanced around, breathed deeply and smiled. She looked at him, and attraction, hot and wild, sizzled. Muzi knew that if he made a move, covered her mouth with his, she would be his for the taking. She wanted him, that much was obvious, nearly as much as he wanted her.

She wouldn't object to skipping dinner to return to his house and get naked.

He was so very tempted.

"Are you guys going to spend the rest of the evening standing there or are you coming in?"

Muzi immediately recognized the gravelly voice and turned toward the man standing off the path leading up to the house, a glass of wine in his hand and a cigarette dangling between two fingers. Muzi grinned when Ro's fingernails dug into his skin on his forearm.

"Uh…that's Pasco Kildare, the famous chef, one of the youngest in the world to be awarded two Michelin stars. He owns a restaurant in Manhattan, and you need to wait a hundred years to get in," Ro whispered, sounding a little starstruck.

The last time he was in New York, about two months ago, he called in on Pasco during lunch service and returned that night to work his way through Pasco's new tasting menu. His food was always stunning, creative and cutting-edge.

Pas, he had to admit, could feed him anytime and anywhere.

Pasco's, Franschhoek, was more down-to-earth, casual

and, because Pasco was Franschhoek born and raised, it was where Pasco could relax. The town still saw him as the younger son of one of the valley's most respected farmers and remembered him for being one of the biggest pranksters the town had ever seen.

It was hard to be taken too seriously when your biggest claim to fame wasn't the Michelin stars or your reputation as a superstar chef, but the fact that you plowed your first car through the floor-to-ceiling window of an exclusive art gallery on Main Street.

"Triple M," Pasco said, in his drawling voice.

"Hey, Pas," Muzi said, exchanging a one-armed hug with his old friend. He stood back and put a hand on Ro's back. "Meet Roisin O'Keefe."

"Call me Ro."

"Hello, Call Me Ro," Pasco said, dropping a kiss on her right cheek, then her left. Done with the Gallic kissing, he kept her hand in his and Muzi fought the urge to rip off his arm. Jealously wasn't his thing, but he'd give Pas ten seconds to drop her hand or else things might turn fractious.

Pasco dropped her hand at nine seconds. "Welcome to my place," Pasco said, sitting on the thick stone wall of the restaurant's old-fashioned wraparound veranda.

"Shouldn't you be in the kitchen?" Muzi asked, not at all happy with the fact that Pasco couldn't keep his eyes off Ro. Pasco finally met his eyes and Muzi saw the mischief dancing in those green eyes. Damn. Pas knew that he was attracted to Ro and was prepared to give him a hard time about it. Muzi knew that if the shoe was on the other foot, he'd mess with Pasco in the same way.

Irritating each other, winding each other up, was what they'd been doing since they were spotty teenagers.

"My team has everything under control, and I'd much rather sit here and talk to a pretty woman."

He could find someone else to talk to and stay away from his woman…wait, what the hell? Ro wasn't *his*, he reminded himself, and he didn't believe in treating women as property. What the hell was happening to him?

"Stop flirting with her," Muzi told Pasco, speaking in Xhosa. Having been brought up on a farm, Pasco was nearly fluent in the language and, even if he wasn't, Muzi's scowl would tell him to back down. Way down.

"You're not the type to get jealous but she is lovely," Pas replied, his Xhosa accent a little rusty.

"It's business," Muzi replied, keeping his tone flat. He knew that Pasco wouldn't believe that whopper, but he had to try.

"Sure, it is," Pasco said with a wide grin.

"Why are you out here and not being a control freak in your kitchen?" Muzi asked him, reverting to English.

"I only flew in yesterday so I'm taking it easy tonight."

"You're welcome to join us," Ro politely told him.

"No, you're not," Muzi snapped. He saw Ro's eyes widen at his harsh retort and shrugged. She raised her eyebrows, looking for an explanation for his rudeness, but there was no way he could tell her that he wanted to be alone with her, to have her complete attention on him.

What a sap.

"Pas is a horrible bore, he just likes to talk about food and wine," Muzi said, wincing at his weak clarification.

Pasco rolled his eyes, picked up Ro's hand and dropped a kiss on her knuckles. "I'd love to join you and I might, *later*."

Now the jackass was just messing with him. He'd pay, Muzi thought. Somehow, somewhere.

Pasco led them into the restaurant, which only consisted of twenty or so tables, with another ten on the patio outside. Pasco threaded his way through the tables, touching shoulders and trading quips as he passed his customers, Muzi and Ro trailing behind.

Pasco stopped a few feet short of the outside dining area and slapped his hand on his forehead, grimacing as he looked at Muzi. "Crap."

"Problem?" Muzi asked him.

Pasco looked embarrassed. "Sorry, I'm jet-lagged but that's not an excuse. I forgot to tell you that Keane is here."

It took all his effort to hide his annoyance, to keep his cool. He shrugged. "No biggie."

Pasco gave him a "Who are you kidding?" look. "I can juggle some tables and put you inside."

No, he wanted to sit in the balmy air and under the twinkling fairy lights and the man he'd once been closer to than anyone else, a man he'd considered his brother, would not chase him away. He hadn't done anything wrong, dammit, and refused to act as if he had.

"He's dining with his mother," Pasco added.

Oh, sweet baby Jesus. That was all he needed.

"It's fine, Pas," Muzi said through gritted teeth. It wasn't but he'd be damned if he'd let anyone see his annoyance or discomfort. Especially Susan.

Muzi reached for Ro's hand and when her fingers slid into his, his heart rate dropped, his shoulders and jaw loosened, and he was able to take a full breath. She steadied him, he realized, just being around her made him feel more relaxed.

Horny but relaxed. A curious combination. He glanced down at their linked hands, dark and pale, and shook his head, wondering why this woman had such an effect on him. He'd met her just a few days ago and here he was, holding her hand as he walked across the patio behind the country's most lauded chef.

Muzi saw Keane, the fairy lights making his deep

auburn hair seem redder than normal, sitting at a four-seater table on the other side of the room. Keane looked up, caught his eye, started to smile and then, as if remembering that he was the enemy, frowned. They locked glances for twenty seconds and then Susan put her hand on his arm, tugging his attention away. Keane's face hardened as she whispered words in his ear and Muzi saw the distaste on his face when Keane looked his way again. Yep, Susan was doing another fine job of poisoning the well…

Pasco pulled out Ro's chair, got her settled, and when Pas looked at him, Muzi saw the sympathy on his face. Narrowing his eyes to make it clear to his friend not to say anything, Pasco gave him the smallest of nods.

Muzi knew that, when they were alone, Pasco would ask him, once again, whether he could talk to Keane on his behalf. Digby had made the same offer more than a dozen times but Muzi was adamant: he was a big boy and he didn't need his friends playing peacemaker or interceding on his behalf. He and Keane would work it out themselves.

Or they wouldn't.

It was between him and Keane. He refused to put his mates in the middle of a family argument.

Either way, he'd be fine. He always was. But Muzi couldn't help opening his fingers and looking at the fine scar on the palm of his hand. A lifetime ago, he and Keane watched a movie featuring friends who made a blood oath and, being ten and stupid, thought a blood oath was a cool idea. They'd sliced their hands open and shaken hands, feeling very cool and very grown-up.

The resulting infections, thanks to the rusty knife they used, hadn't been much fun…

But it turned out blood oaths and promises meant nothing, words even less.

* * *

Ro looked from Muzi to the table where the redheaded man was seated and she felt a tight band of tension between the two tables, an undeniable connection.

But nobody would realize that by looking at Muzi. He embodied the three *C*s: cool, calm and collected. Until she looked into his eyes, turbulent with unspoken emotion. She immediately placed her hand on his, linking her fingers with his. She shouldn't be touching him but, under his implacable surface, she was sure he needed comfort, a little reassurance that she was on his side.

Not that he wanted, or needed her, to stand in his corner—the man was very able to take care of himself—but didn't everyone, at one point or another, need support? She sure did.

"Who are those people?" she asked, hoping but not expecting him to answer her.

Muzi tugged his hand away, pulled his linen serviette off the table and carefully laid it across his lap. "The older woman is Susan Matthews-Reed and she's, despite our age difference, legally my sister. The redheaded guy is her son Keane Matthews-Reed. I don't know who the younger woman is. Probably Keane's current girlfriend."

Muzi waited for the waitress to pour them a glass of red—Ro noticed that Pasco didn't ask them for their preferences but just sent over what he thought they should be drinking—and leave before asking for clarification. "I'm confused. Can you explain that again?"

"My maternal grandmother was Mimi's housekeeper, and they were great friends. Lu died when I was ten and Mimi adopted me. Susan is her daughter and Keane is Susan's son, Mimi's grandson. I'm, legally, Mimi's son but I've always considered her to be my grandmother, not my mother," Muzi added.

Got it, Ro thought. "Where are your parents, your other grandparents, Mimi's husband?"

"Mimi's husband died young. As for my birth parents, I had an uninterested mother and have no idea who my father is."

Right. His "Don't go there" expression and flat voice suggested she not ask any more personal questions.

"Did you have a happy childhood?" Ro asked, trying to keep her question as casual as possible.

Muzi shrugged. "I had everything I could want, and I got a great education."

Good to know but he didn't answer her question as to whether he'd been happy. Ro was about to push for more when he spoke again. "I'm very close to Mimi. She's always treated me like her own."

Ro started to ask him another question, but he cut her off, asking her what she wanted to eat. Right, he didn't want to discuss his family or his place within it. She got the message.

She wanted to find what made this fascinating man tick, but he'd slammed that door shut. Maybe it was better that it stayed closed, she was already ridiculously attracted to Muzi, she didn't want to become completely fascinated by him.

At this point in her life, she needed a romantic relationship like she needed a hole in her head.

"A menu would be good," Ro said, looking around for a waitress.

Amusement returned to Muzi's eyes. "You won't get one. Pasco doesn't care what *you* want to eat, he's going to send us what he thinks we *should* eat."

Ro placed her chin in the palm of her hand and pulled a face. "Oh." She wrinkled her nose and leaned forward. "Look, I know I'm sitting in one of the best restaurants in the country but, damn, I want a hamburger."

Muzi's eyes lightened with amusement. "I can ask Pasco if he'll make you one. He'll probably curse, but he'll do it if I ask."

Ro raised her eyebrows. "Really? You're that close?"

Muzi grinned. "Hey, I fought off boarding school bullies for him, he can make me a damn burger. If he gave me a choice, not that he ever does, I'd just order a steak."

"Rare?"

"Is there any other way to eat steak?"

"According to my mother, the vegetarian, I'm going to hell for killing God's creatures and so is my father. He's, mostly, a vegetarian but occasionally takes a trip over to the dark side. Once or twice a year, or when he's annoyed with my mom, he brings out the barbecue and murders a steak, cooking it until it's the consistency of old leather."

Horror jumped into Muzi's eyes. "Tell your dad to stick to being a vegetarian."

"I have, on numerous occasions," Ro replied. She looked across the patio, saw that Susan was still looking their way, and tried to ignore the ripple of unease running up and down her spine. What was that all about? Why was she having a weird reaction to someone she didn't know and, probably, never would? Susan was part of Muzi's life, his business, not hers.

But if she and Muzi…

No, now she was being over-the-top fanciful. There would be no "she and Muzi," now or in the future. She was avoiding relationships. She didn't need the drama. She had enough trouble in her life already.

"So you and Pasco went to school together?" Ro asked him, running a finger up and down the stem of her wineglass.

"We—Digby, Pasco, Keane and I—all started at Duncan House at the same time. Most of us have been friends ever since."

Most of us? That had to mean that something cata-
strophic must've happened to his and Keane's relationship
along the way. Seeing that Muzi didn't cross the restaurant to greet the man he was raised with, that much was
obvious.

"Tell me what happened between you two…"

Muzi sighed as he leaned back in his chair. His body
language told her that he was trying to retreat from the
question or the subject and when he crossed his arms, she
knew he was feeling defensive. There was no way that
Muzi, proud and reticent, was going to open up to her.

And why should he? If he needed a sounding board, he
could talk to Digby or Pasco…why would he want to confide in a woman he'd only known for a day or so?

Punching above your weight bracket, O'Keefe. Big-
time.

She held up her hands, signaling to him that she was
backing off. Muzi's shoulders immediately dropped and
the tension in his face eased.

Muzi was not going to allow her to delve into his private
business but maybe he could help her with hers. He was
one of a handful of people who knew she was the Tempest-
Vane heir, he'd known Digby for over twenty years and,
best of all, he could give her an outsider's view, a nonpar-
tisan view of her birth parents.

Digby and Radd were too close to the situation and the
press were known to exaggerate. Her brothers called Gil
and Zia materialistic and wild, extreme narcissists, children of Satan. Maybe Muzi could give her a more level-
headed assessment of the people whose DNA she carried.

"Did you ever meet my birth parents? Maybe when they
came to visit Digby at school?"

Muzi looked thoughtful and took a while to answer her
questions. "I think Gil and Zia only came to the school

maybe once, possibly twice in the whole five years we were there."

"They didn't visit him?" Ro asked, appalled.

Muzi shook his head. "Digby was, as the third son, possibly the most neglected of the brothers. They didn't seem to care about him at all."

Ro rubbed the space between her eyes with her fingertips. "What lovely blood flows in my veins," she quipped, trying for sarcasm but failing.

She picked up her fork and drew patterns on the tablecloth. "Digby and Radd do not have anything nice to say about them, and I understand why, but they couldn't have been *all* bad. They must've had *some* redeeming qualities."

She heard the note of hope in her voice, the optimism and cursed herself. She wanted them to be better than what she heard, what she'd read, because who wanted to be the biological daughter of two monsters?

Muzi's eyes connected with hers and she saw the empathy within those dark depths. "Are you waiting for me to sing their praises?"

Ro shrugged. "Not sing their praises but… God, I just want someone to tell me they weren't completely irredeemable."

Muzi stayed silent and Ro scratched her head. "You can't tell me that, can you?"

Muzi topped up her wineglass as he slowly shook his head. "I wish I could but…no, I can't. They were completely, horribly, equally narcissistic."

Ro sighed. "Excellent news."

"Are you worried that you inherited their tendencies?"

Ro shrugged. "Wouldn't you be?"

Muzi placed his forearms on the table and leaned forward, his fleeting expression suggesting that he wished he could remove all her pain and frustration. "If it's any consolation, I choose to believe that nurture is a lot stronger than nature. Tell me about your parents."

Ro smiled. It was easy to tell him about the loving, outgoing, passionate people who had raised her. "They are great, very affectionate and a lot of fun," Ro told him. "They're a little hippy, a little dippy but very warm and very, very smart."

"What do they do?" Muzi asked, looking interested.

"My dad is a college professor, he teaches constitutional law, and a political consultant. My mom is a pediatric surgeon."

Muzi raised his eyebrows, impressed. "As you said, smart. How old were you when they told you that you were adopted?"

"My adoption was always openly discussed between us, so I don't remember them ever sitting me down and telling me I was adopted." Ro ran her finger up and down the side of her wineglass. "I had a very happy childhood and they loved me, they gave me a lot of time and attention."

"But?"

How was he able to discern the hesitation behind her words? He didn't know her but he seemed to be able to look beyond what she said to what she believed, how she felt. Despite being together for eight years, Kelvin never mastered the ability to recognize subtext, to look beyond her words to her emotions. Yet this big, imperturbable, muscled stranger could.

Honestly, it was both sexy and scary.

"But they were so wrapped up and so in tune with each other. So in love." She could tell him everything, she was sure he'd understand. "As a kid, I used to believe that my adoption was the reason I always felt on the outside of their relationship, that if I was biologically theirs, I wouldn't feel like that. And that's why the news of them wanting to divorce rocked my world," Ro added as she stared down at the table. She seldom cried, and never in public, so the burn in her eyes annoyed her.

Muzi's thumb stroked the inside of her wrist. She already felt warm and if she was this affected by him holding her wrist, she was sure to combust if she watched his broad hands stroke her naked body...

"When did they tell you that?"

"Around six months ago. The day after a lawyer contacted me and told me who my biological parents were and that I was the heir to the estate, I went around to tell them that I'd inherited money from my birth parents but before I could tell them my news, they hit me with their divorce."

"Did they know who your birth parents were?"

Ro shook her head. "According to the adoption agreement, Gil and Zia knew who my parents were but they insisted on keeping their identities a secret."

"And your folks were happy about that?"

"They'd been waiting for a child for years and didn't care where I came from." Ro played with the charm bracelet on her right arm.

Muzi topped up his wineglass and sipped, looking deep in thought. "Hearing that you are insanely rich must've freaked your parents out," Muzi stated with a lazy grin. Ro couldn't return his smile. His smile slowly faded. "You haven't told them?" he demanded.

Ro shook her head. "Before I could, they told me they were divorcing and, I'm not proud to admit this, but I lost it. I told them to pull themselves together, that they were going through a midlife crisis. I was, *am*, still angry."

Muzi rubbed his jaw, his expression bemused. He lifted his hand to run his knuckle over her jaw. "Damn, but you've had a lot to deal with lately, haven't you? Hearing about the inheritance, meeting your brothers, your parents' divorce."

Yeah. And she had yet to tell him that her fiancé had cheated on her. She opened her mouth to dish that news but snapped it closed. She'd whined enough and didn't need to appear sadder and more messed up than she already was. She'd deal with her breakup, her parents' divorce and her unexpected windfall in her own way and in her own time.

"I'll be fine," she breezily assured him.

He nodded and squeezed her wrist again before pulling his hand away. "Oh, I know you will. You're strong, smart and sensible. And sexy."

Ro suddenly had a strong awareness of her heartbeat, could feel it pounding in her chest. The room faded and only Muzi remained, a small smile on his face, desire in his eyes. Ro, not one for elaborate gestures, tamped down on her urge to clear the table of its contents, to crawl across its surface to reach his mouth, to put her hands on that hot, lovely skin. She wanted him, completely, crazily...

Obsessively.

She swallowed, then swallowed again. She downed a glass of water that did nothing to assuage her parched throat and lifted her hand to her neck, then to her cheek.

Be careful, O'Keefe, you could be jumping from the frying pan into a very hot fire.

That wasn't something a smart, sensible, strong woman did.

"Sorry for interrupting..."

Ro jerked her eyes off Muzi to see the waitress standing next to their table, holding two slate gray plates. She slid a sizzling steak on a base of potatoes in front of Muzi. It looked divine and smelled even better. Ro felt her taste buds tingling but whether they prickled for the food or Muzi she couldn't be sure. Probably both.

The waitress then set her plate down in front of her. "Japanese Wagyu beef burger, wasabi mayonnaise and black truffles on a brioche bun."

Ro caught Muzi's eye and burst out laughing. "How did he know?" she asked him, astounded.

Muzi shrugged and smiled. "Who knows and do you really care?"

"Not even a little bit," Ro told him and dug into her food.

CHAPTER FIVE

THE NEXT DAY, Ro stood in the tall grass between two rows of overgrown vines on St. Urban and watched as Muzi gently parted the foliage, his focus on the trunks of the vines. She swatted away a fly and wished she'd put on more sunscreen. It was late afternoon, but the sun was still blisteringly hot. She'd finished her bottle of water thirty minutes ago and she was fairly certain some little African creature had climbed up the back of her shorts and was nibbling on her butt cheek.

She'd agreed to walk the St. Urban lands with Muzi before he left for Cape Town, but she hadn't expected to spend the best part of the afternoon stomping through the overgrown vineyard.

She wanted a swim, two liters of cold water and then a glass of Chardonnay, not necessarily in that order.

And a nap, since she hadn't slept much the night before. Not because she'd been burning up the sheets with Muzi but because she'd spent most of the night *imagining* burning up his sheets. There was, obviously, a vast difference between the two.

"The trunks are, mostly, in good shape. Fairly straight and mostly disease-free."

Muzi had been making odd, vine-related comments all afternoon and she'd lost track, and interest, an hour ago.

Ro looked down at him. He was on his haunches peering under a vine, and she admired the muscles rippling under his white T-shirt, and the way his chino shorts pulled over the curve of his perfect, perfect butt.

He was built, sexy and as fit as hell. But she could easily resist sexy and good-looking—LA was filled with good-looking guys—but the addition of nice and smart was harder to ignore. Muzi was also a gentleman. He opened car doors, allowed her to walk into a room before him, stood up when she approached him. His old-fashioned manners were charming and instinctive, they weren't put on or forced, they seemed to be part of who he was.

But underneath the charm, she knew he could be as tough as old leather, ruthless if he needed to be. He was intelligent, cunning and very, very secretive.

He got her talking last night, chatting away about her parents and their divorce but she'd barely scratched his calm surface. She still had so many questions about his adoption by Mimi—strange that they were both adopted—but she still wanted to know more about his grandmother Lu and his childhood.

Ro slapped the back of her neck and looked at her grimy hand. Why was she so fascinated by Muzi and why did her heart jump when she heard his voice, splutter when his deep, intense eyes met hers? Ro scowled at the overgrown grass, remembering that, not so long ago, she was deeply in love with a man with whom she expected to spend the rest of her life.

How could she move on so quickly? Was her attraction to Muzi simply a rebound fling? Was he a bridge to dating again, a way to get over her ex? Or could he be someone special?

Ro knew that she shouldn't be thinking of dating again, that wading back into the messy world of relationships was an unbelievably bad idea. Her judgment could no longer be trusted—she'd never, not once, believed that Kelvin would cheat on her—and she no longer had any idea what love was, what it looked like, how it acted.

Her life was complicated enough without her incredibly inconvenient attraction to a smart, sexy, secretive man.

Ro put her hands on her hips and arched her back, thinking that she needed to get out of her head. What she needed was a project, a distraction, something to keep her occupied. Ro looked toward the mansion, thinking that the neglected house and gardens might be the projects she needed to keep busy.

And her hands, thoughts and attention off Muzi.

But if she was going to stay in Franschhoek for the foreseeable future, she'd need to find a B and B, she couldn't stay in Muzi's house indefinitely. She wished she could move into her house but, while Muzi inspected the cellars earlier, she had walked through the mansion and it was, genuinely, horrible. It was obviously a dumping ground for the Du Toit family's—she'd discovered Zia's maiden name from paging through a stack of ancient bills and letters left on the hallway table—unwanted furniture, books and detritus. The house was uninhabitable, so she'd have to find somewhere else to stay.

"I'm going to book into one of the local B and Bs tomorrow," Ro told Muzi.

She saw him tense and he dropped the vine in his hand, pushing to his feet. "Why?"

"Because I can't keep taking advantage of your hospitality," Ro primly replied.

"I'm leaving for the city shortly and I won't be back until the weekend, or maybe even the next weekend. My house will be empty so what's the problem with you staying there?" Muzi asked.

It would be super convenient, she admitted. "I could pay you a daily rate," Ro suggested, knowing he'd refuse but needing to make the offer.

"Not happening," Muzi said, his tone suggesting she not argue. "There's a Jeep in the garage that you can use, as well."

Now, that was too much. "Muzi, I can hire a car. Or even buy one."

He shrugged, looking unconcerned. "Use the Jeep, Ro."

He started to walk past her, and Ro put her hand on his arm, looking up at him. "Hey, a conversation doesn't just end because you deem it over."

Muzi looked at her hand, then moved his eyes to her face, specifically her mouth. She knew that he wanted to kiss her and wished he would. She hadn't stopped thinking about the hot-as-fire kiss they'd shared and she suspected, *hoped*, he hadn't either.

"What's there to discuss? You need a place to stay, and I have an empty house. You need a car, and there's one in the garage not being used. I don't need your money, so I won't accept payment," Muzi stated, sounding super reasonable. But she caught the "Why are we discussing this?" note in his voice. Yep, he was a little arrogant and very alpha, someone very used to getting his way.

But his self-confidence was deeply, stupidly attractive.

"So, any new thoughts about this property?" Muzi asked her, as they walked back toward the house.

Ro scowled at his back. "I know that you're trying to change the subject," she groused.

Muzi flashed his spectacular grin. "I am," he admitted. "Arguing with you is exhausting. St. Urban, Ro?"

"I think I am going to fix it up and sell it, I guess," Ro replied. The Franschhoek Valley was a beautiful area and the property had enormous potential, but Ro knew this property wasn't her forever place. She couldn't see herself living in the old, rambling house big enough for six families.

No, she far preferred Muzi's modern, light-filled house…
Stop it, Roisin!

"I'll buy it, at your asking price, right now."

Ro slammed on the brakes, her head whipping around to stare at him. "What?"

"You heard me," Muzi stated. "What price did the lawyers put on it? I'll even give you 10 percent more."

Ro felt her head swim, partly because of the heat, but mostly because Muzi was offering to pay her stupid money for this property. She opened her mouth to speak but no words came out.

"Why do you look so surprised? I told you that I wanted to buy it." Muzi placed his hand on her back and urged her forward.

She pointed to the house, just visible through the oak trees in the distance. "You're mad, Muzi! The house is a mess. I'm quite sure it's falling down."

"It's structurally sound, it just needs some work," Muzi said. "Besides, you know I want the land, not the house."

Ro slapped her hands on her hips. "Is that rare cultivar worth so much money?"

Muzi's expression hardened. "To me it is."

Ro watched as he picked a vine leaf and rubbed it between his fingers. He looked at her, his expression intense. And unyielding.

"So, what do you say? Do you want to save yourself the hassle of fixing up and clearing up the house and sell it to me?"

It would be an immediate and easy solution and an offer she should take. Although it had been in Zia's family for generations, she had no emotional connection to the place and she could save herself a lot of sweat and tears.

"Um...*no.*"

Muzi looked as surprised as she felt. "You're refusing my very generous offer? Do you want more money?"

Really? That was where his mind went? "No, I don't want more money, you idiot. I'm just not sure I want to sell. Not yet, anyway."

"Why not?" Muzi asked her. "The place is overgrown, the house is a wreck, and I don't see you becoming a wine farmer anytime soon."

Well spotted.

Ro took a minute to hunt down the correct words. Muzi, thankfully, didn't hurry her along. "For the past few months, I've felt like I'm floating, that nothing seems quite real. I helped Digby and Bay by looking after Livvie but I haven't achieved anything this year. All I've done is meet with lawyers and read reports and go along with Siya's suggestions about how to go ahead with the dispersal of my birth parents' assets. It's all a bit, well..." She hesitated, looking for the right word.

"Unreal?"

Perfect. "Yeah, unreal. But also emotionally taxing. I feel like I need to throw myself into a project, something with a beginning and an end. I need to get my hands dirty and my muscles working. I need to work on something tangible."

St. Urban was that something.

She looked around at the overgrown vineyards, so different from the picture-perfect rows of vines she'd seen on other properties, including Muzi's. Maybe they both could have what they wanted. "What if I leased you the land? And, as we discussed, I give you the first option to purchase it when I am ready to sell?"

In his eyes surprise mingled with relief. "Yeah, that could work."

Ro dragged her trainer through a tuft of grass. "Would a year be long enough for you to work out whether the cultivar is here?"

"More than," Muzi quickly replied.

Ro jammed her hands in the back pockets of her shorts. She could feel her nose burning and hoped she didn't peel. She needed to get out of the sun. "If you do discover the cultivar, we can include an option for you to extend the lease when the year term is up."

"That's incredibly generous of you, Ro. I do appreciate it," Muzi said, his voice deeper than usual. "But you should know that having a lease in place might be problematic if you want to sell the property."

"Not really," Ro replied, smiling. "If you find the cultivar, you'd want to buy the property, right?"

"Right."

"And if you don't, the lease is only for a year. I don't need to sell the property immediately. I could wait for a year. More if I had to."

Muzi stopped, turned to face her and put his hands on her shoulders. "Thank you," he said, his voice tender. "You don't know how much this means to me."

This wasn't just business, Ro thought. His need to find the C'Artegan cultivar went deeper than business, than bringing a new wine to the market, than receiving awards and accolades. It was soul-deep important to Muzi and she wished he'd tell her why. She wanted, needed, to know him on a deeper level.

Good job on keeping your attraction surface-based, O'Keefe!

Muzi looked like he wanted to touch her, his mouth darting to her mouth and back to her eyes. He reached for the band of her shorts, his fingers sliding between the fabric and her skin, anchoring her in place. Ro had no intention of going anywhere.

The only place she wanted to be was in his arms.

"Is my magnanimous gesture enough to make you kiss me?" Ro asked, surprising herself with her boldness.

"You standing there, simply breathing is enough to make me want to kiss you, Roisin," Muzi told her, lowering his head.

Within half a second, maybe less, his mouth was on hers and she wondered how she had lived on planet Earth for so long without having been kissed by him.

He tasted of coffee and sun, of sex and sin. He tasted glorious...

Ro draped one arm around his strong neck and placed the other above his heart. He was hotter than she expected but solid, and she had the sensation that he'd be an impenetrable barrier between her and the world. She was strong and independent, but sometimes even strong and independent women wanted to feel protected.

Muzi cradled her face in his broad hands and his clever tongue slipped between her teeth. Her knees softened as her heart rate kicked up and, perfectly tuned to her responses, he placed a hand on her lower back and pulled her closer, into his long, thick and very hard erection.

The man was big...everywhere.

Muzi cupped one butt cheek and lifted her onto her toes, his mouth plundering hers. This wasn't a gentle kiss, a get-to-know-you kiss; it was wild, intense and a little feral. And every bit of her loved it. She couldn't get enough, she wanted more...

She wanted everything. Right here. And right now.

Ro returned his passionate kiss, moving her hands up and under his shirt as she tangled her tongue around his. She released a small moan when his hand found her breast, his thumb swiping over her nipple. She needed to get naked, to have him inside her.

She wanted to pull back, just long enough to tell him to make her his…

She had barely finished that thought when Muzi clasped her hands and pulled them off his body. He held them to her sides and rested his forehead on hers, breathing heavily.

"You are addictive, Roisin O'Keefe," Muzi muttered, before linking her fingers in his. After swiping his mouth across hers in a brief, hard kiss, he took her hand and they slowly walked back to the house, with Ro wishing he wasn't returning to Cape Town.

Despite having known him for such a short time, she was going to miss him.

They stepped onto the circular driveway in front of the house and Muzi nodded to his car. "Let me take you home, then I need to be on the road."

"Busy week ahead?" Ro asked as she settled into the passenger seat of his SUV.

Do not ask him to stay, Ro. Do. Not.

"Very," Muzi replied as he pulled away. "I'll get a lease drawn up for the land and I'll send it to Siya for him to make sure your interests are protected."

Ro wrinkled her nose at the mention of her lawyer. "I'm sure it will be fine."

Muzi looked horrified. "Jesus, Ro, you never sign anything until you've had a lawyer look over it."

Ro rolled her eyes. "It's a lease from *you*. If you stiff me, my brothers will bury you."

"They would, and rightly so." He frowned at her before returning his eyes to the road. "But don't sign a damn thing, not from me or anyone else without Siya's okay. Deal?"

"If I agree, will you stop nagging me?"

Muzi placed his hand on her thigh and squeezed, his

fingers sending ribbons of heat through her body. She looked at his hand and wished…

Wished that he wasn't going back to the city, that he'd feed her a dozen, a hundred more kisses, strip her naked and do wicked, wonderful things to her. She wanted to share late-night conversations and coffee, early morning whispers and drugging kisses.

She wanted him…

With an intensity that scared her.

Muzi's hand remained on her thigh as he drove back to his vineyard, and after a brief journey, he swung his fancy car down the tree-lined driveway and pulled up next to his front door. Muzi leaned across her and opened her door.

"You're not coming in?" Ro asked him, surprised. "You must be hot and thirsty. I am!"

"They have water in the city and it's a short drive," Muzi told her, leaning his forearm on the steering wheel.

"But—"

Muzi rubbed his hands over his face. "The last time we returned from St. Urban, I was as dusty and dirty and I *just* managed to stop myself from inviting you to join me in the shower. But if I get out of this car, I'm going to start kissing you and I'm not going to stop until we are both naked and you are screaming my name," he said, his voice a low growl.

She didn't have a problem with that, she really didn't.

"I see the way you look at me, the desire in your gorgeous blue eyes," Muzi said, his thumb gently swiping her bottom lip. "I want you, I'm pretty damn sure you want me too, and driving away is going to be the hardest thing I've done for a while."

"Then why are you?" Ro wanted to look around to check to see who was putting words in her mouth. Because this wasn't her, sounding bold and fearless and more than a little wanton.

Muzi's thumb pressed into her bottom lip. "I could tell you that you're Digby's sister and we're doing business together and that it's not a good idea. It's all true." Muzi dropped his hand and lifted his huge shoulders. "But it's more than that. As you know, Digby talks to me. He's worried about you, so is Radd. They think you are more stressed than you realize—that you're feeling vulnerable and a little lost, that you are dealing with a lot. Maybe a temporary fling is *not* what you need."

Pride had her lifting her nose in the air. "Isn't that my decision to make?"

"Sure," Muzi replied, his tone easy. He leaned back in his seat and stared at her, his expression pensive.

She waited for him to speak, hoping he wasn't going to be stupid and try and make decisions for her.

"Your brothers are super protective of you, but I think you are stronger, more resilient than they give you credit for. And yeah, you're an adult who can make her own decisions. So why don't we do this? Why don't you take the time until I get back to relax, to read a book, to hang out by the pool? To sleep and to chill. If you want to pick this up when I come back, then it's game on. But I can't promise you anything, Ro."

She never, not for a minute, thought he could. Being more than a little stubborn, she wanted to argue with him, tell him that she knew what she was doing, that she knew her mind and was perfectly capable of deciding whether she wanted to sleep with someone or not. But…

But his words resonated with her. She had been stressed lately, she was tense and feeling overwhelmed. Maybe a little time spent on her own before they embarked on a no-strings fling would be a good thing. She nodded. "Okay, deal."

But, because she wanted to leave him with a taste of

what he'd be missing out on, she leaned across the seat to drop a kiss on his mouth.

"Drive safely," she told him, turning back to open her door more widely. She dropped to the ground and slammed the door closed. She wasn't surprised when Muzi lowered the passenger window. She raised her eyebrows and waited for him to speak.

"Stay away from Pasco Kildare," he grumbled.

Ro grinned at him. "Not a chance," she informed him. "If the man offers to feed me, I'm going to eat."

"As long as feeding you is all he does. If he tries anything else, friend or not, I will annihilate him," Muzi muttered before lifting a hand and driving away.

She wasn't a fan of possessive men, didn't like them puffing up and beating their chests but, like everything else about Muzi, his jealousy turned her on.

Man, this hole she kept digging was just getting deeper and deeper.

Ro woke up to a message from Muzi, sent at around 6:00 a.m., informing her that he was back in Franschhoek, that he'd gone for a trail run, and that he'd see her later.

His return had been delayed and, after nearly two weeks, she was dying to see him.

Hopefully, he'd be back soon. Instead of pulling on an old T-shirt, her most battered pair of shorts and rain boots—her standard uniform these days—she tugged on a bikini, a short, flowy skirt and a loose, off-the-shoulder top. She swiped on mascara and lip gloss, sprayed perfume on her neck and wrists and allowed her long hair to fall down her back.

Shoving her feet into beaded flip-flops, she left Muzi's guest room.

She'd missed him, of course she had, and staying in his

house without him felt strange but, she reluctantly admitted, she'd thoroughly enjoyed her time alone.

Working hard stopped her from overanalyzing and made time move quickly. The power and water to St. Urban were restored the day after Muzi left for the city and, since then, she'd worked eight-to ten-hour physically demanding days at the mansion, systematically clearing one room before moving on to the next. She now had a system—things to toss, things to keep, things to donate—and she was making slow but steady progress. She'd pulled down curtains, washed exquisite, vintage china, taken heavy and old paintings off walls and ripped up carpets. She'd boxed diaries, thrown away forty years of newspapers and found five cases of a very old, exceptionally fine whiskey.

She wasn't a whiskey drinker but Muzi and her brothers would, she was sure, appreciate a case each.

She was proud of her progress and an unexpected benefit of hard work was that her anxiety levels had plummeted. By the end of the day, she had just enough energy to eat the meals Muzi's housekeeper prepared for her, shower and fall into bed. Worrying and thinking required more energy than she currently possessed, and she was often asleep before nine o'clock, sleeping well until the next morning.

She was still ignoring Kelvin—not a day passed without him trying to connect with her—she spoke to Siya on an as-needed basis instead of constantly peppering him with questions about the trust and, instead of pressuring her parents to save their marriage, she was trying to give them some breathing room.

She didn't waste her time thinking about Gil and Zia.

She felt better, stronger, fitter…more in control.

Yep, Muzi—so damn smart—had been right when he said she needed to take a break.

Ro took her time walking through his house, stopping

to admire a sculpture or the art on his walls. On her way to the kitchen, her attention was caught by the intense colors of an abstract painting to her left. She stopped at the open door to Muzi's study—normally kept closed—and moved her eyes to the painting on the wall opposite his desk.

It couldn't be...could it?

Because she'd spent a lot of time with the Murphy International representative, the auction house selling Gil and Zia's art and collectibles, she immediately recognized the artist as Irma Stern. Gil and Zia owned three of her paintings, one of which she was keeping. She'd put the other two up for auction and each carried an auction estimate of more than twenty million dollars. Muzi's painting, bigger, bolder and better executed than any of the paintings in Gil and Zia's collection, had to be worth more.

How the hell did Muzi afford a painting by one of the country's best artists? Oh, she could understand the impressive house—he was the CEO of an international wine company—and he earned well, but she would've thought that a painting by such an amazing, important artist would be beyond his price bracket.

Ro turned around, saw another smaller painting on the wall next to the window and realized that it was a sketch by Degas, and on the desk was a sculpture by William Kentridge. Not in the same league as Degas and Irma Stern but ridiculously expensive all the same.

So, Muzi had pots of money as well as taste. She didn't give a fig about the money, but she did applaud his taste.

Ro walked out of his study and walked through the lounge toward the kitchen, sighing at the smell of fresh coffee and what she thought might be fresh croissants. She adored Muzi's housekeeper.

If she couldn't wake up with Muzi in her bed, then coffee and croissants were the next best way to start the day.

Ro added boiling water to the coffee carafe and placed it on the tray. The breakfast tray was bulging with goodies and she picked it up and carefully made her way out to the entertainment deck, choosing the small iron table instead of the outside dining table that seated eight.

It was shortly past nine, she'd slept later than usual, but it was Sunday and no one was waiting for her at St. Urban. A gentle breeze danced over the vineyards and the garden and it was already pleasantly hot. She thought she might lie in the sun after breakfast, and do a few lazy laps in the pool.

Unless Muzi had other plans for them…

She still wanted him, Ro decided, slathering her open croissant with butter. She wanted to know what being with him was like, whether reality could ever match her imagination. Ro stared out at the mountain dominating her view, remembering Muzi telling her that he couldn't promise her anything.

After being in such a long relationship, she was fine with that. She didn't know if she was ready for anything more than a bed-based friendship.

She'd always know where she stood with Muzi, he was stunningly honest, and she respected that. After Kelvin's duplicity, she'd rather be hurt with the truth than comforted by a lie. Honesty was a gift she never expected to receive.

She could have an affair with Muzi and when it was time for her to return home—sometime before Christmas—she could leave with a smile and some awesome memories. The thought of going back to the States made her mouth suddenly dry.

She didn't know if LA was where she wanted to be…

"Anyone home?"

Ro turned at the strange voice and watched as an extremely attractive, slim woman walked through Muzi's lounge and stepped onto his entertainment deck. She was followed by a younger man wearing an untucked button-down shirt and black chino shorts, trendy trainers on his feet.

She recognized them instantly, from Pasco's. Susan and Keegan? No, Keane.

She wiped her lips with a serviette and wondered why she hadn't heard them knock, or the sound of a doorbell. It was a big house but not *that* big and she knew that Greta, Muzi's live-in housekeeper, had left to attend a church service in town. Greta normally didn't work on a Sunday but she was on a mission to look after and feed the, in her eyes, too-thin American.

"The front door was open so we came on in," Susan said. She waved a thin hand, her superlong ruby-red nails flashing in the sunlight. "It's the country, we don't stand on ceremony here."

Ro thought she had a great deal of chutzpah to walk unannounced into Muzi's house but she wasn't a South African, maybe they did things differently here.

Ro gave mother and son a quick once-over. It was obvious the two were related. They both had deep red hair, the same green eyes and a long nose. Both wore expensive clothing: their watches and her jewelry could prop up the economy of a developing country.

Their clothing and demeanor screamed privilege, prestige and power. Ro wondered how they'd react if they heard that she could, probably, buy and sell them a hundred times over. The thought gave her courage so she slowly rose, pushed back her shoulders and lifted her chin.

"My name is Roisin O'Keefe, I'm a guest of Muzi's. He's not here, unfortunately," she said, not bothering to hold out her hand for them to shake. They'd probably ignore the gesture.

"Oh, we know," the older woman said. "Take a seat."

Ro, annoyed by her barked order, gripped the edge of the back of the chair. She was about to demand what they wanted when the younger man spoke. "I'm Keane Matthews-Reed, and this is my mother, Susan Matthews-Reed."

He, at least, was attempting to be courteous.

"Susan Matthews," Susan corrected, and Ro wondered if she imagined the flash of embarrassment in Keane's eyes at her imperious attitude.

"Okay," Ro said, "but I have no idea what you could want with me."

"For God's sake sit down and ask the housekeeper to bring us a champagne mimosa," Susan said. "I'm parched."

Keane frowned at his mother. "Not everyone has champagne for breakfast, Mother. And you said that we weren't staying long enough for a drink."

Mother? Who called their mom "mother"?

Susan glared at him. "For God's sake, Keane, you know that I prefer to be called Susan."

Wow. Okay, then.

"I could offer you some coffee," Ro replied, hoping they wouldn't accept her polite gesture.

"We've just had some, thank you," Keane said. He sat down and rested his hands over his flat stomach, his green eyes cool. "Susan, you said you had something to discuss with Roisin, so can you get on with it so that I can get home?"

Susan crossed one long, still slim leg over the other and twisted an enormous diamond ring on her middle finger. That was, if it was real, a hell of a rock. And, judging by her Chanel bag, Louboutin heels and Prada sunglasses, it had to be real.

"I want to know how you are connected to St. Urban and why Muzi recently rented the property's vines," Susan demanded.

Ro stared at her, feeling blindsided. She definitely didn't have enough coffee in her system to deal with Susan. "Uh…"

Keane sat up straighter and glared at his mother. "For God's sake, Susan, you told me we were coming here to welcome her to the valley. And what the hell are you talking about?"

"Muzi signed a lease this week on behalf of Clos du Cadieux to rent over one hundred acres of Merlot vines from St. Urban," Susan told him, her eyes not leaving Ro's face. "I've been trying to speak to him, meet with him, all week but he's been ducking my calls and avoiding me."

Honestly, Ro couldn't blame Muzi; she would do the same thing in his position. "Why on earth would you think that Ms. O'Keefe knows anything about Clos du Cadieux business?" Keane asked, sounding genuinely confused.

"She's been spending a lot of time at the property," Susan replied, her tone defiant. Her eyes connected with Ro's and her ultrathin eyebrows lifted. "Why?"

Ro rested her arms on the back of the chair and held Susan's hard glare. She'd worked at a private, exclusive kindergarten in Trousdale, one of the most expensive neighborhoods in LA, and faced down many an entitled helicopter mommy. Compared to those lionesses, Susan was a toothless tiger.

"I fail to see how anything I do concerns you," Ro told her, her voice dropping below freezing point.

"I am a board member of Clos du Cadieux. I have a right to ask what the CEO is doing here, and why he's here with you," Susan retorted.

"For God's sake, Mom," Keane groaned, obviously embarrassed.

"Why did he accompany you to St. Urban? What is your connection to the trust that owns the property? What are you hiding?"

Keane rolled his eyes and sent Ro an apologetic look, his shoulders lifting in a small "What can I do?" shrug. *Telling her to shut up would be a good start*, Ro silently told him.

"And why do you look familiar?"

Ro returned her gaze to Susan, her mind racing. If this nosy-as-hell woman got wind of who she was, Ro did not doubt *that* bombshell would reach Cape Town by nightfall and she'd be tomorrow morning's headline.

She needed to nip this in the bud, right now. "I thoroughly object to you rocking up here with your impertinent questions but I suspect you won't leave until I answer. I met Muzi through Digby Tempest-Vane when I was working as an au pair for his fiancée's niece." All true. It was best, she'd read somewhere, to stick to the truth when one was lying. Now she needed to fudge a little. "Digby heard that the lawyer looking after his parents' trust—"

"Digby and Radd aren't inheriting a cent from that trust so why are they talking to the lawyer?" Susan demanded in a sharp voice.

Right, well, Susan was well-informed and wasn't a fool. It took all of Ro's acting skills to shrug her shoulders and look puzzled. "I have no idea and it's not a subject I have discussed with him. I know how to mind my own business."

Her pointed comment didn't resonate with Susan, but Keane dropped his eyes and looked away. It was obvious he hadn't inherited his mom's rhinoceros-thick hide.

"The trust's lawyers were looking for someone to oversee the cleanup of St. Urban so that the owner could sell, if he wanted to—"

"How do you know the owner is a he?"

Lord give me strength.

Ro lifted her hands. "I don't—"

"Mother!"

Susan ignored Keane and gestured for Ro to continue. Yes, Your Majesty.

"The lawyer offered me the job, I accepted and Muzi offered me a place to stay," Ro said, thinking that she needed to end this conversation and get them out of Muzi's house. "The lease, if there is one, would be between Muzi and the trust."

"Muzi is the CEO of an enormous wine empire, he doesn't accompany girls to farms," Susan sneered. "I don't believe you, tell me the truth."

Keane slapped his knees and stood up. He gripped his mother's arm to get her to stand up. Susan slapped his hand away and oh so deliberately leaned back in her chair, her posture telling them both that she had no intention of going anywhere.

Marvelous.

"Why don't I believe anything you are telling me?" Susan demanded. When Ro didn't answer her, she stood up. She placed her fists on her skinny hips and her surgically enhanced chest rose and fell with obvious indignation. "I demand to know what Muzi is up to, what you are doing at St. Urban and why you are staying in Muzi's house."

Right, she was done with white lies, she needed one with pink and purple stripes and golden dots. There was only one other explanation she could give—one Susan would believe.

"Not that it is any of your business, but Muzi and I are having an affair. We have been since we met."

Keane's expression hinted at amusement, but Susan looked at her, mouth agape. She opened her mouth to speak, shut it again and shook her head. "Nope, not buying it."

"Right, we're done," Keane said, his face hard. "Mother, you've embarrassed yourself, and me, enough for one day.

I'm leaving and if you are not in the car in five minutes, you'll have a long walk back to the city."

Susan obviously saw something in Keane's expression that convinced her he was being heart-attack serious. She glared at him but picked her bag off the coffee table and pulled it over her bony shoulder. She tossed her head and sent Ro another glare. "Tell Muzi that this isn't over, that I will find out what he's up to."

"Tell him yourself," Ro coldly suggested.

Susan released an annoyed huff, whipped around and strode into the house and out of sight.

Keane rubbed the back of his neck. "Sorry about this, she can be a bit irrational about Muzi."

He looked embarrassed, Ro thought, but also sad. Taking a chance, she tossed out a question, wondering if he would answer it. "Muzi and Susan obviously have a tense relationship—"

"That's a massive understatement."

"So what's your excuse for treating him like crap?" Ro demanded.

Remorse and humiliation flashed through his eyes, across his face, before Keane's expression settled into impassivity. "I'm sorry we intruded."

Ro shook her head as he walked away and a few minutes later, she heard a powerful car start up and drive away.

Well, that was fun, she thought, dropping to sit on the edge of the chair. Seeing her phone on the coffee table, she picked it up and wondered how to tell Muzi that their relationship had shifted.

Had a very unexpected visit from Susan and Keane Matthews-Reed. The story is that I am at St. Urban, employed by the trust's lawyers, to fix up the place to get it ready to sell.

She sent the message and stared down at the screen, thinking how to frame her next piece of news. *Just keep it simple, stupid.*

She didn't believe me, said I looked very familiar—!!!—and kept pushing. So I told them we're having a red-hot affair.

CHAPTER SIX

We're having a red-hot affair.

HE WISHED.

On seeing the message on his phone from Ro, Muzi cut short his twelve-mile trail run and headed down the mountain, skipping over a tree root in the middle of the narrow path. Annoyance skittered up and down his sweaty spine. God, Susan had a tungsten set of balls. How dare she stroll into his house and ambush Ro?

Muzi used the back of his forearm to wipe perspiration out of his eyes and, despite knowing it was dangerous to go too fast on the rock-and-root-filled path—if he fell, he could tumble down a steep hill and, possibly, into the ravine below—pushed himself to speed up.

Bloody Susan.

Most people would think that him accompanying Ro to St. Urban was a perfectly reasonable thing to do, and it was, but Susan always suspected everyone of having ulterior motives. Pity that, in this case, she was right. He expected her to do a little digging into who Ro was, that was just the nature of the beast, but he never, ever expected her to rock up at his home demanding answers.

What raised her suspicions? She knew about him leasing St. Urban's land but Ro's wasn't the first land he'd leased, nor would it be the last. It was the fact that they didn't *need* more land and grapes right now that had obviously raised her suspicions.

He'd made a mistake of avoiding her lately and he cursed himself. If Susan heard he was on the trail of a new cultivar, she'd do whatever she could to derail his efforts. Hurting and hobbling him was more important than Clos du Cadieux.

Muzi, his lungs straining and his muscles screaming, bolted down the path. If the cultivar wasn't growing at St. Urban, or if the vines produced terrible grapes and dismal wine, his reputation would take a hell of a hit, exactly what Susan wanted.

There was no way he'd allow that to happen, he hadn't endured so much to let her win. Muzi, his legs burning and his arms pumping, ducked under a low hanging branch and cursed when a broken stick slashed the skin above his eyebrow.

He swore again, this time in Xhosa, touched the wound and felt blood trickling over his fingertips. Bloody Susan, this was her fault. He took his eyes off the path, looked down at the bright red blood on his fingers, not noticing the tree root beneath his trainer. His foot hooked it and he found himself flying. He went down hard, his shoulder connecting with a rock, sending waves of searing pain up and down his arm. Sprawled on the path, his face in the dirt, he took stock. Shoulder dislocated but no arms or legs broken. A cut on his forehead, scrapes to his face and he'd lacerated his shin.

He'd live. But, damn, he hurt.

Using his good arm, Muzi pushed himself up to a seated position and grimaced at the blood pouring down his leg. He looked around and realized that he was only a few miles from his house. He would call Ro and she could meet him at the bottom of the hill. She could drive him into town and his favorite doc could reset his shoulder.

First item on the agenda, calling Ro. Except that his phone was strapped to his good arm and he couldn't use his useless arm to pull it from its pouch. It took him a few minutes to remember that he could use voice activation...

"Siri, call Ro."

He watched but it didn't light up and he looked at the phone again, cursing when he saw the massive crack across the screen. His phone, thanks to the impact with the rock, was dead.

Muzi cursed yet again, long, low and slow this time. When he was done, he pushed himself to his feet and fought a wave of dizziness. He breathed deeply and, when his light-headedness receded, he started to walk home, dripping blood and swearing up a storm, trying to convince himself that, because he routinely completed ultratriathlons, four or so miles was a piece of cake.

With a dislocated shoulder, four miles on an uneven trail turned out to be the seventeenth level of hell.

It took Muzi much longer than he thought, mostly because he was a little light-headed—he must've hit his head harder than he thought—and he was tired, dirty and goddamn hurting when he walked up the steps leading to his outside entertainment area. Each step sent pain ricocheting through his shoulder, but a flash of bright pink momentarily distracted him.

He stopped, one foot on the step above, and his pain receded at the sight of Ro lying in the sun. Her long body was turning pink and a wide-brimmed straw hat covered her face. Judging by the way her chest and fabulous breasts rose and fell—covered in only two brief triangles—she was soundly asleep.

He could spend hours, days watching her sleep, fascinated by her long, slim legs, her flat stomach, the delicate curve of her hips. But, because he felt like someone was ripping off his arm, he could only give her another twenty seconds before calling her name.

He called once, twice, and when she didn't wake, bellowed her name. Ro shot up, her hat went flying and her head whipped around frantically, trying to find the source of the noise. She didn't think to look behind her and Muzi called her name again.

Ro turned her torso, placed her hand to her face to keep the sun out of her eyes and sent him a smile. "Hi, you're back. Did you get my message… Holy hell, what happened to you?"

Exhausted, Muzi slowly lowered himself to sit on the top step. He watched Ro run across the lawn and, a few seconds later, she stood in front of him, her mouth agape.

His eyes were in line with her belly button and she had a tiny ring in it, classy and stupendously sexy. He allowed his eyes to skim over her brief bikini bottoms, down her long legs and noticed that she wore a silver toe ring and had a small rosebud tattooed on the inside of her ankle. How had he missed that?

"Do you have any other tattoos?" he asked, before lifting his hand. "No, don't tell me, I want to discover them myself."

"You're hurt! Oh, my God, you're *bleeding*!"

Yeah, he knew that. Muzi squinted up at her. "So, we're having a red-hot affair? Cool."

Ro ignored his comment and dropped to her haunches in front of him, looking at the cut on his leg. "This needs stitches."

He figured.

She peered into his eyes, looking far too serious. "Did you hit your head, are you concussed?"

Muzi rocked his hand from side to side. "Maybe."

"Probably," Ro stated, standing up and holding out her hands. "Let's get you up and get you to a doctor."

Muzi looked at her hands and shook his head. "Nuh-uh."

Ro narrowed her eyes at him. "Look, Superman, you need, at the very least, an EMT. That cut needs stitches and while I have been known to apply a butterfly clip or two, this is beyond my area of expertise. I also want to make sure you don't have a concussion, so get up off your ass."

"Can't..." Muzi said, focusing on her pretty blue eyes. "My shoulder is dislocated."

Her mouth dropped open in shock as her eyes fixed on his right shoulder. He'd seen a dislocated shoulder before, knew it looked weird. Because he'd been running shirtless, she'd be able to see the strange bump and sloped shoulder.

Ro pursed her lips and slapped her hands on her hips. "Right," she said, not giving him time to respond. "I'm going to call an ambulance."

Muzi gripped her wrist in his good hand. "I just need you to drive me to Sam."

Ro bent down to thread both her arms through his good arm. "Use your legs to push up and who is Sam?"

Muzi swallowed a yelp of pain as he rose and scrunched his eyes together, sucking in some deep breaths. Ro kept her hands wrapped around his bicep and led him into the house. "Do not brush your leg against any furniture."

He glared at her; he was hurt, not idiotic. He managed to avoid the furniture, kept his bloody shoes off the carpets and walked through the door leading from the kitchen to the garage where he'd parked his Lamborghini before starting on his run. "Are you comfortable driving a stick shift, Ro?"

She pulled a face. "It won't be pretty, but I'll manage."

She opened the passenger door for him. "You didn't answer my question, who is Sam?"

"One of my favorite women, ever," Muzi replied as he pulled himself up into the car's high seat using his good hand. Ro stood on the running board and pulled the seat belt down and across his chest. Her breast pushed into his chest, her hair tickled his chin and neck, and her bare hip connected with his thigh.

And, because his junk had a mind of its own, and didn't care that his shoulder was a lava bed of pain, he felt himself swelling, growing. Any minute now and she would realize it too.

Ro clicked in his seat belt, tensed and turned her head to look at him. One arched eyebrow raised. "Really? Now?"

He lifted his uninjured shoulder in a brief shrug. "You're wearing next to nothing and all I can see is a lot of smooth, feminine flesh. Your scent, a combination of sunblock and perfume is intoxicating and your mouth, and nipples, are in easy reach of my mouth. What do you expect me to do?"

"Act like an adult and not a randy boy," Ro snapped back.

Easier said than done, Muzi decided. He looked down at his arm and saw his cell phone pouch. The edges of the pouch were digging into his skin and he asked Ro to take it off. She pulled apart the Velcro and, when it was off, looked down at the cracked screen. "Well done, Triple M, you've just managed to destroy the very latest, most expensive smartphone on the market."

On the list of his regrets, it was near the bottom. Ro tossed his phone onto the back seat and hopped down from the running board. "Let's get going," she suggested, standing back to close his door.

"Wait!" Muzi stated, holding up his good hand.

Ro pushed back her hair, irritated. "What now?"

"As much as I love what you are wearing, maybe it would be better for you not to ride into town dressed in a skimpy bikini." Despite his pain, he had to grin at her shocked face. "We don't want to attract any more attention than necessary."

He laughed as she cursed and flounced back into the house.

She made it into Franschhoek with a lot of grinding of gears and Muzi's muttering about his poor gearbox and lamenting her treatment of his SUV. Ro, trying to keep the powerful, super expensive and luxurious car on the road, ignored his running commentary and, finally, what seemed like hours later, pulled up outside a home on the leafy outskirts of the town. The house was painted a mellow cream and was set in a lush, extensive garden with what seemed to be acres planted with roses.

Ro, in shorts and a white, flowing top, cut the engine to the car and darted a look at Muzi's gray face. The man was in a lot more discomfort than she'd realized, and her heart pounded in her chest. She didn't like seeing anyone in pain, but seeing this powerful, warrior-like man gripping the seat and biting his lip made her eyes sting. She needed to get him help. And fast.

But she had no idea why they were at a private house and not at a doctor's surgery or a hospital. "Why are we here?" Ro asked as a pack of hounds, of every color and breed, galloped toward the car, barking madly.

"Don't worry about the dogs, they're harmless," Muzi said, his voice thready. "Hit the hooter, Ro."

The hooter? What? "Huh?" Ro asked him, not understanding his request.

Muzi shook his head, turned his torso, and used his left hand to hit the horn of the car. Right, in South Africa, a horn was a hooter, a napkin was a serviette and, strangest of all, a traffic light was called a robot. Weird.

The dogs barked again, danced around the car and within a few minutes, a well-dressed couple appeared around the corner of the house, arm in arm. They waved when they saw Muzi's car and the older man released a sharp whistle that quieted the dogs and made them sit.

Damn, she wished she could do that with her kindergarten kids.

Thinking that she was safe from the dogs, Ro exited the car and, giving the hounds a wide berth, approached the couple. "Hi. Muzi insisted I bring him here. He's hurt."

The woman's expression immediately sharpened, and she pulled her hand out of her husband's, her casual stroll increasing to a fast walk. "What happened?"

"He took a fall running," Ro told her. "He's got a bad cut on his shin, a cut on his head, I think he may be concussed. And he's dislocated his shoulder."

"Right." The woman yanked open the passenger door and glared up at Muzi. "*Really,* Triple M? This is not the way I wanted to spend my Sunday!"

Over her shoulder, Ro saw his tight smile and the fondness in his eyes for this petite but forthright woman. "Sorry, Doc."

Ro released a long, relieved sigh. Thank God, she was a doctor and Muzi would finally get some help. Ro leaned her shoulder against the back passenger door and stared down at the bright emerald grass beneath her feet. She felt like she could, finally, pull some air into her lungs.

Ro held her hand out and saw that her fingers were trembling. She'd pushed back her fear but now that there were others to help him, she felt a little dizzy. His injury could've been a lot worse. He could still be lying on that mountain, his neck broken, his head bleeding.

God...

She couldn't bear the thought. Ro wrapped her arms around her middle, forced to admit that she'd be gutted if something happened to Muzi, that he'd come to mean a lot to her in too short a time.

She'd known him for less than three weeks. How could she be feeling such a connection after so little time? It wasn't normal, not for her, anyway. She took her time with people, sussed them out and looked before she leaped.

With Muzi, she'd just dived on in...

"Cut on head and leg, a dislocated shoulder? Anything else I should know about?" the doctor briskly asked him, her sharp eyes bouncing between Ro and Muzi's injuries.

"I think that's it," Ro replied when Muzi didn't. "I think I mentioned a concussion?"

"Not concussed," Muzi stated, lifting his good hand. "Sam and John, meet Roisin O'Keefe, also known as Ro. Ro, these good people are your favorite chef's parents, John and Dr. Sam Kildare."

John Kildare, Pasco's dad, sent her a warm smile. His wife's smile was there, but cooler. "You had dinner with Muzi at Pasco's recently."

Wow, news seemed to travel at light speed in Franschhoek.

"Pasco told us, and said that he enjoyed meeting you," John explained. He placed a hand on his wife's shoulder and peered over her head to look at Muzi. "How are you doing, Triple M?"

"Hurting like a mother," Muzi admitted. "Is Pas around? I could do with his help getting out of this car."

John jerked his head and Ro turned to see Pasco, wearing a battered pair of shorts, an old T-shirt and rain boots, walking toward them, casually eating a piece of toast.

"What's the idiot done now?" he asked, not sounding remotely concerned.

Ro bristled at his casual tone. The least the man could do was show a little concern or sympathy. She moved so that she could put her hand on Muzi's thigh, giving it a sympathetic pat. He sent her a weary grin. "Much as I like your hand on my thigh, Ro, you need to get out of the way so that the moron can help me down and into the house."

Moron, idiot…okay, so this was how the old friends talked to each other. Noted.

Pasco shoved his last piece of toast into his mouth and gently nudged his mom away from the car. "I've got this, Doc," he told her. Pasco leaned across Muzi to unclip his seat belt and whistled as he caught sight of the jagged wound on Muzi's leg. "Jesus, Triple M. What the hell did you do?"

Muzi swung his legs toward the open door, his lips thin with pain. "I was on a trail run behind the house and I got a text message." His eyes connected with Ro and she knew exactly what the text message was about and she blushed. "I was trying to wrap my head around the text as I flew down the path, but I was distracted and tripped over a root, smacked my shoulder into a rock and hit my head." He glanced down at his leg. "I have no idea how I gashed my leg open."

Pasco linked his arm in Muzi's and shared his strength with him as Muzi slid out of the car. He swayed but Pasco's grip on him kept him upright. "I'll help you inside and then the doc can work her magic on you."

"And not for the first time," Sam muttered as they slowly walked to the house. "Since you are now adults, I thought I was over patching you boys up. Just goes to show that I can be, occasionally, wrong."

"Can I have that in writing?" John quipped.

"Do you want to sleep with the dogs tonight?" Doc Kildare asked her husband, the twinkle in her eye taking the sting out of her words.

Ro caught John's eye, saw his exaggerated grimace, and, caught between the urge to laugh and cry, started to giggle.

Seeing the light under Muzi's half-open bedroom door, Ro gently knocked. When she heard Muzi's command to enter, she pushed open the door.

"Hey," he said, his deep voice washing over her. He ran his hand over his jaw and glanced at the dark night beyond his floor-to-ceiling windows. "I can't believe I slept for so long. What the hell did Sam give me?"

Ro stepped into the room and rested her hand on the back of a black-and-white wingback chair. His bedroom was a study in black and white: the wall behind his head was painted charcoal, his headboard was black and snow-white linen covered his bed. Huge black-and-white photographs depicting wild, desolate beaches decorated the white wall that separated the bedroom from his dressing room, which she presumed led to an en suite bathroom. Opposite him was a huge flat-screen TV attached to the wall. He muted the sound and tossed the remote onto the bed beside him.

"How are you feeling?" Ro asked, noticing that he'd dispensed of the sling Dr. Sam insisted he wear when he left her house.

"Not too bad," he replied, crossing his long legs at the ankle. On returning home, he'd refused her help. He'd managed a shower and to pull on a pair of running shorts, but his chest was still bare. That was okay, she had no problem looking at his big body, muscles on muscles.

"Since it's Sunday, and Greta took the rest of the day

off, I made a chicken salad for supper," she told him, rocking from foot to foot and trying to pull her mind off his fantastic body.

"Sounds good, but I'm not hungry," Muzi said. He patted the bed beside him. "Come here."

Ro moved to the bed and sat down on the edge, sending him a concerned look. A bandage covered the stitches in his leg and a butterfly clip held the cut on his forehead together. He had a scrape on his chin and his shoulder but, despite the hint of pain in his eyes, he looked a million times better than he did before.

"You scared me," Ro said, internally wincing at the fear in her voice.

"I'm tough. My body has taken a lot worse," he reassured, placing his hand on her bare knee. It felt good there, like it belonged. Damn, she could not be developing strong feelings for this reserved man.

She would not let herself fall for another person who would, eventually, end up hurting her. Love was a fallacy, and commitment was a concept that was, as she knew, flawed.

Muzi squeezed her knee and she lifted her head to look into his soulful black eyes. "Thanks for your help today."

Ro nodded and half turned, putting her knee and thigh on the bed to face him. "I'm sorry I abused your fancy car."

"It'll be fine," Muzi assured her, drawing circles on the bare skin beneath the hem of her shorts.

"Do you need me to call anyone, to tell them about your accident?" she asked, trying to ignore his sparking-a-fire touch.

"No, there's no need to get Mimi upset. Or even involved." Muzi frowned. "I hope Sam didn't call her."

"Do they know each other?"

"Oh, yeah. Digby and I spent a lot of time with Pasco

growing up. His folks were still living on the vineyard they own—Pasco's brother is the resident vintner now—and we were always hurting ourselves or hurting each other. Sam had to call Mimi quite a few times to inform her about my latest injury."

"And how did Mimi take those calls?"

Muzi smiled. "With equanimity. She believes that God protects the stupid. To be fair, He did that a lot because we got up to some dumb stuff."

"It was weird to see one of the world's most celebrated chefs in ratty shorts and Wellington boots," Ro commented.

Ro moved to sit cross-legged on the bed, her knee resting against Muzi's uninjured leg.

"Pas is both farmer and chef, he was probably potting around in the greenhouse. It's his way to relax."

"How do you relax?" Ro asked him.

"Working out, reading…" Heat flashed in his eyes. "Sex."

She saw the question in his eyes, knew that if she made the slightest move, she'd be naked in ten seconds and he'd be rocketing her toward an intense orgasm. But she wasn't ready, not just yet. She didn't want to sleep with him until she was very sure that she could treat him as a friend with benefits, a lovely interlude. Before she slept with him, she needed to get rid of these mushy feelings, the thoughts that something could develop between them.

Nothing could. Or would.

She knew that intellectually, but she needed to believe it, heart, body and soul. She just needed a little more time to pull herself together. She dragged her eyes off his handsome face and played with the frayed edges of her denim shorts. "I'm sorry I told Susan that we were having an affair, but I didn't know what else to tell her. She's pretty persistent."

Irritation flashed across his face. "*Persistent* is a nice word for her," he muttered, his tone bitter.

Wow, there most definitely was no love lost between them. Ro placed her elbows on the inside of her knees and rested her chin against her linked hands, ready to listen. "As you know, she's Mimi's daughter and she's on the board of Clos du Cadieux," he began.

"Mmm…"

Ro cocked her head to the side, lifting her eyebrows to get him to explain. Muzi's eyes connected with hers and slid away. His eyebrows pulled together in a deep frown and he looked away from her to the TV, and did she imagine him moving his leg so that it no longer touched hers? Oh, she didn't need to be a psychologist to tell that Susan was not someone he wanted to discuss.

A long silence stretched between them, a little uncomfortable, a lot awkward. Ro sighed, wishing he found it as easy to talk to her as she did him. With her, he just needed to look at her with those deep, intense eyes and she started to gush.

It was obvious she did not have the same effect on him.

Ro started to stand up but he gripped her knee as if he were trying to keep her in place. "It's complicated," he said, his normally smooth voice rough with emotion.

"It always is," Ro softly murmured.

"Susan doesn't like me," he stated. Ro covered his hand with hers, linking their fingers. Muzi looked down at their interwoven digits and she felt him shudder. "I should qualify that, she's never liked me. *Ever.*"

Ro frowned, trying to make sense of his statement. Looking for clarification, she tossed out another question. "You grew up with her, didn't you?"

"I told you that my grandmother worked for Mimi and I came to live with Lu when I was three. I have no memories of my life before that, few memories of my mother. I do not have the first clue who my father is," Muzi said, his voice flat and monotonous. He sounded like he was reading from a cereal box and Ro realized that this was his way to deal with a painful subject.

If he had to explain, he'd do it but with as little fuss as possible.

"Lu was awesome and so was Mimi. Years after I came to live with Lu, Susan divorced her husband and she moved back into Mimi's mansion with her two sons. Mimi treated us all the same—I wasn't treated like her servant's son, she wouldn't countenance that. Rafe, Keane and I became like brothers."

"And Susan?" Ro asked, knowing that he'd left out a huge chunk of this story.

He stared at a point past her shoulder, and pain and anguish danced across his face and into his eyes. "She was the original Jekyll and Hyde."

"What do you mean?" Ro asked, puzzled.

His face, just for a second, revealed long-ago devastation before it settled back into his "Nothing to see here" expression. "Because of our age difference, Susan treated me like another of her sons when we had company. When we were amongst friends, or even when it was just the family, she was supersweet. But…"

She tightened the grip on his fingers, suspecting that she knew what was coming.

"But when she got me alone, she turned into a viper— a cold, angry, vicious woman."

Ah, no. Please, no.

"She told me, often, that she would do everything in her power to see that I left Mimi's house, that I was sent back to my mother's family in the Transkei, people I never met. She told me that I wasn't good enough to live at La

Fontaine, which is Mimi's estate, just a few miles east of here. It's where I grew up, where Mimi still lives."

Ro felt her other hand tightening into a fist as a wave of anger bubbled up inside her. Educating kids, protecting kids was what she did, who she was, and the thought of an innocent Muzi at the mercy of a vicious adult made her want to scream.

But she knew if she reacted with anything but an empathetic expression, if she showed Muzi her anger or her sympathy, he'd take her response as pity and he'd shut down and shut her out.

"She told me that if I said anything, that if I ratted on her, they wouldn't believe me and I'd be sent away. That I would go back to poverty, that I would never be educated, that I would be alone."

Red-hot anger burned the back of her throat. Not able to say anything without revealing her anger, she gestured for Muzi to continue.

"Lu died when I was ten, Mimi adopted me and threw me an official welcome-to-the-family party. Susan hugged me, said everything she should but later on she told me, in no uncertain terms, that she would do everything in her power to ostracize me, to separate me from Mimi. Later, I realized that her intention, probably all along but definitely from the time my adoption became legal, was to separate me from Mimi's money. Mimi's enormous estate is to be split four ways, with Susan, Rafe, Keane and me as her heirs."

"And Susan doesn't like that," Ro said, proud that her voice sounded reasonably normal.

"Susan hates that. Always has, always will."

"There's more to this story, Muzi. Tell me."

He shook his head and Ro touched his masculine jaw,

rubbing her fingers over his short beard. "You know my secrets, Muzi, and you can trust me with yours."

"I haven't told anybody about Susan, not even Mimi."

She could understand that. He was a proud guy. And he loved his adoptive grandmother and didn't want to cause her any pain. "Tell me everything," she insisted.

Muzi dropped his head back against the headboard and stared up at the ceiling. "The teenage years weren't so bad as I spent a lot of time at boarding school and many weekends and school holidays with friends, either at La Fontaine or at their houses. I became adept at avoiding and ignoring Susan. I went to university, and when I graduated Mimi offered me a position at Clos du Cadieux. Susan actively tried to sabotage me at work. Luckily, I learned very quickly to cover my ass and none of her machinations succeeded. Then Mimi appointed me as CEO and informed the family I would inherit her shares in Clos du Cadieux. Susan lost it."

"Publicly?"

"Hell, no. She caught me working late one night and told me, straight-out, that there was no way she'd ever allow me to succeed at this job. And for the past few years, she's openly and actively tried to undermine and ostracize me."

Ro scratched her forehead, puzzled. "And Mimi knows this?"

"Eh...sort of. Mimi has completely retired and is no longer involved at Clos du Cadieux, She's asked me whether we've had a falling-out, but I brush it off when she brings it up."

He caught her "Why didn't you tell her?" expression and threw up his hands. "She's eighty-four years old, enjoying her retirement. What would it help to tell her that her daughter has tormented me all my life? I understand Susan, she's insecure and narcissistic and controlling but

I can handle her. Rafe and I are good—he's in the States and I don't see much of him, he's doing his own thing. But losing Keane's friendship has nearly killed me. Thanks to his mother, he thinks I'm demanding and controlling and that I've been stealing from Clos du Cadieux, and Mimi, to line my own pockets."

"Why would they think that?"

"Because I have a lifestyle that exceeds the income I make from the company."

She'd been wondering about that herself. "I know I'm being nosy but how *do* you afford the very high-end art and the sculptures, the super expensive car and your fancy threads? I'm sure you earn a kick-butt salary, but you own art worth tens of millions—art that only billionaires can afford."

The corners of Muzi's mouth lifted. "I saved every penny growing up and Mimi gave me a whack of cash when I turned twenty-one. After Jack's death, your brothers vowed to have nothing more to do with their parents and, as a result, had no access to the Tempest-Vane cash.

"Radd knew this computer genius who had an idea for a new internet payment system. They used the little money they had to develop the system but soon ran out of seed money. I took my birthday money and invested in their company. When they sold, I, like them, made a fortune."

Right. Now *that* made sense.

"Mimi knows but nobody else does. I didn't think it was any of their business, specifically Susan's. But now, in Susan's and Keane's minds, the most logical explanation is that I am siphoning money from Clos du Cadieux."

Ro remembered Keane's attitude toward his mother earlier that day and shook her head. He didn't come across that way to her. Ro suspected that he was a guy caught between his loyalty to his mom and his lifelong friendship with Muzi. Oh, she wasn't going to defend him, he didn't deserve that, but she genuinely believed that things weren't as dire between them as Muzi thought.

"Why do you think Susan came here today?" Ro asked.

"I've been thinking about that," Muzi replied, looking thoughtful. "First, you've got to remember that Susan is suspicious of everything I do, all the time. She's looking for something to discredit me, a mistake I'll make to get me canned. I'm looking for a reason to get her to resign from the board. Neither of us has yet managed to dislodge the other so we're in a holding pattern. But she's looking for a gap, a way to hurt me.

"I think a couple of things, occurring at roughly the same time, caught her interest," Muzi continued. "You working at St. Urban, you living here and me leasing St. Urban land all raised her curiosity."

"But why would she come *here*?" Ro demanded.

Muzi rubbed the back of his neck. "I don't bring girl-friends home and when I go to Pasco's, I usually go with Digby or Radd, or simply on my own. Us being together was very out of the norm."

Well, well...

"Susan is clever. You're an anomaly and she'll want to find out more about you."

"She told me that I look familiar," Ro informed him. "That worries me."

"It worries me too because she knew your mom, your birth mom. In fact, they were quite good friends."

"Birds of a feather..." Ro quipped.

Muzi nodded. "If she discovers that you are Zia's biological daughter, she won't hesitate to out you. And if she finds out about a supposedly extinct cultivar on your farm, she'll find those damn vines and pull them out herself."

Awesome news. "So did I hurt or hinder our chances

of keeping all our secrets by telling her that we are having a red-hot affair?"

Muzi, for the first time that evening, smiled. "Oh, that helped. But—"

Oh, God, there was a *but*.

"But she, and everyone else—because there will be no way she'll be able to keep such juicy gossip to herself—will gossip about us and how serious we are. They'll talk engagement rings and marriage and speculate about when we plan to have children."

Ro stared at him, a little shocked and very bemused. "Just because I am, theoretically, sleeping with you? Why would they jump to such ridiculous conclusions?"

"Because I never bring women back to my hometown, and I've never, ever shared this house with a woman before. You are a very lovely exception to a long held and strictly enforced rule."

Ro didn't know what to say to that or how to react. She stared at him, conscious that her mouth was desert dry, that ripples of anticipation were running over her skin. The atmosphere in the room changed from confiding to combustible and Ro knew that if she leaned forward and placed her mouth on his, clothes would start coming off.

Her body was demanding the sexual relief only he could give her, but her mind was still throwing a hissy fit, telling her that sleeping with him was dangerous.

"I want you, Ro."

It was such a simple statement, and more powerful for being so unpretentious. He was just a man declaring what he wanted, tossing it out there to see how she'd respond.

"I want you too—" Ro admitted, feeling the heat in her cheeks.

"I can hear the *but*."

When she didn't answer—Ro was having difficulty

forming her words—he sighed. "But it's too soon, but you're not ready, but I'm hurt. Which one is right?"

"All three?" Ro asked, wrinkling her nose.

"Fair enough," Muzi replied. He lifted his lips into that devastating smirk. "But, for your information, I would've still managed to rock your world one-handed."

She saw that he wasn't expecting her to take his words seriously. "Is this California king big enough for you and your ego?" she asked, her tone pert.

"Just," Muzi replied with an easy smile. "Well, if you're not going to rock my world tonight, lie down next to me, and let's watch a movie."

"What about food? You're on medication and you should eat something," Ro protested.

"Maybe later," Muzi told her, tugging her toward him. She lay her head on his shoulder and felt his big hand on her hip, holding her close. "Sci-fi, action or a war drama?"

"Historical romance, a chick flick or a tearjerker?" Ro replied, smiling as she stretched out next to him.

Muzi released a snort. "Can we compromise on a comedy?"

"Deal," Ros said, resting her hand on his flat, ridged stomach. Oh, Lord, being this close to him and not allowing herself to explore his fabulous body was pure, unadulterated torture.

She just needed to say the word and she would know if he could live up to his promise of rocking her world.

But, because she was an adult and tried to listen to her head and not her juvenile libido, she lay there and tried to concentrate on the movie.

She didn't succeed.

CHAPTER SEVEN

MUZI COULDN'T RECALL the last time a woman fell asleep in his bed and then realized he couldn't remember because it had never happened. Not once. Not even when he was younger, at university, or in the years following his studies. He far preferred to share his partner's bed, that way he could control when the evening ended.

He didn't do sex-free sleepovers, neither did he indulge in confessions. Last night he did both. He had never spent so much time explaining his past. Digby knew, or suspected, parts of it but he'd never confessed the full extent of Susan's emotional abuse.

He and Ro knew each other's secrets, and it was as scary as hell.

Muzi lay on his side and watched her sleep. Something else he wasn't in the habit of doing. Being so close he could see a tiny bump on the ridge of her straight nose, how extraordinarily long her eyelashes were and that her skin was blemish-free. When he first saw her, she reminded him of Snow White, but after a few days in her company, he knew the comparison wasn't just. She was so much more than a cardboard cutout character from an old Disney movie. She was determined, sensitive, empathetic and, best of all, nonjudgmental. And, terrifyingly, he felt the urge to spill more of his secrets.

Secrets like…while he was terrified to love, neither did he want to be alone. That, despite having the power in the wine industry he commanded, he was frightened that Susan would achieve her lifetime goal and have him sidelined and made irrelevant. Nobody, not even him, knew how far she would go.

Muzi knew that Susan never expected him to fly as high and fast as he did. And when he joined Clos du Cadieux, she'd encouraged his managers to make his life hell to avoid any accusations of nepotism. She thought he would quit. He'd done just the opposite. When threatened, he buckled down and got more stubborn. He wasn't going anywhere, and he wouldn't let an insecure and vicious woman get the better of him. But he had to do it in secret; Susan's machinations would devastate Mimi and rip the Matthews family apart. He owed it to Mimi not to let that happen.

But Muzi didn't know how to end the long-running battle.

It was early Monday morning and the sun was just breaking over the mountain. This was the time he normally went for a run or hit the gym, but with his injuries—the cut on his leg was throbbing and his shoulder still felt tender—that was out of the question. His other option was to get up and dressed and head back to the city to where a pile of work lay on his messy desk. That didn't excite him either. What he most wanted to do was to lie here and look at Ro and spend the next week discovering her delightful body.

She was, mostly, ready to go there with him, he could see it in her eyes. Normally, if a woman was even a little reluctant he would back the hell away, but Ro was a magnetic force and he was irresistibly drawn to her. He wanted her as he'd never wanted anyone before. He didn't know where to put this new, insistent, demanding desire. A part of him wanted to run away, the rest of him wanted to stay right here and hope she woke with a change of heart.

He recognized that a relationship between them was futile, that whatever was bubbling between them could not be sustained. She wasn't going to stay in South Africa, and he had no intention of living anywhere else. But more than geography separated them—he couldn't see himself handing his heart over to her, or any other woman. His birth mom had taken a piece of it when she decided that he wasn't worth keeping around, another part of his heart died with Lu. When Mimi died... No, he couldn't go there.

Love meant risk and love equaled hurt.

He'd managed to make it into his midthirties without love, or a steady relationship, someone to come home to. He was used to being alone, happy on his island. He had friends, finding a temporary lover was never a problem and being alone was safer.

Then why did being with Ro feel so damn right? It was a question he suspected would never be answered.

Muzi was about to leave the bed—they had both fallen asleep in their clothes—when Ro's hand landed on his stomach. He sucked in a surprised breath and wished, desperately wished, that her hand would move down lower. He couldn't take his eyes off her fingers, imagining them wrapped around his shaft. Just a thought caused him to turn rock-hard and it took everything he had not to release a loud groan.

He needed to leave the bed, get dressed and go back to the city.

But more than that he needed to make Ro his.

He dragged his eyes from her fingers to her wrist, up her arm, across her shoulder and onto her face. Her open, astonishing eyes were the color of old-fashioned blue ink, deep and dark and mysterious. Wide and enticing, and desperately sexy.

"Kiss me, Muzi, please."

Because he wanted to do exactly that, more than he wanted to keep breathing, he lowered his head and gently covered her mouth with his, wrapping his arm around her slim waist. He was lying on his bad shoulder and it instantly started to throb. But he didn't care how much pain this position caused his shoulder, he was kissing Ro.

And that was all that mattered.

She tasted of early morning, or honey and spice, of want and need. Cupping her face with one hand, he traced the ridge of her cheekbone as his tongue tangled with hers. He ran the back of his hand down her neck, across her shoulder, needing to feel her skin. Desire, fiery and demanding, welled up but he pushed it back.

Until she permitted him to take this further, he'd be content to feed her hot, desperate kisses and pray that gave him the green light to love her.

But even if this was all she could give him, he'd take it. Kissing Ro was better than having sex with anyone else.

Ro cupped the back of his neck and ran her hand down his bare back, over his butt. She scooted closer and pushed her breasts into his chest and he could feel her hard nipples through her bra and shirt.

Making out with her, not taking this further, was going to kill him...

Needing her entire body to be connected with his, he used his good arm to roll her onto him, her chest against his, her mound resting on his hard erection. He groaned as she ground down, her body telling him that she wanted more.

Her mouth, and brain, had yet to catch up.

Muzi ran his hand up and under her shirt, up and down

her back, over her butt, sighing when the scent of her skin, citrus and flowers, flowed over him. This was the best way, bar none, to start his Monday, to start his week. Being with her was…what was the word…? Yeah. *Magic.*

He'd never used or thought of the word in the context of a woman before.

He was in more trouble than he thought.

Ro lifted her head and sent him a tremulous smile. "You okay?" he asked, seeing the sheen in her eyes.

She nodded, and he saw her swallow. Her fingers touched his short beard, wandered over his lips and traced the contours of his chin. "You are the most masculine man I've ever met. So strong, so steady."

He placed her hand over his erratic heart. "Not so steady, I feel like my heart is about to explode."

"Mine too," Ro admitted. She lifted his hand and placed it on her breast and he felt her lush roundness, the softness beneath his palm. What he couldn't feel was her heartbeat.

"Uh… Ro, your heart is on your left side," Muzi pointed out.

Ro's smile was just that side of wicked.

"I know," she whispered, placing her mouth on his. He smothered his laugh and his thumb brushed her nipple, causing her to release a little growl at the back of her throat.

He lifted her shirt, pulled down the cup of her bra and finally, finally felt her soft skin. But it wasn't nearly enough.

He wouldn't beg, it wasn't in his nature, but he found himself pulling back from her, his eyes searching hers. Hoping to see the yes he'd been longing for.

Blue met brown, desire skittered across her face, flushing her skin, and hope sparked and burst into flame. He couldn't wait a nanosecond more and released the words he'd been keeping behind his teeth. "Say, yes, Ro, *please.* Put me out of my misery."

Her creamy skin reddened in a blush, heating from the inside out and her eyes widened as she nodded. Nodding wasn't enough, he needed to hear the words. "Talk to me, Ro."

She placed her hands on his chest, ran them down his rib cage, dancing her fingers over his abs. "I want you, Muzi. I want anything and everything you can give me."

Thank God and all his archangels, angels and cherubim. Clasping her face in his hands, he pulled her down, allowing his kiss to turn ferocious. He couldn't hold back anymore, he intended to make Ro his.

Giving in to temptation was such a risk. Ro wasn't just another one-night stand, a fling. She was—could become—important. He was risking his heart again and it had taken many, many beatings in the past. He should pull back, he really should, end this now…walk away. Instead of being sensible, instead of protecting himself, Muzi rolled her over so that Ro was under him. He sat back on his haunches and pulled her upright, swiftly lifting her shirt, pulling it over her head, and throwing it to the floor. He ran his finger down her chest, circling one breast, then the other. Ro reached behind her to unclasp her bra but Muzi pushed her hands away and, with one hand, flicked open the clasp.

Ro pulled her bra down and off her arms and he looked at her, taking in her sweet breasts and rose-red nipples. He touched one with the tip of his finger and watched, fascinated as it hardened under his gaze. Dipping his head, he blew on her bud and when she tensed, pulled her into his mouth. As sweet as, no, sweeter than he imagined, sheer perfection.

Muzi felt his heart bouncing off his rib cage, his lungs straining to get enough air. Sex had never affected him like this before, he'd never been compelled to immediately make her his or to slow time down to a crawl and spend eons discovering every inch of her luscious body.

He wanted to both devour and delay, ravish and ramble.

Muzi moved off her legs and slowly undid the zipper to her shorts, kissing every inch of new skin he exposed. He pushed her shorts down her legs, nipping at her hip bone and nibbling the inside of her leg before tossing them over his shoulder. She lay on his bed in a pair of pale cream panties, nearly the exact color of her skin. He allowed himself the pleasure of running his finger over her mound, between her feminine folds, and felt the dampness of her panties, reveling in the knowledge that he'd made this intriguing, lovely, complicated woman wet.

Leaving her was torture but he needed protection. Since he seldom—okay, never—brought women back here, he didn't have a stash of condoms in his bedside drawer. Remembering that he had some in his bathroom cabinet, he pulled back, smiling at her groan of disappointment.

"I need to find some condoms, baby," he told her before walking into his dressing room, and then his bathroom, glancing toward the huge corner shower, complete with two showerheads and a bench.

He could imagine sitting on that bench, Ro riding him...

But that was for later. He grabbed a strip of condoms and hurried back to her, momentarily stopping in the doorway to take her in. She looked both wanton and wonderful, turned on and temptation personified.

She was going to be his...

And he couldn't wait.

Muzi tossed the condoms near her and sent her a reassuring smile as he lowered himself back onto the bed. "Does that yes still hold, gorgeous?"

"More than ever," Ro murmured, lifting her hips in a subconscious move. "But I do wish you'd hurry up."

"Patience, sweetheart." Not that he had much himself, he was burning up with need. He knew that he could enter her, slide on home, but he wanted this first time to be something she'd remember for the rest of her life. And that meant doing something he'd been fantasizing about.

After dropping a hard, brief, openmouthed kiss on her lips, his mouth traveled down her body, over her abdomen and the fabric of her panties. She gasped and tensed. He pulled aside the fabric and circled her nub with his tongue, causing her to release a harsh scream.

Yeah, she liked that.

Impatient with the barriers, Muzi pushed her panties down her legs and placed his mouth on her core, pinning her to the bed with his hand on her stomach. Needing to give her more, he slid a finger inside her, then another, lifting his eyes to see her head thrashing against his pillow. She reached down and pushed his head closer to her and Muzi widened his fingers and sucked her harder, knowing she was close.

She turned statue still, released a long wail and he felt her gush over his fingers, buck against his mouth as she touched the sun and ignited.

He was torn between giving her more or watching her come down from her intense orgasm, and decided to combine both. Sitting up, he quickly opened a foil packet and rolled the condom down, his skin ultrasensitive.

It wouldn't take much to ignite him. Hell, Ro just needed to look at him and he'd explode.

Metaphorically. And, possibly, literally.

Lifting and widening her legs, he placed himself at her entrance and commanded Ro to open her eyes. "Is this still okay, Ro?"

She smiled at him. "What would you do if I said no... that I was done?"

He didn't return her smile. Consent was too sensitive a subject to joke about. "I'd pull back and…"

"And?" she asked, tipping her head to the side.

"Probably punch a wall," Muzi reluctantly admitted.

Ro touched his jaw with her fingertips. "I think you've been hurt enough, Triple M, so, yes, this is very okay. Or it will be when you…aargh." On hearing her yes, he'd pushed inside, and realized that she was oh so tight. For the first time in fifteen years, he wondered if he'd fit, if he'd be able to seat himself in her. He was a big guy and she was petite…

He reached down and touched her core, and pleasure flashed across her face. He felt her relax, and he sank deeper into her, groaning all the way.

Too good, there was no way he could last.

Muzi recited chemistry formulas in his head, the periodic table and the lyrics to Mi Casa's "Jika." But nothing could stop the freight train of pleasure rushing down on him.

"I can't wait…you need to come," Muzi ground out, knowing he had ten seconds, maybe less, before all hell, the good kind, broke loose.

Ro arched her back, slammed her hips up and came again, her fist to her mouth to stop the scream he knew she wanted to release.

He wanted to tell her he didn't care how loud she got, that there was no one to hear them, but that was for later, right now he was about to be smacked by pleasure and he stepped right into its path.

He'd never had it so good, was Muzi's last thought before he spiraled away.

Muzi missed work that morning. And that afternoon. Of course, having a recently dislocated shoulder, a suspected concussion and a two-inch gash on his leg were great excuses to play hooky. Nobody needed to know—and, according to Muzi, as CEO he didn't need to explain a damn thing—that they'd spent most of the day in bed and used quite a few condoms.

Quite. A. Few.

Ro was, frankly, pretty damn exhausted.

Showered and dressed, Ro walked out of Muzi's bedroom and through his house, and after stopping in the kitchen to pick up a soda—she needed a sugar and caffeine hit—she walked onto the entertainment deck and flopped down into a chair and put her feet up on the railing.

After showering together, and indulging in some heavy petting, Muzi told her that he needed to go into his home office and check his emails and return calls, and Ro was glad for the opportunity to be alone.

She needed to think.

Best lover…check.

Best sex ever…check.

Least inhibited she'd ever been…check, check, check.

Ro sipped her drink and rested her head against the back of the comfortable chair, content to watch the sun dip behind the mountains. It was late, after six and she'd accomplished nothing today, and no, a bunch of orgasms didn't count.

Or did they?

Pulling her thoughts off Muzi and the fun they'd had—and it had been fun—she remembered that there was still so much work to do at St. Urban. The thatch needed to be replaced, she needed to get an antique expert in to value the furniture, and she suspected the place needed to be rewired.

She had weeks, months, of work ahead of her and she was glad to have an excuse to hang around Franschhoek, to be where Muzi, sometimes, was. She wanted to stay in this house, in his bed, in his arms for…hell, the longest time, probably forever.

Ro blew a curl out of her eyes, irritated with herself.

Stop fantasizing and embrace a little bit of reality, Roisin.

She had plans to make, lawyers to meet, things to do but her thoughts kept coming back to the intriguing man a couple of doors away.

Being with him had been earth-shattering, she'd adored being loved by him, she'd so enjoyed giving him pleasure…

Be sensible, Roisin. You're a reasonably intelligent woman, think this through.

She was feeling mushy, attached and emotional.

She knew that great sex produced oxytocin and that the hormone was associated with bonding, trust and loyalty. She was just experiencing a chemical storm, it didn't mean anything.

Unless it meant something…

Argh!

No, that wasn't possible. She'd known Muzi for less than three weeks, she couldn't possibly be feeling more for him than attraction. This was nothing more than rebound sex…

She wasn't the type to fall into bed, or into a relationship, quickly. When it came to her heart and emotions, she wasn't an impulsive person. It took her three months to agree to date Kelvin, another two before she slept with him. She didn't treat love rashly and didn't jump into situations that could cause heartbreak.

No, she wasn't falling in love. She was in lust…that was totally, utterly different. But if she was…

Hypothetically, she was sort of…kind of…okay with the concept and she wasn't completely freaked out. Ro tipped her head back and released a long breath. She reminded herself that she no longer knew what love meant, she'd been disappointed by Kelvin, her parents were divorcing, and Gil and Zia were the most screwed-up couple *ever*. One night with Muzi and she was prepared to ignore all rational evidence that love was a farce and dive on in?

Anyone would think that she'd banged her head, not Muzi.

Ro heard his footsteps behind her and smiled when he dropped a kiss on top of her head. He came into her direct view and Ro noticed that he was holding two wineglasses and a bottle of red.

"It's a fifteen-year-old bottle of Shiraz, from a vineyard we own," Muzi told her. "Can I interest you in a glass?"

Ro nodded, taking in his fresh pair of navy blue chino shorts, his white linen shirt and expensive flip-flops. He opened the bottle, poured an inch into each glass and handed one to her. She didn't bother to smell or swirl, causing Muzi to roll his eyes good-naturedly, and took a hefty swallow. "It's good," she told him.

"It's bloody fantastic," Muzi corrected her, sitting down in the chair next to her. Muzi dropped his head back to stare at the sunset. He sighed and when Ro looked at him, she caught his smile. "Today was a damn fun day."

"It was," Ro agreed.

"So why, then, were you looking a little lost when I came out here?" Muzi asked. His next question was typical Muzi, direct and honest. "Do you regret us sleeping together?"

Ro lifted her eyebrows. "What? *No!*"

Muzi sipped his wine and returned his gaze to the mountain and the setting sun, skepticism on his face.

She could explain, Ro thought. He'd understand. "I was just wrapping my head around the fact that I'd never had such good sex in my life, not even with my fiancé."

He shot up so fast that her head spun. "What the hell? You have a *fiancé*?"

Ro lifted her hand and shook her head. "Calm down, Triple M. It's been over for a few months."

Muzi scowled at her, his lips pulled into a thin line. "For future reference, feel free to use the prefix 'ex' whenever you mention the word *fiancé*," he muttered before sitting down again.

He sounded properly upset. "I'm sorry." She eyed him over her glass. "So, judging by your hot response, I take it that you don't sleep with women who are in committed relationships?"

He didn't need to answer, she saw his reply in his narrowed eyes and tight expression. Right, Muzi didn't poach on other men's territory. That was honorable, respectful and his response was another tick in her He'd Make a Fantastic Boyfriend column.

For someone else, obviously, but not for her. There were too many ticks in her Why This Would Never Work column to consider him as anything other than a lovely, exciting diversion.

Muzi placed his feet on the railing in front of them and watched the light changing over his lands, his tension sliding away. "What happened? Why did you guys break up?"

"He sent me a text message meant for her, saying how much he enjoyed the night they spent together. And that he liked her pink panties." Ro wrinkled her nose. "I don't own pink panties. And, big clue, I was already in Cape Town when I got the text."

Muzi muttered something underneath his breath but although she couldn't hear him distinctly, she knew it wasn't a compliment. His immediate instinct to defend her made her feel warm and squishy. She was being ridiculous.

"I presume you were devastated when he cheated on you?"

Ro nodded, then scrunched up her face, questioning

her response. Had she been? She mourned the death of her dreams, the future she'd created with him, the wife she intended to be, the kids they'd have. Did she mourn him? She wasn't so sure.

"He changed my thoughts about love and relationships," Ro explained, pulling her heels up onto the edge of her chair and wrapping her arms around her bent knees. She rested her cheek on her knee as she looked at him. "Actually, everything that has happened over the past few months has changed what I thought I knew about love and commitment."

Muzi reached out, ran his hand down her arm before pulling back. "Tell me more."

"I had my life planned, we were going to get married at some point and, in time, we'd have kids. Our lives were jogging along, same old route, same old path." The wind picked up and blew a strand of hair across Ro's eyes and she irritably pushed it away.

"As it does," Muzi murmured.

"Until a hurricane whips you off said path and into a whirlwind."

"The whirlwind being your inheritance?" Muzi asked. "Bet your ex is pissed that he's not part of that action now."

"I never told him and no, my inheritance wasn't the hurricane."

"What? You didn't tell him?"

Ro shook her head.

He whistled, his astonishment obvious. "I'm sure a psychologist would have a lot to say about why you didn't trust him enough to tell him, but I digress… What was the emotional hurricane?"

Ro's chest lifted and fell. "My parents wanting a divorce. I genuinely believed they had a rock-solid marriage. I'm still in shock."

Muzi tipped his head to the side. "These things rarely come from out of the blue, sweetheart. Are you sure that you didn't miss the signs?"

She'd thought about this, often. And hard. "Nope, I don't think I did. Every time I've seen them, they've acted like they always have, super affectionate, super touchy. I never suspected anything. Then the lawyers contacted me and told me about Gil and Zia and I went online and read all about them—"

Muzi mimicked putting a gun to his head and pulling the trigger. She managed a small smile. "Obviously, my parents' situation was still on my mind and I couldn't work out how two serial cheaters managed to stay married for so long when my seemingly hopelessly in love parents were calling it quits."

"And then you discovered that your ex cheated on you. Slap number three."

"And that's without going into the whole I-don't-know-why-my-parents-didn't-keep-me suck-fest. I no longer know what love means, what commitment is and, given that both sets of parents are incapable of both, whether I will be able to commit to anyone ever again."

Muzi's hand skimmed over her hair. "Ah, Ro."

"No words of wisdom?" Ro asked him, needing something, anything, to hold on to, to make her believe again. She wanted to, she realized. She wanted to be the woman she'd been, the one who was happy and hopeful, who was excited to be a wife and a mother. To grow old with someone.

Muzi grimaced. "Not having had a long-term relationship in my life, I don't hand out advice on love." He looked away, obviously deep in thought. "My only contribution to this conversation is that I think you should discard anything your birth parents did or said. They were outliers, two exceptionally flawed people who found each other and who encouraged the other to be the worst version of themselves. If you discard them, who they were and what they did, you can, maybe, see your parents' marriage in a better light."

Ro kept her eyes on him, fascinated by his every word. He was thoughtful and compelling and, so far, his words were full of wisdom.

"Your parents probably agreed not to let you suspect anything about their problems, to protect you. But marriages do fail, people do grow apart, few people manage to stay married forever. People change and so does what they feel for each other."

That made sense.

"And just because they don't love each other anymore, doesn't mean that they don't love you," Muzi told her, with compassion in his eyes.

She wrinkled her nose. "I've said that to quite a few of my kids when I heard that their parents are divorcing."

"Whether you are three or thirty, it doesn't make it any less true," Muzi assured her. "As for your ex, he's an idiot who never deserved you," he added, scowling. "Did he tell you that it was an accident, that he never meant it to happen?"

"Yep."

"Then he's a double idiot. It's never an accident. He *chose* to let it happen—he could've stopped at the first inappropriate conversation, the first time they flirted, when they first kissed—and a consequence of his choice was losing you. He bought the ticket—he gets to take the ride."

Ro sat up, dropped her legs and held out her hand for him to take, sighing when her hand disappeared in his. "Thank you. You've given me a lot to think about."

Muzi squeezed her fingers and lifted her knuckles to his mouth. "I have something else for you to think about..."

Desire, sharp and delectably fizzy, skittered through her. They hadn't been naked for more than an hour and it was far too long. "Mmm...yes, please."

His laugh was rich and deep. "I like the way you think but, sorry, I'm not offering to take you back to bed. Mimi called and she wants to see me, to see if I'm okay."

"You're very okay, I can attest to that."

He grinned. "Thank you, but Sam, the big mouth, called her and told her that she had to patch me up again. Mimi has summoned me to La Fontaine and she's ordered me to bring you. And to stay for dinner."

Ro pulled a face, not sure if she was ready to meet Muzi's grandmother. Meeting the family made her think that this...*thing*...between them was moving too fast.

"I don't know, Muzi."

Disappointment jumped into his eyes. "Her chef cooks like a dream and she's a character but if you're not keen, I'll just head over there and have a quick drink with her." He drained his glass of wine and put it on the coffee table to his right. He glanced at his watch. "If I leave within the next ten minutes, I could be back by eight."

"And you are going back to the city in the morning?"

"Yes, I'm so behind and I have a series of meetings I have to take."

"And do you have any idea when you will be back?" she asked, trying to sound nonchalant but knowing that she missed it by a country mile.

Muzi's look was rock steady. "Is that your way of asking whether I want to see you again, to sleep with you again?"

He was so straightforward. And, after Kelvin's dishonesty and the confusion around her adoptive parents' marriage, it was a nice change. "I guess I am."

He stood up and gripped the arms of her chair, caging her in. "No promises, no expectations, but yes, I'd like to see you again. When that changes, you'll be the first to know. And, unless something major happens at work, I'll be back here Friday night."

Ro nodded, relieved. She stroked her thumb across his bottom lip and sighed when his mouth covered hers in a brief, hard kiss. Ro pouted, disappointed when he stood up and moved away to stand by the railing.

"Talking about work, your lawyers should have the lease agreement by now, can you sign it sometime soon so that my farm manager can put a cleanup crew in the lands?"

"Let him do it, I'm not going to change my mind," Ro told him, not liking the change of subject. When Muzi talked business, his expression turned implacable and a curtain fell in his eyes. He wasn't robotic but he was unreachable. And if she only had a few hours until he left her here in Franschhoek for five days she didn't want to waste a minute of that time.

She wanted to be with him. "I'll come to La Fontaine with you." She gestured to her casual shirt and shorts. "Should I change?"

He nodded. "Mimi is old-school and expects us to dress for dinner. Nothing fancy but shorts and flip-flops are not acceptable."

"Got it," Ro said, climbing to her feet. Then a thought occurred, and she hesitated. "If I go with you, your grandmother is going to believe the rumors are true."

"What rumors?"

"That we are having a red-hot affair!" Ro retorted.

Muzi smiled. "Sweetheart, we *are* having a red-hot affair. If it got any hotter, we'd both be dead, burned to a crisp."

She swatted his arm and he laughed. "You know what I mean! She'll think that there's something between us!"

Muzi placed his hand on her lower back and pushed her in the direction of the lounge. "There is something between us…" He hesitated, and Ro's heart rate sped up and her brain froze. What was he about to say? And was she ready to hear it?

"Let's take it slow, see where it goes. Right now, we are friends. Enjoying some earthshaking benefits."

Stupid girl for even entertaining the thought of more. She wasn't ready for more, and he didn't want it.

Right. They were both on the same page. That was good…

Wasn't it?

CHAPTER EIGHT

THREE DAYS LATER, Ro sat in the library at St. Urban, morosely contemplating the floor-to-ceiling shelves of books, wondering who would take a roomful of old and dusty books. And, because the Du Toit family had been über-wealthy, she suspected that there were a couple of first editions on those shelves.

She needed to find someone who specialized in old books. Ro sighed and picked up her phone to add the item to her long to-do list.

Ro tucked the phone into the back pocket of her jeans and contemplated the rolltop desk standing between two long narrow windows. If the other two desks in this room were anything to go by, it would be stuffed full of old papers, crumbling bits of newspaper and ancient pens and keys.

She slapped her dusty hands together and sat down on the ancient leather chair in front of the desk. Somebody had to do it and she was here and might as well make herself useful.

And keeping busy helped the hours go faster...

The truth was, she couldn't wait for Muzi to come home. *Home.* Ro turned the word over in her head and realized that his house did feel like home, in a way that Digby's barn conversion or even her apartment back home didn't. It shouldn't as it was filled with Muzi's possessions and she didn't have anything of her own to make it feel familiar but…

It was his favorite place and she wanted to be anywhere he was. God, she missed him. Missed seeing that half smile, hearing his deep voice, feeling safe when she fell asleep on his broad shoulder.

Wherever he was, was where she wanted to be.

She had a life back home and, if she wasn't mistaken, her lease was up for renewal. Christmas was a few weeks away and she needed to make plans to go back to LA, to be with her parents. The auction for her parents' art and collectibles would be held in the first week of January and Carrick Murphy wanted her to do a visual inspection of what she was selling, to make sure she would have no regrets later. Her teacher colleagues and college friends were demanding to know when she'd be back home… Ro cursed under her breath, feeling like the real world was intruding and that her time in this magical valley was running out. But she had so much unfinished business here.

But, really, was that true? She could hire people to sort out this house, she could talk to her lawyers about the estate via emails and phone calls, she could do electronic signatures from anywhere in the world.

No, the reason she was hanging around in Franschhoek was because Muzi was here—well, here on weekends. And she was using clearing out St. Urban as an excuse to hang around, to be with him.

Pathetic? Maybe.

Ro heard footsteps on the wooden floor outside the study and then heard an imperious voice calling her name.

Ro instantly recognized Mimi's voice and looked down at her dirt-streaked pale yellow shirt and grubby jeans. She looked, as she did most days, like she'd been rolling around in the dust.

Ro pushed back her chair and saw Mimi standing in the doorway to the library. She wore a tangerine-colored suit over a white T-shirt and funky, fashionable trainers on her feet. Designer glasses covered her eyes and she wore a gold necklace as thick as Ro's thumb.

"Dear God, child, what do you look like?" Mimi demanded, stepping into the room.

Ro greeted her before telling her that she dressed like this most days. "Not that I'm not happy to see you but why are you here?"

Mimi folded her arms across her chest. "I came to invite you to join me and a couple of friends for lunch."

Ro looked down at her dirty clothes and grimaced. "Sorry, I'm going to have to pass. Not only am I dirty, but I'm expecting the antique furniture expert to drop by soon."

"Pity," Mimi replied, walking into the room and heading for one of the long windows. The view outside was amazing, with rows of vines and the mountain looming over the farm.

"What is going to happen to St. Urban? Do you know?" Mimi demanded, turning back to face her. "I heard that Muzi signed an agreement to lease the land, and the vines, but what do you think the owner is going to do with the property?"

Was Mimi putting an emphasis on the word "owner" or was that just her imagination? Was she questioning whether she was who she said she was, an employee of the trust? Or was Ro's paranoia running away with her?

Ro wiped her dusty hand on the seat of her pants. "Muzi has expressed interest in buying the land so the owner is thinking of subdividing the property and selling the house. It's what he's done with all the other properties." Had she said too much? Was she supposed to know that much?

"He?" Mimi raised an eyebrow.

Oh, yeah, she definitely suspected something.

Mimi sent her a penetrating look. "What do you think the owner should do with this property?"

Ro joined her at the window. She shouldn't answer but she would. After all, she'd given this topic a lot of thought. "I would tell him to turn this house into an exclusive, very upmarket boutique hotel. It has over ten bedrooms, more if you converted some of the outbuildings. The place is furnished with exquisite antiques, amazing art and it's a throwback to the early 1920s."

"Carry on," Mimi instructed her.

"I'd… I'd suggest to him that he renovate the cellars and set up a tasting room and, if he was feeling brave, establish a restaurant on the property. Something ridiculously upmarket and expensive."

In her mind's eye, Ro could see the house restored, its windows gleaming, its furniture polished and the art displayed proudly. She could see guests reading in this library, sitting under the wonderfully old oak trees, sleeping in enormous beds covered with white linen, eating in a fabulous new restaurant.

It was so real she could smell the newly cut grass, the blooming roses, beeswax polish intermingled with the expensive perfume of the female guests.

Mimi took her time answering. "It's not a bad idea," Mimi eventually answered.

But was it a good one? Ro wanted to ask her—she had been, after all, a powerhouse businesswoman—but Mimi asked her another question before she could. "What's my grandson up to today?"

Uh…

Ro took a moment to switch gears. She and Muzi had spoken this morning, as they did most days. He was better than an intravenous dose of caffeine for getting her blood moving and her heart rate spiking.

"He's in meetings, I think. And he's going to have dinner with Digby and Bay tonight."

"It's been far too long since I saw Digby," Mimi complained. "He used to practically live at La Fontaine and now I have to beg him to come and see me."

Ro knew that wasn't true. Digby and Bay made a point of visiting Mimi and called her often. "What do you mean Digby spent a lot of time with you?"

Mimi looked around for a seat and Ro pushed the leather chair over to her. Mimi sat down, crossed her legs and pulled her bag onto her lap. "Damn, I want a cigarette."

Ro glanced at her piles of old paper, horrified. "No smoking in here!"

"I gave up years ago," Mimi grumbled.

Ro leaned her hip against the rolltop desk. "You were telling me about Digby." Then she realized that she shouldn't sound so interested in her ex-boss. Damn. But this was her *brother* Mimi was talking about, she was interested in anything anyone had to say about him.

"Instead of going home, Digby spent many school holidays at La Fontaine. Basically, that meant he, Muzi, my grandsons Keane and Rafe—and that scoundrel Pasco—would terrorize the neighborhood."

Ro smiled. "I can imagine."

Mimi rested the back of her hand against her forehead, acting dramatic. "You really can't. They made me old before my time."

Mimi, as Muzi told her, spent a lot of time working so she probably didn't know half of it. "Did Digby stay with you because his parents were overseas?"

Zia and Gil had, as she read, traveled constantly.

Mimi snorted. "Partly, but mostly because they weren't

interested in the boys and didn't want anything to do with them. The only reason they had children was because they were paid to do so."

What on earth was she talking about? She was about to ask when Mimi, surprisingly given her age, jumped to her feet. "I need to go. I'm going to be late."

When Mimi refused to meet her eyes, Ro knew that she was regretting her words. "Wait, hold on...explain what you meant about Digby's parents being paid to have him."

Mimi tried to wave her words away. "Nothing, I'm old and confused."

Not damn likely, Ro thought. Mimi's expression turned sly. "Why are you so interested?"

Yeah, very *not* confused.

Ro forced a smile onto her face, knowing she couldn't argue the point without raising Mimi's suspicions. "I'm just being nosy, forget about it."

Mimi nodded, sent her another piercing look before smiling. "Talking about being nosy, what exactly is happening between you and my grandson?"

Good question and one she didn't have the answer to. Friends with benefits didn't normally spend hours talking before bed and for at least a half hour in the morning before they started work. Sex buddies didn't exchange texts and voice messages or send each other silly memes and jokes.

"Is this serious or are you just knocking boots?"

How did she answer that question?

Ro could only think of one reply. "I don't feel comfortable discussing that with you."

"Pfft!" Mimi scowled and pursed her lips. Then she smiled sweetly, and Ro felt a prickle of apprehension skitter up and down her spine.

"I like you. I do."

But…? Because there was a glittery pink and purple neon *but* heading her way.

"But know this, if you break his heart, I will break you."

All righty, then.

Muzi stood in Digby's office at The Vane and scowled at his two best friends. He should be back in his office, putting out fires, but here he was, arguing with the Tempest-Vane brothers, trying to convince them to tell Ro the truth about why she was adopted.

Earlier in the day, he'd taken a break between meetings and frowned when he saw a couple of missed calls from Ro. When he picked up his voice messages, she told him that Mimi—his gossipy, garrulous grandmother—told her Gil and Zia had been compensated for having children. Was Mimi right, she'd demanded to know. She was also, she told him, going to call her brothers to get to the bottom of Mimi's bizarre claim.

"It will hurt her, Muzi," Digby said, after slamming his fist against his desk. "How do you think she's going to feel hearing that our parents gave her up for adoption because they weren't going to get paid the millions they did when they produced a boy?"

He understood their concern. But what Ro's brothers didn't realize was that she could handle it. That she was strong. Oh, it would hurt, but it wouldn't make her buckle or bend.

Ro was tougher than that. She was…

She was amazing. Strong and sexy and sensible and… *lovely.* She was everything he'd ever want in a woman. Intelligent, empathetic, hardworking and independent.

Sweet and so heart-stoppingly sexy. And stubborn…

And because she was stubborn, she would hound them,

and him, until she had an answer to the question of Gil and Zia being paid to have kids.

Bloody Mimi and her big mouth.

Muzi ran his hand over his jaw, recalling the puzzled looks Mimi sent Ro when they dined with her earlier in the week. She looked at Ro as if she couldn't place her and had mentioned, on at least two occasions, that she looked familiar.

To him, she looked like a feminine version of her brothers but no one had yet, as far as he knew, commented on the similarities between Ro and the Tempest-Vane siblings. Muzi had also seen pictures of a young Zia and Ro looked like a carbon copy of her birth mother.

Mimi would eventually make the connection, would figure out that she was a Tempest-Vane but he knew that if he asked Mimi to keep her identity a secret, she would.

Mimi could be a vault when she needed to be.

But that was a problem for the future. They had to resolve the one in front of them first.

"I'm heading up there tomorrow and she is going to bug me for an explanation," Muzi said, slapping his hands against his hips and scowling. He knew that he looked big and intimidating but he didn't, sadly, scare the Tempest-Vane brothers.

"I'm not lying to her, guys," Muzi said, annoyed at the desperate tone in his voice. "Please don't ask me to do that."

Digby placed his palms flat on his desk and glared at Muzi, his expression thunderous. "What is going on between you?" he demanded.

God only knew.

They talked, a lot. They discussed movies and books and covered all the subjects couples talked about when they wanted to get to know each other. But they also ventured into deeper territory and shared their fears and childhood memories, both good and bad. He told her about how he saved every penny he was gifted or earned, how terrified he was of Susan's threat coming true, of him being alone. And poor.

She told him that she often felt on the outside of her parents' marriage, that they were so into each other and seemed to, occasionally, forget about her.

He told her about his travels, his daredevil adventures with Digby, and she told him how much she missed teaching and her students.

He couldn't define what they were, but they were more than friends. Ro had crawled under his skin, into his heart. He'd told her more than he'd told all his friends, and Mimi, combined. She knew his fears and his failures and his insecurities, the jagged pieces he never revealed to anyone. The thought, and realization, terrified him.

She was not only his lover, but she was also his best friend. Yet she was supposed to be returning to the States soon, leaving him behind.

He wanted to ask her to stay but couldn't give her a good enough reason to do that. He wouldn't, couldn't commit to her—he was not prepared to throw himself off that cliff and not have her catch him—yet it wasn't fair to ask her to stay if they were going to simply continue their sex-based friendship. She deserved more...

She deserved *everything*.

But he couldn't give her what she wanted. He wasn't brave enough to ask her to be his family, to have his kids... not without an unbreakable guarantee and, as far as he knew, relationships didn't come with warranties.

"Well?" Radd demanded, pulling Muzi back to their conversation.

He and Ro were adults, they didn't owe anyone an explanation. Not even her siblings, the men he considered to be *his* brothers too. This was, and always would be, between them.

"None of your business," Muzi ground out, heading toward the door before turning and raising his index finger to point it at Digby, then Radd. "Tell her. I'm not going to lie to her."

Muzi closed his office doors on his words, hoping that he was right to insist that her brothers tell her. And that Ro could handle more awful news.

On Friday, the day after her conversation with Mimi, Ro worked at St. Urban, trying to decide whether she should make the drive to Cape Town to confront her brothers. When she'd called them, both Radd and Digby professed innocence about Mimi's comment, with Radd stating that Mimi was old and confused. Digby told her that all sorts of wild stories and rumors circulated about their parents and, if she wanted to remain sane, it was best to ignore them.

Ro knew they were both lying.

Mimi wasn't confused and her offhand comment wasn't the result of unfounded gossip. She'd heard her brothers' swift intakes of breath when she raised the subject, heard the forced note of cheer as they tried, using a lot of fake casualness, to dismiss her question. There was something to Mimi's comment, she was sure of it. She'd tried to call Mimi, to ask her to join her for a coffee at one of the many cafés in town but, curiously, Mimi was ducking her calls.

She needed to know, Ro thought, carrying a box of papers toward the skip that stood under the old oak tree. It was an important piece of the missing puzzle, something that would greatly contribute to her understanding of her birth parents. But nobody was talking.

Even Muzi, when she'd raised the subject with him over

the phone, switched subjects. The more they fudged, the more determined she was to find the truth.

And she would—*somehow*.

Ro heard a powerful engine and turned around to watch Muzi's car navigate her still bumpy driveway. She glanced at her watch, happy he was, by her count, at least five hours early.

Her heart bounced off her ribs as she dropped the box into the skip and, yanking off her work gloves, ran to meet him, thoroughly overexcited. Damn, she needed him. Preferably naked and on top of her.

Muzi, clutching a stack of papers in his hand, exited the vehicle and Ro threw herself at him. He wrapped his free arm around her and found her mouth, his tongue immediately sliding past her lips. Ro sank into him, pressing her breasts against his chest, pulling his shirt from his tailored suit pants to find his skin.

God, they'd only been apart for five days but she'd *missed* him.

Muzi spun her around and pinned her to the back passenger's side door, papers fluttering to the ground when his hands slid up her rib cage to cover her breasts. His thumbs brushed over her already hard nipples and he pushed his erection into her.

Well, it seemed like he'd missed her too.

They kissed and groped for the longest time, long drugging kisses that made her forget her name and it was Muzi who eventually pulled back to rest his forehead against hers.

"Hi," he murmured.

"Hi back," Ro lazily replied, loving the way there wasn't space enough for a paper between them. "Did you miss me?"

Muzi pushed his hips into hers and she sighed at how

hard he was. "What do you think?" he murmured, dropping light kisses on her jaw.

Ro caught his chin and tried to bring his mouth back to hers but he shook his head. "Seriously, if we don't stop, I'm going to take you right here and right now."

The idea of making love outside made her shudder with pleasure. "I'm okay with that."

Muzi grinned. "I'm not because my farm manager has a crew in the fields, and they are going to be breaking for lunch soon."

Damn, Ro thought. "There are numerous bedrooms inside, most of which have beds."

Muzi grimaced. "That would be like making love in a dust storm." He kissed her nose and pulled back. "We're adults, we can wait."

"Being an adult sucks," Ro grumbled.

Muzi bent down to pick up the papers he'd dropped. He waved the papers under her nose. "Here's your copy of the signed and notarized lease between Clos du Cadieux and the trust."

Ro squinted down at the papers and nodded. More paper, she was already swimming in the stuff. "I'll get it from you later."

As Muzi opened his car door to toss the lease onto his passenger seat, Ro noticed a group of men coming up from the field. She blushed. If she and Muzi hadn't slammed on the brakes, the poor men would've had to bleach their eyeballs.

Good call, Triple M.

"How is your day going?" Muzi asked her, loosening his silver tie—Hermès?—and rolling up the sleeves of his deep gray button-down shirt. He wore a different watch today, a vintage Rolex.

"Good," Ro answered, tucking her hands behind her,

between her butt and the car, so that she didn't reach for him. "I spent some time this morning drawing up a list of steps I would have to take to turn this into a boutique hotel."

She'd told him about her plans for the house and he'd listened but not given her much encouragement one way or the other. "You haven't given me your opinion on whether you think it's a good idea or not."

Muzi wore his implacable expression, the one she was coming to hate. She couldn't read him when he pulled on his "You can't see into me" cloak.

"I don't have an opinion on the house, it's yours to do what you wish." She started to protest but he cut off her words by holding up his hand. "My biggest question is how you are going to manage the process from the States?"

What was he talking about? Of course she couldn't do this from the States. She'd have to be here, staying in Franschhoek, preferably in his house. "Obviously, if I decided to do this, I'd have to stay." Not wanting to scare him, she sought to reassure him. "For at least another six months, maybe a year."

A tiny frown appeared between his eyebrows. "But then you'd go back, right?"

What did he want her to say? That, yes, she'd go back? Or, no, she wanted to stay here forever? She didn't know so she remained silent, hoping he'd help her out by giving her a hint on what he wanted. Where he saw them going.

She hated being in limbo, not knowing which way they were heading. She coped better with people, and life, when she knew where she stood, how to get from point A to point B. She wasn't a person who could waft in the wind.

Sometime soon, she and Muzi would need to define their relationship so that she could envision the road ahead. But did she have a right to ask that of him when she didn't know what love was, what it meant or what it could be? She could love him, she admitted. Probably did already. But did that matter when she couldn't define where and how to place that love, where and how to let it grow?

Damn, she was so confused. But she was sure of two things: she and Muzi needed to talk—sometime soon—and that she only wanted to stay in South Africa if she could be with him.

Living in this country, without him, would be untenable.

Muzi watched her eyes, saw the confused thoughts jumping in and out of all that dark blue. He could, if he was stupid enough to do so, take some comfort in the fact that she seemed to be as rattled by what was happening between them as he was, but it didn't negate her words.

She might want to delay her departure, but she would, at some point, now or later, go back to LA. Her life was there. His was not.

"I'd appreciate your input on whether it's feasible to turn this place into a guesthouse or boutique hotel, Muzi," Ro stated, her tone subdued but her voice clear.

Muzi gave himself a mental slap. He was a businessman and she, at the very least, was his friend. A friend who didn't have any business experience where he had lots.

Muzi sighed and turned to look at the house. The contractors had painted the exterior, and the windows were clean, and the house seemed happier, more cheerful. Man, he was losing it if he was giving inanimate objects human traits.

"This valley already has a lot of hotels, Ro, so it would have to be pretty special."

Ro nodded. "It needs something to set it apart from the rest, something to encourage people to stay here. So many wine estates have restaurants and coffee shops, galleries and gift shops, I don't want to imitate them."

An idea popped into Muzi's head, born out of a conversation he'd had earlier in the week with Pasco, who'd bitched to him about having to return to New York. Pas was tired of working sixteen-hour days and, having won every award he possibly could, was over the finicky, stressful world of fine dining in New York. He wanted to kick back and relax...

Would Pasco consider returning to Franschhoek and opening a smaller version of his NYC restaurant here? At St. Urban?

He could only ask. But he wouldn't mention his idea to Ro, not until he spoke to Pasco. He didn't want to get her hopes up.

"Let's sit down this weekend and draw up a business plan, crunch the numbers," Muzi suggested.

"I have no idea how to draw up a business plan," Ro reluctantly admitted.

"I do," Muzi assured her. He turned to face her and gently gripped her chin and jaw with the fingers of one hand. "But that will only be after I've had my way with you, several times."

There was no way he could concentrate on doing anything pertaining to business until he'd rid himself of the gnawing need to have her under him, over him, up against a wall.

First things had to come first.

"I can live with that," Ro said before lifting her mouth to receive his hard, brief and openmouthed kiss. Thinking that there was no time like the present, he spoke again. "Shall we get going, then?"

Ro glanced at her watch and shook her head. "I wasn't expecting you this early and the gardening crew is working a half day. They should be done in fifteen minutes or so. You go home and I'll lock up behind them and I'll join you there as soon as I can."

He shook his head. "I'll go and inspect the vines while we're waiting," Muzi told her, happy to be in the fresh air, feeling the sun on his face.

Ro nodded. He was about to turn away when she put her hand on his arm to stop him. When he looked down into her face, he saw the determination in her eyes. "Muzi, I also need to talk to you about us, where we are going and about what Mimi said. Also, I think she suspects who I am."

Damn, he'd been hoping to dodge both those bullets. No such luck.

"Even if Mimi did suspect, she'd respect your privacy and would never tell anyone. But if you are so worried about being outed, why don't you get ahead of it and issue a press statement to tell the world who you really are?"

"And have them hound me and dig into my life? Radd and Digby accept me, that's all I ever wanted," she retorted before flinging up her hands. "Look, I'm not an idiot, I presume that someone at some point will connect the dots but I'm not releasing any information before I need to."

Fair enough.

"Now, what did Mimi mean when she said that my parents were paid to have kids?" Ro asked him, *again*. Damn, he'd hoped his question about her true identity would distract her, but it hadn't worked.

"Can you not let this go, Ro?" Muzi asked, a little desperately. This was between her and her brothers, he shouldn't even be involved in this!

Ro folded her arms across her chest, defiance in her eyes. And all over her face. "Would you?"

Of course he wouldn't. Muzi sighed. He yanked his phone out of his pocket and pulled up Digby's number.

The phone rang twice before he heard his friend's cool voice. Right, Digby was still pissed. That was okay, he was pissed too. No doubt they'd get over it at some point.

Muzi locked eyes with Ro as he spoke into the phone. "She wants to know, and I told you I wouldn't lie for you."

"You can't tell her," Digby insisted.

"Then you tell her!" Muzi told him and, not waiting for an answer, passed his phone to Ro. She held it up to her ear and held out her other hand to him, needing the contact.

Muzi linked her fingers in his and watched as the color drained from her face, her eyes turning a dark and tumultuous blue. From where he stood, he could hear Digby's voice but not his words. Still, judging by Ro's reaction, he assumed Digby was telling his sister the abysmal truth.

Her birth parents only kept her brothers because they were paid a couple of million for each son they bore and— *snort!*—raised. Gil's Tempest-Vane grandfather hadn't thought girls were worth that amount of money, or any, so there was no financial reward for producing a girl.

And, to Gil and Zia, why keep her around if there wasn't anything in it for them?

When the call ended Ro dropped her hand, stared down at the screen before eventually handing him his phone. Seeing the devastation on her face, he started to pull her into him, needing to comfort and reassure her, but she stepped back abruptly, lifting her hands to ward him off.

"No, please, don't." She pushed her hair away from her face and held it back, her eyes extraordinarily dark in her ghostlike face.

Digby and Radd were right, this had been a bad idea. Ro was knocked sideways, emotionally drawn and quartered. What the hell had he been thinking?

"Tell me how I can help you, Ro," Muzi pleaded, wishing she'd let him hold her.

"I need to be alone, Muzi," Ro said, her voice hollow. "I need to digest this, wrap my head around it."

"I'll wait—"

Ro dropped her hands and violently shook her head. "No, go home. Please!"

"I don't want to leave you alone, sweetheart," Muzi told her, sounding and feeling desperate.

"But that's what I need, Muzi," Ro replied, and he heard tears in her voice. One tear hovered on the rim of her right eye, but she blinked rapidly and it went away. Muzi watched as she sucked in a deep breath and straightened her spine.

She wouldn't let him, or anyone else, see her cry.

She had her pride, as did he. And if she needed time alone, he would respect her wishes and give her what she wanted.

Later, he'd hold her. For as long—fifteen minutes or for the next year—as she needed him to.

CHAPTER NINE

RO WAS STILL trying to make sense of the bombshell Digby dropped nearly five hours later.

Over the past couple of months, on reading or hearing something about her parents, Ro often thought that she'd heard the worst of what they were capable of. Then a new story would surface, one she hadn't heard before, and she'd be shocked to her core, thinking that *this* had to be the worst of them...

But this was, absolutely, as low as they, or anyone, could go.

She'd been tossed aside, dispersed of because she was a girl and didn't come with the right equipment. Holy, holy hell.

Now she understood why neither her brothers nor Muzi had wanted to explain Mimi's odd comment. They hadn't wanted to hurt her. But she'd pushed and pushed and here she sat, in the corner of the low stone wall, hurting.

She'd been looking for reasons to like Gil and Zia, to understand them, to find justifications for their revolting choices. But, with this soul-shredding news, she was forced to accept that Gil and Zia were twisted, probably evil, utterly narcissistic and a waste of oxygen. And she carried their genes.

Dear God, the knowledge hurt.

The fact that they thought she wasn't worth keeping hurt. And knowing that she loved Muzi and that he clearly didn't love her...

Hurt worst of all.

Ro stood up, brushed the seat of her pants and told herself to pull herself together. Muzi never promised her anything other than a fling, her birth parents did her a favor by giving her up for adoption—her parents adored her and gave her a wonderful life—and her roller-coaster life would even out, hopefully sometime soon.

Ro leaned her butt on the concrete wall and stretched out her legs. She needed to go home, have a shower, drink a glass of wine and spend time with Muzi.

She didn't know how much time she'd have with him and sitting here, moping, wasn't productive.

Or fun.

Ro heard her phone ring and pulled it from the back pocket of her shorts, wrinkling her nose when she saw it was Kelvin video calling her. She'd been ducking and diving his calls for ages, maybe she should just answer, speak to him and move on.

She swiped the screen and their eyes connected through the power of technology.

"Hi, how are you?" Look at her, being so adult.

"I'm good," Kelvin replied, a smile lifting his lips.

He had a great smile, Ro admitted, but it seldom reached his eyes. Muzi smiled less often but she always caught the laughter in his eyes, the amusement turning his brown-black eyes luminous. His smile could power the sun.

And God, those dimples.

Muzi's, not Kelvin's. Kelvin didn't have dimples.

Kelvin peered into the screen, his eyebrows pulling together. "Good grief, you are filthy, what on earth have you been doing?"

Ro turned the screen and panned her camera over the outside of her house before turning it back to face her. "I'm renovating this house."

"Why?" Kelvin asked, horrified. His distaste amused her. Kelvin did not like to get his hands dirty.

Ro jumped up backward to sit on the veranda wall, the heels of her trainers banging against the rough wall. She shrugged. "It's a job."

He nodded. "You must be running low on your savings by now. Isn't it time you came home?"

If he only knew. "I'm thinking about it," she told him. She was thinking about many things, including how to incorporate a big, bold African man into her life. And how to get him to include her in his.

"Why did you call, Kelvin?"

He rubbed his hand behind his neck, looking contrite. "I wanted to say that I'm genuinely sorry. I messed up but I want you back."

"Yeah, you did," Ro said. "And I'm sorry, but I'm not interested."

"I made a mistake, Ro. We can make this work, I know we can."

How to get through to him? Ro thought about and discarded a few options and decided to hit him with the truth. "Kelvin, I don't love you anymore. I don't know if I ever did. I don't know what love is, what it means for me, how it's supposed to be. But what I do know for sure is that you are not it, that you no longer have a piece of my heart."

Oh, God, were those tears in his eyes? "Does that mean that you've found someone who does own a piece of your heart?"

She could lie and tell him no, but she couldn't deny what she felt for Muzi anymore, the feelings bubbling and burning, rippling and roaring. Neither did she want to, because those crazy feelings were demanding to be explored, to be *acknowledged*.

"I have found someone new. I don't know if I'm in love with him but I'm pretty damn close," she admitted. "I'm feeling like I am standing on the sharp edge of a knife, that one misstep will slice me in two. He has the power to hurt me, Kel, in a way that you never did."

Ro stared at her grubby shoes, the streaks of dirt on her jeans. "You cheated on me and it pissed me off, I was so mad at you."

"You had—have—a right to be. I was an idiot," Kelvin said.

Ro smiled. "That's exactly what Muzi called you." Ro turned, propped her phone against the wall, lifted her legs and placed her chin on her knee, her eyes on the small screen. "The point is…my pride was hurt but your betrayal didn't touch my heart. I shrugged it off. I shouldn't have felt so little, been so blasé. I'm not trying to hurt you but Muzi makes me *feel*, Kel, in a way you never did. He makes my skin tingle and my heart feel like it's going to jump out of my chest. He makes me think and laugh and when I'm around him, I feel the best version of myself."

"And if he cheated on you?" Kelvin asked her, his tone subdued.

The idea was too horrible to contemplate. She bit her lip, her eyes brimming as sadness and devastation flowed over her. "He'd break my heart. He has the power to emotionally chop me up in little pieces, to rip me in two. I've never had such a strong reaction to anyone in my life and I doubt I ever will again." Ro released an unhappy, tiny laugh. "He's phenomenal."

"And you're telling me that you're *not* in love with him?" Kelvin said, sounding unconvinced.

"I'm trying not to be, I'm trying to protect myself," Ro

told him, knowing it was true. "I'm trying to do anything and everything I can to stop myself from tumbling into this crazy situation I don't understand, one I can't figure out and most definitely can't control. Feeling like this is terrifying."

"I'm sorry I couldn't be that person for you, Ro."

She nodded, not knowing what else to say. Kelvin cleared his throat, sat back in his chair and touched the perfect knot in his tie. "I went to see your folks, by the way."

Ro knew him well enough to recognize that he'd closed the door on their emotional conversation. "They look pretty relaxed for a couple who are divorcing. Honestly, I really thought they'd last forever."

"You and me both," Ro told him. "Do you think there's any chance of them reconciling?"

Kelvin frowned. "Ro, they've legally filed, their documents are in the system. I've split their assets and they've put their house on the market. Their marriage is over."

So they were going ahead with their divorce. It was more than they'd told her. Then again, she couldn't complain about their lack of openness, she was keeping a couple of big and bold secrets herself.

"I'm sorry," Kelvin said, sounding sincere.

"Yeah, me too," Ro whispered.

Kelvin cleared his throat and gestured to his desk. "I need to get some work done. Thanks for taking my call." He looked down before forcing his eyes back to her face. "Again, I'm sorry. I'm sorry we didn't work out, and I'm so sorry for cheating on you. I wish you a good life, Ro."

It was over, they were fully done and from this moment on, Kelvin would be a memory. "You too, Kel."

"I hope he makes you happy, kiddo, you deserve it."

Ro's smile wobbled. "I hope so too. Be happy, Kelvin."

Feeling a tear slide down her face, she jabbed her finger

on the red button and Kelvin's face disappeared. And just like that, he was gone. Permanently.

Ro rested her cheek on her knees and watched as Muzi crossed the verandah to sit next to her on the wall. He'd arrived as she took the call and she'd known he was standing there, just around the corner. She always knew where he was, felt his energy, could sense his eyes on her.

And maybe that was why she'd been so open with Kelvin, said the things to him that she couldn't say to Muzi, knowing that her emotional words would force them to confront their feelings, to jolt them out of this holding pattern they were in. To move them along.

To get them from point A to point B.

Beside her, Muzi stretched out his long legs. Ro didn't prod him, knowing that he'd speak, eventually.

"You knew I was there," Muzi stated, his voice low.

"Yes. I was waiting for you, I knew you'd come back to check on me, to comfort me and to tell me that my birth parents' decisions have nothing to do with me," Ro replied.

"And you used your ex as a conduit to talk to me."

His tone was so bland that Ro couldn't decide whether he was angry or not. Ro felt his eyes on her face and lifted her head, forcing herself to meet his eyes. "I never planned it, he asked me the question and I responded with the truth."

"Next time, say what you need to say to my face, Roisin."

Ro winced. Yep, okay. Noted. She waited for him to rip into her some more, but he just rubbed the back of his neck, then the side of his jaw. He was feeling uncomfortable, Ro realized, unsure. Good, she wasn't feeling too confident herself.

"You said that I have the power to rip you apart. Is that true?" he finally spoke again, his voice as deep as the night.

Right, they were going to do this. Ro sucked in a breath and held it, suddenly wishing she could backtrack. But Muzi, she knew, didn't dodge or duck, he faced situations head-on. And she'd shoved theirs into his face.

In a few minutes she'd either be sinking or swimming, dancing or drowning.

"Yes," Ro whispered.

"You have the same power, Ro. More than anyone I've ever known."

She knew that and was humbled that she could affect this strong resilient man in such an emotional way. "So let's not hurt each other, Muzi," she softly suggested. "Let's promise each other that we won't."

She heard the clang of desperation in her voice, the way her voice rose and fell, coated with anxiety.

"I can't promise that, Roisin. You can't either."

Sadness coated his words, and Ro's heart plummeted to her feet. Her intuition told her that this wasn't going to end well.

"You are braver than I am, Ro, willing to wade into these dark waters even though you don't understand them and have no idea how to navigate them, how to protect yourself."

She held her breath, knew what was coming next.

"But I'm not that brave, not that strong. I don't trust love to stick around, I *can't* trust it. I lost my mother when I was three, my grandmother when I was a young kid. I lived under the threat of losing my family my entire life. I will, hopefully not anytime soon, lose Mimi. I survived my childhood, I didn't let Susan break me and when Mimi's time comes to move on, I'll mourn her, and I'll miss her. But I'll cope."

Ro held her breath, waiting for the hammer to fall. "But I can't survive losing you, Roisin. Like you, I am standing on that knife-edge, ready to fall. But I'm not going to do that. I *can't* and I *won't*. I'm going to be sensible and back away, while I still can."

Muzi stood up and dropped a kiss on the top of her head. "I could love you, Ro, we both know that. And yeah, I'm scared of being hurt. But more than that, I can't bear the thought of doing something to hurt you. I would rip any-one in two who caused you one tear…"

He hesitated, took a breath and forced the words out. "But the hell of it is, I know that I have the power to hurt you the most, to hurt you *again*. Nobody gets to do that, Ro, especially not me. I hope you find love, Ro. I hope you find a man who can give you everything you want, every-thing you need, what you deserve."

She didn't want anyone else, she wanted *him*. But Ro was old enough, and wise enough, to know her wants and needs didn't matter. She couldn't demand him to be brave, to take a chance, to love her as she did him.

Love, not given freely and courageously, wasn't love at all. So Ro bit her lip and watched him walk away.

And slowly, so very slowly, she started to sink, knowing that she was about to, mentally and emotionally, drown in the sadness enveloping her.

CHAPTER TEN

Ro TOSSED STAINED and ratty blankets into the skip, once again dirty and dusty. The cleaning crew had been back yesterday, and they'd swept and vacuumed the inside of the property, mopped the floors and cleaned the windows but she still found ways to get filthy.

Today she was sorting through the piles of linen. The finely embroidered tablecloths, stitched by her great-grandmothers, would be hand-washed and placed into plastic containers to protect them from moths and other vermin, but sheets and duvets and stained tablecloths were all going in the skip.

She wished she could toss out her problems as easily, but life didn't work that way.

More than a week had passed since that night she couldn't stop thinking about. The night Muzi left, she'd curled up on a couch in the library and white-knuckled it, thinking that this was true heartbreak. She'd cried until a soft dawn broke over the mountain.

The next day she'd forced herself to swing by Muzi's place to collect her stuff. He wasn't there, Greta told her, and the housekeeper had been instructed to pack up Ro's bags.

Refusing to cry—knowing that if she started again, she might not stop, *ever*—she went into Franschhoek, picked up food and fresh linens, and organized to have a bed delivered to St. Urban. She hadn't left her property since.

She wasn't eating and she wasn't sleeping, and was, she decided, a walking, talking zombie. She'd been so desperate to sleep last night that, sometime around midnight, she decided to take a long walk through the vineyards, hoping the fresh night air would help her to get some rest.

Leaning against the skip, she remembered her walk through the section of the vines that had been cleared by Muzi's farm crew, the moonlight so bright she hadn't needed a torch to navigate her way. When she came to the property boundary she'd video called her mom and was pleasantly surprised to find her dad with her.

She hadn't spent a lot of time on pleasantries, she'd simply jumped right in and asked them what was happening with their divorce.

"We're going ahead with it," her mother told her, "and we expect it to be finalized within a few months."

"We are good friends, Ro, and we intend to stay that way," her dad assured her.

"And you will always be our daughter. We've just changed, moved on from each other," her dad added. "Love doesn't always last forever, pumpkin."

"But it should, I want it to! I need to believe that love can last forever!" she'd shouted, tears on her cheeks. "I want to love someone and to *know* that it will last forever. Look, I know that I am being overly romantic and highly unrealistic," she continued. "I know that having a relationship that lasts a lifetime is something rare and wonderful and the chances of it happening to me are extremely unlikely."

"You and Kelvin—"

"Kelvin and I are over." Ro sat down between the vines and watched the moonlight dance across the leaves. After taking a deep breath, she told her parents that she was the biological daughter of two of the most dysfunctional people the world had ever seen and that she'd inherited their fortune.

She told them she was obscenely rich, that they had to keep her identity a secret and that she'd decide, when the time was right, to reveal to the world that she was the long-lost Tempest-Vane heir. Or she might not. She'd see what worked best for her sometime in the future.

Oh, and that she'd fallen for another man. Her explanations took time, and it was over twenty minutes before she could return to her point about relationships.

"If my decent, lovely parents can't make their relationship work, what chance do I have? My parents, my real parents, the two people who made me believe that happily ever after in love is possible, are splitting up. My birth parents routinely cheated on each other but stayed married. My fiancé cheated on me two weeks after I left home, and I've fallen in love with a man who's everything I want but he's commitment-phobic and has abandonment issues."

She could see the long look her parents exchanged— saw the love in their eyes—and a few of the many knots in her stomach eased.

"We loved each other wildly, intensely, wonderfully," her dad said, emotion coating every word. "Do I regret that? Not for a second. Your mom has given me so much pleasure and I've loved every moment with her. And you were a gift from heaven above."

"We loved each other, Roisin, and we still do. It's just... changed," her mom said, resting her temple on her dad's shoulder. "Will that happen to you? With this man or someone else? I don't know, life and love don't come with any guarantees. But do we think you should walk away from love, now or in the future, because we're getting divorced and your birth parents were lunatics? No, that's…*nuts*."

"You decide your future, who you love and how you love that person," her dad told her, sounding a little cross. "You don't get to walk away from love because of something that might or might not happen in the future."

Shocked by her normally easygoing father's harsh words, she'd nodded. Growing up, her mom was the whip-cracker but when her dad waded in, she never argued. "That's all very well, Dad, but he won't let himself love me."

And that's what it came down to: she might be prepared to take the risk of loving him, to see where this went but a relationship needed two people to be courageous, to take a chance, to make it work.

Muzi wasn't prepared to put any skin in the game and she couldn't force him to. Love wasn't love when it was demanded or coerced.

Muzi wouldn't allow himself to love her and she needed to accept that. But, God, it *hurt*.

When they disconnected, Ro remained seated on the damp grass, thinking of her dream to be the center of a man's world, the glue that held a family together. But the only man she could see herself being with was Muzi. And he didn't want her…

Feeling the burn of tears—she'd never cried so much in her life—Ro climbed to her feet, her attention caught by the sheen of moonlight on the leaves of the vines. She touched a leaf on her left, smiled, and looked right…

The moonlight looked different on those leaves. Ro frowned, thinking that she was going mad. Rubbing her eyes, she inspected the vines again and stepped away to look at them from another angle. The vines on her right definitely didn't reflect the moonlight in the same way the vines on the left did.

And were the vines on the right a little bigger, with bigger veins running through them? In the moonlight, they looked dissimilar.

Ro decided that they were...

Could these subtle differences mean that she'd found Muzi's precious cultivar? She didn't want to get his, or her, hopes up but...

Maybe. Just maybe.

If she couldn't give him her love, at least she'd be able to give him the gift of securing his position in Clos du Cadieux. It was something, she supposed.

Nine long-ass days after last seeing Ro, Muzi strolled into Pasco's at lunchtime and found an empty seat at the bar, wondering if noon was too early to get slammed.

He lifted his hand to his head and remembered that he'd just managed to get rid of remnants of last night's hangover and he didn't know if his poor head could take another beating. Tomorrow was Monday, and he had a board meeting, where he expected to take flak for leasing land comprised of Merlot vines.

He planned to tell the board that, according to his research, he was convinced a good portion of those vines weren't Merlot, and in a few years, Clos du Cadieux would launch an exceptionally rare, award-winning wine on the market.

They'd be excited to hear that, and pretty damn pleased with him. And as soon as their excitement bubbled down, he'd make another announcement...

They needed to choose between him or Susan. If they wanted him to run Clos du Cadieux and to bring a new wine to the market—an expensive, rare, hugely profitable wine and one only he could produce—Susan needed to step down.

Or else he would resign. And, as per the contract he'd signed with Ro, the St. Urban vines went with him. Thank God that she'd insisted on including that clause in the agreement—she'd only wanted to deal with him and nobody else—it gave him a safety net. If they did choose Susan over him, he'd still have the vines and could still bring a wine made from the C'Artegan cultivar to the market.

He held all the cards to get Susan out of his life and Ro had given him most of them.

And that just pissed him off.

How had she, in such a short time, flipped his life inside out? Because of her, he'd started, just a little, to dream of accomplishments outside of his career, being a husband, having kids. Growing old with someone.

For the millionth time since leaving her alone at St. Urban he remembered that night, the pain in her deep, dark eyes.

After she'd spoken to Digby on the phone, he'd given her some time and space to process the reason for her adoption but when she hadn't returned home by dusk, he'd headed back to St. Urban, needing to see if she was okay.

On the drive over, he reluctantly admitted he was already in love with her and if she stuck around, happy to continue their no-commitment fling, he'd only fall deeper and deeper in love with her. And when she finally left—and she would, she'd told him she was only sticking around for another year—he'd fall into a bubbling, flesh-and-soul-stripping volcano.

He knew he should put distance between them, to create a barrier between them, but he couldn't leave her alone, not when she was upset and in pain. He'd try to be sensible later…if he could.

On arriving at St. Urban, he'd expected to find her crying but that wasn't the case. She sounded fine, *normal*, and the realization that she was talking to her ex had literally stopped him in his tracks.

He'd stood there out of her sight, trying to control his jealously. But then her words started to make sense. They said that eavesdroppers never heard anything good about themselves but Ro's honest and emotional declaration of how she felt nearly dropped him to the floor, in a good way. A bright, warm rush of love and a dose of happiness barreled through him and he'd hurried down the long veranda to get to her, prepared to yank the phone out of her hand and kiss her stupid…

She loved him, or something damn close to it.

Jack. Pot.

You're not good enough, you're unlovable, you're nothing…

Those long-ago phrases had him placing his hand on the wall, needing to steady himself.

What the hell are you thinking, Triple M? Have you lost your damn mind?

Terror immediately replaced tenderness. Love, he reminded himself, was the greatest weapon of all, dangerous because it lulled one into complacency before it proceeded to slice and dice you.

He'd thought his mother loved him, but she'd shipped him off. Lu loved him, but she'd died. Susan pretended to love him in company and verbally annihilated him in private.

Muzi stared down at the wooden bar top, his eyes blurry with fatigue. Love confused and baffled him. He never knew which way was up. And that was why he avoided it.

And, Jesus, was it too much to ask for it to come with a guarantee or two?

"Hey, you're going to frighten my customers with your sour face," Pasco told him from the other side of the bar.

Muzi lifted his eyes and thought about asking Pasco for matches to prop open his eyelids. He hadn't slept and he was exhausted. But as soon as he closed his eyes, he started to think of Ro and how much he missed her. Unable to deal with that suck-fest, he moved on to thinking about Susan and her lifelong campaign of terror and all that did was increase the volume of noise in his head.

By tomorrow, at least one of those problems would be solved. But getting Ro out of his head and soul was going to require a lifetime of effort.

Pasco placed a drink in front of him and Muzi nearly gagged at the sight of a Bloody Mary. "I can't," he muttered, pushing the glass away.

Pasco pushed it back. "'You can and you will. And when you are done drinking that, you will go upstairs to my private apartment and take a long shower. I'll send some food up and then you will sleep."

Muzi heard the tough note in his voice and wondered whether he had the strength to argue. He didn't, so he picked up the Bloody Mary and downed it, trying not to gag.

"I'll go home, have a shower there and try to sleep," Muzi told Pasco, sliding off his barstool.

"Upstairs, *now*," Pasco ordered, sounding like Gordon Ramsay in a very bad mood.

He didn't have the energy to argue. "Yes, Chef." Muzi took a step toward a door marked Staff Only. He stopped, turned around and slid his hands into the pockets of his rumpled shorts.

"By the way, if you are serious about wanting to move

back here, I heard that the owner of the Tempest-Vane trust is thinking about converting St. Urban into a luxurious boutique hotel and wants a restaurant on the premises. It might work for you."

Pasco's eyes widened in surprise. "That's *interesting*. I'd wondered why Ro was putting her heart and soul into restoring that wreck."

Muzi winced when he comprehended Pasco's meaning. "Pas, *crap*. How did you know?"

"I've got eyes, don't I? She and Digby are two peas in a pod."

Dammit. "You can't...don't...nobody is supposed to know."

Pasco looked him in the eye. "And nobody will. It's her secret to share, not mine." Muzi released his death grip on the doorframe. When Pasco gave his word, he never reneged on it.

"So, is she sticking around?"

"I don't know, you'd have to ask her," Muzi said, his tone bitter.

Pasco's eyebrows rose. "What the hell have you done, Muzi?"

"Why do you automatically assume it's my fault?" Muzi demanded, knowing that his tone lacked conviction.

"Because you're a moron," Pas replied. He rolled his eyes. "Go upstairs, shower, have a nap. When you've slept, things will look better."

Muzi rolled his eyes at him. "Sure they will."

He was completely sober, and his life looked pretty bleak.

Muzi was tempted, so tempted, to get drunk again.

Unbelievably, after a shower in Pasco's apartment upstairs, and a bowl of hearty chicken soup, Muzi stretched out on

Pasco's long leather couch and drifted off to sleep. He woke six hours later, feeling…if not better, then more human.

After washing his face, he snagged some of Pasco's toothpaste and rubbed it over his teeth. He rinsed his mouth and stared at himself in the mirror, noticing his roadmap-like eyes and the gray pallor of his complexion. He needed to pull himself together and move the hell on.

But the thought of doing that without Ro made his stomach churn. How could he live his life without her in it? He lifted his chin and reminded himself that this wasn't his first rodeo: he'd survived after being separated from his mom, coped after Lu died.

He could do this. He *would*. But maybe he should go back to having shallow affairs with innocuous women. He ignored the thought that that was how his relationship with Ro began, with him thinking it was all about the sex.

It had been so, so much more. Ro was laughter and color, warmth and wit. She was the sunrise, her presence was the breaking of his night. She was midnight comfort, as her head used his shoulder for a pillow, his early morning jolt of energy, his reason for, well, everything…

Muzi placed his hands on the side of the basin and closed his eyes, sinking under the knowledge that she was everything to him. And that he'd let her go.

He knew, intellectually and through experience, that every day got a little easier, that heartbreak did eventually fade.

He hoped it faded before he did…

But, right now, he knew what he needed to do. He needed to go home, walk his lands and breathe in some warm, sultry air. When he'd done that, he'd spend some time working in his study and on something he could control, and that was work.

He could heal, he *would*. He just needed to be alone and to process the past few weeks. Everything would be fine in the end, he reminded himself, and if it wasn't fine, then it wasn't the end.

He entered the bar and saw that Pasco had been joined by Digby and, God, *Keane*. What the sodding hell? Standing in the doorway, he caught Pasco's eyes and scowled.

Pasco just motioned him over and nodded to an empty barstool to the left of Digby, who turned and gave him an up and down look. "So, you look like crap."

He knew that already. "What the hell are you doing here?" He growled the words, deliberately ignoring Keane.

Digby gestured to Pasco. "Dr. Phil here sent out an emergency SOS, telling us that you needed us, that you were falling apart."

Muzi considered wrapping his big hands around Pasco's neck, but settled for a threat. "I'm gonna kill you."

"You can try," Pasco told him, sliding a bottle of water across the bar.

Muzi, needing to do something with his hands, cracked the top. "And what the hell is he doing here?"

Muzi saw the long look Digby and Pasco exchanged. Digby, to his credit, was the first one to step onto the battlefield. "This cold war between you two has got to stop. We're tired of it."

Right now, Muzi didn't give a rat's ass about their feelings, he had too many of his own he was trying to corral. "He chose to believe the BS his mother has been spouting about me, about me running the business into the ground and stealing money from Clos du Cadieux."

Pasco and Digby both turned accusatory looks toward Keane. He lifted his hands and, to his credit, met Muzi's eyes. "Susan is a difficult woman and, with Rafe in the

States, I'm all she has. In my defense, I didn't believe any of those wild claims."

"And yet you still walked away from me and our friendship," Muzi muttered, shocked at how much it still hurt. Keane abandoned him, just like his mom. And in a sense, like his grandmother did. Death was the ultimate abandonment wasn't it? Everyone he loved could, would and did, hurt him…

And that was why he ended it with Ro.

Keane rested his elbows on the table and pushed his hands into his hair. "Jesus, Triple M, I was *trying* to protect you. I always felt that, under her smiles, my mom didn't like you—"

Like… Such a small word for what she put him through.

"But her hatred of you bubbled over when we left university and joined Clos du Cadieux. And it went through the roof when Mimi appointed you as CEO."

"You're not telling me anything I don't know," Muzi pointed out.

"She told me to choose between her and you," Keane told him, his shoulders rising in agitation. "Honestly, I would've chosen you. But Susan is a basket case and, with Rafe leaving, I knew that if I sided with you, there would be no one to curtail her worst impulses. When Mimi retired, she told the family that she didn't want to hear of any squabbling at Clos du Cadieux. I am the only one who can talk sense into Susan, to make her consider her actions. I sided with her to protect you!"

"I don't need protecting!" Muzi said, his voice rising.

"From Susan you do," Keane insisted. "She hates you— she always has. Looking back, I think I've only just realized how much."

Muzi didn't want to think about that, didn't want to acknowledge the guilt and sorrow in his brother's eyes. The past couldn't be changed.

"So, you detonated our friendship to protect me?" Muzi scoffed.

Keane looked him in the eye. "Yeah, I did. Susan has had some wild schemes over the years concerning you but I, mostly, managed to deflect her."

"So why are you telling me this now?" Muzi demanded. "Why are you here?"

"Because when I get a message telling me that your life is falling apart and that Pas has never seen you so defeated, I will always come running," Keane told him, his voice strong and sure. "My mother is mad but you, *you* are my brother."

Muzi felt the prickle of tears at his sincerity, still trying to wrap his head around what he was hearing. "You could've come to me and told me what you were doing, Keane. Losing you..." He couldn't continue, it hurt too much.

Keane placed a hand on his shoulder and squeezed. "I know, I'm sorry. It was just supposed to be for a few months, but the gap I created just kept getting wider and wider until I didn't know how to bridge it. Can you forgive me, Triple M? I *am* damn sorry."

Before they got to that point, there was something else Keane should know. "I'm going to bury your mother tomorrow at the board meeting."

Keane's expression remained inscrutable, but curiosity jumped into his eyes. "How?" he asked, his tone careful.

Muzi, knowing that he was taking the risk that Keane would take what he was about to say straight to Susan, explained his plan and Keane nodded. Muzi held his breath, waiting for his response. "I think that's a perfect plan. The board will vote to keep you."

"You think?"

Keane nodded. "Trust me, there have been rumblings for a while that Susan's animosity toward you is hindering rather than helping the situation. I have been asked to persuade her to retire."

Muzi felt one of the many boulders sitting on his chest roll away.

"The board, and I, will all vote for you," Keane told him. He lifted his glass of whiskey, sipped, and Muzi saw regret and fear roll across his face. "I messed up, and I'm tired of being on the outside of your life. Can we…is there any chance…"

His words trailed off but Muzi knew what he was asking. Could they go back? Could they try again? Could they repair their relationship? It would take time, effort but… yeah. He thought they could. Because he did, somewhere where truth resided, believe that Keane had been trying to look after his best interests.

He nodded and held out his hand for Keane to shake. Keane took it a step further by pulling him into a one-armed hug.

"Cut it out, you're acting like two overly emotional teenage girls!" Pasco broke the soppy moment with his sarcastic quip but Muzi could see that he was pleased. As was Digby.

Muzi raised his bottle, thinking he needed something stronger. "Can I have something with alcohol in it?" he asked Pasco.

"Hell, no," Pasco told him, pulling the whiskey bottle out of his reach. "You still have work to do, my friend."

Muzi lifted his hands, confused. "What work?"

"My sister," Digby stated, his tone hard.

Ah, crap. He might've regained one friend, but, judging by Digby's face, he might be losing another. He looked for something to say, found nothing and opted to keep his mouth shut.

"What? No explanation?" Digby demanded.

"I'm not sure what you need me to explain," Muzi carefully replied.

"Well, according to Bay and Brinley, my sister is currently sleeping at St. Urban because you kicked her out of your place. And your bed, and your life."

True. He didn't need to be a rocket scientist to know that Radd and Digby's women were not impressed with him.

"I should take you outside and pummel the hell out of you," Digby muttered.

That was okay with Muzi, he needed an outlet for his stress and he couldn't possibly feel worse than he already did.

"Why did you kick her out? Especially after she was ambushed by the truth of her adoption?" Keane asked him, ignoring Digby.

Hell, did everyone now know who Ro was, her real connection to Radd and Digby? She was going to eviscerate him when she found out. With a blunt teaspoon. He threw up his hands and scowled at Digby, who winced.

"I told Keane," Digby admitted. "Pasco worked it out for himself."

"If either of you tells anyone, I will break you," Muzi told Keane and Pasco. They wouldn't but a strong warning was warranted.

Muzi shook his head, feeling like he'd stepped into a world where nothing made sense. "I gave her time to be alone, as she asked. When I returned, she was on the phone with her idiot ex."

"If you are about to tell us that she's still in love with him, I will deck you," Digby threatened.

"No, she told him about us…that she's this close—"

Muzi held up his thumb and index finger an inch apart "—to falling in love with me."

All three faces reflected confusion. "And that's a problem?" Digby asked.

"Yes! The way we feel about each other is crazy! It's insane, intense, intimidating!"

"Incredible, irrational… I can't think of any more words starting with an *i*," Pasco drawled.

Muzi had the feeling that Pasco was taking the piss. When he had the energy, he would make him pay for that remark.

Muzi thought he'd try, once again, to explain. He didn't hold out much hope that they'd get it. "Look, we have the power to hurt each other, badly. I'm not thrilled at being in that position but, worse than that, I couldn't live with myself if *I* hurt *her*."

Digby lifted his beer bottle to his lips and took a long swallow. "So don't hurt her, half-wit."

"Poor Ro, she's had a tough few days—ambushed by her ex and dumped by the man she's crazy about," Pasco mused. "I should go and comfort her."

"Only if you want to be buried in a shallow grave," Muzi growled.

"I should kick your ass for sleeping with her and then treating her like crap, man," Digby told him, and Muzi saw his bunched fists.

"It wasn't like that… I didn't…" God, he was a reasonably erudite man, why couldn't he find any words today? He stood up, reached across the bar, grabbed the whiskey bottle and took a slug. He felt the burn down his throat and, resting the bottle against his forehead, groaned.

"In my defense, it was a crazy day. I thought—assumed—that she was going back to the States. A little earlier she told me that she was going to stick around for another six months, maybe a year, and I was happy, I thought I had time to persuade her to stay forever. But then, hours later, she hits me with the possibility of love and forever and trying for more…and… God… I…"

"Take another belt, Triple M," Pasco suggested.

Muzi took another sip of whiskey and passed it back to Pasco, who put it under the counter, out of his reach. "She terrifies me. What I feel for her scares the hell out of me," he finally admitted.

Digby nodded, looking satisfied. "Good, it should scare you. Love is terrifying but that's no reason to run from it."

"Yeah, *that*," Pasco said, pointing his beer bottle at Muzi.

"Shut up, Kildare, you only have one-night stands and have no idea what you are talking about," Digby told him.

Digby turned his intense gaze, his eyes the same color as Ro's, on him. "Falling for someone is a big deal and it should cause your breath to hitch and your heart to stop. Look, you can carry on being a coward or you can face that fear. Step into the unknown and trust that the way you feel for each other, that the love you have for each other, your desire not to mess up and hurt each other, is enough to carry you through.

"I've never known you to be a coward, Triple M," Digby said, his voice silky with challenge.

God, was he trying to dare him into a relationship with his sister? And was he tempted? He was. He really was.

"I didn't expect or plan on her. I never expected to feel this way."

"We all think we can control what we feel but, when the right woman comes along, we're bowled over," Digby said. "Radd did, I did, it looks like you have too, M."

"I didn't mean to," Muzi grumbled.

"Neither did any of us," Digby cheerfully replied before

his expression sobered. "But what I can't forget is that my sister is alone in an old, huge house, probably crying her eyes out because you are a cowardly dipstick. So, are you going to do something about that, about *her*?"

Doing something meant telling her how he felt, asking for another chance, telling her that he wanted so much more than he ever had. It meant putting his heart into her hands, taking a chance.

Being brave.

"At the risk of repeating myself, love is scary, Muzi. Terrifying, actually," Digby told him, his voice vibrating with emotion. "It's hard, but so is being alone, so is not having her in your life. Choose your hard, Triple M."

CHAPTER ELEVEN

CHOOSE YOUR HARD...

Muzi thought about Digby's words as he drove over to St. Urban. It was fully dark and his headlights cut through the night, showing him only the next few yards of the road.

But that was okay, he didn't need to see hundreds of yards ahead, he just needed to navigate what he could see.

It was, he realized, a metaphor for life. He couldn't see into the future, there were no guarantees that Ro wouldn't die or disappear, but that was far in the future, shrouded in darkness. He needed to navigate life as it was in front of him, the few yards he could see.

If he wanted Ro, and he did, he needed to live a little more in the present. The past, as Mimi often declared, was a memory and the future was imagination. Only the here and now mattered.

And Ro mattered most of all.

Because he didn't want to scare her—and because he wasn't a complete moron—Muzi texted Ro to tell her he was on his way. But his warning would also give her the chance to avoid him and he hoped he didn't have to start chasing her all over the country. Or the world.

He would but it would be a pain in the ass.

Muzi pulled up in front of the steps leading up to the

front door, his headlights catching the small figure sitting on the wall, dressed in a pair of skimpy shorts and a cropped T-shirt. Her long hair hung down in waves and even in that glance he had, he could see her pinched face, her wide eyes.

Her wariness.

He shut down the car, climbed out, and kept his eyes on her as he walked over the gravel drive and up the steps. As his eyes became accustomed to the darkness, he saw her pull her knees up to her chest, her pose defensive.

"What do you want?" she demanded.

He stopped a short distance from her but close enough to realize that she'd recently showered and that her long hair was still wet. And that her eyes were red from crying.

He thought about how to respond to questions and decided that he might as well start with what was important.

"You. I want *you.*"

Ro, her heart thundering in her chest, heard his simple statement and stared up at him, not knowing what to say or how to react. What did that even mean?

How did he want her? In bed, up against a wall? As a fling, his partner or a significant other? Did he want her for now, for the next few months, or forever?

Why did men have to always skimp on the details?

"I think you need to explain that statement," Ro carefully told him.

Muzi nodded, crossed his arms and widened his stance. He looked big, powerful and intimidating but, even in the low light—the moon wasn't quite as bright as it had been—she could see the emotion roiling beneath his surface. It was in his eyes, in his tense jaw, in the way his nostrils flared every couple of seconds.

He didn't speak and she didn't know how to broach the

subject of their relationship—or current lack thereof—so Ro broke their silence by telling him that she'd taken a walk in the vineyard the night before.

Muzi frowned. "I'm not crazy about you walking the lands alone at night."

Ro waved his concern away. "I was on a video call to my folks—and yes, they are still divorcing—"

"And how do you feel about that?"

Fine. Better than fine. "They explained that they still love each other but that their love has changed. They are still the best of friends and still plan to stay in each other's lives so there won't be any awkwardness or taking of sides. I'm grateful for that. And, of course, they still love me as much as they ever did."

Muzi's mouth lifted in that sexy half smile she so loved. "Of course they do."

Ro waved her hands in the air. "But that's not what I wanted to tell you. So, I was sitting there, in between the vines on the east side of the property where your guys have been working. And I was watching the moonlight on the vine leaves and, you're going to think I'm crazy, but I think I might've found your cultivar. I saw some distinct differences..."

His expression didn't change and Ro frowned. "Why aren't you happy about this?"

Muzi shrugged. "I am, I guess. But, honestly, the C'Artegan cultivar is way down on my list of important stuff right now."

Oh, man, this was bad. If Muzi wasn't reacting to her news about finding the cultivar he was desperately looking for, then their night was going to go downhill fast.

She took a deep breath and forced herself to verbalize her thoughts. "Then what's at the top of that list?"

Muzi sat down on the wall next to her and stretched out his long legs.

"Did you not hear me say that I want you?" Muzi asked, his tone gentle. He sighed and linked his hands behind his head. "God, could I be any worse at this if I tried?"

Before she could reply—not that she had a response to his rhetorical question—he spoke again. "Let me back up a bit and start with this... I'm so sorry you were hurt when you found out what Gil and Zia did," Muzi quietly stated. "I thought you could handle the truth. But, in hindsight, maybe I should've protected you from that knowledge."

"You were right to tell me, and the last of my illusions have fallen away. In my head, they are sperm and egg donors but not my parents." Ro put her hand on her heart and smiled. "My parents are pretty damn wonderful, actually."

"I'm sure they are. They raised an incredible woman."

His words washed over her, but they weren't enough, she needed more. "What are we doing, Muzi? Where is this conversation going?"

Muzi pulled his thigh up onto the wall and turned to face her, his expression pensive. "I didn't plan for you, Roisin, I didn't plan for *this*. I was quite happy to be alone, content to have the occasional affair. I convinced myself that I didn't need anybody, that love wasn't worth the risk.

"And that I don't need anybody..." Muzi added.

Ro's heart, which had started to soar, stalled and plummeted back down to earth.

"But I do need *you*," Muzi said, his voice rough with emotion. "I know that you are still recovering from being in a long-term relationship, that another relationship might not be what you want but I'll be here—I'll take anything you can give me—hoping that you will love me the way I love you."

Ah...*what?*

"You love me?" Ro squeaked.

Muzi rubbed the back of his neck, looking uncomfortable. "I wish what I felt for you was that simple. Yes, I love you but it's more than that." He hesitated and Ro held her breath, unable to catch her heart, which was on a death-defying roller-coaster ride.

"I've fallen into you...into a dream of a future we can have together. I can see us creating a life together, living and loving together, creating babies and memories." He managed a small smile, moonlight in his eyes. "I've been scared before—scared that I'd be alone, abandoned by Mimi and the family—but losing you, it's a level of fear that can drop me to my knees. *You* drop me to my knees..." Muzi added.

She wanted to reach for him, to tell him that she wanted what he did, but there was something she had to get out first.

"We both want, or wanted, guarantees that our hearts would be safe, that we won't hurt each other but—" Ro hesitated, emotion closing her throat. She pushed the words past the tightness, and they came out a little rough. "But as I've recently discovered, love doesn't come with a guarantee."

"I *know*. And it's so damn terrifying," Muzi said, his hand coming to rest on her bare foot. "The thing is Ro, I'll take you, I'll take whatever you can give me. I choose you without any guarantee. That's true right now and I have to believe that it'll be true tomorrow and ten years, twenty, from now."

His thumb brushed the instep of her foot and heat rolled up her leg. She lifted her head and stared at him, unable to believe that this reticent man was saying exactly what she most needed to hear.

That he loved her, that he wanted her in his life…

"Put me out of my misery and tell me that I have a chance, Ro," Muzi begged. "Stay here with me, create a life with me."

Ro nodded and knew her smile was tremulous. "Okay," she whispered.

Muzi bent his head toward her. "Sorry, I didn't hear that?"

Oh, he absolutely did, the man had excellent hearing. Ro's smile grew stronger. "Yes, Muzi. Yes, to the life and babies and the vines and living in your house. But mostly yes to loving you. As hard as I can…"

Muzi closed his eyes and rested his forehead on her bent knees. "Thank God."

Ro kissed the top of his head, and when he lifted his face to look at her, she kissed his lips, unable to stop her smile. "I'm so insanely, wonderfully, utterly in love with you."

Muzi clasped her face in his big hands. "And I you." He stared at her and at that moment, the brief slice of time before his lips met hers, the world stopped and they were the only two people on earth, standing under a suddenly bright moon. Anticipation danced between them and she waited, not wanting the intense, powerful moment to end…

Then he kissed her, and she realized that it wasn't the end but simply the beginning.

Ro pulled back and sent him a cheeky smile. "Want to take a walk and look at the C'Artegan vines?"

Muzi stood up and scooped her up, cradling her against his big chest. "Again, not anywhere near the top of my 'Things that are most important right now' list."

Ro sighed, linked her arm around his neck and kissed his jaw, and he strode into the house. She did not doubt that she was priority one on that list, just as he was on hers.

And they'd both work damn hard, for the rest of their lives, to keep it that way.

* * * * *

THE ITALIAN'S
BRIDE ON PAPER

KIM LAWRENCE

MILLS & BOON

PROLOGUE

Eighteen months previously, Zurich

Maya and Beatrice had set out early, not alone, as the minibus ferrying tourists from the small ski resort to the airport in Zurich had been full of fellow travellers. They had all been stranded by the severe storm front that had resulted in the ski slopes being closed for the previous four days.

The storm was over now but *early* as a strategy had not worked—the minibus had been diverted before they'd even reached the terminal. The update texts the sisters had received so far from the airline had not been particularly encouraging or helpful and the details of the *airport security issue* mentioned in news reports remained worryingly vague.

There were rumours floating around on the Internet and also in the hotel bar situated within a short taxi drive of the airport where Maya and Beatrice had decided to wait out the delay.

They were not the only stranded travellers to take this option; the place was full of easy-to-spot tense, grumpy and frustrated airline passengers, who were waiting to be given news.

'A response some time this side of Christmas would

be good.' Beatrice's remark was not leavened with any of her normal humour. Her smooth brow was creased in a frown as she acquired a spare bar stool and sat down, arranging her long legs with casual elegance before turning her gaze back to the screen of her phone, as if willing their airline's promised update to appear.

'I might just go and check—'

'Fine,' Bea snapped, tight-lipped, without looking up.

Maya sighed. No sign of a full thaw just yet. They'd had the biggest row ever back at the ski resort, and, although they'd made up, the atmosphere was all a bit frigid. Some of the things her sister had said to her... Maya just couldn't get them out of her head; they kept playing on a loop.

'Really, Maya, relationship advice from *you*—what a joke! You've never even *had* a relationship. As soon as any half-decent guy gets within ten feet of you, you push him away,' Beatrice had said accusingly.

Maya had been stung. 'I dated Rob for months!'

'And you sabotaged that one just like all the others— and there have hardly been any others, have there? So *you've* never had your heart broken, for the simple fact that you won't take a risk—'

'*You* took a risk and look where it left you!' Maya had regretted the hasty words the moment they'd left her lips, and her swift efforts to de-escalate the situation had not exactly been a success. 'Sorry, Bea, but I hate to see you so unhappy. I know you chose to leave Dante, but he is clearly still messing with your—'

'Do not badmouth Dante to me...' her sister, who had spent the last few days doing just that herself, had growled back. 'Yes, I left him, Maya, but people do sometimes leave! And people die, we both know that too. It's called real life—and at least I have one.' Tears suddenly filled Beatrice's blue eyes. 'Sorry... I'm so sorry. I didn't mean that.'

After that final riposte, they had hugged and made up but Maya knew her sister had meant everything she'd said, and it was probably all true.

She considered saying something bright and cheery to lift the mood but decided that optimism would go down like a lead balloon. There was nothing she could say to make Beatrice feel any better, so it was probably better not to say anything at all.

She hitched in a little sigh and wished she'd remembered that saying nothing was an option last night. As she drifted away to stretch her legs, she threw the occasional glance over her shoulder at her sister, feeling the heavy weight of her total helplessness on her slender shoulders in the face of Beatrice's overwhelming unhappiness.

It was hard to watch someone you loved hurting.

She loved Beatrice, and no matter how often they squabbled or disagreed she knew that they had an unbreakable bond and that Beatrice would always be there for her.

The connection could not have been stronger if they had been biological sisters instead of Maya having been adopted by Beatrice's parents. Actually, Maya believed that it was stronger because she had a *real* sister out there and she had no connection with her. Her sister— actually, half-sister to be accurate—remained only a name and a face in a photo... *Violetta*. Her half-sister was clearly someone who, like their shared birth mother, apparently did not want to know Maya, did not want to be *embarrassed* by Maya's existence.

Searching out her birth mother was one of the few things she'd done that Maya had never shared with Beatrice or her adoptive mother, her *real* mother. When she had reached out to Olivia Ramsey, she had not been sure what to expect. And when the response had been an invitation to meet up for lunch, Maya had almost confided her very mixed feelings about the prospect of finally putting a face to the name of the stranger who had given her life and then immediately given her away. But she hadn't told Beatrice or their mother, and now eighteen months had passed, and so, she told herself, had the moment for sharing the secret.

Maya eased the vague sense of guilt she still felt for keeping that particular secret by convincing herself that this way there was no risk of Mum or Beatrice thinking that they were not enough of a family for her. Because they were her everything.

If she was being totally honest with herself, her reluctance to confide in them ran side by side with her reluctance to relive in the telling Olivia Ramsey's rejection all over again. Once had been more than enough to have it spelt out that the well-dressed, clearly well-off woman who had given birth to you only wanted to meet up with you years later to tell you, categorically, that there was no place in her life for the daughter she had given away. Showing Maya a photo of the daughter she *had* chosen to keep—Violetta—had been the last nail in the coffin of Maya's hopes of building any kind of relationship with her.

Maya couldn't remember exactly how she'd responded to Olivia's deliberately calm statements of fact…something along the lines of, *No problem, but I'd be grateful for any family medical history that might be relevant to me,* which her birth mother, who had not seemed overburdened with empathy, had accepted at face value.

So she hadn't inherited her own empathy from her biological mother—but what about her father? Well, when she had finally worked herself up to asking the question of his identity the answer hadn't left her any the wiser. Apparently her mother hadn't known his name—but he'd been good-looking, *very* good-looking. Normally, Olivia had drawled, she didn't date men under six feet.

The other woman had volunteered her reason for giving Maya up without any prompting in the same emotionally tone-deaf style: she'd admitted she would almost *definitely* have kept Maya if her married wealthy lover at the time had accepted her story that the baby was his. Only how was she to know he'd had a vasectomy? And surely Maya *had* to agree that saying you are single mother is a total turn-off for a real man?

'Ouch.'

The person wielding the trolley bag like a lethal weapon didn't even acknowledge the collision—of course they didn't, she thought darkly as she took refuge behind a potted palm. It turned out to be a perfect vantage point to watch the progress of an enterprising young artist who was based in the hotel foyer banging out a production line of cartoon portraits of new arrivals.

She rubbed her bruised shin and sighed. This last-minute skiing break had been doomed pretty much from the get-go; it had started badly and gone steadily downhill from there.

They had not even reached the chalet that had held so many good memories of long-ago childhood holidays when Maya had felt a migraine coming on.

It had definitely been a sign of things to come and proved, she reflected grimly, that it was a fatal mistake to try and recapture the past. But when the owner, an old family friend, had offered her and Beatrice the place for a song after a last-minute cancellation it had seemed too good an offer to pass up. So they'd eased their consciences by calling it a working holiday; after all, what better place, Beatrice had said, for Maya to get some inspiration for the winter collection she was trying to put together for the long-delayed launch of their fashion label.

But they had got very little actual work done, not due to Maya's migraine, or the lure of the ski slopes or even the après-ski fun, but solely thanks to the arrival of Beatrice's nearly ex-husband, Dante, who had turned up without the royal fanfare befitting his status as the Crown Prince of San Macizo and thrown her sister's life into chaos yet again.

Maya could forgive him for being the reason that their fashion label had not got off the ground first time around, but she couldn't forgive him for making her sister—who, until she'd fallen in love with Dante, had been the most optimistic and glass-half-full person Maya knew—so damned miserable. These days, even when Beatrice did smile, it was obviously an act; the shadow of misery visibly remained in her eyes.

From her vantage point beside the potted palm, Maya pushed away the thoughts of her sister's doomed marriage and watched in fascination as the young artist's hand moved across the paper managing in a few bold confident lines to pick out the essential features of his victims and magnifying them to comical proportions.

Maya had once thought she had artistic talent, but her youthful confidence in her ability had not withstood the campaign of mockery and humiliation waged by her stepfather.

The man was no longer in their lives and Maya had recovered most of the self-belief he had systematically destroyed, but never regained her uncomplicated joy of expressing herself in charcoal or paint.

In retrospect she could see that the dreadful Edward had probably unintentionally done her a favour—*goodness, but he'd hate to know that*—because there were so many artists far more talented than her who never made the grade and she didn't want to be one of the ranks of *nearly* good enough.

But this guy, she decided, was pretty good. Though to her amusement it was obvious that not everyone was happy with the frequently unflattering though always amusing portraits. But he was doing brisk business and he took the few knockbacks he received in his stride.

'Quantity over quality.' The youthful artist threw the comment towards her over his shoulder, making her start guiltily.

'I think you're very talented,' Maya said with a smile. She came out from behind the spiky palm fronds and moved in closer as the young man scrunched up his last rejected creation and attacked a fresh sheet.

'It pays the bills, or at least some of them, and beats starving in an attic. That is *so* last century or maybe the one before. God, not again!' He groaned as the hotel lights flickered and went out.

'Is it a power cut?' There had been a moment of total silence but now the place was filled with a jabber of voices, most saying much the same as she just had.

'Who knows? It's been doing it all morning. Ah, and now we have light.'

His clever hand was flying over the paper again, the caricature coming to life like magic. With a few brief strokes a face began to appear along with, and this was the most magical part, a personality.

Head tilted, she studied the face that was taking

form. A razor-sharp blade of a masterful nose made for looking down on the rest of humanity bisected a face with impossibly high cheekbones; a mouth with an overtly full, sensual upper lip contrasting with a firm, slightly cruel-looking lower, a deep chin cleft and a squared-off jaw that looked as though it were carved from granite completed the strikingly austere effect.

If the owner of those heavy-lidded eyes with exaggeratedly long curling eyelashes had in the flesh a fraction of the arrogance, self-belief and authority that was looking back at Maya from the paper, he was surely not going to be a potential customer of the artist.

In her private estimation, the subject of the cruel, clever portrait did not look like someone who could laugh at themselves.

Her warm dark brown eyes lifted, sparkling with amused speculative curiosity as she searched the room for the real-life inspiration, but the half-smile curling her lips quickly faded as she recognised the model for the unsolicited portrait.

It wasn't hard to spot him and that wasn't just because he stood inches above most people in the place. An imposingly tall, athletic figure in a long black wool trench coat that moulded to broad shoulders. His jet-black wavy hair was pushed back from a broad brow, nearly touching the snow-crusted collar of the coat as he moved through the press of bodies with a seemingly inbuilt exclusion zone. He was *not*, she mused, someone who could easily fade into the background.

Maya was conscious, not just of the uncomfortable in-your-face aura of alpha-male authority that he projected even from this distance, but the skin-tightening prickle of antagonism it produced in her. She chose to focus on that aspect while trying to ignore the pelvic flutter of awareness she felt as she watched him. He really was the living, breathing definition of compulsive viewing.

Love him or loathe him—there was no in between, she suspected. What was not in dispute was that there was something totally riveting about the man. Maya found herself both repelled and fascinated in equal measure, but then beauty always was fascinating—even if you were only trying to find a flaw in it—and he *was* pretty aesthetically pleasing!

The artist was good, but the closer his subject got, the more the limitations to his technique became apparent, though to be fair no amount of exaggeration could turn this subject into a joke. Everything about him, from the sense of restrained power in his panther-like fluid stride to his perfectly chiselled profile that combined strength and sensuality in equal measures, suggested he was *more* in every sense of the word.

The artist moving forward, sketch pad in hand to waylay his quarry, re-awoke Maya to her surroundings. She blinked and shook her head. The noise of the crowded space gradually filtering back, she was disturbed and embarrassed to realise just *how* hard she must have been staring at the man, as though she were... She lowered her eyes and felt the heat climbing to her cheeks as the mocking term *sex-starved* popped into her head.

It was not a description she could dispute in the literal sense, but the phrase somehow implied that the situation was a bad thing. Maybe it was for some people, but in her own personal situation celibacy was a conscious choice and not bad luck or, as Beatrice suggested, because she was frightened... She closed her eyes briefly, trying not to think about what Beatrice had said. Her sister was hurting badly, and was just lashing out.

Beatrice had passion, and Maya, well, she had…*caution*, and what she suspected was a pretty low sex drive, so she didn't envy poor Bea in the slightest.

She sometimes wondered if her sister had thought she had found with Dante the rare thing their parents had enjoyed before their father had been snatched away from them.

How would you even know if you found it? It seemed to Maya it was much more likely that—always supposing that special someone even existed in the first place—you would walk straight past your soulmate in the street. Maybe it was why most people, or so it seemed to her, either *settled* or, like Beatrice, imagined that they had found their soulmate, only to end up miserable and alone when things went wrong.

Or maybe Bea was right? Perhaps Maya was just scared—scared of offering her love to a man only to have it rejected, or loving and losing him as Bea had… Pushing away the unhelpful thoughts before they could set up home in her head, she allowed herself to be further distracted by the advancing tall, powerful subject of the caricature.

No chance of mistaking him for a soulmate, she mused, rubbing her hands hard against her upper arms to ease the dark prickle she felt under her skin even through the layers, a sensation she had only previously experienced in the prelude to an electric storm.

She decided not to over-analyse this unexpected physical response to a total stranger, because though some people, her sister included, might suggest that *choice* was not involved where attraction was concerned, Maya firmly believed that you always had a choice. So as far as she was concerned, her head would always rule her heart and her hormones, not the other way around.

And there was also the purely practical side to consider. At this point in her life, romance or sex—*what was the difference?*—would have been a complication too far.

She and Bea were trying to start up a fashion business and one of them had to stay focused. Her sister was going through the trauma of a divorce and Maya needed to take up the slack. Her eyes slid briefly to where Bea sat, her death-ray stare glued to her phone, but Maya saw the sheer misery underneath the anger and her tender heart ached. Bea *really* wasn't the best advert for love right now, but, if it ever crept up on her, Maya was determined she was not going to allow her happiness to depend on a man—not *any* man.

She couldn't conceive of feeling that way, *ever*, she was not that person, but if a man made her unhappy there would be no looking back for her. She'd vowed to herself that she wouldn't be weighed down by someone else's baggage.

The heat, the crush of people, in here was unbearable and Samuele almost turned around and walked straight back through the revolving glass doors and into the street where the snow that was melting on his hair and overcoat had started to fall in earnest. But he had two hours to kill if his cautiously optimistic contact with inside information on the unfolding situation in the airport was to be believed, and suffering from hypothermia was not going to help the situation.

Was anything?

It deepened his sense of grinding frustration to know that there was a private flight ready for him on the runway—*so near and yet so far*—but waiting here remained his best bet of getting back to Rome in time to be with his brother before Cristiano went in for his scheduled surgery.

His fingers curled around the phone in his pocket as he thought about ringing Cristiano again, but on reflection he decided to wait until his revised travel plans were confirmed; he didn't want to make promises to his brother that he could not keep.

His facial muscles tightened in response to an explosion of laughter off to his right, and the sound of happiness grated on his nerve endings. He didn't want to hear it, he didn't want to be here, he wanted, no, he *needed* to be with his brother.

Cristiano was in the worst kind of trouble, trouble not of his making, and he was alone going through this ordeal, because the wife he adored had a *problem* with hospitals. Violetta did not do the *ugly* things in life, or, it seemed, *do* supporting the man she had married while someone cut into his brain to biopsy the reason for the blinding headaches and other assorted symptoms he had suffered in silence for the past six months.

'She cried when I told her,' Cristiano had said.

Female tears did not affect Samuele; well, not all female tears. Even now, after all these years, the memory of his mother's tears, mostly silent, still made his gut tighten in an echo of the remembered helplessness he had felt as a child. But tears that were purely cosmetic or used to manipulate left him cold, and Violetta's were both. Sadly, his brother was not as immune.

Samuele embraced the anger and contempt he felt towards Violetta even as it deepened the frown line that was threatening to become permanent between his thick slanted brows.

His hand came away wet as he dragged it across his

dark hair, before clenching it into a fist. *Dio*, what was it with the men in his family and their bad choices in wives?

He supposed that he was just lucky he had never found the so-called *love of his life*. One thing was certain, if he ever saw her coming he'd sprint in the opposite direction. Samuele gave a thin cynical smile that left his dark eyes cold. He was reasonably confident he would not need his running shoes any time soon, because love was a complete work of fiction, and he was not living in the final scene of a Hollywood romantic comedy.

As he made his way over to the bar thoughts of what his brother was going through alone crowded in, dominating his thoughts, so it took a few seconds for the question being directed at him to penetrate.

Samuele glanced at the face of the young man, then looked down at the sketch being held out to him. He flinched inside. It was good, *too good*, for on the paper he saw a man who was clearly too unapproachable for even his own brother to confide in.

The anger he felt at himself, the frustration he felt at being unable first to save Cristiano from a toxic marriage and now from this disease that had sunk its claws into him, surged up inside him. The release after the past hours of enforced calm was volcanic, though it erupted not as fire but ice.

'Is that really the best you can do?' He allowed his blighting stare to rest on the caricature before he trained his hooded gaze back on the artist. 'The future is not looking bright for you, is it? I sincerely hope you have a plan B.' For a split second he felt a surge of satisfaction but then the kick of guilt came fast on its heels.

Talk about finding a soft target, he derided himself, contempt curling his lip, but this time it was aimed purely at himself. The only thing the guy had done was to be in the wrong place at the wrong time and to have a future for him to mock, unlike his brother, who might not.

Bleakness settled over him like a storm cloud, sucking away any form of hope.

'No problem.'

Instead of releasing the sketch to the young man who was backing away, Samuele held onto it, reaching in his pocket for his wallet with his free hand.

Always easier to throw money at a problem than say sorry, Samuele thought cynically, but before any conscience-easing exchange could be quietly made a small figure appeared, her dark hair a riot of flying Pre-Raphaelite curls, her sweater beneath a padded coat a flash of hot orange. She virtually flung herself between him and the young artist, who let go of his sketch and took a step back to avoid a collision.

She had moved so fast that Samuele had no idea where she had come from as she stood there, glaring up at him, her hands on the slim supple curves of her hips.

With a sinuous little spin that rather unexpectedly sent a slither of sexual heat through his body, she directed a warm look at the boy before turning sharply again and continuing to vibrate scorn towards Sam. 'He, *he* has more talent in his little finger than you...*you*... do in your whole body!'

She didn't raise her voice but every scathing syllable reached its intended target—him.

To say Samuele was taken aback by the sudden attack would have been an understatement. On another occasion he would have liked to have listened further to her voice, which, in contrast to her delicate build, was low and husky.

He could imagine it having a rich earthy tone, he could imagine it whispering private things for his ears only…which said a lot for his state of mind, considering that at that moment it shook with the emotions that were rolling off her—emotions that were neither warm nor intimate.

Samuele found his initial shock melting into something else equally intense, as enormous brown eyes flecked with angry golden lights narrowed on his face. The further kick of attraction he felt was suddenly so strong that the pain was actually physical as it settled hot in his groin. There were not many inches involved here—she did not even reach his shoulder—but every single one packed a *perfect* sensual punch.

She was so gorgeous that she couldn't have faded into the background if she'd tried, but she wasn't trying.

He really liked that.

He took in the details in one swift head-to-toe sweep. Her outfit appeared to be a glorious clash of colours; the only subdued element was her fur-cuffed snow boots, the velvet-looking close-fitting jeans tucked into them a deep rich burgundy, her sweater orange, the padded jacket that hung open turquoise.

She was either colour-blind or making a point; either way it worked, though, having reached her face again, he lost interest in colour coordination because the face occupied by those fire-spitting eyes was beautiful—heart-shaped, surrounded by long dark drifting tendrils of glossy hair that had not been confined in the messy topknot of curls pinned high on her head.

Her delicate bone structure and warm colouring conveyed a sense of both fragility and sensuality. The glowing flawlessness of her skin stretched across smooth, rounded high cheeks projected youth and vitality, the slight tilt of her neat nose gave it character and cuteness. Her mouth, however, was not cute at all; it was full and plump and at that moment pursed as she scowled at him.

He found his eyes lingering overlong on their pink softness, unaware that the hunger he was feeling was reflected in his hooded stare; he couldn't remember ever having experienced such an instant, intense visceral response to a woman before.

The way this man was looking at her… It was only her angry defiance that stopped Maya turning and running, letting him see that she was only brave on the outside.

If she was really brave it would not have crossed her mind even for a split second to remain a silent observer to this public display of cruel bullying, to pretend she hadn't seen.

The knowledge that she had been tempted to do just that made her almost as mad with herself as she was with the target of her wrath as her eyes were met and held by the piercing stare of the man in front of her, who was towering over her. She embraced her anger as well as the rush of blood to her head, only now she was experiencing another rush of blood, pounding all around her body, because the way he was looking at her made her feel totally exposed and shaky inside.

With a sharp blink of her eyes, she pushed back at the sensation of vulnerability, clenching her jaw as she gathered herself, deliberately focusing on what had triggered such an intense reaction.

As she opened her eyes again and met his stare head-on she was relieved that the *raw* expression she had just seen in his gaze was gone. She lifted her chin; she wasn't the kind of woman who melted into a puddle because a man looked as if he wanted her.

She focused instead on the soul-destroying contempt she had seen in his eyes as he'd spoken to the artist, the dismissive curl of his lips…every contemptuous syllable an eerie echo of ones she had heard so often from her stepfather. The situation had varied but the meaning was always the same: you are useless, worthless, don't even try.

She was no longer a child sitting there with her head bowed taking it, having her self-belief stripped away by her stepfather, and she wasn't about to watch it happen to someone else. She couldn't live with herself if she didn't call out that sort of bullying.

'Everyone's a critic,' she said hotly. 'Especially those who are incapable of understanding artistic talent. You wouldn't recognise quality if it bit you on the—' She felt her focus slipping away like wet rope through her fingers as one of the lights that had lagged behind the others suddenly burst back into life, shining like a stage spotlight directly at the object of her contempt. He was under the spotlight but *she* was the one who dried.

He sighed and stamped the last of the snow off his boots. 'This has not been the best of days for me.'

His voice was deep and edged with gravel, the slightest of accents only upping the fascination factor he held for her.

Her chin jerked upwards. 'Is that a *threat*?'

'How much?' He tossed the question to the youth over her head.

'You think you can buy your way out of anything, I suppose,' she muttered bitterly. Everything about him screamed money and exclusivity, she decided, as her glance lingered on the breadth of his shoulders.

But the realisation that anger was no longer solely responsible for the dizzying adrenaline rush coursing through her body hit her.

He was objectionable and a bully, but she was ashamed to admit she was a long way from being immune to the waves of male magnetism he exuded.

Taking a deep sustaining breath, she broke the spell of those eyes and felt a trickle of moisture snake down her back. She was *not* about to fall in lust with some random stranger. 'You have talent.' She threw the words over her shoulder at the artist. 'And *you*,' she added, killing her smile, 'won't destroy anyone's confidence or fill them with self-doubt.' She lifted her chin a defiant notch and thought, *Not on my watch!*

Samuele had been on the receiving end of a few unfriendly looks in his time, but nothing that came close to the sheer loathing that he was being regarded with by this total stranger.

He found himself wondering what it would take to make her smile at him… *Possibly seeing you lying dead at her feet*, suggested the sarcastic voice in his head.

'And never,' she ground out through clenched pearly teeth to the young man, 'let *anyone* tell you otherwise.'

'I'm fine—' began the artist.

She cut across him unapologetically. 'Never apologise for someone else's rudeness, and don't let *anyone* gaslight you. You have to believe in yourself.'

Samuele was caught between annoyance and amusement. She clearly had issues, but they were none of his business. 'What are you, his girlfriend or his life coach?'

'Just someone who doesn't like bullies,' she sneered. 'What do you do for an encore, show kittens who's boss?' She widened her eyes in mock admiration. 'A big tough man like you, what inadequacy are you compensating for?' she wondered. 'Dumped by the girlfriend?'

'Wondering if there's a vacancy?' he shot back.

He couldn't help his satisfaction as she flushed bright red. 'In your dreams.'

'Oh, I have very interesting dreams,' he drawled in a voice like warm honey.

'I am not interested in your dreams, thank you,' she retorted haughtily. 'Or your suggestive comments.'

The lights went out again with no warning flicker and in the blackness there was the sound of a glass breaking and several giggles and shouts.

In the darkness Maya felt a whisper of sensation on her lips, light as a butterfly's wings. She sighed and shivered, and began to stretch upwards towards the touch, but just as suddenly it was gone, making her wonder if she'd imagined it.

The lights came back on.

He'd disappeared.

She blinked as the young artist handed her the sketch he had done with an admiring look. 'Man, you are fierce!'

'You bet you she is!'

It was Beatrice who'd rushed over and enfolded her in a hug. 'I am so, so sorry what I said before. I know you were only trying to help me and I was a monster.'

'No…no…'

'Utter and total. Really, Maya, I think you have it right; you never want to feel as rotten as this. So, who was that hunk you were just yelling at?'

'I have no idea.'

CHAPTER ONE

Maya put down the phone and eased her bottom on the edge of the table where she had perched for the duration of the call. She pushed a section of hair that had escaped her casual topknot back from her face with her forearm and yawned. If she hadn't been waiting for the call she would have already been in bed, which, given it was a Friday night, she was twenty-six, single and living in London, probably made her what most people would call sad.

She knew she was going to have to do something about her social life, or rather the lack of it, although the irony was she'd actually had an invite tonight: a group from work had been going out for cocktails to celebrate someone's engagement. She had had to refuse, explaining her mum was travelling overseas to stay with her sister and had promised to contact her the moment she arrived.

'A long trip?' someone had asked.

'San Macizo.'

She didn't have to elaborate further. The exotic island had been the location of a recent blockbuster movie and had been very much in the news, as well as the subject of numerous articles. Like the articles the conversation had swiftly moved on from the stunning scenery to Maya's brother-in-law, with his film-star looks, bemoaning the fact that the hot heir to the throne of San Macizo, the delicious Dante, was no longer available; he'd married an English girl, who everyone wanted to be.

If Maya had contributed to this part of the conversation she could have explained that the English girl was her own sister Beatrice, who, after being reconciled with her husband, had now happily taken on the role of Princess and mother, making both roles her own.

Bea was pregnant again and suffering severe morning sickness, so Maya was glad their mum was there to offer support and also fuss over her delicious little granddaughter, Maya's goddaughter.

But Maya had stayed quiet, not because she wasn't proud of her royal connection, but because it was easy to predict the questions they might have asked, like, *If your sister's a princess, how come you're working as a window dresser for a department store?*

The answer, according to her sister, was that Maya was too damned proud, stubborn and stupid to take help when it was freely offered to her. Maya had really appreciated the offers of help, and she knew they were well meant and sincere, but, though it might take longer, when she finally got to where she wanted to be, it would mean so much more to know she had done it herself and not just used her connections and their bank balance.

She yawned, easing one fluffy mule back on her narrow foot, and caught herself thinking about making a mug of cocoa... *Oh, God...cocoa...get a life, Maya!* Would the wine she had opened last weekend still be drinkable?

Cocoa or last week's wine? She had not completely decided when the doorbell rang.

This time of night the only person who rang her

doorbell was the pizza delivery service and she had definitely not ordered one.

Puzzled but not alarmed, she went to the door.

She tightened the belt on her robe before she opened the door a crack—one of these days she really would get a safety chain.

It was not a pizza, it was a woman, and she was not alone. Before becoming a proud aunt, Maya wouldn't have been able to guess the age of the dark-haired baby the woman carried, but if asked now she would have estimated him at somewhere between three and four months. But she wasn't in any state to guess; behind the flickering of her silky, sooty dark lashes, the eyes they framed were blank with shock as she stared at her visitors.

She hardly noticed the door swinging wide as she took a tiny step back, but finally she breathed out a shakily incredulous, 'V... Violetta...?'

Because although it really *couldn't* be, the woman standing there—tall, slim, looking as though she had just stepped out of the pages of a fashion magazine, her river-straight waist-length hair with a mirror gloss, her make-up perfectly highlighting her china-blue eyes—was the same woman she had seen in the photo her birth mother had proudly shown her—her half-sister. Maya still had it—it was the only thing her birth mother had ever given her.

'You're Mia?'

'Maya.'

'Of course, Mummy described you perfectly...but I'd have known you anywhere!'

'You would?'

'Absolutely! There's just this *connection* between us; I can feel it, my little sister. Can't you?' As she bent forward to kiss the air either side of Maya's face, Maya instinctively leaned back, not to avoid contact, but to stop the baby being sandwiched between them. 'Although you're older than me, aren't you? But I'm sure you look lovely with some make-up on.'

Maya blinked rapidly, unnerved by Violetta's rather Siamese cat stare and too utterly confused to even register the implication that she clearly did not look lovely without it.

'No…yes, that is, I'm…' Maya shook her head. 'You…here…' She took a deep breath and focused on forming an entire sentence. 'Just what is happening?'

'I needed help—' Maya watched with horror as her half-sister's slender shoulders began to shake, and her lovely face crumpled as tears began to roll in slow motion down her cheeks.

Maya's wary antagonism melted into genuine concern. 'Is there anything I can do?'

'I shouldn't be here, really… I'm so sorry. I should have rung you, I know, but I was afraid you'd say no and I had nowhere else to go. You're our *only* hope, so please don't send us away,' she begged plaintively, hugging the sleepy baby so tight that he gave a little cry of protest.

It jolted Maya free of her shock. 'Oh, no…no, of course not—' She broke off at the sound of heavy breathing a moment before a figure carrying luggage under both arms came into view.

'There's no lift, and you don't travel light.'

Maya, who was feeling as though events were getting way ahead of her, took in the numerous bags now filling the doorway and the panting, sweaty-faced new arrival, who did not look happy, though his frown vanished when Violetta looked at him with tears shimmering in her beautiful eyes.

'Oh, you poor thing! Mia was just about to help you, weren't you?' she assured him, an emotional hitch in her voice as she turned to Maya. 'This man—George, isn't it?—has been a total angel… Now, where is my purse…? Oh, Mia, would you get it for me? And don't forget to give George a healthy tip.'

Mia? Ah, well, she'd been called worse, and she had other priorities, like locating her purse, paying the driver and dragging the luggage wedged in the doorway inside. By the time she had accomplished these tasks Violetta and the baby had transferred themselves to the sofa in her living room, and while the baby dribbled and chewed his fist his mother was giving her attention to the interior decor. It was patently obvious from the flare of her nostrils that shabby chic was not her thing.

Maya waited. There were just so many things to say she didn't know where to start, though it seemed she didn't need to.

Her visitor whispered a tremulous, 'I'm sorry.'

'For what?'

The literal response drew a tiny frown and the intense blue gaze narrowed calculatingly on Maya's face. 'Turning up without warning this way…but I was desperate, although I swear I've wanted to reach out to you for so long…'

'You have? But I thought your mother… *Olivia* said that neither of you wanted anything to do with me…' Maya bit her lip, hating that telltale quivering of her voice.

'When Mummy met you, I was…*vulnerable.* It's a time in my life that I still struggle to talk about. And Mummy always was…*is* very protective of me. Later on, I must admit I was afraid that you'd resent me, even though—' Her lips quivered this time, and her voice

cracked. 'Even though Cristiano said that I should...
I'm sorry—'

She looked around helplessly until Maya located a
box of tissues on the desk behind her. The practical gesture seemed pretty inadequate given the situation, but
it was better than nothing.

'Cristiano?'

'My husband.' Violetta took a tissue and dabbed it
gently to her miraculously smooth and unblotchy cheek.
Maya couldn't believe there wasn't even a smudge to
her make-up. 'But he died without ever seeing our dear-
est Mattio.'

Maya's wide, shocked eyes went to the little baby—
her nephew!—and her heart ached for him and his
mother. How on earth did someone recover from a trag-
edy like that?

'I am so sorry to hear that.'

The baby chose that moment to grab a strand of his
mother's dramatically coloured hair in his chubby fist.
Violetta let out a squeal, her expression of tragic suffering suddenly morphing into annoyance.

'Let me.' Maya leaned forward and unwound the tiny
yet tenacious fingers from the glossy strand that started
auburn at the root and went through an extraordinary
range of shades ending in a deep strawberry blonde at
the tip. It was hard, given the artistry, to guess what her
natural hair colour was.

'And now I... I have nothing!'

Struggling to respond with anything that didn't
sound lame and shallow, Maya offered another tissue,
which was refused as her half-sister shook back her
glossy hair.

'You have this little one and he has you,' Maya finally said hoarsely as she felt her throat thicken with

tears. She swallowed hard; if *she* started crying it would not be as pretty as Violetta's efforts. 'All a child needs is to be wanted and loved,' she added, even as she reminded herself that love did not pay the bills. 'I know it must be hard financially being a single parent and—'

'But Mattio is an Agosti!'

Maya shook her head, confused.

Her ignorance appeared to shock the younger woman, whose blue eyes flew wide. 'He is heir to half the Agosti fortune.'

'Oh, right…' Maya nodded vaguely, getting the picture, though to her mind, as useful as silver spoons might be, surely a child would be better off with a living father?

'Of course, the money should have come to me as his widow, but Cristiano changed his will, and I know exactly who to blame for that,' she said darkly. 'Not that I have a problem with the money going to Mattio,' she added hastily, seeing the look on Maya's face.

Maya nodded, feeling uncharitable that she had trouble believing this claim. How could she blame the woman? It must be hard if she had expected to inherit.

'I have a problem with having to go to *Samuele* for every penny. *He* saw to it that Cristiano left financial control of our child's fortune to him.'

'Who is Samuele?' Maya asked, seriously struggling to keep up.

'He is Cristiano's older brother. He's always hated me—he was jealous because Cristiano stopped letting him make all the decisions. Oh, I don't blame my darling Cristiano, he was vulnerable and Samuele dripped poison in his ear and turned my own husband against me… I can tell you don't believe me, but then no one does!' she cried, her voice rising to a shrill hopeless note. 'They don't understand—they think that Samuele is caring of his family, including me.'

Maya pressed her fingers to the throbbing in her temples. With each word a picture appeared that was horribly familiar to her, channelling her anger into a quiet resolve.

'Oh, I understand. I understand *perfectly*,' she said, 'how someone can appear one thing on the surface and be something very different.'

Before he had married her and Beatrice's mother, Maya had believed her stepfather was the person that the world thought he was: caring and considerate and, most importantly, making her grieving mother happy again. Then they had married and the abuse had begun, so subtle, so insidious that her mother hadn't seen that she was being isolated from her friends, her support network, and in the end even her daughters, until it was almost too late. Maya had not known then but she did realise now that Edward had seen her own closeness to her mother as an obstacle to his all-consuming need for total control over his wife.

Golden girl, he had mocked as he'd deliberately set about revealing to the world and her mother that she was not golden at all; she was useless, she was deceitful.

'They call it coercive control,' Maya said grimly. 'But you're not alone.' And neither had she been; Beatrice had been there for her. Now it was Maya's turn to offer support to another woman and she was glad to be able to.

'You understand!' Gratitude shone in her half-sister's eyes that was quickly replaced by despair. 'But there's nothing you can do to help me, because he has everything. Samuele has money and power, and now I think…' She faltered, kissing the top of her baby's head before revealing, 'No, I *know* he's trying to take my baby away from me, but no one will believe me. But maybe they are right?' she cried wildly.

'No, don't believe that, ever! Believe in yourself,' Maya replied fiercely, her voice shaking with emotional emphasis.

'Coming here was a total act of impulse. It all became too much for me and…well, I just need some space to work out what to do next.'

'You can stay here with me. Take all the time you need.'

'Really?'

What are you letting yourself in for?

Immediately ashamed of the momentary flicker of uncertainty, Maya lifted her chin and she smiled. 'Really.'

It had been the early hours of the morning before Maya had finally crawled into bed, but despite being exhausted she slept in fits and starts, repeatedly waking and remembering all over again that Beatrice's room was not empty any more. It was occupied by a half-sister she did not really know, a half-sister whom, given what she was going through, Maya *ought* to feel a connection with, and she was confused by the fact she didn't.

But then maybe it was unrealistic to expect emotions like that to just materialise out of thin air, and it obviously didn't help that she found herself comparing Violetta to Beatrice and finding her blood relative coming out second.

Whatever she did not feel for Violetta was more than compensated for by what she *did* feel for Mattio. She had felt nervous when Violetta, pleading utter exhaustion, had handed over the baby to Maya to feed and change.

Maya had been surprised by the little ache in her

heart when she had eventually handed him back, and it had made her wonder if her own birth mother had felt that way when Olivia had given her up? Had the sound of her crying triggered the same instinct that had Maya leaving her warm duvet cocoon as she heard Mattio wailing in the next room? Dragging both hands in a futile smoothing motion across her wildly tumbled dark curls, she swung her feet to the floor.

Maya closed down the useless speculation over her birth mother and caught sight of herself in the mirror as she grabbed a robe off the hook behind the door, the sleep-deprived face that stared back at her bringing a fleeting grimace to her face.

On the plus side, her disturbed night had not been troubled by the recurrent dream that she half dreaded, half longed for. She never remembered specific details. On waking all that remained was an erotic blur; the sense of deep yearning, the memory of a deep honeyed voice and a strong sense of shame that usually lingered until she'd had her second cup of coffee.

It hardly seemed possible that a chance encounter so many months ago with a tall, arrogant stranger should leave such a strong imprint on her unconscious. She lifted a hand to her suddenly tingling lips. Had he kissed her or had that been a fiction invented by her overactive imagination too?

An extra loud baby cry had her shrugging off the memory of temperature-raising dark eyes. Once outside her room, she thought she could hear the distressed baby cries even more loudly, but then her experience of crying babies was not what anyone would call extensive.

Her niece probably *did* cry, but whenever Maya saw her, which was too infrequently, little Sabina Ella, a deeply contented child, always seemed to be smiling or examining the world around her with big solemn enquiring eyes or giving the deep little belly chuckle that was impossible not to react to.

There was a wistful element to the small smile that played across the fullness of Maya's soft mouth in response to the memories of her last visit to San Macizo. She was really glad her sister had found the happiness she deserved, and that she was finally reconciled with her husband, but she couldn't help wishing that Beatrice had found all those elements a little closer to home.

Approaching the bedroom door, she paused and after a moment knocked, raising her voice to make herself heard above the distressed bawling inside.

'Is there anything I can do or get for you, Violetta?' she asked, directing her question to the closed door. She paused again and waited, head tipped to one side in a listening attitude, but the only thing she heard was Mattio.

Pitching her voice louder, she repeated her question and was not really surprised when there was still no response; she could barely hear herself above the crying. Tapping on the door again, she called out the other woman's name several times to give her some warning as she pushed it slowly open.

'Violetta?' Maya scanned the room, empty but for the travel cot that held the baby, his wailing subsiding into a series of gulping, heartbreaking breathy sobs as he heard her voice.

Maya walked across to the cot and whispered a tentative, 'Hello there.' The baby's face was red, his eyes puffy with prolonged crying, and when he saw Maya he didn't quiet completely but he did stretch out his chubby little hands towards her.

Maya felt something tighten in her chest, the strangest sensation.

'Oh…' She swallowed, feeling the unexpected heat of tears pressing against her eyelids. That's all we need, more tears, she told herself sternly as she blinked hard. 'So where is your mummy?' she asked, refusing to think about the significance of the undisturbed decorative pillows on the bed until she actually had to. 'Violetta!'

The baby, clearly objecting to her raised voice, started crying in earnest again.

'No…no, don't do that! I'm sorry, don't…oh, God!' Taking a deep breath, she leaned into the cot and lifted out the warm, damp baby. 'Righto!' she said, channelling slightly desperate cheer as she settled him awkwardly against her hip. 'So, let's go find your mummy, shall we?'

The knot of panic in her chest had expanded to the size of a heart-compressing boulder as, jiggling the baby in her arms, she walked through every room in the flat. It didn't take long—there was nowhere a cat could hide, let alone a person—but she retraced her steps anyway.

'This is not happening,' she muttered. But it was, and she had to deal with it. 'Don't worry, it'll be fine,' she said to the baby, and saw that his little head was propped on her shoulder. He had fallen asleep, exhausted by his crying.

There had to be a perfectly logical explanation for this, she thought, and then spotted the note propped behind a framed photo of Beatrice with Dante, who was looking at his wife with an expression of total adoration. There was a name scrawled across the front of the envelope.

Not her own name, but *Mia*.

Well, some people were just bad with names. Weren't they?

She stared at the envelope with a sudden sick feeling of dread in the pit of her stomach. Probably, given the situation, it was totally justified.

Why prolong it, just do it! Better to know the worst.

Or was it, was it really? There were occasions when blissful ignorance had a definite appeal and Maya had always struggled with the 'rip the plaster off and get the pain over with' mindset.

One arm supporting the sleeping baby, she glanced down at his sweet, tear-stained face and wished she could copy him. She blew out a gusty breath and decided to put him back in his cot.

Baby settled, the next thing on her checklist—because this wasn't about delaying, it was prioritising—was the formula sitting in the fridge to inspect. While the letter wasn't going anywhere, when he woke Mattio would need feeding and, of course, changing. Locating the changing mat and nappies and clean clothes took another few minutes, but the letter was still sitting there and now she had run out of more important and less potentially explosive things to do.

With a hiss of exasperation, she snatched at it and ripped it open, but she had barely scanned the contents when the doorbell rang, making her jump.

Samuele lifted his hand off the doorbell and applied his clenched fist to the wooden panel, fighting the urge to batter his way through the last barrier between him and his nephew.

Instead, he took a deep breath and reminded himself that, while Violetta was a piece of work, selfish, cold and manipulative, she would not harm her own child. This small soothing piece of positivity didn't lower his levels of frustration because, though it might be true, Samuele also knew that she would not hesitate to use Mattio to further her own agenda. This particular vengeful widow had never put anyone's needs above her own self-interest and motherhood had not altered that aspect of her one iota.

Samuele's hand lifted to the fading red line that ran down from his cheekbone to his jaw, glad that the one on the other side had already gone. *He* was the target of Violetta's spite, not the baby, but that didn't mean the innocent child could not be collateral damage. His gut tightened with guilt that he had not seen this, or something like it, coming.

He had promised Cristiano so easily that he would take care of his child. Pulling himself up to his full height, he fixed his steely gaze on the door. He would make good on that promise.

He heard the sound of a key in the lock and took a step back—waiting for…who?

The words of the note still echoing in her head, Maya's unsteady hands were shaking so hard she struggled to get a good grasp on the key in the lock, not realising until a lot of fumbling later that it wasn't locked, it couldn't be locked, because Violetta had left it open when she left.

Just thinking of how *desperate* Violetta must have felt to leave her own baby with a virtual stranger sent a fresh surge of emotion through her body. She'd said in the brief note that she would come back for Mattio…and she *would*, Maya was sure of that. Perhaps she already had?

Relief that Violetta had realised she couldn't desert her baby washed over Maya in a heart-steadying wave.

She gave the stiff door an enthusiastic tug, stepping forward as it swung open to reveal, not her half-sister, but a shockingly familiar imposing figure. The welcoming smile of relief vanished from her eyes as reality collided with her dreams.

Her voice shook with the sheer impact of recognition that nailed her to the spot, leaving her feeling as though she had just run full pelt into a wall.

The seconds ticked away as two sets of eyes locked. It was Maya who finally broke the tableau, her chest heaving as she gasped for air before giving voice to her unedited reaction at being faced with the person who had unlocked something inside her so many months ago that she still refused to acknowledge.

'Oh, no... *You!*'

No matter how many times you skydived, there was always that moment of shock in the split second when you actually launched yourself into space. This was the first time Samuele had experienced that same sensation with both his feet still on the ground.

His hooded gaze moved in a slow sweep upwards from her bare feet to the top of her glossy head, taking in everything in between. He clenched his teeth, the twist of lust in his belly that crossed the border into pain all too familiar.

His reaction to this woman was just as visceral as it had been the first time, when her liquid dark eyes had flashed fire at him for being rude to that artist. The same eyes now were glazed with shock. His glance lingered on the soft full outline of her mouth... He had thought about that mouth a lot since that day, wished he had followed through with his instinct and actually kissed her, so he'd know what she tasted like.

A muscle clenched in his jaw. '*You* are the *sister*?' And presumably a part of Violetta's plan to extort money from him.

Not ready to admit to anything just yet, Maya countered this accusation with her own question.

'*You're* the *brother-in-law*?' The man in her dreams, the man she had met for only moments eighteen months ago, and yet who had imprinted himself indelibly inside her head, was Violetta's persecutor!

One dark brow arched upwards as with a contemptuous curl of his lips he announced, 'I am Samuele Agosti, and, as I'm sure you know, I am here to return my nephew home to Italy.'

He had lost none of the arrogance she remembered from Zurich, and, unfortunately for her, none of his rampant maleness. She folded her arms protectively across her chest.

'Well, you've had a wasted journey.'

'Where is she?'

The question was not directed at her but past her, unlike the fleeting scornful glance that she was definitely the intended recipient of.

Her chin went up. 'I'd like you to leave now.' The door only moved a couple of inches before it met the immovable obstacle of his size-twelve foot shod in handmade leather. 'Home for a child is where his mother is—' Maya stopped, unable to prevent the self-conscious dismay from spreading across her face as she realised that even if this were true, Mattio's mother wasn't here.

She was the only thing standing between this man and her baby nephew.

'You don't sound too sure about that,' he remarked.

'You know what I *am* sure of—that I'm going to call the police if you don't leave in the next ten seconds.'

'The thing about threats is that you have to be willing to follow through with them, or at least convince the person they're directed at that you are.'

Maya found her eyes following the motion of his long fingers as they moved from the open-necked collar of his white linen shirt and the vee of olive skin at the base of his throat, up his neck and across the dusting of dark stubble on his firm, square jaw.

There was a challenge in his smile, and the male aura he radiated—his *presence*—could fill an entire arena. This was not an arena, it was a very small, unglamorous hallway, and it made her feel very small and insignificant.

The recognition of the feeling made her square her shoulders. She didn't care who he was, this was *her* space! She drew herself up to her full diminutive height, managing to project a sense of confidence, which was a miracle in itself, considering she was not dressed for dignity—a fact that was just hitting home to her.

Without taking her eyes off his face, she casually reached for the tie on her robe and knotted it around her middle before smoothing down her hair, but it was a pointless exercise, she knew, so she gave it up. Dignity was more than skin-deep.

'I don't bluff.' She tightened her belt another vicious notch and pushed out abruptly, 'Just go away.'

CHAPTER TWO

'Where is she?'

The question flustered her and put her on the defensive.

'She who?'

This drawn-out innocent act tried his temper, but not as much as the unwelcome recognition of his own initial shock reaction to the sight of the woman barring his way. God alone knew how long he had stood there literally in the grip of a hormonal rush worthy of a teenager.

Or a man who had gone too long without?

He found the latter explanation far more palatable and very easily solved. Sex was like any other hunger. It was not at all complicated as long as you didn't start imagining there was anything other than a mutual attraction there. No matter how strong, no lust had a shelf life beyond a few weeks.

'I think we should take this inside, don't you?'

Sam swallowed as an image of her wide dilated eyes and messy hair floated through his head. Just how responsive would she be in bed…? Frowning in response to the sly voice of his libido, he pushed the images away to focus on the reason he was here.

She panicked. 'No!'

Her response was so unexpected it stopped him and

his thought processes dead in their tracks, and it took him a few moments to actually take on board what she was doing.

She stood there stubbornly, a hand braced against either side of the door frame.

'I *don't* think we should take this inside,' she said firmly.

'You've got to be joking,' he said, feeling an unexpected stab of admiration as she tightened her grip on the door frame, blocking his way with, what, an entire seven stone nothing?

Stronger than his admiration was the mental image of placing his hands around her ribcage and bodily removing her from his path. His thought lingered on the image long enough to count as self-indulgent and he frowned slightly.

Maya compressed her lips and maintained her defiant stance even though, truthfully, she was starting to feel a little foolish. As gestures went this one was pretty futile, and she was still suffering from the weird feeling of having entered a conversation midway through.

Forget about the why, and the how, just focus on the now, she told herself, and in the now she physically represented no obstacle to him. He could have lifted her out of the way with one hand tied behind his back... It was far more worrying that the idea of him doing that made her breath come a little too fast as, under the protective cover of her lashes, she made a covert scan of his long lean length. It only revealed what she already knew: he had the physique of a Greek god who worked out a lot—or in this case an Italian god.

So nothing has changed in the twenty seconds since you last drooled over him, Maya!

'Violetta!' He pitched his deep voice to carry and Maya groaned.

'All right,' she sighed out. It was easier to admit the truth, or at least this portion of it, than have him wake Mattio. Dealing with one Agosti male at a time was enough and this one was way too big to rock to sleep. She cleared her throat and pushed away a deeply distracting image of his dark head on her breast. 'She isn't here, but—'

'And Mattio?'

'Well, you can't have him...because he's not here either.'

Sam's brows lifted at her obviously panicky tack-on. 'You are a very bad liar,' he observed, unaccountably disgruntled at the discovery. 'Look, enough.' He brought one long-fingered brown hand down in a slashing motion. 'I really don't care who you have in there, beyond my nephew, who belongs with me.'

'I don't have anyone in there!' she retorted.

But in his mind's eye, Samuele was seeing a lover sleeping in her bed. Grimly, he found he had no problem disturbing this exhausted, sleeping boyfriend.

'You always walk around dressed like that after midday?'

Catching his drift, Maya blushed. 'My sex life is none of your business,' she countered, thinking, *It's just as well he doesn't know I haven't got one.*

Life might be interesting if it were his business.

As he veiled his eyes with his ludicrously long lashes she glimpsed a gleam before he delivered a flat statement that came out sounding a lot like a threat.

'I can stay here all day.'

'No, you *really* can't.'

'I—' He stopped at the unmistakable sound of a baby cry.

'Oh, my God, look what you've done now!' she exclaimed.

On the receiving end of a 'rot in hell' glare, he did not immediately respond to the opening as she stood there, hands pressed together as though she were praying.

A moment later she breathed out. 'I think he's gone back to sleep.'

'I am not going away without Mattio.'

There was no hint of concession in his voice or on his chiselled features. Thinking hard, she considered his beautiful fallen-angel face, her eyes drifting over the angular contours of his lower jaw and hollowed cheeks, which were dusted with dark stubble that emphasised the razor edge of his carved cheekbones and the sensual curve of his upper lip.

'So, I think this is where you invite me in.'

'Or what, you'll barge your way in? I'm warning you, I really will call the police.'

He lifted his eyes from where they had drifted to the gaping neckline of her silky nightshirt, and she couldn't help the shiver of excitement that sizzled down her spine.

'Feel free if Violetta actually isn't here.' He subjected her face to a speculative laser-like scan. 'I'm quite sure this situation will be of interest to them.'

It suddenly occurred to her that this might well be the case. She weighed her options and discovered she didn't have many.

With a tight-lipped sigh she stepped to one side and without another word he shouldered his way past her.

'Come in, why don't you?' she drawled, sarcasm masking her apprehension as she glared at the man who now dominated her small living room.

Samuele scanned the modest space that had probably been dominated by the stacks of books and a dressmaking dummy draped with fabric, only now they took second place to a baby buggy, a stack of disposable nappies and general baby detritus. But the item his eyes zeroed in on was a stuffed rabbit. He felt his throat thicken, remembering when it had been new, his brother's way of telling him that he was going to be an uncle.

'Don't you mean you're going to be a father?' Samuele had responded.

'Maybe.' His brother had handed him the toy. 'The cancer's back, Sam. I start chemo next week. So, you see, this kid is going to need you to be around.'

'You'll be around for them! You beat it once, you'll beat it again.'

'Sure, I will.'

They had kept up the pretence, dancing around the truth, right up until the last minute. Sometimes he thought that his little brother had been protecting him, rather than the other way around.

Maya watched a muscle jump in his cheek as he bent forward, pausing before he straightened up with a soft toy in his hand. For a split second she saw something in his face that made him seem almost vulnerable. She experienced a troubling moment of what felt scarily like empathy, but then he looked at her, and his eyes were not those of a man who needed her empathy, they were hard and cold and ruthless.

'So where is Violetta hiding?'

'She's not hiding anywhere...' Unable to sustain eye contact with the darkness in his, she transferred her gaze to the toy trailing from his fingers. 'She's... gone out.'

'Where and when will she be back?' he asked as he arranged himself in the nearest chair.

Maya struggled to contain her panic as she watched him stretch his long legs out in front of him. 'I don't exactly know,' she said, pretty sure she was sounding as lame as she was feeling.

His eyes narrowed. 'Don't know exactly what—where or when?'

'All of those.'

'You know very little,' he observed unpleasantly.

'I know you are sitting in my chair and I didn't invite you in... I'm sure that's against the law.'

He grinned. 'Only if I'm a vampire.'

Her lips tightened at the flippancy but she couldn't help thinking that it wouldn't actually be such a stretch to see him in the role of a sexy vampire!

'Look, this is ridiculous.' *So was imagining offering him your neck.*

Ridiculous would be him allowing himself to be fobbed off. 'I'll wait for her.'

'No!' She gulped and added, 'I'm expecting some—' She broke off as the sound of a low murmur amplified by the baby monitor on the coffee table filled the room. 'Oh, God, he's woken up again.'

Her eyes widened as her uninvited visitor vaulted to his feet in one smooth stomach-clenching action. Maya was only a heartbeat away from throwing herself physically in his path as he approached the door leading to Beatrice's bedroom. It was crazy; she still thought of it that way, even though her sister had only spent a few nights there before her life had taken a very different direction.

What would Bea do?
She wouldn't have let him in.

Get a grip! Beatrice wasn't here, she was, and she couldn't let Beatrice fight her battles any more. Maya was never going to give in to a bully, not ever again.

She got between him and the bedroom door, and she turned to face the advancing figure, who suddenly seemed about ten feet tall, raising her hands as if she could actually physically stop him. She knew she'd have had more chance of stopping a hurricane! It struck her that the analogy was very apt—there was something truly elemental about him.

'There are rules,' she said, refusing to give ground. 'Ground rules.'

He looked astonished. *'Rules...?'*

'If Mattio has fallen asleep again, don't wake him up—please.'

She held her breath, once again seeing in her head the image of herself being lifted bodily by two strong hands—which produced another worryingly ambiguous reaction low in her stomach.

She cleared her throat. 'It took a long time for him to settle.'

Sam looked from the door to her pleading face and after a moment he nodded.

Her relief seemed genuine. 'So, what is Violetta playing at? What little scheme have you two been hatching?' he asked.

'I hate to ruin a conspiracy theory with inconvenient things like facts, but there is no scheme or hatching, there is no *us two*.'

'She is your sister, isn't she?' The fact that she looked sexily wholesome on the surface made her far more dangerous than her overtly glamorous but entirely toxic sister.

'Half-sister, actually.'

'She ran to you, left her baby with you, so you two must be close.'

A little laugh escaped Maya's parted lips. 'I hadn't even met her before last night when she turned up with Mattio.'

Unlikely as it sounded, Samuele found he was inclined to believe the ring of truth in her voice.

'So she's using you. Typical.'

'No, she's not… Do not twist everything I say.'

'So when did she leave?'

There seemed very little to gain from not telling him. 'I'm not sure. I woke up, and there was a note…' Maya's hand went to her pocket. 'She seems really desperate.'

He laughed and said something that sounded pretty rude in Italian before he tacked on a polite translation in English. 'She is *really* devious.'

'She's probably suffering from postnatal depression—new mothers need *support*, you know.' As if he'd know the meaning of the word, she thought, throwing a look of seething contempt at him.

'She left her baby and you're *still* defending her. You really don't know your sister very well at all, do you?'

'I know enough, about her and about you too…'

His dark eyes narrowed on her flushed face his expression assessing as his long lashes rested briefly on the cutting angle of his cheekbones. 'Ah, so my reputation precedes me,' he drawled with a slow smile that Maya found almost as disturbing as his apparent ability to read her mind. 'So what has the absent mother been saying? Actually, don't bother, I can guess most of it, but maybe you should allow for a little bit of artistic licence on her part.'

'You probably make her feel inadequate!'

'Projection, much?'

The hot angry colour flew to her cheeks. 'You don't make me feel inadequate.' Her chin lifted to another defiant angle as she claimed boldly, 'Nobody makes me feel inadequate.'

The overreaction hinted at a vulnerability that was none of his business, he told himself, swiftly closing down that line of speculation.

'You don't strike me as an inadequate woman,' he mused, allowing his eyes to move in a slow sweep up her slim body before settling on her vivid heart-shaped face inside the frame of wild silky waves. The delicate features qualified as high on the catch-your-breath index but there was a determination to the round chin and a fierceness in her direct gaze that he seriously admired.

Taken aback by his response, Maya took an involuntary step away from him.

What do I strike you as, then? She pushed away the question as irrelevant and reclaimed the space she had given up. She tightened the sash on her robe another breath-restricting inch while somewhere in the back of her mind a voice reiterated, *It's past midday and you're still in your night clothes.*

'I wasn't talking about me.' Would he have been saying that if he'd seen the person she had been? Her defensive wall wavered and then held against the wave of self-disgust, and she met his dark stare with a semblance of calm.

He arched a dark brow. 'No?' His broad shoulders lifted in a shrug as his gaze moved beyond her to the closed bedroom door. 'If you say so...' He sighed and scrubbed a hand through his hair. 'I am here to see Mattio. Is he in here?' He tipped his head towards the right of the two doors they stood outside.

'That's my bedroom.' *God, Maya, how old are you?* she thought as she felt the heat rise up her neck. Deciding the best way to deal with the juvenile blush was to pretend it wasn't there, she glared up at him.

'You're not here to *see* him, you're here to take him away and I won't let you,' she asserted, sounding more confident than she felt at her ability to follow through with this claim.

'I haven't made any secret of what I'm here to do and if you're about to threaten me with the law again...' The prospect didn't alarm Samuele overly. 'I'd think that one through if I were you. Bring in the authorities on this one, and, red tape being what it is, I probably won't walk out of here with Mattio, but he *will* leave in the arms of some child protection social worker. And then when my court order granting me temporary guardianship comes through—which it will—I'll be able to take Mattio home.'

'You have a court order...?'

'I will have, soon.' It was not *strictly* a lie, but it would not have bothered Samuele if it had been.

'But,' she quavered out defiantly, 'Violetta is his mother! Don't courts *always* give a child to the mother?'

He gave a hard laugh and slung her a pitying look. 'That's often true—but it does kind of depend on the mother, don't you think?'

'Violetta's not here to defend herself,' Maya argued, knowing that words could be weaponised and a disparaging word here, a scathing comment there, could over time alter people's perception of someone, as she knew to her cost.

'Isn't that the point?' he suggested drily, looking bored with the discussion. 'She dumped a baby on a virtual stranger in a foreign country. That might raise a few legal brows.'

'*Foreign...?*'

'Mattio is Italian, he is an *Agosti*!'

'So is Violetta.'

'Not if Charlie has any say in the matter,' he shot back.

'Charlie?'

'Her next meal ticket,' he outlined with a thin smile.

'I'm not listening to you,' she bit back through clenched teeth.

'Because the truth hurts?'

'You twist everything I say.'

'Twist,' he echoed, raising his hands in a gesture that reinforced the scornful incredulity written on his face.

'For a woman to leave her baby...' Shaking her head, she scanned his face for any sign that he was capable of understanding what a massive thing that was. 'Have you *any* idea of what a terrible place she must have been in?'

'You really are determined to see her as some sort of victim, aren't you? I promise you that is the very last thing Violetta is. Look, Mattio is not your responsibility—'

'It's not about responsibility,' she retorted. 'It's about—' Struggling to put her feelings into words, she clenched her hands and tried to focus.

'It's about what?'

'It's about...' She made herself meet his eyes even though she knew the experience would not be comfortable. 'A child needs to be loved, to be wanted, and you don't really want him.'

'Now you're telling me what I want?'

'You just want to control everything.'

Samuele sketched a thin-lipped smile that he knew didn't reach his eyes. At that moment he'd settle for controlling his own baser urges, which at that moment… He shook his head slightly and thought, *Better not to go there.* The main thing was that he *was* in control.

'You really have swallowed Violetta's fiction hook, line and sinker, haven't you?'

'I haven't swallowed anything!' she fired back. 'I'm not some sort of gullible idiot—though I can see that it would suit you if I were!'

He didn't react immediately to her claim…there seemed little point. As he studied her face it was obvious she believed everything she was saying. His frustration levels threatened to bubble through his enforced calm.

He'd thought that he'd mentally prepared for every scenario he might face to get Mattio back, but in all of those he'd been dealing with Violetta, a known quantity.

This woman was definitely *not* a known quantity; in fact, she was the biggest unknown quantity that he had encountered—ever. A woman who looked as she did but made no conscious effort to use her allure was a mystery to him. She could bewitch a man with a flutter of her eyelashes if she wanted to, but all she did was try and batter him into submission with her totally flawed logic and stubborn arguments.

If he didn't have more important things on his mind, he might have been tempted to find out more about her, against his better judgement, though instinct told him that Maya Monk came with serious complications and possibly not the ones that he was armoured against.

All the same, she was intriguing and quite incredibly beautiful.

How was it possible to want to taste a woman and at the same time want to…? He shook his head, despairing that anyone could be so wilfully stupid. This would have been a hell of a lot easier if she *hadn't* believed everything she was saying, and the fact he had not detected the sort of artifice he always expected from a beautiful woman made him uneasy.

His unease deepened when without warning a Eureka smile spread across her face.

'What about Violetta's mother? Could she come and look after Mattio until Violetta gets back?' Maya knew it was a compromise but maybe one that he might accept. 'What…why are you looking at me like that?'

'Your mother too, if I'm understanding your relationship correctly.'

'We're not in contact. Olivia has her own family.' Some of it was in her spare bedroom. 'And I have mine.' What would she not have given for her mum or sister to be in the same time zone right now?

If they had been, they would be here in this room offering her back-up and some much-needed baby advice.

'It's tough being rejected.'

She flinched, really disliking his ability to wander around inside her head. 'I'm not a victim. I was adopted as a baby, and, I told you, I have my own family now.'

'Olivia died six months ago.'

CHAPTER THREE

It was like watching the life story of a flower in time-lapse photography on a natural history programme; blooming, fading and shrivelling in mere seconds.

It was irrational, but he felt as guilty as hell for killing her hope.

'Sorry, I didn't know that.'

She was apologising to *him*? 'There's no need to be sorry, she was nothing to me.' From what Samuele had seen Olivia was a vain, selfish woman who had passed on all those delightful qualities to her daughter.

'Oh…no…me neither, I suppose… I mean, I didn't really know her either. How—?' she began and then stopped.

'She didn't suffer, did she?'

Samuele only knew the bare clinical facts, namely that Olivia had died after complications from a botched cosmetic surgery. He opened his mouth to share these when he met her anxious eyes and paused.

'No, she didn't,' he heard himself say.

Samuele caught a look of relief on her face before she tipped her head in acknowledgement, and her expression was concealed by her wild mass of dark hair as she lowered her head.

So this was what lying to make someone feel better

felt like—a novel experience but not one that he was likely to repeat any time soon.

'So this was something your *sister* clearly didn't share with you before she dumped her kid on you.'

Maya sighed. 'She was upset, and she probably assumed I already knew.' Even as she gave voice to the excuse Maya was thinking of the occasions that that there had been for her half-sister to tell her that their mother had died. 'She was desperate.' She felt ashamed of the doubt that she struggled to conceal but could hear in her own voice.

Not desperate, no—Samuele's eyes moved around the room—but the woman he knew would have to be very determined indeed to consider spending a night here.

'She is a widow with a baby, who is being undermined at every move.'

'You don't appear totally naive.' In his view, being idealistic was probably worse. 'So please listen to me when I tell you that this was totally planned, *cara*. She played you, as they say, for a sucker.'

'That's ridiculous!' *Was it?* Little details of the previous evening surfaced in her head that she would not even have thought about if it hadn't been for him planting seeds of doubt. 'I saw her, she was... Why would anyone...?' Her eyes suddenly widened. 'What did you call me?' Not Mia at least, said the catty voice in her head.

He shook his head in a pretty unconvincing attitude of bewildered innocence—she was pretty sure that Samuele Agosti was neither; it was hard to imagine he ever had been.

When she replayed it in her head the casual endearment on his lips sounded like honey, liquid and warm.

Just thinking about it ignited another burst of heat low in her belly.

'She isn't coming back, you do know that?'

His expression came as near to sympathy as she'd seen, so she looked over his shoulder, refusing to allow the suspicions he had planted growing room in her head, worried because her hormones could be skewing her judgement. On the other hand, if what he said was true… Despite her determination the thought dropped into her consciousness and the ripples spread.

'I'm not leaving without Mattio,' Samuele stated.

I'm not leaving without Maya.

Maya swallowed past an emotional occlusion in her throat. She could suddenly see her dad so clearly, standing there smiling sunnily in response to being told that there was no parent accommodation available at the hospital—and besides, his little girl would be discharged from the overspill ward attached to the accident department after the cast that encased her broken arm had been checked by a doctor in the morning. She remembered willing him not to go and leave her in this big scary place and being glad he'd stayed even when she had cried that she wanted her mum, not him.

Mum had wanted to be there, he'd told her, but the rail strike meant she and Beatrice couldn't get back from the town where her sister had been competing in an athletics competition until the next day.

Her eyes lifted. There was no resemblance at all between the gangly dad of her memory, with his beard and untidy gingerish hair, and this tall, impossibly handsome man. But nevertheless, they had something in common.

'I need to see him,' he reiterated.

She offered up a suspicious look but couldn't bury

the memories rising up in her...seeing the expression in her dad's eyes—the one that had made someone produce a chair for him to sit on.

After a moment she found herself nodding, not, she told herself, because of an expression in *anyone's* eyes, but because there was nothing she actually could do to prevent him.

She stood back and opened the door.

The curtains were drawn in the room; she had never reached the point of opening them. Light seeped between them and there was a lamp on the bedside table that cast more shadow than light.

Hovering uncertainly in the doorway, she watched him move across to the travel cot. He was not a man she would associate with hesitancy, but if he'd been anyone else that was how she would have termed his approach. As he reached it and looked down at the sleeping baby he was half turned to her so she could see his face in profile.

The subdued lighting exaggerated the dramatic bone structure of his face, and maybe it did the same to his expression, but what she saw or *thought* she saw was an almost haunted look of loss that made her feel almost as if she were intruding. Shaking her head at her irrational response as if to loosen the grip of the uncomfortable feelings, she quietly left the room without a word, wishing she could unsee that look. Empathy for him was the last thing she needed to be experiencing; she already felt bad enough for even imagining a fleeting similarity to her dad, who had been her hero. It felt like a betrayal.

She refused to concede that maybe Violetta's monster wasn't a *total* monster, so she focused on the indisputable fact that he quite definitely wasn't a hero, not her definition of one anyhow. She would save her empathy for the baby caught in the middle of a conflict.

Conscience pricking, she walked into her bedroom, musing over her struggle to feel anything sisterly towards baby Mattio's mother, despite her hot defence of the woman. She closed the door behind her, knowing that, as the walls were paper-thin between the two rooms, she'd hear a pin drop let alone someone making off with a baby.

Not that he would do that... On her way across the room she paused as she realised this confidence in him was actually based on nothing more than a very non-evidence-based gut feeling. Her self-reflective line of thought was abruptly terminated when she caught sight of herself in the mirror on the wardrobe door. *Just* when she thought things could not get worse!

She thought longingly of a shower as she left a trail of clothes in her wake, struggling to open a drawer in the tall heavy chest of drawers of stripped pine to reveal the neatly folded and brightly coloured selection of sweaters inside.

Walking out of the adjoining bedroom, Samuele was struggling to suppress immense waves of sadness, anger and guilt after looking at the child his brother had never met. Life is unfair; live it, he'd been told, except his brother hadn't lived and life wasn't just unfair—it was *bloody* unfair.

He hadn't been able to protect Cristiano, but he was sure as hell going to protect his child no matter what it took. Still lost in his thoughts, he turned his head in response to a sound at the exact moment he was in line with a crack in the slightly open door, delivering an image of a slim, graceful and totally naked figure sitting back on her heels as she pulled open a cavernous drawer.

Smooth, sleek, supple, with perfect curves, she looked like an iconic art deco figure made warm flesh.

He turned his head sharply away, a stab of self-disgust piercing his conscience as his body reacted independently of his brain to the indelible image printed on it.

Flinging the pair of jeans she had grabbed backwards onto the bed, Maya sifted through the sweaters and hastily selected one.

Still resisting the pull of the shower, she turned the basin taps on full and washed her face. She fought her way into her clothes and cast another despairing glance at her image in the mirror as, brush in hand, she decided to just give up on her hair, choosing instead to secure the wild mass of dark curls at the nape of her neck.

She was halfway through brushing her teeth when she heard a noise from the living-room monitor, followed by a gentle whimper from the adjoining bedroom.

'I think Mattio has woken up again!' Samuele called.

'I'll be right there!' she replied, hastily rinsing her mouth and remembering wryly not taking seriously Beatrice's claim during the early sleep-deprived days of motherhood that she'd struggled to get dressed before midday.

She erupted into the living room like someone reaching the finishing line of a sprint. 'What...why are you looking at me like that?'

He shook his head and crossed the room in a couple of fluid strides. Holding her gaze, he reached out and, before she could react, gently touched the corner of her mouth.

For a breathless moment their eyes clung as she tried desperately to hide the shuddering skin-tingling awareness that his touch had awoken.

If that was only a touch, imagine what a kiss would do to you, said the wicked voice in her head.

She already knew...the memory of the whisper of an almost-kiss surfaced from the place she had consigned it to and an uncontrollable shiver traced its way down her spine.

'Toothpaste,' he explained, sliding a tissue back into his pocket.

Her hand went to her mouth. Wearing clothes was meant to make her feel more confident and in control but they offered no protection whatsoever from his penetrating stare. 'Oh...right, thank you.' She shook herself and said briskly, 'I need to go and sort out Mattio.'

Samuele watched as she left the room. He could hear the gentle murmurs of her talking to the baby through the monitor and a moment later she returned carrying his nephew.

'Could you put that on the floor?' She nodded to the brightly coloured plastic mat beside the nappy stack. 'Yep, just unfold it for me, thanks.'

He continued to observe as she dropped to her knees and laid the baby on the padded plastic surface and jiggled with one of his feet before she unfastened the all-in-one affair he was wearing. The entire time she chatted unselfconsciously to Mattio, discussing what she was doing with the baby boy, who seemed to be listening to everything she was saying.

The change of nappy and clothes completed, she settled back on her heels and gave a little grunt of satisfaction.

'You are really good at that,' he remarked thoughtfully. He knew he was not, and it was not exactly a short trip back to Italy.

'Beginners' luck,' she admitted. 'I do have a niece, although she is a few months older than Mattio. Beatrice, my sister, is already expecting another.'

'So were you both adopted?'

She shook her head as she got to her feet. 'No, Beatrice came along when I was one, a kind of miracle baby. Mum and Dad had been told they couldn't have children.'

'That must have put your nose out of joint.'

She smiled, clearly unoffended by the suggestion, which, he realised, had probably been made to her numerous times. 'No, our parents made absolutely sure we both knew we were special. Beatrice is my best friend.'

A muscle in his jaw clenched. 'Tell her that often,' he heard himself say.

Maya's liquid eyes held the beginning of understanding.

Although one of his rules in life was that he didn't explain himself, he inexplicably felt impelled to add abruptly, 'Because now I can't ever tell my brother that he was my best friend.'

'I should think he knew that, don't you? Sometimes you don't have to say anything.'

The gentle way she was looking at him, as though he was no longer the enemy, unsettled him—or was it the fact that he liked the feeling that they might be coming to a better understanding of each other? No, that was far too dangerous. He didn't appreciate the way his thoughts were going. 'Could be. After all, he knew his wife cheated on him, but we never discussed that.' The closest they'd come was when they'd overheard a group of women in an adjoining restaurant booth discussing the latest rumour concerning Violetta, but Cristiano had cut him off before he could say a word. Subject closed—for ever.

I know you don't understand, but it's my life and I love her.

Her expression immediately froze over at his dig about Violetta. 'You just never give up, do you?'

'I have that reputation,' he responded coolly, accompanying his words with a lethal smile.

Lips tight, she glanced down at the baby, who was happily kicking his legs and blowing bubbles. 'Can you watch him while I go and get his feed?'

She didn't hang around long enough to see his nod of assent.

Samuele got to his feet. He could watch him but he could do very little else. Whenever he had tried to see Mattio, Violetta had always had a reason why it wasn't convenient. Perhaps he hadn't tried hard enough, which was why he was now little more than a stranger to his own nephew.

When Maya returned with the warmed bottle, Samuele was kneeling beside the baby, one large finger in the tight baby grip of a pink chubby hand, but it was the long thin red mark down the side of his face that suddenly caught Maya's attention.

'He has sharp nails,' he mused, standing up and looking slightly self-conscious.

'He isn't the only one,' she said, looking at the scratch on his face and wondering if there were others on his back... The idea of him lost to passion like that left a sour taste in her mouth.

'It's definitely not what you're thinking,' he said drily as she settled with the baby in a chair.

She flashed him a startled look before bending her head over the baby to hide the mortified heat that was stinging her cheeks. 'You have no idea what I'm thinking,' she mumbled, focusing on the baby as he eagerly attached his rosebud mouth to the teat and began to enthusiastically suck.

Samuele knew *exactly* what she was thinking but he didn't say anything until the bottle was empty and she had carefully placed the baby over her shoulder and was patting his back.

'This happened at the will reading.' He touched the mark. 'The others have faded. It was Violetta's reaction to hearing that she would not have control of Cristiano's money, the money that, according to her, she had *earned* as Cristiano's wife, and that apparently *I* am stealing. Running away with Mattio is all part of her vow to make me *regret it.*'

'That's a terrible, wicked thing to accuse someone of!' she exclaimed, horrified. 'You really would say anything to get what you want, wouldn't you? That's slander!'

'Only if it's not true, and there were witnesses there, including the lawyer.'

She shook her head, but Samuele could see, once again, the doubts about Violetta creeping into the edges of her previous certainty. Cuddling the baby in her arms, she got to her feet. 'There are two sides to every story.'

He sighed out his frustration as she settled Mattio in his little rocking chair. Maya eased her own chair protectively closer.

'I agree. There are always two sides, but it seems to me that you are only willing to hear one. Why are you so determined to believe that I am the one in the wrong? How do you think I knew you existed, knew your name, found this place?'

The groove between her feathery brows deepened as she shook her head.

'I had inside information from Charlie. Believe me or not, but the truth is that Violetta has a new, extremely wealthy boyfriend who very much wants to marry her.' Deluded fool.

'So you don't want another man bringing up your brother's baby?'

'The point is the other man doesn't want to bring up another man's baby or, for that matter, any baby at all.' He spelt out the situation with brutal brevity. 'Charlie wants Violetta but not Mattio. He has no interest in any child restricting his lifestyle.'

'So it was him who told you that Mattio was here?'

He nodded, seeing more cracks appear in her conviction and pushing home his advantage. 'He told me exactly where to find Mattio because it would suit him very well if I claimed the baby.' He held up a hand, the action drawing attention to the thin red line on his face and the tension round his sensual mouth. 'Yes, I know this might be another one of my very wicked lies, so how about you call her and hear the proof from the merry widow's own lips?'

'I can't call her because she left her phone here.'

'That was a nice touch. Let's face it, Maya, you are in no position to negotiate and there is a time limit on being awkward. Not that I'm suggesting you don't do it very well.'

Maya slung him an unamused smile, realising that if he did take the baby, it was going to be harder for his mother to reclaim him. Violetta needed to come back right now, and Maya was sure if she could just talk to her, her half-sister would understand.

'If you know who she's with and have his contact details, then let's call him, but let *me* speak to her. I'm sure by now she'll be feeling...' She petered out. She really wasn't qualified to guess how a woman who had walked away from her child felt. 'Guilty probably, so saying the wrong thing could tip her over the edge.'

'You think I can't be sensitive and tactful?' Maya pulled a face, which drew a reluctant laugh from him.

To hide the effect the unexpected sound had on her Maya channelled chilly disproval. It was a pity it only went skin-deep; to her shame, just under the surface she was all quivering, melting warmth. 'This isn't a joke.'

The smile in his eyes vanished, snuffing out like a candle. 'No, it isn't,' he said, producing a phone from his pocket. 'How about I put it on speaker? Then if I get too insensitive you can rescue the situation.'

He was being sarcastic, she could see that, but what she didn't understand was what he imagined he could achieve. Did he think he could bully Violetta into telling Maya to hand over her son? Even *imagining* such a situation brought her protective instincts to high-alert level and she'd only known the child existed for hours. Imagine if you'd carried and given birth…being apart from your baby would be like losing a part of yourself. Wouldn't it?

'You must see that the baby *needs* his mother.' She searched his face for any hint of understanding but, after a moment, sighed.

There was more give in a granite rock face.

'It depends on the mother. I don't know how well you knew Olivia, but you were far better off without her, I assure you. Just look how Violetta turned out.'

'We're not talking about me.' And they never would be because she would never invite this man into her head. 'I have no abandonment issues.'

She bit her lip. She was getting familiar with his

expressive shrugs; he was able to convey a range of emotions with the slightest movement of his broad shoulders.

'What?' she snapped querulously, because he was staring at her in that unnerving way again.

'You have…' Samuele half lifted a hand and then shoved it safely back into a pocket. The last time he had touched her mouth— No, he wasn't going there again. 'Blood on your lip.'

A man who made a mistake could be forgiven, but if he knowingly repeated that mistake, he was a fool who didn't deserve forgiveness.

Samuele had never had any time for fools. Did it count as foolish, with the very recent memory of the heat that had stung through his body when he'd touched her mouth still fresh in his head, for his eyes to follow the tip of her tongue as it licked the pinprick drop of blood from the plump, pink outline of her bottom lip?

Probably not, but he hadn't followed through with the impulse to replace his finger with his mouth and continue the exploration. He knew his reasoning bore all the classic hallmarks of rationalisation, but there was such a thing as overthinking something.

He accepted that looking at her mouth, or any other part of Maya Monk, wasn't ever going to lead him down a path to inner peace. Luckily, he wasn't looking to take away inner peace from this encounter—just his nephew.

There was a tension in the room that Maya chose to ignore as she nodded pointedly towards the phone he held.

After a moment he punched in a number and laid the phone on the coffee table between them. It was picked up almost immediately and a man replied, sounding distracted, possibly by the owner of the husky female laugh Maya could hear in the background.

'This is Samuele Agosti. Put Violetta on, will you, Charlie?'

There was a silence before the man on the other end began to babble. 'Samuele, it's great to hear your voice, but actually I can't help you—she's not with me…'

'Oh, for God's sake, give me that thing and get out.' There was the sound of rustling and banging and then what sounded like a door closing.

'He's gone. How did you know where I was?'

There was no betraying quiver in the voice; it was hard and cold and annoyed, but Maya knew without doubt that she was listening to her half-sister.

'Well, you're not with your child so where else would you be?'

'You found him! Damn, that was quick,' she snapped petulantly. 'Clever old you. I really wanted you to sweat.'

The most shocking thing for Maya was that Samuele didn't look even slightly surprised by this vicious, vindictive statement. Instead, he looked…she searched the angles and hollows of his face and the word *dangerous* floated into her head. The ruthless, relentless quality she had been aware of in him was in sharp focus as he allowed the moment to stretch before responding.

'You succeeded.' His glance shifted across to where Maya stood like a frozen statue, her hand pressed to her mouth, horror shining in her eyes.

Breaking eye contact, he shifted his weight from one foot to the other to move her into the periphery of his vision, ignoring the weight of uneasy guilt in his chest.

He had no time to be gentle; she *needed* to hear

this. The truth was brutal—everyone learnt that lesson sooner or later. Yes, sometimes having your eyes opened hurt, but walking around with them tightly shut was dangerous, and a woman who'd reached her age should have stopped believing that every person was good and honest.

'I was hoping you'd have to suffer for much longer than this.' The petulance was now laced with viciousness. Maya felt almost numb now as she heard her half-sister hiss, 'Because you deserve it after you turned my own husband against me and stole what's mine. I deserve that money!'

'Would that I could have turned him against you, but he was loyal to you to the end.'

The bone-deep weariness and despair in Samuele's voice finally penetrated Maya's own personal misery. It had all been an act and she had fallen for it.

'You wanted to see me suffer, I get that, but isn't this all a little bizarrely complicated, even for you?'

'If I'd tried to vanish in Italy your contacts would have found me in thirty seconds and I needed to be in London to get my hair done—my colourist here is simply the best.' Her laugh that made Maya think of glass breaking rang out before Violetta added, 'And anyhow London definitely solved the babysitting problem. It was a toss-up, I thought, between that and having someone burn down your bloody castle, but this was more of a "two birds with one stone" thing. I told you that you'd regret cutting me out of the money. Next time I'll get even more inventive, so don't relax just yet, will you, darling?'

'Cristiano left you very well provided for.' Samuele struggled to keep his voice free of the disgust churning in his belly. 'You don't need Mattio's half of the Agosti estate as well.'

'Your brother always did what you told him, but at least your investment advice paid off. I do have a very nice sum, you're right, but half the estate is worth a fortune.'

'It's Mattio's.'

'And Mattio is mine, but maybe now that you've found him I might let you keep him.'

'How much do you want?'

'Oh, darling, you can be so crude. You may hold the purse strings but I hold the baby, so play nice or I might change my mind.'

'I'm listening.'

'So you've met Mother's little mistake, have you? Mummy said she wouldn't be a problem or try and encroach in our lives, but it never occurred to me that she'd actually be useful.'

Samuele was glad that Maya had moved out of his line of vision; he didn't want to see her reaction to that disgusting remark. 'Get to the point,' he bit out.

'I see my future with Charlie.'

'And his millions,' he added contemptuously.

'Well, I wouldn't marry a poor man, would I?' she cooed.

He didn't bother replying.

'It suits me for you to have Mattio right now. Charlie is not really into babies, but there's always the possibility that I might just change his mind about that.' And with that, she hung up.

After any conversation with Violetta, Samuele usually felt as though he needed a shower and this was no exception. He didn't know at what point Maya had left the room or how much she had heard.

She was standing in the kitchen, her head bent. She had dragged her hair across one shoulder and was anchoring it there with her forearm, revealing the sculpted hollows of her collarbones, the delicately defined angle of her jaw and the elegant length of her neck.

She didn't immediately turn when he entered but the added level of quivering tension in her body made it clear she knew he was there.

'I don't know how much of that you heard…?'

Maya's arm fell away and her hair tumbled free as she spun around to face him.

'Enough to know you were right, I was wrong, she was using me and now you've got what you want.' She struggled to keep her voice flat, and struggled harder to push away the overwhelming self-pity, ashamed she was making this personal because the only person who should be considered in this scenario was the baby in the next room. 'I suppose you want me to pack up his things?' Without any warning her dignity was drowned in a rush of blinding anger.

'Is it all about the challenge for you? The winning? I suppose you'll lose interest in him now you've won,' she threw out, not even sure she believed it but wanting to hurt him because—well, she was not about to give him the benefit of the doubt.

Or maybe she just didn't want to be the only one hurting here.

Samuele tensed, every muscle in his face clenching as his face blanked, and anger bit deep at the insult. She had unerringly targeted his pride, questioning his integrity and implying he had no conscience.

He knew many men who were successful because they possessed little or no conscience. When it came to making money a conscience was something of a hindrance so he hid his, which made it doubly ironic that he was insulted now because he'd succeeded.

But when their gazes connected there was no spite in hers, just a mixture of sadness and pain, a pain so deep it took a real effort for him to detach himself from the emotions he saw there. His own anger deflated, leaving a vague sense of utterly irrational guilt in its place.

'This child doesn't have a father, which is not my definition of winning.' He arched a brow. 'What's yours?'

Maya's brow puckered, the muscles on her face quivering as her eyes softened and went liquid. 'I'm so sorry, your brother must have been very young when he died.'

He watched her fighting back tears and struggled to imagine just how uncomfortable that degree of empathy must be to live with as he found himself revealing, 'He tried to hang on to see his son, but he didn't make it. He was the bravest man I have ever known.'

Samuele had never discussed his brother or the battle he had fought with anyone, so why was he suddenly opening up to Maya, of all people? He dodged the answer and swore under his breath. 'You don't have anything to be sorry for.'

'When I lost my dad I bottled up my feelings, but when I actually talked about them—'

In a voice that could have wilted green shoots on a plant, he cut across her. It was for her own sake really; if she started wandering around in his head, she would definitely find more than a few things that she didn't like. 'I appreciate the sharing,' he drawled sardonically, 'but—'

This time it was Maya who shut him down. 'I get the message.'

She did. If he was one of those people who thought

admitting to emotions was a sign of weakness, that was his business; it was the baby her heart ached for. Being taught by example that to *suck it up* was what real men did... God, it was so depressing.

As she thought of the baby her eyes softened. She might have been abandoned but there was never a moment in her life after she was adopted that she had doubted she was loved. It was those early years that had made her tough enough to survive Edward's concerted campaign of destruction.

'What will you ever tell him about his mother?' *Oh, God, I said that out loud!*

Bracing herself for another one of his icy put-downs, she maintained a defiant stance as she slowly turned to face him.

'I would write her out of his life if that was possible.'

No ice, just a cool statement of fact, and while she sympathised with his attitude, she still didn't think it was the right one. But then it wasn't her business, was it? she reminded herself.

'Isn't it possible? Isn't she giving you custody of Mattio?' Giving him away as if he were simply a piece of excess baggage. That was when she'd had to leave the room; if she'd stayed there another moment her feelings would have got the better of her and she'd have started yelling down the phone at her half-sister.

'Nothing is ever that simple with Violetta. It suits her now to have me take Mattio back to Italy, but she won't relinquish her maternal control willingly,' he predicted. 'And once she's got Charlie to the altar... Let's just say she can be very persuasive indeed,' he finished grimly, no doubt thinking of the custody battle that lay ahead.

'Oh... I'm sorry.'

He arched a sardonic brow.

'Well, you'd be better for Mattio than she would be. Actually, anyone would,' Maya said honestly.

'Wow, faint praise indeed,' he drawled, the smile in his voice warming his eyes and making her want to smile back.

She fought the urge and dived for the door. 'I'll start packing his things up.'

CHAPTER FOUR

Mattio had dozed off in his little chair. Coming into the living room behind her, Samuele watched as Maya tenderly tucked a light blanket around him and began to pick up the baby items strewn around.

Feeling a stab of self-disgust that even in a time like this he could appreciate, actually more than appreciate, the tightness of her behind under the snugly fitting denim, he cleared his throat.

'I have been thinking.'

One hand on her thigh, the other outstretched to scoop up a soft toy that had found its way under a side table, she lifted her head and looked up at him from under the frame of curling lashes. She was oblivious to the fact the action made her square-necked cobalt-blue sweater gape, giving him a tantalising glimpse of her lacy bra and the suggestive creamy swell of her smooth cleavage. The shadow of her nipples under the lace might have been his imagination which was, to his own annoyance, clearly working overtime.

'Come with us.' The offer was made not because of his recent testosterone rush but *despite* it—it was a purely practical suggestion, he told himself, devoid of any personal feelings.

Purely practical would have been putting an ocean

or three between this woman and you, pointed out the voice in his head.

He ignored it and the insulting implication he was not totally in control. For someone who had been born with a hot temper and a tendency to act before his brain was in gear, he was conscious of the need to maintain control at all times. Allowing their emotions and appetites full rein had been the downfall of both his father and brother, so Samuele's life was ruled by his determination to ruthlessly suppress any similar tendencies when and if they ever surfaced in himself.

Maya dropped the toy and came upright with a jerk that made her hair bounce angrily before settling in a silky tumble down her back. 'Is that some sort of joke?'

'No, it's... Have you been crying?' he asked, observing the dampness on her cheeks with a tightening in his chest.

Maya was always alert and very defensive about anyone assuming that, just because she looked delicate, she *was* delicate. There was something patronising in people thinking she needed to be given special treatment.

So she had zero qualms about lying.

'No, I have not.'

It was crazy! This time yesterday she had not even known this baby boy existed. Maybe it was the fact they had both been abandoned that had brought out these painfully intense protective feelings in her?

'Well, you look—'

'I have *not* been crying—though God knows the way this day is going, it would be small wonder if I had!'

He lifted his hands in an open-palmed pacific gesture. 'Fine, you have not been crying.' He shrugged. 'I have a flight home arranged.'

She had been prepared to hear him out in stony silence,

but her curiosity won that battle. 'Where is home?' Where would she imagine Samuele living? She wouldn't be imagining him at all, she reminded herself, but who knew if his voice might continue to seep into her dreams...?

She gave a little shiver. On any measurement scale their first chance encounter had not exactly been a cosmic event and yet it had lingered in her mind. More than lingered, if she was honest, thinking of that voice in her dreams, the touch she woke up remembering, which was an invention of her subconscious, because he had never touched her. Did that merest whisper of a kiss even count?

Now fate, or whatever you liked to call it, had thrown them together once more. Not just a nudge this time, but a full-on red-light collision, and they were connected for ever by Mattio.

He still hadn't touched her.

'Tuscany, outside Florence. The estate has been in our family for generations.' And very briefly large sections temporarily not. The realisation that his father had been selling off piecemeal vast tracts of the estate and splitting up the world-renowned Agosti art collection, just to keep his second wife, Samuele's stepmother, in private jets, luxury yachts and jewels to wear when she lost yet another fortune at the gaming tables, had caused Samuele to abandon his medical degree course midway through.

Medicine might provide status, respect and job satisfaction, but if he wanted to succeed in his determination to restore his family's heritage he needed money, the sort of money that the financial services sector could provide for someone who was successful. And Samuele was hugely successful, his rise had been meteoric and he had never regretted his decision, not once.

Before his father's death he had discreetly, through a series of anonymous holding companies, managed to reacquire seventy per cent of the estate that his father had sold. After his death there had been no need for discretion and the restoration of the Agosti villa in Florence had been completed the previous year.

He had expected success to feel more...*victorious*? He pushed the thought away. The truth was, it was hard to be enthused about anything since Cristiano's death. And now he had someone to hand the reclaimed heritage on to. He had Mattio.

He would always put Mattio's needs ahead of every other consideration, including his own conscience.

'I have a private plane waiting.' He said it in the casual way that, in Maya's experience, only people with a lot of money spoke about such things. 'I'll need a nanny for Mattio.'

'I'm not a nanny!'

'*Dio*, I wasn't offering you the job.'

He was secure in his self-control, but inviting this woman to live under the same roof as him on any sort of permanent basis, given the chemistry that existed between them, would break too many of his self-imposed boundaries when it came to allowing women into his life. And if ever he'd met a woman who was incapable of recognising a boundary, let alone staying the right side of one, Maya Monk was it.

He didn't need a woman like her in his life—actually he didn't need any woman. Of course, there were women he had sex with occasionally—he needed sex, the same as any man—but they never threatened his inner peace.

Another word for loneliness, mocked his inner voice, but he didn't care if it was true. Isolation was preferable to the option both his father and brother had embraced:

marrying wives who'd taken them for every penny and made them smile while they did it.

Embarrassed heat stung Maya's cheeks. There was nothing like refusing a job you hadn't been offered to make a girl feel stupid. 'Oh, well…my mistake.' Her firm little chin lifted, defiance exuding from every pore as she added mutinously, 'But it sounded to me like you were.'

His gaze drifted from her narrowed eyes to her sensuous mouth that couldn't look thin and mean, even though she was clearly trying. When it came to a live-in nanny, he would definitely not choose one that looked like Maya Monk. A world where she was a permanent feature in his life without her sharing his bed was an absolute non-starter… No, the person he had in mind was sturdy and no-nonsense, radiating a comforting, calm, kind vibe. Would it be sexist to put any of those things in the ad?

'I travel light, and I have no experience of babies,' he admitted, thinking he had even less experience of women who made him laugh. 'Let alone travelling with one.' Logic told him there had to be more to that endeavour than there appeared. 'And it's going to take me a little time to find a suitable nanny. In the interim, I was thinking that you could…help out with Mattio. I've watched you with him—you're good with him, he knows you and you seem like a…safe pair of hands.' With a soft heart, which of course was what he was counting on.

'So you don't want a nanny, you just want an unqualified, unpaid dogsbody!'

'Are there qualifications for doing someone a favour?' he asked with a shrug. 'And payment isn't an issue—name your price.'

She reacted huffily to the suggestion that she could be bought. 'I can't be bought.'

He fought the impulse to share his cynical view that that fact alone made her unusual, if not unique.

'Not a very practical response, but fine, if that's what you want, I won't pay you.'

She threw him a narrow-eyed look of dislike. 'I suppose you assume that just because I'm female I know about babies.'

Female... Yes, she was... The provocative blood-heating image of her slim, smooth, naked body, *very* female naked body, floated into his head, making it hard to stick to his point. 'You really could do with some lessons in selling yourself.'

'I'm not trying to sell myself,' she said, her voice barely audible beyond the sound of her low shallow breaths, which made the subsequent decibel rise all the more apparent as she suddenly added, 'And I really don't care what *you* or anyone else thinks about me. I care what *I* think about me.' To his ears it had all the hallmarks of a classic *she protests way too much* denial.

She was too busy trying to inject some much-needed neutrality into her voice to notice the thoughtful expression that slid across his face. 'And I've already said no.'

'Yes, you did.'

You didn't have to do much reading between the lines to work out that once she *had* cared about what someone thought, and that someone had done some serious damage to her self-confidence.

She had recovered because she was obviously a strong woman, but there were always scars...even if they weren't visible. He'd come across men like that; ones who made themselves feel big to disguise the fact they were hollow and weak. He would have liked to get his hands on—

He forced himself to de-escalate his growing antagonism towards this faceless creation of his imagination, the man who'd probably tapped into the passion he sensed in Maya, who had maybe made it harder for her to enjoy it with the next man who came along.

But he was not that man.

'You wouldn't be doing it for me,' he emphasised. 'You'd be doing it for Mattio. What's a few weeks out of your life? The poor kid hasn't had much continuity in his so far.'

Even a compulsive liar had to speak the truth occasionally, Maya thought sardonically as her half-sister's words floated through her head. *You don't know what Samuele is capable of.*

Well, she now knew one thing he was capable of after this breathtakingly blatant attempt to play on her feelings for Mattio.

'For future reference,' she told him crisply, 'I don't respond well to moral blackmail. Not that there will be—a future, I mean,' she tacked on, wincing, because the only thing she'd managed to do was make it sound as though they had a past.

They didn't have a past, present or future. She had spent more time in the company of the woman at the checkout till at her local supermarket than this man, and she actually knew more about her!

It was just the entire off-the-scale hothouse weirdness of everything about the last few hours that had fed this strange feeling of intimacy between them, utterly misplaced intimacy, she told herself.

'Sorry, that was below the belt.'

She suddenly caught an expression in his face and wondered if he felt guilty. If he did, it couldn't be *that* guilty. It wasn't in his nature to give up, and when one tactic failed you tried an alternative one. He didn't disappoint her.

'I need your help and if you can put aside your dislike of me... I mean, you don't have to like me or trust me, and any practical inconvenience I will sort out with your employer or whatever. Will you promise to think about it?'

She struggled not to feel disarmed by his sincerity, but knew she was losing the battle as she felt her antagonism melting away. 'How long before you need to know?'

He glanced at the thin metal banded watch on his wrist. 'Five...no, make that four minutes.' He looked at her, one dark brow arched, and produced a white grin that would have given the devil a run for his money— a very attractive devil.

She gave a small laugh of disbelief.

'And I would really appreciate your input into the recruitment of the nanny too,' he said, dangling the suggestion like a carrot of temptation.

She breathed out heavily. 'I just can't...' Her voice trailed away as the exhaustion she'd been holding at bay with sheer willpower suddenly hit her, like walking into a wall, and bone-deep weariness came flooding in.

'Are you all right?' He stood braced, looking as though he was fully prepared to catch her if she fell, which was a good thing because she really felt as if she might go down.

She pulled herself to her full height, but she still had to tip her head back a long way to look him in the face.

'I'm fine,' she grouched irritably, wishing she could throw something more than his concern back in his face, then sighed as she felt impelled to add, 'Thank you.'

'You need to sit down. You're having a vasovagal attack.'

'A what?'

'You're going to faint.' Taking matters into his own hands, he took her by the shoulders and manoeuvred her onto the nearest sofa. One finger pressed into the middle of her chest sent her backwards while he lifted her legs onto the cushions.

'I don't faint.' In her head it was a firm, calm statement, but sadly it emerged as a weak little whisper. Maybe she would just lie there until the world stopped spinning. Things were a bit vague and hazy, and she couldn't even work up the enthusiasm to react when she felt cool fingers taking the pulse on her wrist. 'Who made you the expert on fainting anyhow?'

Eyes closed, she missed the look that crossed his face.

'I suppose you've been making girls swoon all your life,' she observed waspishly as she experimentally opened her eyes to discover the world had stopped spinning.

'Take it slowly,' he cautioned as she lifted herself up onto an elbow.

A massive surprise when she ignored him and sat up, swinging her legs to the floor. 'Did you get much sleep last night?'

It seemed like a century ago since she had opened her door to her half-sister, and the memories were already meshed into a kaleidoscope of intertwined images.

It had been one hit on top of another. The exhaustion she was feeling was not just about sleep deprivation; it was emotional.

'Take this.' She curled her fingers around the warm teacup. 'You can sleep on the plane.'

She flung him a look and grimaced as, cradling the cup between her two hands, she lifted it to her lips and drank. 'I don't take sugar.' She took another sip anyway. 'I can't just drop everything...my job...' Her voice trailed away. She was expecting her redundancy notice to arrive any day now, not that that made any difference.

'Where do you work?'

She named the department store. 'I'm a window dresser.'

'But I saw the sketches...'

Her glance went to the folders stacked behind the folded architect's table, which she'd intended to put away in the spare room. 'My sister and I had plans to start a small fashion label, but she got back together with her husband, and start-up businesses need some serious capital and time investing in them... In the meantime, I do actually like my job.'

'Don't married women work?'

'It would be a long commute. Beatrice lives in San Macizo.'

His mobile black brows lifted. 'Yes, I can see that would be pushing it...' He paused, a frown corrugating his brow. '*Beatrice?* As in the—'

She cut him off. 'Yeah, I have royal connections.'

'Who could surely give you the capital you need to start up your business?'

At the hint of criticism in his voice she fired back angrily, 'They have offered and I refused.'

'Interesting.' She didn't ask what was so interesting and he didn't elaborate. 'So you have a niece, and now you have a nephew too.' He watched closely as the shock of recognition flickered in her eyes.

'Yes.'

'I imagine that you'd do anything for your niece?'

'Obviously,' she responded, indignant that there

could be any doubt about that before she saw the point he was making.

It was true she would do anything for little Sabina, who had an adoring mother and father, who would never ever be abandoned or made to feel she was not worthy of love. She looked up at Samuele over the rim of her teacup, feeling lighter as she shrugged off the invisible but very real weight of indecision.

Why would she do any less for her nephew, who was so much worse off than her niece?

'I'll do it.'

It would be fine, she told herself. All she had to do was remember that she could not fall too deeply in love with her nephew because, in reality, parting was inevitable.

The uncle…well, there was no danger of love being involved there, but she would have to keep some sort of check on the surges of attraction that might put her in danger of doing something stupid.

Like flying off to Italy with a man you barely know where your lack of childcare skills is going to be outed very quickly.

CHAPTER FIVE

She struggled to shake the feeling that she was there under false pretences as Samuele's staff deferred to her on every matter to do with the baby on board.

Apart from an interval when he became fretful, which, according to one sympathetic steward who seemed knowledgeable about such things, meant that he was probably teething, he'd been no trouble at all.

'Look at those hot little cheeks, bless him. We didn't sleep for a week when our eldest was teething,' she said, setting out the bottle of formula Maya had not needed to request, but had magically appeared.

As Maya jogged up and down later, Mattio in her arms, she could appreciate how much harder this might have been if there were more than the one other passenger on board. Samuele was certainly not going to complain about the noise of a grizzling baby, but even he had spent most of the flight locked in a private cabin where she presumed he was working, only appearing when they were about to land to ask, in what she felt was a critical way, if she'd had any sleep.

Did she look that bad?

'He's teething,' she said stiffly, nodding to the baby, who had just nodded off himself.

'Oh.'

Maya quite enjoyed seeing him look out of his depth. She could imagine that it was probably a once-in-a-decade thing, so she didn't let on that she was too.

Once they disembarked a well-oiled machine seemed to spring into action, making the transfer into a luxury four-wheel-drive painless and swift.

The only blip in this process was when the passenger door was opened by one of the team whose sole purpose in life appeared to be saying *'sì'* to Samuele. Though to be fair his attitude did not suggest he required deference. He was relaxed with all his staff, who seemed pretty at ease with him too. Maya, whose nervous system was on permanent red-alert mode around him, felt quite envious. She hesitated at the car door. She had intended to sit next to the baby in the back seat, though perhaps there was no such safe distance when it came to Samuele.

'Is there a problem?' Samuele sounded impatient. She noticed he had got changed on the flight and the black jeans that greedily clung to his muscular thighs seemed a very valid reason not to sit beside him. God knew when he'd found the time to swap clothes, but then it seemed to Maya that he did everything at a million miles an hour. He was not, she decided, the sort of person to take time out to appreciate a sunset or a view. Did he ever actually relax?

'I was wondering if we'd see much of Florence. I've never been there but I understand it's very beautiful.'

'Another day I'll give you a guided tour.'

'Oh, I didn't mean—'

'Get in, Maya.'

She got in rather than make a fuss and any concerns she had about making stilted conversation were unnecessary because they were barely outside the city limits when she fell asleep.

When she woke, confused, her head propped against the padded headrest, a blanket from the back seat thrown over her, she was too muzzy-headed to think about how it had got there. Samuele wasn't in the car.

She rubbed her eyes, knowing that it was a given that her hair would look as though there were small animals living somewhere in the wild mass of curls. She took in her surroundings. The car was stationary and they were parked at the side of a narrow empty road where the trees lining the road ahead and behind had thinned to reveal what was the most incredible panoramic view she had ever seen in her life. She'd clearly been wrong: Samuele did stop to look at the view.

She gave the peacefully dozing baby in the back seat a quick glance before she unfastened her belt and exited the car. Her nostrils flaring at the pungent scent of pine and the wild thyme that released its sweet scent into the air, she picked a path across to where Samuele stood, his tall figure dark against the backdrop of a deep cerulean-blue sky.

'Sorry I fell asleep...oh, my, it's so beautiful.' She sighed, her eyes drawn to the view that stretched out before them. Against the distant backdrop of the purple hills the undulating fields were a patchwork of colours, gold with wheat and green grazed by animals impossible to identify at this distance. The separate areas were defined by rows of statuesque pine and dotted with sculptural cypresses, and ribbons of water gleamed as they wound their way down the sloping hills that, to her uneducated eyes, seemed to be covered with the regimented neatness of vineyards.

For a long time she said nothing. 'It's almost... *spiritual.*' The words emerged without any conscious thought and a moment later she gave an embarrassed little laugh and angled a look up at him. Samuele was no longer staring at the landscape, but looking at her, the expression on his face making her insides quiver.

'That probably sounds stupid.'

'Not at all. It's taken some people a lifetime to see that, and some,' he added heavily, 'never do.'

He redirected his stare to the vista but there was a brooding quality to his stare now that hadn't been there before.

'When do we reach…your home?'

'We have.' He opened his hands wide to encompass the land that stretched out before them. 'We have actually been on the estate for the past twenty minutes, and the village is about five minutes back there. You'll be able to see the house once we come out on the other side of that copse.'

'I had no idea that it was so…vast,' she admitted, making some serious adjustments to her preconceptions of the Agosti heritage. 'You own an entire village?'

'My family has cared for this land for years and it has cared for us…and many others in return. Until recently.'

'Recently?' she probed warily, wondering if he was alluding to his brother's death.

'My father stripped everything of value he could and sold off the rest to keep his wife in private jets and fuel her main hobby which was—and presumably still is—gambling,' Samuele said heavily. 'She went into rehab after my father's death, where she met her new husband; in a twist of irony, he owns a string of hotel casinos.'

'When you said his wife, was she not your mother?'

'My mother is dead. My father's second wife was Cristiano's mother. I remember that she adored him as a baby but as soon as he passed the cute baby stage she treated him pretty much like an out-of-date handbag.'

The calming effect of the beauty of the land he loved so much, the land that would never hurt him, evaporated as he dwelt on the destructive emotion his father had called love. Even at the end, when he'd known that the woman he'd worshipped was having affair after affair, he'd still defended her to his eldest son. And then, to Samuele's despair, exactly the same fate had befallen Cristiano.

'She didn't consider she had an addiction problem so my father didn't either. His duty to the land, his tenants, his family…he sacrificed them all for this insanity of selfishness, which went disguised as love.'

The delivery was flat and even but despite, or maybe because of, his measured neutrality Maya could feel the emotions throbbing in every syllable.

'But the land—you said this is yours now…?'

'I started buying it back anonymously as soon as I could afford to, and now it is almost back to what it once was.' He still had hopes of tracking down the last few elusive classical sculptures that would complete the art collection that had rivalled many museums.

'Wow, that couldn't have been cheap…' She flushed as his eyes swivelled her way. 'Sorry, I didn't mean to sound nosy.'

'Yes, it wasn't…er…*cheap, cara*.'

To her relief he seemed amused, not offended.

'I am an investment banker, so raising capital is what I specialise in, and the finance industry pays extremely well.' He had not drifted into finance, he had deliberately plotted a course, and the rewards, not the job satisfaction, had been his motivation for doing so.

He inhaled, drawing in the sweet clean air as he scanned the horizon. To Maya, it seemed as though he was letting the peace, the sense of continuity over the ages, visibly seep into him.

'So the estate is a hobby?'

He continued to look into the distance. 'No, finance is my hobby. The estate is my life.' He turned to face her. 'So, are you ready?'

Caught staring at him, she shifted guiltily and began to move towards the four-wheel-drive. 'I'm sorry I fell asleep...' she said again, skipping to fall into step beside him.

It was a subject he did not particularly want to think about. He closed it down with a light teasing reply. 'Relax, you don't drool.' But he couldn't close down the images that stubbornly remained inside his head or the memory of the scent of her hair as it tickled his neck.

After the second time of nudging her head back onto the headrest, he had finally let it stay where it kept falling against his shoulder.

'Sorry, I wasn't much company.'

'A woman who doesn't talk while I'm driving is my kind of perfect.'

Maya huffed a little as she tried to keep pace with his long-legged stride. 'Did you take classes in sexist chauvinism?'

He flashed her a look, all white teeth and testosterone.

'No, I am totally self-taught.'

The exchange had brought them level with the luxury off-roader that stood in the sculpted shade of a cypress tree. 'Your mother must be so proud of you,' she muttered, raising herself on tiptoe to look through the back window she had cracked open before she'd left the car. Mattio had not moved an inch.

'She's dead, remember.'

She shot him a contrite look. 'That was a stupid thing for me to say!'

'Oh, I don't know, it was quite funny. Relax,' he said matter-of-factly, opening the passenger door for her. 'I barely remember her.' Sometimes a memory would surface, triggered by a scent or a familiar object. 'And my life did not lack female influence for long,' he added in a tone hard enough to cut through diamond. 'She was barely cold in her grave before I had a stepmother and, four months later, a half-brother.'

Her eyes, widened in comprehension, flew to his face. 'Four months?'

His fingers curved around her elbow to give her a steadying boost into the seat of the high-level vehicle, which brought her face level with his.

'A married man having an affair...' he mocked. 'Who'd have thought?' Not Maya, clearly, and her naivety made him perversely want to shock her more. 'When I was going through my father's papers I found some of my mother's things.' Untouched and gathering metaphorical dust, since they'd been consigned to a filing cabinet with the other *unimportant* items.

'There were some legal documents dated the day before her death. It turns out he had served her with divorce papers, something that was not revealed in the inquest, I would imagine, seeing as I think they might have had a bearing on their verdict of accidental overdose. Maybe if there had been a suicide note...?'

The way he relayed the details, with a total absence of any emotion, was somehow almost *more* shocking than the story itself.

It made her wonder just how deep he'd buried the trauma. She never doubted there *was* trauma because Maya knew from experience that it never, ever went away, not until you faced it.

'I suppose there are some things you can never

know.' Given the story, his attitude to marriage and women was hardly surprising.

He met her sympathetic gaze with a look that was dark, hard and unforgiving. 'Oh, I know, I know full well that my mother killed herself because she was being traded in, because she didn't give a damn about what or who she left behind—namely me.'

He'd thought the words plenty of times, but he'd never actually said them out loud before. The pity he could see shining in her luminous eyes was the reason why.

Samuele looked away from those eyes, asking himself yet again what it was about Maya Monk that made him open himself up this way. He had revealed more about himself in the space of the last few hours than he had told anyone—ever.

'I don't need your pity.'

'Good, because you haven't got it. There's a difference between pity and compassion, you know! You're angry with a parent for leaving you—believe you me, that doesn't make you unique around here, Samuele. Your mother found it impossible to carry on living but that doesn't mean she stopped loving you.'

He climbed into the vehicle after her, staring stonily ahead as he reversed out of the clearing at speed.

'Sorry,' he said as they hit a particularly bad pothole that almost jolted Maya out of her seat. 'Resurfacing this road is due to start next month. If we were approaching from the other way, the road is almost civilised.' He was watching her as he turned the corner; he liked to see people's reactions as they got their first glimpse of the castello.

Maya's jaw dropped as she took in the square towers in each corner of the massive sandstone edifice and the teethlike projections high up along the walls between them. It seemed to ramble, if you could use such a word for such a formidable-looking building. 'You live in a palace!'

'Castello di Agosti is classified as a castle. My family have lived here since the thirteenth century, apart from a short period when it was used as a hospital during the Second World War.'

'It's…'

'I have never seen a ghost.'

'I wasn't going to ask that.' But, of course, now she was thinking it. 'Are there many suits of armour?'

'A few, hopefully not dusty. Relax, the place has been totally renovated with all mod cons. You look more apprehensive than the tenants did when I introduced some new eco-farming methods. We have a long-term strategy here.'

They were driving along a wide, smoothly surfaced driveway now that wound its way through lush parkland. As the road divided she saw a field with horses in.

'Years ago our stud was world-renowned. We've just started building up a breeding programme again in a small way.'

It seemed to Maya that nothing here was built on a small scale.

'Oh, my!' She twisted her head to see the gardens that they were passing, stone terrace after stone terrace spilling flowers above a formal walled garden with a series of classical looking fountains.

She settled back into her seat as they drove away from the castle and through an archway into a gravelled area surrounded by low stone buildings.

The car stopped and a small welcoming party appeared: two young men in white shirts and dark trousers, who began to unload their luggage; a woman with no visible waist and a lovely smile and another young man, who were introduced by Samuele as the housekeeper, Gabriella, and his private secretary.

While the housekeeper got tearful over Mattio, Maya watched Samuele and his secretary talking quietly. A few moments later she could almost see him shrugging off his city persona; here he was king of the castle, though a very chilled-out king. In fact, he looked more relaxed than she had imagined possible.

'I have some things to attend to, so I will see you at dinner. Gabriella will look after you,' Samuele said, turning to her.

'I don't expect you to look after me,' she blurted.

He tipped his head. 'You are our guest.' There was nothing in his words, but the light in his eyes made her stomach muscles quiver.

'*Our*…is there a…do you have a…? Are you married or anything?' She paused awkwardly, the idea he wasn't single sending panic that was quite out of proportion with the possibility through her body as she stood there kicking herself for not asking earlier.

'Not even *anything* at this present moment. It was just a figure of speech.'

At the outset Maya had no idea what her role was classified as being while she was here, and she had half expected to be accommodated in the servants' quarters. Although if what she had seen was any indication the servants' quarters would be pretty five star.

There were several gasp-out-loud moments as she was led by the housekeeper, who'd offered to carry the travel seat that Mattio was snuggled in, an offer Maya declined, through the vaulted hallway with its stone walls and up a grand staircase that divided into a gallery at the top.

'The frescoes are in the west wing,' Gabriella explained as she led the way along a long corridor that could have easily accommodated a couple of football pitches.

Maya nodded, as though she knew about wings or frescoes.

When they finally reached the suite of rooms she had been allocated it was clear that she was not expected to slum it. She was given the tour of the additional nursery first, which was decorated in lemon and blue and was utterly charming, as was the well-equipped mini kitchen stocked with enough baby formula to feed ten babies.

'It's all wired for sound,' the housekeeper explained as she led her through to her own private sitting room, which was palatial in size and charmingly furnished with antique furniture, but nothing heavy or dark.

The bedroom, with its balcony, was dreamy with a four-poster and the same delightful feminine furniture, but it was her bathroom that stopped her in her tracks. Massive enough to dwarf the double-ended copper tub built for sharing, it boasted a stone fireplace complete with a wood burner, and a walk-in shower that had more touch buttons than a space module and a shower head the size of two dinner plates!

Setting Mattio's seat down on the marble floor, she sniffed a couple of the oils in the crystal flagons set along the matching marble shelf and turned on a tap in one of the twin sinks.

She could, she decided, picking up a fluffy towel from the top of one of the stacks, quite happily just live in here.

In the meantime, it was time to check out the kitchen for Mattio's feed.

'So, kiddo, what do you think of your place...not bad, hey?'

CHAPTER SIX

The knock on the door pulled Maya away from the mirror. Did people actually dress for dinner outside movies and royal palaces? Where did castles fit into the scheme of things? Maya did have some experience of palaces and, though her sister had instigated a more casual approach since she'd taken up residence, when it came to family dinners at least, her life still involved a number of tiara occasions.

Luckily here Maya was not the hostess, family or a guest, in any proper sense of the word, so it was just as well she didn't possess a tiara or even a formal dress, at least not one she'd packed. She was normally a meticulous minimal packer and had not adapted well to the 'throw everything into a case in five minutes flat' approach.

But you worked with what you had, and her choice tonight had been between a good pair of jeans—aubergine velvet—an orange minidress she had worn once for a christening and a mid-length silk slip dress in a jewel-bright turquoise that could be dressed up or down.

The lack of jewellery to accessorise equated with dress-down, but the spiky-heeled ankle boots in a leopard print, which had involved the death of no leopards or, for that matter, any animals whatsoever, were definitely dress-up. They also made her appear quite tall, which although an illusion still felt quite nice.

She had worried when she'd first paraded in front of the massive ormolu framed mirror. True, the high neck of her dress revealed her collarbones, but nothing else. It was only when she turned around that you got the *wow* factor or, depending on your viewpoint, the *too much* factor. The back of the dress dipped dramatically almost to her waist and, while she *normally* didn't flinch from being slightly in your face clotheswise, tonight she had to admit to having some doubts.

Twisting around to look at her rear view, she frowned, then caught herself thinking, *What am I doing?*

Self-doubt was something she had left far behind her, and it had not been easy to do. She was no longer that person, the one who had felt as if she were fading into the background. It was no figure of speech—there had a point in her adolescence when she had *literally* felt almost invisible, thanks to evil Edward. Rediscovering her love of colour had been a visible reflection of how she felt inside—and how well she'd recovered from the abuse he'd heaped on her.

But there was bold and then there was all that flesh... She solved this problem by leaving her hair loose so her exposed shoulder blades and all but the lowest section of the small of her back, just before the dip to her waist, were concealed beneath a curtain of curls ruthlessly tamed—with her hair there was no other way— by the brilliant product she had dragged through it with her fingers.

She took a deep breath, and pasted on a smile. She *could* do this, she'd just think of it as having a solo takeaway in front of the telly, except of course it wasn't either. It was the solo thing that bothered her most, which was insane. This categorically *wasn't* a dinner date, or for that matter any sort of date at all!

The woman on the other side of the door was young, more a girl, really, and was wearing the sort of informal uniform adopted by most staff that involved a white shirt and dark trousers.

Maya struggled to keep her smile in place as the girl's eyes widened in shock, doing a face-to-floor-and-back-again sweep. Her response was not *quite* a jaw-drop, but it came very close.

'Hello,' Maya said.

At the gentle prompt she flushed and rushed out, 'I am Rosa and I am here to sit with the little one.'

'Of course.' Maya stood back to allow the girl to enter the room. 'He's asleep.' She paused; it seemed ironic, considering the number of times she had been asked for ID to confirm her age, but this girl did look *very* young. 'Are you sure...?'

Rosa seemed to correctly interpret the hesitation to hand over the care of the baby that Maya didn't totally understand herself.

'After school I worked in a pre-school nursery for a year. I begin my pre-nurse training at the university next month and I'm the eldest of seven.'

Which makes her much better qualified than me to take care of a baby, Maya mused wryly.

'Wow, that's, well... I've made a few notes for you if he wakes up.' She handed over the sheets she had jotted down some notes on.

'Thank you. Would you like me perhaps to get someone to show you down to the dining room...?'

It was an offer that Maya would have definitely appreciated had she not decided during the last ten seconds not to go down to the dining room at all.

'Actually, no, would it be possible for me to have a sandwich here?'

The girl looked confused.

'I'm feeling just a little tired and not so very hungry after all, so a sandwich in my room…that would be just fine.'

The girl tipped her head in compliance, very obviously struggling to hide the fact that she thought Maya was insane as she backed out of the room.

When the door closed, some of the tension left Maya's shoulders. She was, she told herself, totally comfortable with her choice.

It was important for her to believe it was a decision that had nothing to do with backing away from a challenge. It had been one of the things she had promised herself that she would never do once she had rebuilt her confidence one painful brick at a time after her stepfather had destroyed it with his insidious campaign—a person got told they were worth nothing on a daily basis and eventually they began to believe it.

She told herself that she had recovered fully from what had happened, but the questions Samuele had asked about her business hopes had shaken loose some uncomfortable possibilities she had been unconsciously avoiding. She did not regret refusing Beatrice and Dante's offers of assistance, but there were alternatives she could have taken. There were business loans available for new start-ups; she had done all the research into them, but at the last minute she had always backed away, telling herself that she didn't want to start out weighed down with debt. But she could see now the truth was that she was scared. Somewhere in the back of her mind she could still hear her stepfather telling her she was hopeless, useless.

It wasn't about pride or practicality; she was just scared, even if she hid it well.

And tonight? The strong reluctance to leave Mattio was totally genuine, and it had taken her by surprise, but wasn't there an element of her using it as an excuse not to spend the next couple of hours with Samuele?

In her defence, even if there was, she couldn't really be blamed; being around him was very exhausting because she couldn't lower her guard. She wasn't quite sure what she was guarding against, but she knew it was essential that she do so.

There were times when she decided to be brave and this wasn't one of them. Despite being more relaxed now she had made a decision—admittedly her jaw was still aching, but her teeth had unclenched—the static buzz of panic in her head had not gone away but it was less deafening.

Samuele would probably be relieved by her no-show. If he hadn't actually said that small talk wasn't really his thing, she felt it was a safe assumption to make, and she wasn't here to socialise anyway so starting as she meant to go on seemed a logical choice. In retrospect the entire 'what am I going to wear?', 'do I look good in this?', butterflies-in-the-stomach fizz of mingled excitement and anxiety was rather embarrassing, more suited to a date than what this was.

What was this?

She quickly gave up on finding a definition. It was far easier to say what it was not, and that was a date in any sense of the word.

She was just hoping that they were generous with the sandwiches because she had lied to Rosa—she was starving.

She wasn't really sure how long she'd been standing there lost in thought, but when the polite knock on the door came she still hadn't got around to kicking off her heels. Opening it wide ready to receive the tray—probably silver—she felt her smile fade and her hand drop to her side as she found herself facing not someone bearing a tray, but someone pushing a trolley, and another someone swiftly bringing up the rear.

'Oh, that is...' She gave a shrug, thinking it might not be a bad thing that there was wine when she spotted the cooler. She wasn't really much of a drinker but something to take some of the tension out of her shoulders would be good. 'Lovely,' she tacked on, stepping back to let them enter. It was easier than arguing and she wasn't about to send back good food when she was this hungry!

Hovering to helpfully close the door behind the waiters, who had their hands full, she found herself being pushed backwards as the door opened even wider to admit a tall figure. Her heart jolted.

Oh, dear, this wasn't going as planned!

Samuele had chosen to dress down but in a 'not as we know it' way, in black jeans that clung to his narrow hips and a pale blue linen shirt. Only a strong sense of self-preservation stopped her giving a little whimper of appreciation. It was the artist in her, she told herself. *The woman in her,* countered the voice in her head.

Samuele paused, registering her presence—how could a man not?—but resisting the very strong impulse to turn and stare. He conversed casually with the two staff members, delaying the moment just to prove to himself that he could. He was attracted to her, absolutely, but nothing had essentially changed; he was in perfect control of himself.

* * *

Maya was playing catch-up. Caught off guard by the sudden turn of events, her brain had lagged behind. The door was still open and she caught herself actually considering in a half-hearted joking way if anyone would notice if she just slipped away.

Man up, Maya, she told herself sternly. *You're the one who always says face your fears*—but her internal pep talk came to an abrupt halt when she realised she didn't want to know what she was afraid of.

Her eyes went to where Samuele stood looking impossibly handsome. He was smiling in response to something one of the waiters was saying, responding a moment later with a comment that made them both laugh. The informality she had noted since they'd arrived continued to surprise her; she had assumed that he'd be a remote authoritarian employer who demanded deference.

But then he didn't have anything to prove, did he? He had already their respect, so he didn't have to *demand* deference, it was just there. Watching the exchange made her think of the times when her stepfather would get huffy when people didn't use his full academic title.

She could remember squirming with embarrassment when he would speak over someone with a corrective *Professor* Edward Tyler.

In the time it took for her thoughts to slide through her head the small table beneath the window had been covered in a pristine white creaseless cloth, the finishing touches of crystal wine glasses and silver cutlery laid with geometric precision.

All impressive, but she barely noticed the crystal or silver; the thing that was registering with Maya was the fact they had laid two places. On one level she was aware that the light-headed fizz of excitement she was feeling at the thought of dining alone with Samuele in her suite was not an appropriate response.

She planted a hand against her throat, feeling the frantic pulse leap and twirl, and wondered if this was what a panic attack felt like, soothing herself with the reflection that even if it was it wasn't fatal—at least she didn't think so...

He turned, acknowledging her presence for the first time as the door closed behind his staff. 'I said we'd serve ourselves.' He offered the translation even though during her ridiculous panicking she had barely registered they were talking Italian.

'This is all...' she paused, clearing her throat as he reached for the bottle in the ice bucket. Popping the cork with a practised twist, he raised an interrogative brow and she hastily added faux-calmly, 'Very kind of you, but it's totally not... It isn't necessary.' She tried channelling a cool she was a million miles from feeling. 'I would have been fine with a sandwich,' she said, allowing her eyes to touch his but not making the mistake of maintaining eye contact.

'What? And leave you all dressed up and nowhere to go?'

He smiled slowly, and his eyes, as they swept up her body from her toes to her head, left a tingling trail of heat across her skin. 'You look lovely.'

She pulled in a tense breath and smiled nervously. 'I feel a bit overdressed.' *That* embarrassment she could shrug off; less easy was coping with the suffocating thud of her heartbeat, and the tingling sensation under her skin, as though a million butterflies were beating madly to get out.

Samuele was pretty sure he could have dealt with her

overdressed problem in no time at all, but that would be playing with fire, so he closed down the visuals that went with the thought.

And you're not playing with fire already?

He closed down the inner voice too and dragged out a chair for her. He watched her hesitate before moving forward gracefully on those crazy heels, her slim thighs pushing against the silky jewel-bright fabric with each stride, forcing his pulse rate even higher. She looked sleek, sexy and exotic with her dark hair streaming like a glossy cloud down her back, just allowing him a peek of her naked lower back. The painful effort of not allowing the desire he felt to show on his face sent a trickle of sweat down his back.

What the hell are you doing here, Sam?

If his life was a roadmap, he felt that right at this moment he was standing at a crossroads. There were two paths ahead. He could see them perfectly clearly: one led to a businesslike short-term arrangement involving looking after Mattio for a few weeks, the other led straight to the bedroom.

One involved the short-term pain of self-denial, the other led to short-term, incredible pleasure... Ironically it was the degree of desire he felt to pursue the second option that made him hesitate. He'd already accepted that Maya was not the same as any other woman he had ever met.

Or was it just his own reactions to her that were different?

It wasn't just the utterly ridiculous level of attraction he was experiencing, it was *her*... *She* was different. When she was around he could not rely on the neat compartments that made his life run smoothly; nothing was contained.

He was so, so tempted to ignore the red warning signs in his head. If alcoholism ran in his family, he would have avoided alcohol; with his particular family history there were certain situations and women he avoided...and he certainly didn't need distractions in his life at the moment, as he focused on putting the last few pieces of the Agnosti estate back together. True, his work ethic had never stopped him having sex before, the difference being—he knew full well—that he had never had sex that touched his emotions.

And she already had, without them even kissing properly...but the admission came reluctantly. It had to be the same reason it had been almost *too* easy for him to open up and tell her such intimate, long-held secrets.

He was confident he *could* stay in control and have her at the same time, he would not admit to a weakness that suggested otherwise, but he didn't want to look at a woman when he left her, and see the shadows under her eyes and worry.

Who was he kidding? She had long-term relationship written all over her beautiful face! She would need things he didn't have to give because he had chosen his path in life. Loneliness was an infinitely preferable option to living his life being manipulated—and humiliated—by the woman he loved.

'I didn't expect this.' Maya paused, trying not to breathe in the clean masculine scent of him as she felt the warmth of his breath on her cheek. 'I just didn't want to be too far away from Mattio the first night we were here.' It was at least part of the truth; actually, it continued to amaze her every time she realised how deep the baby had burrowed his way into her heart so quickly.

Logic told her that it would be foolish to grow too

fond of Mattio when very soon she would be walking away from him.

He wouldn't remember her, he was only a baby, but that didn't matter; she would still feel guilty when she left him, and she would always remember him.

Sadness filtered into her dark eyes as they lifted just as Samuele extended the wine bottle towards her glass. Unfortunately logic did not really play a part when it came to genuine emotions.

'No...yes,' she stuttered, struggling to keep the sudden rush of desperation from her voice as she removed her hand from the top of the crystal glass and pressed it close to her chest instead to hide the fact it was shaking; *she* was shaking.

Anyone would think you'd just made some sort of profound discovery, she mocked herself. *But you just fancy the man—it's hardly a shocking newsflash.*

Having never before felt a physical attraction this strong to any man, she could now see how some people mistook lust for something much more profound. But it was not a mistake she was about to make.

'Sorry to invade your space.' He looked around the room. 'Are you happy with your suite?'

'Absolutely.'

'And apologies again for the candles.' He cast an amused glance towards the lights flickering in the candelabra and gave a light laugh. 'I think my request to have dinner here with you was misinterpreted.'

Maya gave a laugh that she hoped sent the message that she had not for one moment misunderstood what this was. Absolutely *not* a date.

'I was thinking that dinner might be a good time to debrief one another each evening—would that work for you? Though obviously, should a problem arise re

Mattio, I am available at any time. His well-being is my top priority.'

It was utterly irrational, given the circumstances, to feel chagrin. 'Of course, it is, and I have to eat,' she said, discovering her appetite had pretty much vanished despite the mouth-watering smells wafting towards her. 'So here's to the evening version of a working break-fast,' she said, raising the glass to her lips and taking a large mouthful.

She regretted now not taking the option of eating in more formal surroundings, not that the private lavish sitting room was exactly an intimate space. It was the company not the location that was the problem, she re-alised gloomily.

'My reputation would not survive if you leave here a shadow of your former self.'

'It all looks delicious,' she said brightly. 'But I'm afraid that there isn't much to report as yet. Mattio took his feed and he settled into his nursery pretty well. Do you want me to sleep in his room?' She had noticed the divan in the corner of the nursery.

No, I want you to sleep in my room. 'Of course not!' he snapped.

'Fine, I was only wondering—'

She stopped as his phone began to shrill, a look of annoyance crossing his face. 'Sorry, I meant to turn it off.'

'No problem.'

He glanced at the screen and grimaced. 'I have to take this.'

She shrugged and nodded.

His English was so syllable perfect, his accent barely there, that she had almost forgotten that it wasn't his first language. So when after listening for a few moments he launched into a heated diatribe in his native tongue she was jolted back to the reality of the situation.

Which was that he was Italian to his fingertips. Yes, he probably could make a shopping list sound sexy, but his sudden urgent passion as he spoke was utterly transfixing...in a stomach-quivering sort of way.

A few moments later he slid the phone back into his pocket and, with a face like thunder, hammered out staccato fast what was presumably a shortened version of the conversation. In Italian.

She waited until he had finished, or at least paused to draw breath, to remind him quietly, 'You know I didn't understand a word you just said?'

He swore then in several languages and dragged a hand through his hair, ruffling the dark strands into toe-curlingly sexy spikes.

'Sorry, it's just that there are problems with one of our tenants. By the time my father died the place had been starved of resources for years, not to mention that there were entire areas where the trees had been razed... Ancient woodland raped for a quick profit.' The disgust in his voice was also etched in the bleak lines of his face, and his jaw was clenched so tight she could almost hear it grinding.

'Nothing replanted, land over-fertilised and the village was depopulated. There was nothing left for young people any more. A small investment meant ecotourism produced some almost immediate profit, but it's a long-term game. We'll start to see the benefits of the green approach soon, and in two years we might start to see some profit. Most of the tenants are on board with the plans but...' His expression darkened. 'There is a tenant who is not on board, for reasons I don't quite understand. He's not one of the old school, he is young and ambitious—exactly the sort of person I thought would be behind us.'

'But he isn't.'

'No, he isn't. There's an area of marshland which is important ecologically, as it's home to...' He paused and looked at her, suddenly seeming to remember who he was talking to. 'I'm so sorry, this must be boring you.'

'No, it isn't.' She was fascinated by this evidence of his connection to the land. 'It sounds like a difficult situation.'

'You could say that. I have been informed that some heavy machinery has arrived and his intention is to drain fifty acres of the marshland and put cattle on to graze. Apparently the concrete foundations for a barn arrives in the morning. Everything I'm working for will be destroyed for a quick profit. I have to go.' He got to his feet. 'I must stop this.'

Maya laid down her napkin and got to her feet and walked with him to the door. 'Well, goodnight.' She held out her hand. 'And good luck.'

He angled a sardonic dark brow. 'I'll probably need it—' The lights suddenly dimmed and went out completely, leaving the flickering candles as the only illumination in the room, highlighting the angles and planes of his face. 'Does this remind you of anything?' he murmured huskily.

Mesmerised by his dark stare, she nodded. 'The airport hotel. I wondered...'

'What did you wonder, *cara*?'

The words, uttered in a low gravelled tone, were almost like a physical caress. She swallowed. 'Did you kiss me?' she whispered.

He shook his head. In the semi-light his teeth were very white as he produced a slow smile, even while his eyes stayed dark and intent. Maya was too mortified to notice. Why, oh, why had she aired her fantasies out loud? Of course, he hadn't kissed her!

'No,' he confirmed. 'That was not a kiss.'

'Oh…?' she said, glad of the shadows to hide her embarrassed blushes.

He moved in a step and looked down into her face, murmuring something in Italian under his breath as his hand went behind her head. 'But this *is* a kiss.'

In the private theatre of Maya's thoughts and dreams he had already kissed her a thousand times, but this was different; it was so much better, it was *real*. Her initial pliant shock as she melted bonelessly into his arms suddenly gave way to a hunger that matched his own. One muscular arm banding her ribs, he lifted her feet off the floor as the kiss became more combative, more urgent.

Maya focused on not sliding to the floor as he placed her back on her feet and took a step back. She stared straight ahead, her eyes level with the middle of his heaving chest.

Yes, she had imagined what a kiss from him would be like, but it was nothing at all like that. She gave a wild little laugh. 'Yes, that was definitely a kiss. Oh, God!'

'Exactly.' His chest lifted in one last soundless jagged sigh before he turned and walked away with the sweet taste of Maya in his mouth.

CHAPTER SEVEN

She tensed at the tentative tap on the door, but only slightly. She didn't associate Samuele with tentative, so it was unlikely to be him. She had thought this morning might be awkward after their kiss, actually she had thought of spending the day in her bathroom, but it wasn't, because he didn't put in an appearance, and she ate her breakfast alone.

It had been a solitary sort of day. Maya had spent most of it in the nursery suite, although she had walked around a section of garden with Mattio in a pushchair, longingly eyeing up the extensive parkland and the oak woods beyond. She knew they were oak trees because she'd asked a gardener who was working outside. Their conversation had involved a lot of hand gestures, his English being only slightly better than her Italian, but she thought he'd understood her when she'd said she'd like to walk in the woods. There had been a moment when the communication had broken down and he had been particularly emphatic, saying *cinghiale*, and getting quite agitated, repeating it until in the end she'd nodded simply to soothe him.

Her visitor was Rosa, who would have been the babysitter of choice last night. Her English was excellent and Maya would have quite enjoyed a chat, but the girl was here to relieve her from baby duties. It was not presented as an option and the instructions had come directly from Samuele.

'Rafael will show you to the leisure suite. Do you swim?' Rosa asked.

'I don't have a costume.'

The girl gave a little giggle. 'There will be no one else there, but of course there are costumes available for when there are...guests, you understand.'

Maya did understand, of course she did, and she was instantly determined not to wear a swimsuit that had previously been worn by one of Samuele's female *guests*.

'You are not like them. I mean...'

Maya took pity on her confusion. 'I wouldn't mind an hour or so's break,' she admitted. 'But Mattio hasn't had a nap yet or—'

The girl dropped down beside the chair where the baby kicked his legs and continued to chew on a teething ring. 'Me and the bambino will be fine, you go, or I will be in trouble.'

Maya nodded and Rosa beamed. 'Shall I call Rafael?'

'No, it's fine, I'll find my own way.'

The girl looked doubtful. 'It is in the below part of the castello, in the cellar. There are lifts, which are quite well hidden.'

'I'll be fine,' Maya promised.

Had she actually intended to take advantage of the pool she would have accepted the services of a guide. The castello was a warren of rooms and corridors and even making her way to the dining room for breakfast she had got turned around twice, but she intended to head outside to explore the oak woods and maybe even the vineyards beyond.

As she made her way through the parkland heading towards the wooded area she saw the elderly gardener in the distance and waved cheerily at him as he waved back enthusiastically.

It was good to be outside. She might have escaped the luxury of the castello, but the thoughts in her head were less easy to escape. She speeded up, ignoring the jeering voice in her head that was playing on a loop... *You can run but you can't hide.*

She didn't slow until she reached the trees. To her relief there was a definite pathway and she felt confident that she wouldn't get lost. The confidence began to ebb as the trees got denser and began to close in on her, but the path was still clear even though it was darker here, so she pushed on, breathing in the pungent scent of warm earth underfoot. Several times she imagined she heard rustling, and once a flicker of movement in the periphery of her vision but, peering through the branches, she saw nothing.

She was actually on the point of turning back when the trees began to thin and the path opened up into a small clearing. She let out a small cry of delight, and had crouched down to examine the tiny flowers that carpeted the floor when she heard a snap of twigs and a snuffling sound.

She froze, this time knowing it was definitely not her imagination. She wasn't alone.

'Is somebody there?' *What are you going to do if someone says yes?* that voice jeered again.

Run!

She huffed out a laugh of sheer relief when out of the undergrowth a little pig appeared, furry and ginger with stripes down its back. Utterly charmed, she rose to her feet and approached it slowly so as not to frighten it.

'Hello there, little one, are you lost? Ooh, hello there as well,' she added, moving forward, her hand outstretched as three more of the cute creatures appeared, making little whining noises.

She reached into her pocket to find her phone, as she had to have a photo of these, when a loud grunting and squealing behind her made her jump. She almost dropped the phone as she spun around expecting to see more piglets.

She froze. This was not a cute creature, though it might once have been. She knew she was looking at the adult version, and a prickle of fear made the hairs on the nape of her neck stand on end. The tiny eyes gave it a mean look as it stared at her past its long, hard snout, and the piglets started squealing even louder. The parent—mother?—started forward, letting out another angry snorting noise.

Samuele was petrified. 'Do not run, Maya,' he said as quietly as he could, struggling with the image in his head of her being run down within seconds.

Maya was frozen to the spot.

'I can't.'

'Oh, *cara*, you can,' he insisted softly, cold sweat slicking his skin as he watched her poised like a gazelle about to run. 'Now, don't make any sudden noise but start to back away from her very slowly.'

She began to turn her head to look at him. 'No!' His voice dropped back to a low, soft, soothing monotone as he emphasised, 'Do not turn around or look at me, just keep moving backwards, perfect, perfect…very slowly…'

She clung to his voice like a lifeline, each calm yet emphatic syllable stopping her succumbing to total panic.

'Samuele…'

'You will be fine, I promise. I won't let anything happen to you, but be careful and do *not* fall over.' He had seen the damage a female wild boar could do in defence of her young; she might lack the tusks of the male, but she was fast and those teeth could inflict some wicked wounds. The idea of them tearing into Maya's flesh filled him with a fear that was visceral in its intensity.

One of the piglets rushed towards Maya and he clenched his teeth against a groan as the mother's angry squeals intensified—she was going to charge.

Without taking his eyes from the animal he reached down for the fallen branch his boot was balanced on.

'Maya.'

She was shaking, her chalk-white pale face dotted with beads of cold sweat. Being paralyzed with fear had taken on an entirely new meaning.

'Can you hear me?'

'Yes,' she whispered.

'You are going to do what I tell you, when I tell you and not before…do you understand?'

She nodded. 'Yes.'

'Good girl. There is a track behind you and to the left—it goes uphill. I want you to run, but not until I say. Run and don't look back, don't stop until you reach the observatory.'

'*The what?*'

'You will know when you're there.'

'What about you?'

'I will be fine if you do what I ask you to.' The rustle as he tightened his hand over the branch turned the boar's mean red eyes his way, and she began to move away from Maya. 'That's it, come over here, Mama Boar. Now get ready, Maya.' He lifted the branch and banged the ground, yelling like a banshee, the infuriated animal charged and he shouted, 'Now, Maya! Run, *cara*, run!' He waited just long enough to see that she had taken off before he hit the ground running, still yelling as he did so.

There was no way he could outrun an enraged boar who, despite her bulk, could really move, and he knew that his only chance was getting high enough up…once he was sure that Maya was far enough away from those teeth.

Maya ran, her heart pumping, self-preservation giving her feet wings as she ran, instinct rather than a recollection of his instructions putting her on the right path. Panting tears sliding down her cheeks, she ran on uphill, stumbling over roots but knowing that she could not fall… She barely noticed when a stray overhanging branch delivered a glancing blow to her cheek. More tears blurred her vision as she refused to look back— *don't look back, and don't fall.*

Her lungs felt as though they would burst when the trees cleared quite abruptly and she saw her goal. The small, square stone building with the domed roof of glass was an incongruous sight, but she wasn't asking why it was there. She was only focused on the sanctuary offered by the metal-banded doors, thinking… *Not locked, please, not locked!*

It wasn't.

One side of the double doors opened without any effort on her part as she slipped inside the sanctuary and closed it fast behind her. She leaned against it, eyes closed and shaking with reaction, her laboured breathing gradually slowing.

Oh, God… Samuele!

Her eyes flew wide and she turned and pushed the

doors she had just closed open again. She was sobbing again, loudly, but she didn't hear as she was seeing him banging the ground with his stick, deliberately drawing the vicious animal to him... She had left him, deserted him, *abandoned* him; she was *that* person, the person she despised.

If he was harmed she would never forgive herself.

Self-disgust settled over her like a black cloud as she waited, her eyes trained on the woods, alert to any sign of sound or movement. If he was hurt or worse it was on her.

He could be lying out there slashed and bleeding, needing help. She became so convinced by the lurid images in her head that she had just made the decision to go out and find him when he appeared.

She didn't immediately see him, just a movement in the periphery of her vision. She had been willing him to appear, but he came from a totally different direction.

The relief was so intense she thought she was going to faint, then she realised the faintness was probably associated with the fact she was hyperventilating.

Consciously slowing her breathing, she took a step towards him.

'You're not dead!' Even as she spoke it crossed her mind that she had never seen anyone look more alive. His eyes were burning bright, the glitter in them almost incandescent, though one leg of his trousers was ripped from the ankle almost to the thigh, revealing olive-tanned hair-roughened skin and long slabs of muscle.

There were scratches on his face, some oozing blood, but he looked totally relaxed as he drew level with her and he wasn't even breathing hard. It struck her that he looked more dangerous than the boar.

A danger that anyone with a pinch of sense would

run away from, but his hands lay heavy on her shoulders and she couldn't have run even if she had wanted to, which she didn't.

'Dead?' He laughed and shook his head. 'The cinghiale rarely kill but they can cause some serious damage and ugly scars. Some hunters say boars are more dangerous than bears, though we don't have any of those here.' His white grin appeared. 'Just wolves.'

He was giving her a natural history lesson! She had been half out of her mind and he was telling her it wasn't so very bad...cinghiale...why was that Italian word ringing bells?

Sam's eyes moved swiftly across her face, noting the bruise developing on her cheek, his jaw quivering as he felt a twisting sensation in his chest, a tenderness that he was reluctant to name.

'You did good,' he said roughly, releasing her.

'I did,' she agreed breathlessly.

Her eyes widened, and she stood there visibly trembling as he reached out again. She stayed statue-still, her eyes connected with his, swaying slightly as his fingers pushed into her hair, lightly grazing her scalp.

He felt her shiver and watched the pupils of her eyes dilate, the longing in her eyes... It was hard to not see danger when it was literally staring you in the face.

It was just seeing her here safe and sound, the relief, the elation after the not knowing, the nightmare scenarios that had been going through his head while, Madre di Dios, he'd been trapped up a tree until that damned boar had finally given up the hunt.

They were all good reasons for the way he was feeling but not excuses... Control...he needed control.

'Got it! Did you leave any forest out there?' he asked,

opening his hand to reveal the twig he'd gently pulled out of her hair before he dropped it and ground it underfoot, his eyelashes lowering to hide the burning desire in his eyes.

The anticlimax was as shocking as a slap, and the subsequent mood change as dramatic as it was intense. She wanted to cry again, and she could actually feel the tears pressing at the backs of her eyes. You're in shock, she told herself, glad to put a name to the roller coaster of emotions and her heightened mood.

'You found it, then.'

He was looking past her, and she turned her head, not even pretending an interest as her glance moved through the open doors of the observatory to the interior. She was seeing the cedar-lined walls within for the first time, hung round with bookcases and with a sumptuous day bed just to the right of the spiral staircase. From where they stood, she could see just make out the glass dome above the telescope set in a mezzanine observation platform.

'My grandfather was a stargazer. Actually, he was quite a well-respected amateur astronomer, so he restored the observatory and—'

'You enjoyed it, didn't you?' Maya interrupted ruthlessly. She could feel the emotions building up inside her, feel the pounding in her temples like a hammer hitting a crumbling wall…each thud destroying more of the mortar and her self-control.

He recognised the antagonism shining in her eyes, but he didn't really understand it. He hadn't exactly enjoyed the heart-pumping run here, seeing as every step had been burdened by the *not knowing*, the fear eating away at him that she might have been hurt. Every second he'd had to spend up that damn tree not knowing if she was all right had felt like a century, so when he'd seen her standing there unharmed it had felt like... He actually had nothing to compare the feeling to, it was way more complex than anything he could imagine, but perhaps akin to the sheer elation you felt when you emerged from the icy water after wild swimming.

'Well, it's always good to get the better of a boar,' he responded calmly, sticking to facts, not feelings. 'The thing to remember is you can't outrun them, so don't try. Your best bet is to climb a tree. I did,' he admitted, working on the theory that while he was talking he couldn't be kissing her, and he wanted to, he really wanted to... He needed to taste her, and the greedy need was hampering his ability to frame coherent sentences. 'They are incredibly destructive beasts. They cause total havoc. Last year they took over a thousand gallons of grapes and it's virtually impossible to keep them out. We put down miles of electric fences around the vineyards but they just jump them, and I'd take the tusks of a male over the protective instincts of a female any day.'

'You think I want a natural history lesson?'

He bent in, struggling to catch her quiet words, but a second later he was leaning back out again, because he had no problem hearing the next thing she said— they probably heard her in the village five miles away.

'You were enjoying yourself beating the piglets in some macho game while I,' she shouted, stabbing a straight finger hard into his chest, 'I,' she repeated with another stab into his muscular chest, 'I thought you were dead!' she shrieked. 'And it was my fault.'

The fight left her without warning; her legs sagged and she would have slid to the floor had the arm wrapped around her ribs not taken the weight. She looked up at him through the overflow of luminous tears that started to seep out from the corners of her eyes.

'You're crying…' Samuele really didn't know how to deal with the protective surge he felt as he watched the tears silently slide down her cheeks.

'No, I'm not,' she denied fiercely, as though he had insulted her by caring.

Fine, he thought, adopting a heart-of-stone expression, although it was incredibly hard when she looked so fragile…so sexy. 'You're in shock.'

Maya wanted to lash back and tell him he had no idea what she was feeling, only neither did she.

The beginnings of a bewildered frown froze in place as he reached out and cupped her face, his fingers cool on her skin. His expression was fierce his concentration total as he followed the path of his thumb as he slid it across the red mark that stood out against the smooth skin of her cheek.

'Sorry,' he said, clearly misinterpreting her shiver. 'You were very stupid—'

She could not in all honesty deny this.

'And very, very brave…' He brought his face in close, his nose grazing hers, his breath warm on her cheek. 'You are driving me totally crazy, you know,' he rasped, ignoring the voice in his head that told him he was finally losing control of the situation, losing control of himself.

Why bother fighting? said that wicked voice of temptation in his head. *Just relax, enjoy it while you can…*

His face was so close Maya couldn't focus, so she closed her eyes and felt his lips against her eyelids.

'Look at me!'

She responded to the fierce command at the same moment he settled his mouth on hers, the sensuous pressure drawing a whimper from her throat, then, when his tongue slid across the outline of her lips, she grabbed hold of his shirt in handfuls just to stop from sliding to the ground. His lips were cool but she could feel the primal heat coming off him in waves, smell the musky scent of arousal.

Shocked by the fist of need in her belly and the surge of desire that was tangled in with a mess of emotions, she reached up instinctively, her arms curling around his neck, pulling him down to her while arching upwards, wanting...wanting more... Reacting with a fierce little gasp of shock to the very explicit proof of his arousal as she felt the imprint of his erection grinding into her belly.

She was plastered against him, but then with no warning at all the sensual connection was broken and the heat was gone as he physically put her away from him, the only warmth his big hands that still spanned her waist.

'You understand that this is just sex, right, Maya?' He'd never slept with a woman where the warning had been needed, because they'd always understood the game; he'd never needed to hear the words to give himself permission to continue, either. It was just sex, he reiterated to himself, panic bolting through him as he imagined her saying no to his question, because she wanted more from him. Because he couldn't give her more.

The more she totally deserves, taunted the voice of guilt pricking at his conscience.

His eyes were dark and smoky, his skin when she placed a hand flat on his chest was hot too... This was not a rejection, she understood that; it was just him laying out the rules before they started.

As she had never had sex before, she doubted she would notice the difference between that and…anything more. *Just sex,* he'd called it. But it wasn't as though she'd asked him for more, was it?

Not as if she deserved more!

Not as if she deserved love.

No wonder your biological mother rejected you…

'What is it?' he asked, watching the expressions flicker across her lovely face and feeling a rush of protective emotion that was so intense he felt as though someone had reached inside his chest and squeezed his heart.

She shook her head and smiled, feeling suddenly liberated. She would *not* allow Edward to spoil this moment or any other moment for her. She was not a child any longer with no self-esteem and Samuele was not trying to diminish her, he was only being honest.

'I was just remembering something someone used to say to me.'

Her stepfather had been so clever at locating a weak spot and exploiting it. He'd clawed at the one tiny shadow inside her heart that still grieved because she'd been abandoned by her own mother, and by the time he'd finished with her, she had carried an echo of that fear into adulthood. It had prevented her having any intimate relationships because she was afraid of being rejected, for being made to feel like that little girl who didn't deserve love.

'I will make you forget him, *cara.*'

She smiled. 'I've already forgotten. I want you, Samuele, you are exactly what I need right now.'

A low growl was released from his throat as the last shreds of control he had placed himself under snapped.

It felt as though she were being swept away by a

fast-flowing river as his mouth came crashing down on hers; his grip on her waist tightened as he lifted her up against his tense, hard length. Not thinking through her actions, because she was deep in instinct territory now, she wound her arms around his neck, sinking her fingers into the hair on his nape and kissing him back hard as her legs wrapped tightly around his waist to hold herself there.

He broke off the kiss long enough to give a fierce grin as he slid his hands beneath her bottom and they stumbled the few steps to the stone building.

On the receiving end of Samuele's deep, drugging, sense-shredding kisses, she barely registered him kicking the door closed behind them, but she knew that they were alone and common sense, along with the rest of the world, was locked outside.

Samuele pushed aside all the plump scatter cushions on the day bed with one sweep of his hand. He sat down on the upholstered edge and Maya, with her legs still around his waist, landed sitting on his lap.

Her head had slid to his shoulder and he hooked a thumb beneath her chin and tilted her face up to his. He could see that her eyes were big and unfocused, the velvety pansy-brown glazed with passion.

With an almost feral groan he kissed her hard, lowering her back onto the day bed, which was wide enough to accommodate them both side by side, but he fell on top of her, a knee braced either side of her body. He pulled himself up just far enough to free his shirt from his jeans and fumbled with the belt. Clenching his teeth with frustration at the delay, he tore at the buttons on his shirt, before tugging at his zip, giving only partial relief from the painful constriction.

Maya placed her hand flat against the ridges of his

belly. Simultaneously shocked and excited by the hardness and heat of his skin, she grabbed the loose ends of his belt and tugged. He resisted, drawing a cry of protest from her aching throat that faded into a whimper as he took the edges of the long-sleeved T-shirt she wore and pulled it over her head.

She didn't have the strength or the will to move her hands, so they still lay splayed above her head in an attitude of submission. Her breath, coming as a series of uneven shallow gasps, snagged on a moan as he slid the straps of her bra over her shoulders, massaging and kissing the skin stretched across the angle of her collarbones before he traced a moist path down the valley between her breasts with his tongue.

He lifted himself off her just enough to fight his way clear of his shirt, and she came up on her knees to help him, kissing his chest as it was revealed, tasting the salt in his sweat as she slid her hands over his golden skin.

Her bra of tartan satin followed his abandoned shirt, sailing somewhere over her head as he threw it away.

'*Dio!*'

The peaks of her breasts hardened and tingled under his scrutiny. She arched at the first touch of his hand and fell back onto the day bed, gasping, at this, their first intimate, skin-to-skin contact. She twisted and squirmed against him as her small hands went to the half-open zip of his jeans. She struggled with it until he rolled away and, lifting his hips off the bed, peeled the jeans off along with his boxers. He snatched his wallet from his jeans pocket, before kicking his clothes away until they fell with a thud and clatter on the other side of the room.

Maya swung her legs over the side of the bed and unfastened her cotton pedal pushers. She stood up for a moment to pull them down over her hips and step out of them.

Turning, she reached up to find Samuele's hands curling around her upper arms, knowing as he found his eyes on her, devouring the abandoned look of her, that it was an image that would stay with him for ever. Her skin was like silk, her body as beautiful as her face, and he knew she was a perfect fit for him.

She *was* perfect and utterly oblivious to the fact, too. There was nothing feigned about her natural sensuality that made her every move provoking and exciting to Samuele.

She made him feel utterly insatiable… He drew her to him, greedy to touch her everywhere, feel her, explore the smooth softness of her slender, toned body, unable to imagine ever having enough of her.

Lying on top of him, Maya could feel the deep ripples of his muscles as she touched him, exploring the hard counters of his body. Surrendering to the urgency that was burning her up from the inside out, she revelled in the freedom he was giving her to express herself, the lack of any boundaries, as his hands and mouth were everywhere, drawing gasps and moans from her.

When he asked her what she liked she told him with breathless honesty.

'Everything…every part of you.'

His control broke and then she was beneath him, her legs parted, as he teased her with the pressure of his erection against her damp mound until finally he couldn't hold out any longer. Grabbing a packet from his wallet, he sheathed himself quickly and surged smoothly into her.

The pleasure that rushed through her as he entered her drew a deep moan of ecstasy from her lips. Gasping and trembling with an overload of feeling, she reached up and kissed him on his mouth before trailing her tongue along the damp corded skin of his throat.

Then it began in earnest, the slow delicious torment of his fluid, sensuous advance and retreat. The intimacy of being joined with him was like nothing she had imagined it could be; she could literally *feel* the thudding of his heart against her own. Having him inside her felt so incredibly *right*, and with each thrust he touched a part of her that no one had ever touched before, winding her tighter and tighter until she felt as if she were going to explode into a million stars.

She opened her eyes and saw the raw naked need in his eyes; it was like looking into a mirror and seeing exactly what she felt on someone else's face.

The sudden intensity of her release was shocking, like free falling without a parachute but with no impact, just waves and waves of bone-deep drowning pleasure that was better than even the most vivid of her dreams…

CHAPTER EIGHT

Maya slowly floated back down to earth. There was sound and light, and she could see an expanse of blue through the incredible domed glass ceiling.

What would it be like to just lie here with your lover and do nothing except make love under this roof of stars? Well, she didn't have a lover and she hadn't made love either. She'd just had sex, and now it was over.

He rolled away from her and as she looked at his sweat-slicked face through the veil of her lashes she could see that the distancing was not just physical.

Was it wrong to want to prolong the moment, hold on to the image of delicious warm intimacy for a little while longer, even if it wasn't real? Well, it was what she wanted, even though she knew a clean break would be less painful, so she closed her eyes and went for the masochistic option.

Not that she had any room for complaint. This was exactly what she had signed up for and she'd do it again in the blink of an eye.

As her breathing gradually slowed, she knew there was probably a *'You should have told me'* coming, but she wanted to both delay the moment...and stretch out this moment at the same time.

It said something about her day when discovering

an observatory in the middle of a forest was the least surprising thing that had happened to her!

She turned her head and looked into the eyes of the most surprising thing. His expression was veiled, and it didn't alter even when she reached out and laid her hand on his chest, feeling the thud of his heart through her fingertips, still wanting to keep a connection, any connection, between them.

'I keep thinking, what if you hadn't been in the woods at exactly the moment that I stumbled across the boar?'

He looked at her sharply and gave a harsh laugh that faded quickly. 'Stumbled,' he echoed. 'You think it was a lucky coincidence or fate maybe?'

'Wasn't it?'

'No, it was not. It was because old Santino nearly gave himself a heart attack running to get help,' he said grimly. 'The only coincidence involved was him bumping into me first. He was totally desperate. He said you were going into the woods even though he had warned you about the boars, and explained how dangerous the females were when they had litters in this season, and how one boar had killed his dog last year.'

The gruesome details made her flinch. 'The *gardener*, Santino?'

'Yes, the gardener, Santino. How could you be so foolish, so arrogant, as to ignore his warning and put yourself in danger like that?' He'd been so angry, he'd intended to shake her when he found her; instead he'd made passionate love to her.

'But he doesn't speak much English and I...oh, God...*cinghiale*. He was warning me. I didn't understand. I just pretended to because he seemed so upset.' There was a slightly hysterical sound to her laughter, and she had to literally bite her tongue to stop it.

Beside her Samuele had gone very quiet; he had rolled onto his side, and now he lay propped on one elbow looking down at her. She refused to meet his eyes, because she knew exactly what was coming.

And it came, although his voice was not as cold as she'd expected; it was totally neutral, which was somehow worse.

Samuele had to force himself to unclench the muscles in his jaw so he could speak. 'You know that can't happen again, Maya,' he said. Inside his head, he was thinking, *You knew it shouldn't have happened even once, Sam! Virgin, she'd been a virgin!* God, this was utter madness. He'd used the *'This is just sex'* line on her as though it were some sort of magic talisman that let him break his self-imposed rule about sleeping with her, and now look what had happened!

'Why didn't you tell me I was your first?'

Maya sighed, retracting the hand that had still been touching his hair-roughened thigh, and finally met his penetrating gaze. 'It wasn't relevant.' She felt him stiffen and saw the outrage flare in his eyes...which jolted her temper into life.

'It was *my* choice who I slept with first, Samuele. Mine. When, where and with whom, and I made my choice. I don't think I owe you any explanations, do I? Because, like you said, it was just sex and that happens to suit me perfectly.'

'I don't believe you,' he said flatly.

She saw no reason at all to give him the psychological advantage of being the one looking down on her, so she sat up in one fluid motion, with only her tangled dark curls to hide behind.

If things had been different she might have felt self-conscious about being naked, but ironically lovemaking with the patently enthusiastic Samuele had made her even more confident about her body, and anger, which she had fully embraced by now, was a very good antidote to shyness.

'Fine. So you were present for the most important moment of my life. Is that what you want me to say?' She rolled her eyes but didn't quite meet his—that would have required better acting skills than she possessed. She even delivered a laugh, hiding the truth inside a joke and a series of increasingly desperate lies. 'Look, maybe you think every woman you meet is looking for love, but me, I'm not. I'm actively avoiding it. I mean, why should you be the only one?'

Through the veil of her lashes she could see the jibe had found its mark, and she felt a stab of bleak satisfaction. 'Virtually everyone I have ever cared for, and even those I didn't, have abandoned me at some point in my life. Why would I set myself up for even more pain by falling in love?' she pointed out, embracing what she had never admitted to herself before and feeling weirdly liberated because of it. 'My own mother rejected me— *twice*, actually, when you think about it. She clearly never loved me, and neither did Violetta.' Sadness filled her face as she admitted quietly, 'My dad died when I was only a child and I was devastated because I loved him so much. My mum remarried and—well, let's just say you're certainly not the only person who's seen a parent make a terrible second marriage. What did love do for her? And while my sister Beatrice is happy now, she went through absolute hell to get there.

'*She* thinks love is a price worth paying, but *I* don't. My mum and dad were blissfully happy for a few short years but when he died, I think a part of her did too, and she ended up marrying a man on the rebound who was a total control freak. He tried and almost succeeded in isolating her from everyone who cared for her, and he practically ripped our family apart doing it.

'The truth is, I owe you a sincere debt of gratitude, Samuele.' She saw surprise move at the backs of his eyes and felt a stab of triumph. 'I thought that I couldn't have sex without a relationship, that it would feel cold and wrong. But it didn't, and it was incredible. So you have opened up a whole new world of possibilities for me.'

He isn't rejecting me—I'm rejecting him... She repeated the confidence-enhancing mantra inside her head over and over. It didn't matter if it was true, because it was always about how it *looked* rather than how it actually *was*, and she looked totally confident as she surged gracefully to her feet. Displaying an almost balletic poise, she moved around the room, unhurriedly gathering her clothes.

It was hard to project dignity while you were untangling your bra from a lampshade, especially when you could feel a pair of jet-dark eyes following your every move, but Maya thought she pulled it off. Cool and businesslike might have been preferable, and she might well have said more than she'd intended to about her past, though the details of her big speech were already a bit of a blur. But what she *had* done was establish that she was *not* crushed by his declaration that he wouldn't sleep with her again. Because she was his equal. Actually, she decided, she was *better* than him.

Sam watched as she turned her back to him and he had a last flash of her small, high, coral-tipped breasts that had fitted so perfectly into his hands before she covered them with the tartan silk bra. Then she pushed her hair out of the way, drawing it over her shoulder to gain access to the fastening.

The Pre-Raphaelite mass of curls always made him think of an old film... He remembered it being themed rather appropriately around a young woman with incredible hair who discovered her sexuality, a view and the Italian scenery all at the same time.

Well, Maya had certainly discovered her sexuality, he thought grimly, and now she was going to be exploring it with someone else. The image of these faceless recipients of her loving sensuality sent a knife thrust of something acidic that he *refused* to admit was pure, undiluted jealousy.

Recognising the source of the feeling in his gut when he imagined someone else pushing his face into her hair, breathing in the scent of her, of that someone feeling the brush of the silky cascade against his chest and belly, exciting nerve-endings into painful life, would be to admit to a vulnerability that he was unwilling to own.

Pushing away the images, he rose to his feet, watching the flexing of her shoulder blades cause a little ripple of delicately sculpted muscle under the surface of her creamy skin.

'I need to get back to Mattio now.' Maya tossed the information over her shoulder, feeling a stab of shame that he was her only reason for being here, and yet she'd so easily forgotten her responsibilities.

As the fastener clicked home and she was able to drop her arms, she turned to see him standing there stark naked. Her mood of defiant confidence slipped away as she stared, literally transfixed by the sight of him. There was not an ounce of surplus fat beneath his olive-toned skin to disguise the delineation of his athletic frame, the deep muscles on his long thighs, the powerful muscles of his broad shoulders and chest, and the washboard corrugation of his belly.

Things newly awoken inside her tightened and clenched. Who was she kidding? Samuele had not opened her up to a world of sensual possibility, he had just *spoilt* her for any other man! She couldn't even bear to contemplate the idea of another man touching her as intimately as he had...

'Mattio will be fine,' he said quietly. 'And you will be a celebrity once everyone knows what happened.'

The colour slid from her face. 'You're going to tell them?'

'You will, I would imagine.'

She stared at him. Why would she tell everyone she'd slept with Samuele?

'The bruise on your face is going to take some explaining if you don't tell them about the boar.'

She reached for her shirt then, crushing it to her front as she felt the wash of embarrassed colour rise up her neck. She would have died rather than admit the misunderstanding.

He watched her from under his lashes as he pulled his jeans up over his narrow hips, knowing the conclusion she'd just jumped to. Boast about sleeping with a virgin? Ignorance, in his mind, was no defence; he certainly wasn't going to expose his shame. It didn't matter which way you looked at it, he had the experience, and he'd made a move on her when she'd been at her most vulnerable, shocked and upset after almost being badly injured.

The terrible truth was that he would do it again in a heartbeat...and now he knew that Maya Monk could very quickly become his drug of choice, the only option was to go cold turkey. It disturbed him that for the first time in his life his contempt for his father, his despair for his brother, both locked into marriages that amounted to contractual humiliation, was now leavened with the smallest kernel of understanding. Not that Maya bore any resemblance to his toxic stepmother... but that only made her more dangerous to him, not less.

Having her under the same roof as him for several weeks might be a challenge, but maybe he deserved to suffer after what he'd done? Keeping an emotional distance from her wasn't going to be painless either.

'I'll go first,' he said as she walked through the door ahead of him.

'Because you're big and male and I'm a weak little woman?' she jibed.

No, because I can't take looking at your delicious rear all the way back without wanting to have you up against the nearest tree. He shrugged. 'If you like.'

Even though he didn't turn around he must have sensed her hesitation as they approached the trees again. 'Don't worry, that family of boars have probably moved on,' he lied. In actuality he didn't have a clue if they had or not. He'd protect Maya even if he had to pick her up and run all the way back to the castello with her.

'No, it's not that. It's just...you saved my life and I didn't say thank you.'

He paused and looked back over his shoulder. 'I think you said thank you very nicely indeed. In fact, it was one of the nicest thank-yous I have ever received, *cara*.'

He winked at her, then watched the angry colour stain her cheeks. He turned away thinking, *Job done.* Having her angry with him was no bad thing. He resolutely ignored the hollow feeling in his stomach.

CHAPTER NINE

It was two weeks and the bruise on her cheek had almost faded. She had woken the next day to find she had a black eye and her face had gone through some lurid colour changes since then; now a light touch of concealer and you wouldn't know it was there.

If only other things that had happened that day had faded so easily...though a part of her didn't actually want them to. Samuele had been right: her encounter with the wild boars had made her a bit of a local celebrity.

She had a lot of sympathy and was repeatedly told how lucky she was. It seemed everyone had a story of someone who hadn't been as lucky: the hiker who had nearly lost an eye and had been massively disfigured; the farmhand who had fallen and been trampled coming out of his encounter with several broken ribs and a smashed leg...he still walked with a limp, she was told darkly.

Maya had made a point of going out to the gardens to search out the gardener and offer her thanks and apologies. She took Rosa with her to translate and showed Santino the app on her phone she would use to translate for herself in future.

She stayed and won a friend by asking about the gardens that he and his team kept so beautifully, and he was eager to tell her about the years when he had been the only one left to tend them and how it had simply broken his heart to see the historically important landscapes being taken over by Mother Nature.

'Now,' he proudly explained, 'I have every resource I ask for and a team.' He spoke at length about last summer and the massive party with famous people and the filmmaker who had wanted to make a documentary about the gardens. 'The son,' he finished, cryptically tapping his nose. 'He is nothing like the father...'

It was the first time she'd heard this opinion actually voiced, but it was implied in so many other conversations she had had. Samuele was more than simply well regarded; he was flat-out adored by the people of the estate.

She wondered what the high-flying financiers in their smart suits—not that any of them filled out a suit like Samuele—would make of the man she had seen last week?

Her thoughts drifted back to her solo walk she'd fitted into her daily routine, which no longer involved intimate dinners with Samuele. Sometimes Rosa, who had become her official helper with Mattio, stayed to eat with her, which involved far less tension.

Maya's walk that particular morning last week had taken her past the stables. She was a bit nervous of horses, or at least the height they were from the ground, so she had been far enough away to stay unseen, or at least that was what she had thought until that final moment when Samuele had turned and looked directly at her. To her eternal shame she had ducked down behind a hedge, a bit like a child who covered his eyes and thought no one could see him.

Only she wasn't a child and she had sat there and sworn under her breath, waiting for her humiliation to be complete when he came over—but he hadn't.

While it had lasted, the show she'd seen had been quite a masterclass in horsemanship; if anyone had filmed it on their phone it would have gone viral in hours!

How could it not? It had everything: a tall, gorgeously handsome man radiating authority standing there, seemingly oblivious to the slashing hooves of the young horse he was trying to tame.

Maya's initial gut-chilling fear had given way to fascination as she'd watched him. It had been like a ballet really, the horse advancing and retreating and Samuele standing there completely unfazed, radiating the sort of confidence that you couldn't learn or fake or buy, and gradually, almost by osmosis, it had seemed to infiltrate the animal's panic.

She hadn't been the only one watching the show, the fence had been lined with stable hands who had seemed as fascinated as she'd been.

Samuele hadn't appeared to *do* anything except talk softly. Nothing had happened fast but by imperceptible inches he'd won the horse's trust until he was able to stroke his silky face, after which he'd trotted around the exercise ring quite happily.

That was when he'd turned and looked at her; that was when she should have walked calmly over to him and said something bland, talked about the weather, anything but what she'd done.

She still cringed when she thought about what she must have looked like.

Would he comment on it this morning? she wondered, gathering up the folder containing the nannies' CVs and sticking it into her shoulder bag. She assumed that that was why he had requested her presence this morning, via email, which had been the form of communication he had favoured since they'd had their...sexual collision. It was how she'd decided to think of it, like a traffic accident that had happened because you hadn't been paying attention to the road, or because you'd allowed yourself to think about something else instead, like him, standing naked in front of you... Which wasn't going to happen today, she told herself firmly.

It would be their first meeting that wasn't accidental in two weeks. They'd occasionally passed one another in one or other of the maze of corridors and once she had been going into the magnificent leisure suite when he'd been coming out, his hair wet... She'd felt dizzy for quite a while after that. A few minutes earlier and she would have seen him sleek and semi-naked in the pool, maybe even joined him there...? Then who knew what might have happened? Her vivid imagination had supplied several possibilities in glorious Technicolor.

She had not ventured back there since.

Their paths had almost crossed a few times when he'd come to see Mattio, but each time he had she'd been taking her walk and Rosa had been in charge. The girl had given her chapter and verse of how good he was with the baby and how interested he was in Mattio's progress.

Maya couldn't decide what was worse: the possibility he was avoiding her, or he'd forgotten she existed and moved on.

Another one of his personal secretaries, the woman, appeared as Maya approached the office door. Maya suspected that being psychic was probably a required qualification for working closely for Samuele—that and an inbuilt immunity to his intellect-dampening aura of raw masculinity.

That disqualified her on both counts. She was almost as miscast as an employee as she was a lover, even though technically she wasn't either. She'd just been a steamy one-afternoon stand for him, and, far from feeling as if she worked for him, she was actually treated more like a guest by everyone she encountered here. Everyone except the boss, who acted as though she were invisible. Yes, it suited her too, but she didn't have to be happy about it, did she?

'Just give him a minute and then go right in.'

She probably hadn't meant it literally, but Maya got her phone out to time it anyway, and saw she had a missed call from Beatrice. She felt a pang of guilt.

Beatrice and her mum knew she was in Italy but not where or why. When she'd initially told her sister her destination, Bea had immediately concluded that Maya was there in connection with the embryonic design business that had once been their joint project.

'Oh, so that supplier you were talking about, they lowered the costs, did they? That's marvellous! The samples you sent me, the colours of that wool are just perfect. The offer of the start-up money still stands, you know, it's not charity. Dante and I, we believe in you.'

The opportunity had been there for Maya to put her right, but she'd been afraid that if she started talking about Samuele and Mattio and Violetta, it would all spill out, and then the moment had passed. She had allowed the misunderstanding to go on, and the longer it had lasted the more difficult the idea of coming clean had become, and now it weighed heavily on her conscience. She would tell Bea and Mum soon, but it seemed easiest to wait until she could explain the situation in person.

Then perhaps they could explain it to me, she thought. Because when she lay awake at night wondering how she'd got herself into this situation, the answer was no more clear-cut than her feelings for Samuele were.

She was sitting with her back to him and the doorway, unaware of his presence as she slid her phone back into the big leather bag with a file sticking out that she wore slung over her shoulder.

Samuele couldn't see her face, but he'd spotted the tension in her narrow back and he found himself wondering about the person on the other end of the line who had put it there.

'Good morning, Maya.'

She got to her feet as though shot and spun around, her colour-clash statement relatively sedate today. She had on an acid-green shirt tucked into a pair of black pedal pushers, and she wore flat black pumps embellished with embroidery on her narrow feet. Her glorious hair was confined at the nape of her slender neck by a leather lace.

Samuele could almost see the boundaries that he had spent the last two weeks constructing dissolve. In his mind he was immediately unfastening the tie and spreading out her hair down her back—which in this fantasy was naked.

She was naked quite a lot in his mind. Actually, she was in his mind far too much, full stop.

'H-hello,' she stammered out. 'She said to come in but I…wasn't sure.'

He had not been sure either, but he was now.

You did not need to have second sight to see what was coming down the line. Violetta was already hinting—

taunting might be more accurate—the fact that she felt she held the winning card. But her inability to resist turning the knife in his back had actually worked in his favour this time.

He had given himself time to stall by paying her latest thinly disguised blackmail demand, but he had no illusions that it would be the last one. And when she got bored with taking money off him, she would move in for the kill.

It was not really about money or maternal feelings for Violetta; it was all about revenge and power plays.

The money didn't matter to him, but Mattio did, and he was prepared to go to any length to fulfill his promise to his brother—including marriage.

He'd sworn to Cristiano that he would always do what was best for Mattio, and he was ashamed that he'd been willing to deprive the baby of the sort of mother he deserved just because Samuele hadn't looked beyond his own fears of becoming like his father or brother.

But he wasn't either of them, and he could see now that it had been ridiculous to compare his situation with theirs. For starters, poor Cristiano had not been able to see a single fault in his toxic bride and his deluded father's obsession had made him similarly blinkered. While *he* was perfectly aware of Maya's flaws—it was hard not to be when she was the most challenging female he had ever met!—he was certain she would make the best mother to Mattio, and the fact that there was already a blood tie between the two could be an important factor in securing her agreement to his plan.

'Do you want to come through…?'

Maya's heart flipped at the sound of his voice, but before she could respond he was already moving towards the door, taking her agreement as a given. And who could blame him? She hadn't been resisting much of late; maybe once a people-pleaser, always a people-pleaser.

Taking a deep breath, and hating the idea she might be a pushover, she clutched her bag containing the folder and followed him through to his inner sanctum.

As with three quarters of the sprawling castle, this was a room she had never entered—it was probably the first and last time.

She hadn't been sure what to expect, but it was actually pretty modern and utilitarian, dominated by a massive desk with several computer screens. One wall was book-lined, and there was a stack of free weights on a purpose-built stand. She pushed away the mental picture of a sweaty Samuele taking a break from the stress of moving around billions by stretching his muscles to the limit, and focused on the only decorative touch, which was a black and white framed drawing of the castello.

He saw her looking at it. 'The artist is disputed but it shows the place before the more contemporary additions, as in sixteenth-century contemporary.'

'It's very striking.'

He had moved to stand in front of the full-length window, and she tried hard not to sigh wistfully. He was wearing a beautifully tailored dark suit, making him looking formal, exclusive, distant and quite incredibly gorgeous.

'Th… This is a very nice room…'

He cut across her stuttering opening and nodded to one of the leather chairs set on the opposite side of the desk from him. 'Have a seat.' He took his own seat behind the massive desk, which occupied a large section of the pretty large room.

Right…so far, so formal—very formal, Maya thought uncertainly, feeling as though she had been sent to the headmaster's office, though the analogy had some major flaws.

She had never felt this sexually wound up in her school days or for that matter her adult days until the day she'd met Samuele. In her head, her life was pretty much divided into the pre-and post-Samuele days, and now his presence and the knock-on effects seemed to have altered every aspect of herself.

She kept pushing away the intense feelings he aroused in her, but they just kept pushing right back. It felt like an emotional tug of war and, as much as she might call for a referee's intervention, she had already been pulled well and truly over that red line, she thought with a despairing surge of self-realisation.

Well, it was done now; she had finally allowed herself to care enough for someone and had been rejected… and she'd survived the experience. Well, for an entire fortnight she had… She took a deep, steadying breath. See, she was still breathing so it wasn't terminal! So long as he *never* discovered that she lay in bed every night *longing* for him, she could cope.

At a distance he'd sent her nervous system into meltdown; this close to him there was no possibility she could pretend, to herself at least. But although she might have lost the ability to lie to herself, she could still fake it with the best of them in front of him.

'Would you like coffee?'

'No.' She took out the file and put it on his desk. 'I've made some notes,' she offered.

He looked at her blankly.

'The applications for the nanny,' she said, all business. 'Your message didn't say, but I assumed this was what we were going to discuss?'

'Ah, yes… I thought I might go and see Mattio later, take him for walk maybe?'

'It's Rosa's afternoon off, I'm afraid,' she said, unable to resist the dig.

Did he get it or had she been too subtle? It was hard to tell. The planes and angles of his face were designed to be inscrutable, though on anyone else she would have called the dark bands along the slashing angles of his cheekbones a blush.

'You could come too.'

'Come where?' She regarded him warily, thinking that this encounter was all as tense and awkward as she'd imagined. Maybe he was working up to some sarcastic remark about her ducking out of sight at the stables the other week?

'You like the rose gardens, I understand.'

Understand…understand from who? 'What, have you got a spy network watching my every move?' She was only half joking. 'Fine, you really don't have to ask my permission to take Mattio for a walk. Tomorrow?' She raised a cool brow. The significance of his suit, beside the fact it made him look even more exclusive and unattainable, had not been lost on her.

'I've obviously caught you on your way to…'

It could have been just about any place; he seemed to commute to many of the world's capitals the way some people took a bus to the next town, only for him it was a private jet.

'I just got back actually.' Samuele reached for his tie, loosening the constriction at his neck. 'I'd like to know how you think Mattio is getting on. If there are any changes you think should be made…any improvements…?'

He was delaying bringing up the real reason he wanted to talk to her, and he knew it. Finding the right words was not something that he normally struggled with but, in his defence, these particular words were of the life-changing variety. 'Is there anything you need?'

'Wouldn't that be something better discussed with the new nanny? There are some very good candidates here, several with rave reviews.' She was glad, of course, she told herself fiercely, that Mattio would be in the care of someone who came highly recommended by satisfied previous parents, who knew a lot more about child development than she did. She'd always known she had been a brief stopgap in a desperate situation, but the knowledge that her time left with Mattio was coming to a swift end felt like a heavy weight pressing on her chest.

'I have…a…' He paused and dragged a hand down his cleanly shaven cheek before clenching his long fingers into a fist. It was so unlike his normal cool, articulate self that she stared. Perhaps his thoughts were still on whatever high-powered business had taken him away from home this time.

The tension in the room was almost a physical presence; suddenly she couldn't stand it any more and surged to her feet.

'Look, shall I come back if you're…busy,' she hastily substituted, thinking *distracted* was nearer the mark.

He watched silently as she turned and moved towards the door, offering no opinion on what she'd just said… She stopped and swung back, the feelings that she had been suppressing suddenly bubbling to the surface and spilling out into hasty speech.

'Look, I *know* it was just meaningless sex and I *know* that it's not going to happen again, so treating me with simple basic *civility* is not going to raise my expectations for a repeat performance.' Her dark angry eyes raked his face. 'Are you *punishing* me for sleeping with you by ignoring me? I wasn't stalking you the other morning, you know—I was just passing by. How was I to know you were some sort of horse whisperer? Oh, God!' She finally ran out of breath but not nearly soon enough.

Her horror-filled eyes met his momentarily before she squeezed them closed, and with nothing to duck down behind this time, she covered her face with her hands instead.

She kept them there as his hands on her shoulders guided her back to the chair and then pushed her into it again.

'It was the best meaningless sex I have ever had—*you* were the best meaningless sex I have ever had.' Maybe meaningless sex was all he was capable of, Samuele thought bleakly. Not that he envied his father or his brother, but at least they had been capable of feeling a deep unselfish love for someone else, even if it had been based on lies.

Her hands fell away. 'Am I meant to be flattered—?' She broke off when she registered the expression on his face.

His eyes were filled with emotions too intense and complex for her to even begin to guess the cause and his grin lacked its normal voltage.

'I could have phrased that better,' he admitted, but that was clearly as much as he was prepared to admit.

'It's always nice to be good at something. I could put it on my next CV. Good with children and great at meaningless sex...'

He didn't smile, but then she didn't smile either; it had been a very bad joke.

The look in his eyes was really worrying her—he'd probably reject her concern, but what the hell? 'What's wrong?'

She didn't really expect a response to her blunt question, not one so unambiguous, or immediate, or sad.

'It would have been my brother's twenty-ninth birthday today.'

The last vestiges of her animosity and resentment shrivelled away and her tender heart ached with empathy for the pain etched on his face.

'Hearing people here talk about him, he sounded as if he was a good person.'

He nodded. 'He would have been a wonderful father and I think he would think you are acting like a wonderful mother—'

Was this his subtle way of saying she had overstepped her authority?

'I know I'm not Mattio's mother.'

'You're more of a mother to him than the one he's had,' he pushed out in a bitter voice. 'I've never previously thought that a mother figure was essential for a child's well-being and development, but I think I was wrong.'

'You're not going to give him back to Violetta!' she cried in horror. 'I know that legally she is his mother but—'

'No, I'm not letting him go back to Violetta,' he promised, the metallic glint in his eyes as hard as his voice.

Some of the tension left her shoulders but Maya, who had surged to her feet, stayed standing. Samuele moved around the desk and sat on the edge facing her, now at eye level, his long legs stretched out in front of him.

'And apparently, we are to expect a wedding invitation from her soon.'

'So what does that mean? Do you think that she'll try to take Mattio back?'

'I would say that's inevitable.'

'But she doesn't love him!'

'You know how convincing she can be, Maya.'

Her eyes fell as she remembered how easily her half-sister had fooled her. 'Oh, God! But this Charlie she's marrying…didn't you say he doesn't want children?' she cried, clinging to this straw of hope, not wanting to contemplate Mattio being caught up in a toxic tug of war.

'I have no doubt that before long Charlie will do anything she asks just to keep her happy. It's what Cristiano did.'

'But she'll abandon Mattio again! And this time, you might not find him.' Her face creased in anguish at the thought. 'You *can't* let her do that to him,' she declared fiercely.

'I have no intention of allowing her to do that. I intend to make a full custody claim. In the meantime I will keep paying up just to keep her quiet. It's better for now if she thinks she is winning.'

'Paying up?' Comprehension hit her. 'She is *blackmailing* you?'

He shrugged and gave a dry smile. 'Very carefully worded blackmail, but essentially yes.'

'But isn't her Charlie disgustingly rich…?'

'It's not about the money for Violetta—this is about her wreaking revenge on me for thwarting her claim to half the Agosti estate. And it's about power. Remember, she does hold a trump card, actually more than one. You said it to me yourself back at your flat, didn't you? Any court will initially favour a mother over other family members, and Mattio needs a mother in his life at least for the early years.'

She fixed him with an unwavering gaze and wondered at what age he imagined that you *stopped* needing your mother.

'The obvious solution is for me to marry.'

'So have you changed your mind about marriage?' she asked, taken aback.

'Not about marriage as an institution, no, but about being married, yes.'

'Is there a difference?'

'I think if *true love*,' he drawled contemptuously, '*really* existed, then marriage would be redundant. Two people wouldn't need a legal framework to trap them together.'

'Trap…?'

'Oh, I know divorce is relatively simple nowadays, but so many hang on in there when it's obvious it's beyond hope of saving. Marriage is just a contract, not some sort of magical spell that grants eternal happiness and joy. If it's drawn up with both parties' interests in mind, the duration of the contract is flexible and there are no unreasonable expectations like monogamy, then I see no reason why it couldn't be successful.'

'Successful maybe, but it's not really marriage, is it?' This cold-blooded description horrified her.

'An open marriage.'

'So not really marriage at all, then! Because marriage is about faith, trust…' She couldn't bring herself to say *love* or even think the word while she was in the same room as Samuele.

'Marriage in this case is about securing the future security and happiness of my brother's child.'

'Of course, but—' Her thoughts skidded to an abrupt stop and she had to try and conceal a gasp of shock. She had been hanging onto a rock wall of denial by her fingernails for weeks and she'd finally lost her grip.

Not being able to say the word in a man's presence wasn't exactly one of the most recognised symptoms of being in love, but, nevertheless, she was.

She had fallen in love with a man who was capable of giving his love and loyalty to a child that carried the bloodline he was so proud of, and to the land that was his heritage. A man who thought marriage *might* work, but only if you took love out of the equation. There was no room in his life for a woman, no room for her.

She wasn't sure if it was a bitter laugh or a despairing sob that was locked in her throat, but it hurt as she remembered that she'd always believed *not* falling in love with the wrong man was a matter of choice. She marvelled now at her own arrogance and was suddenly deeply fearful for her future.

'So you see that I didn't ask you here to talk about nannies, because I am very much hoping that there will be no need for one.'

She had started shaking her head. 'You want me to stay on here until you've found a suitable wife?'

'I want you to stay on here—but as my wife.'

He watched her drop down into the chair she had recently vacated. Luckily it was still there, though he doubted she would have noticed if she'd landed on the floor.

'That is *insane*!' Her laugh was edged with hysteria. 'The only thing we have in common is Mattio.'

'Isn't that enough?' His shoulders lifted as his dark eyes moved over her face, lingering on the plump curve of her lips. 'But actually it's not true. We also have a similar sexual appetite, don't we? What we have, between us—that kind of chemistry is rare, *cara*, and exceptional sex is even rarer.' Two years of enjoying the pleasures of Maya's body and exhausting his hunger for her would surely compensate for any temporary loss of freedom.

Breathing hard by the time he finished speaking, Maya shook her head in an effort to free her mind from the spell of his smoky voice and the erotic images his words had evoked.

'Yes, we *do* have Mattio.' His delivery was now flat and cool. 'And he deserves the very best. You are the best for him, and there is the blood connection between you, which, given the circumstances, could be a significant factor.' He paused, his crazily long lashes veiling his eyes momentarily.

'I know he's the last bit of your brother you have left and the heir to—'

'He is the heir to the Agosti name,' Samuele cut in. 'And the responsibility that goes with it. But he is not Cristiano's child.'

The blood left her face and her heart went into high gear. She could hardly hear past the dull thud in her own chest; whatever she had expected to hear, this was definitely not it. 'What are you saying?' she whispered, her eyes trained on his face.

'That, unlike you, I have no blood connection with Mattio,' he said roughly, in a voice that cracked with the effort to keep it free of emotion.

'This is the thing that Violetta is blackmailing you about.'

He shrugged. 'It's her trump card.'

'How long have you known?'

'Cristiano told me before he died, when he asked me to keep Mattio safe, to take care of him.'

'Your brother knew that the baby wasn't his?' Her thoughts raced to process the flow of information.

'Violetta couldn't hide it—the dates made it utterly

impossible. Cristiano told me he was out of the country for a significant amount of time when Mattio was conceived. If my brother had lived he would have been the child's father and that is all that mattered to him...'

Would he have been as big a man as his brother? It was a question Samuele had asked himself many times. How could any man know the answer until he was faced with the situation himself?

'Mattio *is* an Agosti, he *is* my heir and I will do anything it takes to keep him safe and keep my promise to my brother.'

Including marrying me.

'Who else knows about this?' she asked.

'I have told no one but you.'

His trust and giving her joint responsibility for the secret he had shared with her changed things in a way she could not put words to—it altered the dynamic between them.

Samuele trained his gaze on her face. 'I'm asking for two years of your life... You would still be young enough later to go on and have a family of your own,' he pointed out, conscious of an odd ache in his chest at the thought of her holding children she'd created with another man. 'There would, of course, be the option to extend that period should both parties be agreeable, and the golden handshake you'll receive at the termination of the marriage would obviously mean that you'd be able to maintain the living standards you'd have become accustomed to.'

'I don't give a damn about money!' she snapped. She wanted his love and he was offering her a soulless marriage.

He watched as she covered her face with her hands again and felt a tug of guilt.

'We have nothing in common… Look at this place,' she said, spreading her hands wide to encompass the room and everything beyond.

'We do. We both love Mattio.'

The response cut right through her defences and directly into her weakness. *Love*… She did love Mattio, but she loved Samuele too. Only what the heart wants the heart can't always have… *But isn't it better to enjoy what the heart can have while it lasts?* that insidious voice tempted.

Halfway through the internal dialogue she realised that she was actually considering it. Maybe he read the self-revelation on her face because he put his hand in his pocket and pulled out a small box.

He opened the box, flicking the catch up with his finger to reveal a velvet lining that was old and worn. Maya wasn't looking at the box, but the prize it contained, a prize that would be a great big fat lie on her finger.

'This was my grandmother's, with a few greats added, who was Russian originally. I repurchased it quite recently.' Along with several other items with a similar Russian royal family provenance. He could already see in his mind's eye the emerald necklace in the stunning enamelled setting sitting comfortably between Maya's lovely breasts… The image came with a distracting rush of that mix of painful yet pleasurable heat.

With a tiny gasp she put her hand to her mouth, her big eyes going from the ring to his face and back again. Even he could see that the square-cut emerald surrounded with clusters of brilliant diamonds, set on a wide gold band etched with a scroll pattern and inlaid with yet more precious stones, was stunningly beautiful.

She shook her head.

'People often marry because there is a baby,' he

pressed. 'The baby might not be ours, but is this situation so very different? The principle is the same, securing the welfare of a vulnerable child.'

Maya looked up at him, loving every line, every carved angle and patrician hollow of his face... She also loved Mattio and she knew her heart would break if she left him. She had so much love to give, so wasn't it genuinely better to give it even knowing that, in this case, it would never be returned?

It was as if all her secret dreams of love and her worst nightmares about abandonment had collided. She couldn't possibly see how this would end well for her, but Samuele was right about one thing: Mattio had to be protected.

Her hand shook as he slid the ring on her finger. It was a perfect fit.

'I have one stipulation. *I* don't think that monogamy is an unrealistic expectation.' She could stand many things, but that was the one betrayal that she knew would totally crush her.

There was a pause, then he said slowly, 'I think I can accommodate that.'

She immediately started tugging the ring off her finger. 'What are you doing?' he asked sharply.

'Taking it off. I can't walk round with a fortune on my finger. We can wait until things are official and I've told my family.' *Oh, God, my family!* she groaned inside.

'Things are already official, so I see no reason to wait. It is the formal opening of the Villa Agosti gallery in Florence in two weeks, so your first official role as my bride-to-be will be to act as hostess.'

'I'm not really a front-of-house sort of girl, Samuele. I am more backstage, prop moving, that sort of thing. I thought I'd just be doing nursery things.'

'You will be doing all the things that would be expected of my fiancée,' he said flatly.

The emphasis on *all* made her sensitive tummy muscles quiver. 'What,' she asked, her alarm shifting up a gear as he framed her face with his hands, 'are you doing?' Silly question—it was pretty obvious what he was doing.

The kiss was long and hard and depleted her of any final remnants of resistance. 'I am making it official,' he rasped throatily, before picking her up and sitting her on the desk, then slowly pushing her back until she lay there watching through half-closed eyes as he threw his tie across the room.

'What if someone comes in?' As resistance went it was pretty half-hearted.

'If you even notice, *cara*, I will be deeply insulted.'

Her breath quickened. 'You make a lot of assumptions…'

He gave a wolfish grin, oozing arrogance from every perfect pore as he planted a hand flat on the wooden surface either side of her face. 'I don't think it is an *assumption*—' she whimpered low in her throat as his scorching lips moved up the column of her neck '—to say that we definitely do not need a rule book in our bedroom.'

CHAPTER TEN

Maya smiled, and a low husky laugh vibrated in her throat as her fingers tangled in the dark hair of the man whose head lay nestled between her breasts in the bed she had shared with him for the last two weeks.

'What are you laughing at?'

'You... No, not really,' she added quickly. It was just she had never imagined that sex could involve humour.

The depth of the sharp soul-piercing tenderness she felt for Samuele was something she had never dreamt of either. As for the desperate raw passion he could awaken in her, she sometimes didn't even recognise herself in the woman she became in his arms.

His head lifted, his dark heavy-lidded eyes still slumbrous from their recent lovemaking.

'I just remembered you saying we didn't need a rule book in the bedroom.' She gave a languid sigh as he slid his way up her body until their faces were level.

'I remember that too.'

Samuele could count on one hand the times he had spent more than one night with the same woman, because the next night would have been much the same and, put quite simply, he had a low boredom threshold.

He had heard it suggested that he was attracted by the thrill of the hunt but in reality there rarely had been a hunt. He didn't make the mistake of putting that down to his own irresistibility; he believed women were attracted by what he represented to them, which was money, power and his supposedly glamorous lifestyle.

He looked at the lovely face inches from his own, no make-up, hair wild, flushed cheeks. No two nights were the same with Maya; her glorious lack of inhibition, her innate sensuality and the fact she gave everything of herself every single time they made love made her the sexiest woman he could ever have imagined.

He quite simply could not get enough of her. His idea of heaven was being stranded on a desert island and having her five times a day, but even that wouldn't be enough; where Maya was concerned, he'd discovered he was insatiable.

'You taste of me,' he said, dipping his tongue into the warmth of her mouth.

'You taste so good too,' she husked against his lips, meeting his tongue with her own.

Sometimes during moments like this Maya could hardly believe the level of intimacy between them, and how natural, how *right* it all felt.

'I should get up,' she said, not moving.

'You're still worried about tonight?'

Samuele felt a by now familiar surge of tenderness as she grimaced and gave a little shrug. Maya never went for the sympathy vote.

'Don't be, *cara*,' he said, pulling himself into a sitting position and dragging a hand through his tousled hair.

'Easy for you to say—you're used to being stared at.' *And lusted after,* she added silently as her eyes followed the liquid glide of perfectly formed muscles under golden skin as he stretched hugely.

'And you're not?' There was a lack of vanity and then there was blindness. 'You must know that you are an incredibly beautiful woman and you certainly don't dress to be invisible.' He sensed her stiffening and tagged on quickly, 'Which is good—I really like your sense of style.'

'I don't want my self-worth to be based on the way I look, Samuele, because looks fade.'

'I think you have a few years left yet,' he teased, taking pleasure just from studying the delicate lines of her face. It was young and smooth now but, gifted with a bone structure like hers, experience and time would only enhance what she had.

She flashed him a quick glance from under her lashes before looking away and muttering, 'I was invisible once.'

His fingers, moving in a sensual sweep down her spine, stilled. 'Your stepfather?'

Astonished eyes flew to his face. 'How on earth did you know it was him?'

'A couple of things you've said.'

And he'd remembered? *Do not go there, Maya, do not start seeing what you want to see.* He's observant, that's all. A skill that had helped make him a respected name in the world of finance. Her Internet research had revealed that about him, also that the respect came tinged with a healthy dose of fear; he had a reputation for total ruthlessness.

He was certainly a ruthlessly efficient lover.

'Edward seemed nice, kind, caring before they were married, but afterwards he changed, at least when Mum wasn't around, towards me and Beatrice. I was so afraid of him—'

Beside her she could feel Samuele stiffen, and he swore and said something harsh in his mother tongue.

'No…no…' she said, laying a pacific hand against his heaving chest. 'There was nothing physical and it was only little things at first. Everything I did he mocked, like a birthday card I made for Mum once. He looked at it and laughed and threw it in the bin saying that I couldn't give her that sort of rubbish.'

Samuele's big strong hand came to cover hers, his fingers sliding in between hers. She smiled her gratitude; the warm pressure was comforting.

'He chipped away at my self-esteem until in the end I didn't have any, no confidence at all. He used to say the only thing I had going for me was a pretty face and when I started getting teenage acne he had an absolute field day!' She felt Samuele's fingers tighten around her own. 'I would dread him coming in and finding something about me to laugh at. I wanted so badly to be invisible and I eventually became a grey little mouse scared of her own shadow.

'I don't know what would have happened if it wasn't for Beatrice. She was tougher than me, and she gave as good as she got, so he didn't pick on her as much. Mum had it bad too. He wanted a child that was *his* child, and she went through cycle after cycle of IVF to try and please him. It affected her health terribly but he acted as if he was the injured party.

'Maybe that was when she started to see what he really was, and she began actually listening to what Bea and I told her, and believing us. I will always remember the expression on his face when he arrived home and she'd packed his bags.'

'I saw a therapist.' She glanced at him to see how he took this. There were still some very outdated views out there about mental health.

'That's really good,' Samuele said, struggling to keep

the burning anger that was consuming him from his voice at the picture she'd painted that he knew only hinted at the true extent of all she had suffered. The need to reach out and comfort her was alien to him and he wasn't quite sure what to do. 'Did it help?'

'It did help, yes, but Mum still tries to compensate. She feels guilty that she didn't see what he was doing. I hate that she and Bea still feel like that, as though I'm weak or fragile and they have to protect me.'

'So you became the unbreakable Maya Monk.' In her bold, bright colours and her hit-the-world-head-on attitude. But underneath all that armour, she was the little girl who had been the victim of a coercive, controlling bully.

She was, he decided, the strongest person he had ever met.

Maya blinked, realising with a sense of shock just how much she had told him, more than she had ever admitted outside the therapist's office, probably more than she had admitted inside it too!

'I suppose I should get up,' she said, suddenly feeling shy and exposed...although *exposed* was a funny word to use when he had seen every little bit of her, loved every little bit of her.

It was moments like this, when everything felt perfect, that she often heard Edward's voice telling her she wasn't good enough, that she didn't deserve to be loved by anyone.

She listened and there was nothing.

She rolled back to Samuele and took his face between her hands. 'Thank you!' she said fiercely.

'For what?'

You made me believe that I'm worth loving.

There was a quizzical furrow in his brow as he studied her face and tried to interpret her silence. 'The gallery opening will be hard for you, won't it?'

'I'll be fine.'

He recognised her factory-setting response for what it was—a cover for the fact that she was not all right at all. He felt guilty for the times he had taken it at face value because it had suited him to do so.

'You'll be fine, I know, and I'll be there for you tonight. You won't be alone because I will be with you every step of the way. Oh, and if you *really* want to say thank you, I can think of several ways...'

She gave a sultry smile. 'So can I.'

'I haven't seen anyone older than nine years old literally press their nose to the window like that before.'

She sniffed and rubbed the fading mist from the window before settling back into her seat. 'I'm sure it's very *uncool* to be excited, but you know what?'

'You don't care,' he completed seamlessly.

'Not even a little bit. Florence may be your backyard but to me it's...' She mimicked one of his shrugs when words failed her.

'I don't take it for granted, though. Actually I *like* seeing the world through your eyes, though only occasionally. Otherwise I'd have given away all my possessions by now to a charity for donkeys.'

'It was a worthy cause and you shouldn't have been looking at my bank statement!'

'You left your laptop open on my desk.'

She gave a little snort and looked out of the window again. They had left the river and the cathedral behind when the car in front slowed. As they approached a building with a classical facade set back from the road behind an elaborate wall, Mattio stirred slightly, his sleepy brown eyes opening briefly before they closed again. They took a sharp right and drove through the archway into the private internal courtyard, and Maya straightened in her seat, bracing herself for the inevitable meet and greet.

'You'll be fine, *cara*, you have nothing to prove.'

Only she did, and he had to know it. He couldn't be that naive, could he? She was about to marry Samuele Agosti, not only the most handsome man on the planet, but also a legend in his own lifetime. The interest in their engagement wasn't just trending on social media, there were several column inches devoted to the upcoming marriage in all the serious financial journals.

She tried to focus on the pluses, which included the fact that Beatrice wouldn't be here tonight. She loved her sister dearly, but not the awkward questions she would inevitably ask.

Poor Beatrice's morning sickness had got worse, necessitating bed rest and an intravenous drip, so she had been admitted to hospital for a while. Back home now, she was being fiercely guarded by Dante and their mum.

Maya's mother was set to meet Samuele next week when she would fly out to spend a couple of weeks at the castello.

So all she had to do tonight was cope with the world's press, half of whom seemed to want to know up front *who* she would be wearing tonight.

The only thing that was stopping her running for the hills was the security of knowing that Samuele would be at her side. His support made all the difference to her.

As she slid out of the air-conditioned car into the fragrant afternoon warmth she knew her mind should have been on higher things than wondering which of the outfits she had brought with her to wear tonight.

But first impressions counted, and photos that were taken tonight would be images the whole world would look at tomorrow and in the days and weeks to come.

Also her choice of dress was one of the few things she felt she had some control over. She tucked her finger, weighted down by the beautiful heirloom ring, into her pocket and emptied her mind of worries. She was determined to take pleasure from the beauty of the cloistered space with the rows of fountains, their spray catching and reflecting the light as it fell into a long central pool.

As she tilted her head to examine the seemingly endless number of windows that looked down from the wrought-iron balconies on three sides of the space, the sun dazzled her and made her blink as she brushed stray strands of hair off her face.

'Good journey?'

Maya smiled as she identified the familiar lanky figure of Samuele's male private secretary, Diego, a nice, friendly reception committee of one. A combination of his youth and his ready smile made Diego, who had travelled ahead with all the bags and baggage—one small child and a white tie event meant they were not travelling light—someone she could relax around.

'And you?'

'Fine—' His glance drifted to where Samuele stood, a phone pressed to his ear, a daunting frown pleating his brow visible for a moment before he turned, presenting his broad shoulders to them.

Maya tried not to register the obvious tension in his back and widened her smile to include Rosa, who had stayed the night with relatives in the city and volunteered to help out tonight. 'Hi, Rosa, I hope your family are well.' She glanced towards the open door of the car and the sleeping child. 'He slept all the way here. I probably should have woken him but he looked so peaceful.'

On cue Mattio opened his eyes and started squirming in his seat. Maya moved to unclip his belt but Rosa, neat in a practical pair of chinos and blue shirt, beat her to it. 'I've already scoped out the nursery. Shall I give him his feed?'

'Would you?'

Rosa opened the stroller that had been unloaded with a practised flick of her wrist. 'We'll be in the nursery when you're ready,' she said as she snapped open the safety harness, ignoring the wail of protest from her passenger.

Maya, who saw that Samuele had finally pocketed his phone, pressed a kiss to the top of the increasingly tetchy child's head. She felt secure in the knowledge that he was safe with Rosa. She was so good with him, to the point when there were times she made Maya feel like an amateur.

Maya began to weave her way through the fountains towards the spot where Samuele stood, conscious as she did so that Diego had hung back discreetly.

As she got closer she sensed a tension in Samuele's stance, but also an excitement, which made sense. Tonight was important for Samuele, she knew that, it was the culmination of the years of rebuilding the lost family heritage that meant so much to him, not just to preserve it, but to make it relevant to the twenty-first century. Could it be that despite his seemingly laid-back attitude he was more worried about tonight than he'd let on?

'Good news, they have finally located the missing Agosti statues.'

'Oh, that's terrific!' She knew how much this news meant to Samuele, in a symbolic, end-of-the-journey sort of way.

Locating and acquiring the entire Agosti collection had been the singular most difficult element of his self-imposed task and one that many doubted was achievable.

Officially tonight was all about the Agosti collection, the largest number of ancient Roman and Greek statues in private hands in the world, now housed in the newly restored Villa Agosti, and to finally be shared with the world.

The fact that there were only half a dozen missing pieces was considered a miracle by many, but for Samuele, who did not cut himself any slack, it had constituted a failure.

'The thing is I have to go right now, because there's a Russian collector after them too...'

She pulled in a tense breath and brought her lashes down in a self-protective sweep. 'Now? But...couldn't you send Diego? Why do you have to go in person?'

Impatient to be gone, Samuele shook his head. 'I'll be back in plenty of time before it starts tonight,' he soothed. 'It's an hour there and an hour back tops. The vendor is a pretty eccentric character, who doesn't seem so much interested in an advantageous offer as she does my star sign. She insists on meeting me in person, something to do with a *planet alignment*...?'

Maya swallowed, struggling to inject a suitably amused note into her response and failing miserably.

'She sounds pretty *interesting*. Obviously you must... It's fine, I understand. Obviously you must go,' she said. But as she spoke she was aware that her response implied he was asking her permission; the fact was he was going whether she liked it or not.

'So you're fine with this?'

She could see from the look in his eyes that he was

already not here—*she* wasn't here. She clamped her teeth over the words he wanted to hear and flung out a cold and resentful response instead. 'And if I'm not would it make any difference to you?'

His lips tightened with annoyance and he sighed. 'You're making this into a big thing and it really isn't. I'll be back before you know it, certainly in time for the speech-giving later on. Diego will look after you. I'm sure I'll even make it back for the photoshoot. They want some footage of us in the gallery. Look, here's Diego now.'

The young man punched the air in triumph when Samuele outlined the developments.

'Sure...sure...' he said when Samuele told him the plan. 'Anything,' he said, turning to Maya. 'And I'm your man.'

No, she wanted to say, *you're not my man...and my man isn't really my man.* Letting herself believe otherwise was the road to madness. She was probably going to have a lot of moments like this one, so she'd better get used to it.

Moments filled with suppressed resentment. Moments when she felt very alone.

'So it's all good, then?' Samuele said distractedly.

Without replying she turned with a brilliantly insincere smile to Diego so that she wouldn't have to watch Samuele turn and walk away from her. Which of course he did.

After a prompt from her Diego was only too happy to launch into an explanation of what a feat the restoration of the villa had been.

'Restoration is a delicate balancing act, too much and you lose the authenticity. I can never get over the fact that standing here you're literally yards from the most famous historic sights of Florence.'

Maya walked alongside him as he displayed his knowledge, only hearing one word in three. She knew that the restoration of the collection was important to Samuele so she had hidden the extent of her nerves about tonight.

They kicked in hard now.

CHAPTER ELEVEN

There was no *us* involved in the gallery photoshoot. Just Maya, dwarfed, despite the high heels, by the pale statues around her, a flash of colour in a monochrome backdrop in the cerise silk shirt dress that was one of the new additions to her wardrobe, as were the dramatic thirties-style drop earrings.

To complete her transformation into a sophisticated stranger her hair had been tamed, with the help of Rosa, into a smooth ponytail. Perhaps sensing the importance of the occasion every curl stayed in dutiful submission during the mercifully short photoshoot.

Back in their private suite on the top floor of the villa, Maya reviewed her performance. While she had not said anything witty or wildly interesting, settling instead for polite, she had not said anything too stupid either, and she had neatly sidestepped the couple of questions that were invitations into controversial subjects.

Diego had said that Samuele would be proud of her.

She had wanted to retort that she didn't want his pride, she required his presence.

He had promised her he'd be there, and he had let her down. She didn't even rate a call or text to say he was running late.

'Any luck?' Maya stood up, the tulle layers of the dress she'd changed into for the speech-giving flaring around her as Rosa returned to the room.

The girl shook her head. 'No, I'm sorry, Diego can't get through to him either…it keeps going to voicemail.'

Maya compressed her lips. Five minutes ago the news had come that everyone had arrived and, with it, the gentle suggestion that it was not done to keep royalty waiting was left hanging in the air. She had felt a clenched fingernail away from total panic.

Fortunately, her mood had moved on. She no longer felt like hiding in a cupboard, she felt like hitting someone—all right, not someone, just the one person who had let her down, abandoned her to her fate, after he had *promised* to be there with her.

Just as her dad had promised he'd be back to watch her in the Christmas nativity play, but he hadn't come back, had he? They'd told her that he wouldn't be coming back, ever, but she had refused to believe them. She'd sat on the window seat looking down into the street, sure that his car would appear, totally sure because he had promised… Finally she'd fallen asleep and someone had put her to bed.

She'd waited the next day and the next but he'd never come.

She'd never forgotten the feeling, and all her life she'd been guided by a determination never to experience it again, until Samuele!

Even as she embraced her anger she knew it would eventually ebb and she'd just be left alone again.

There was a tentative tap on the door and the person who appeared in response to her *come in* revealed breathlessly, 'The royal party has arrived.'

'I'll be right there.' She knew etiquette meant she

as hostess should have been there to greet them…but, thanks to her experience on San Macizo, ironically royalty was one of the few things that didn't spook her about tonight. The same could not be said for everything else.

'Right then, Rosa, he's a no-show so let's do this.' She glanced at herself in the mirror, and decided she looked like a cross between an old-fashioned Southern belle and a lampshade. 'But no, not in this meringue of a dress. Help me out of it, will you, Rosa?'

A wide-eyed Rosa obliged, helping Maya to slip into her second choice for tonight, which had actually been her first choice before she'd doubted herself.

Five minutes later she looked at her reflection in the same mirror and a very different Maya looked back, a much more edgy, sexy Maya.

The pretty froth of pale lemon tulle was gone, and in its place was a scarlet full-length silk slip dress; simple and dramatic, it clung lovingly to the curves of her body.

She had added a dash of old red lipstick on top of the frosted gloss she had previously applied and it didn't take much to intensify the grey eyeshadow she wore to give it a smoky effect.

If she'd had time she would have put her hair down again, but while she had pretended an indifference to the waiting royalty, she was aware that she really didn't have time to hang around, so her hair would have to stay in the classic chignon that it had been tamed into, emphasising the length of her slender neck.

She stood poised at the top of the stairs underneath the spotlight of a chandelier, conscious of a sea of eyes looking up at her, her heart thudding frantically. There was a split second when she wanted to pick up her skirts and run away as fast as she could.

Then she focused on one face, she had no idea who it was, but blanking out the rest worked. She got down the stairs, and the rest was a blur. She parried the obvious questions about Samuele's absence without actually giving a straight answer, but luckily most people didn't seem to realise it until she had moved on.

Every lie and prevarication had only built the resentful head of steam that was choking her. Perhaps he was making a blatant point that her importance in his life came way below a bunch of statues?

Her homework on the collection paid off; she was able to give intelligent responses to several questions. There were a few speeches, people said complimentary things about the evening and her…and then she was told it was her turn.

'What?' she whispered frantically to Diego, who had pretty much been her shadow all evening.

'Well, officially it is—'

'Samuele's turn,' she bit out.

Diego gave her an understanding look. 'There is no need for you to do it. I could make a small speech apologising—'

She was tempted—oh, my, but she was *so* tempted to let him do that—but she shook her head. 'No, that's fine, I can do this.'

'I'll introduce you, shall I?'

'That would be good, thank you, Diego.'

She actually had no idea in the world what she was going to say until she started.

'I'm sure you're all wondering where Samuele is— well, so am I!'

She paused for the ripple of laughter, which came satisfyingly on cue. Sometimes the truth worked better than a lie. Samuele didn't ever explain himself to anyone, so why should she do so in his absence?

'The fact we are here tonight is a testament to one man's determination and single-minded vision, not to preserve this collection, but to celebrate it. Because the past is an organic living thing, which has shaped all our presents and our futures...'

She sensed Diego, who up until that point had looked ready to stage a face-saving intervention, relax. And she continued to speak.

The adrenaline was already fading before she reached the privacy of her room, having checked on Mattio and been assured by Rosa, who had an adjoining room to the nursery, that she would get up in the night if needed.

By the time Maya had closed the door it had gone completely. She could barely stand and she was shaking with anger.

She looked at the champagne in the silver bucket, the two glasses clearly ordered earlier before Samuele had got a better offer. Presumably he was somewhere celebrating his latest acquisition with someone else. A female someone else.

She walked across and picked up the bottle.

During the evening she had imagined, numerous times, the pleasure of throwing his ring in his face and walking away.

But the moment she had looked at the sleeping baby she'd known that was not an option open to her. The trouble was she'd made the mistake of equating great sex with caring, possibly even love. She shook her head at the extent of her own wilful stupidity.

She had allowed herself to believe that Samuele had started to care for her, that his tenderness in the bedroom and the closeness they enjoyed there had translated to them as a couple outside the bedroom too.

Well, tonight her self-deception had been revealed in all its horrific glory, and she only had herself to blame. She was convenient in bed; outside it, she was only there for Mattio. In fact, she was little more than a nanny with a ring.

Samuele fought his instinct to go straight to his room, but fortunately he almost immediately bumped into Diego.

The other man's jaw dropped in shock. 'What happened to you?'

Samuele dragged a hand across his hair to remove some of the excess moisture. 'I fell into a river. Could you get me some dry clothes? I'll get changed before I—'

'Of course, of course…did you get the statues?'

'Never actually got there,' Samuele admitted, not adding that he'd got halfway there and turned back. With every mile he had driven the image of the expression on Maya's face that had said she was far from fine hadn't faded; it had got clearer, as had the excuses he had used to assuage his guilt.

Yes, the acquisition of those statues would finally give him closure over what his father had done, but at what cost? People broke promises every day, and yet he'd convinced himself he would be back in time, and that, even if he wasn't, it would be good for Maya to face her fears.

Like you're facing yours, had mocked his inner critic as the small pokes attacking his conscience had become a sharp knife blade.

Cursing, he had taken the return exit at the last moment and, ignoring the recalculations of the onboard satnav, he'd headed back to the city.

He'd almost made it too. He would have done, if he hadn't glanced across at the exact moment that guy had climbed onto the railings of the bridge.

By the time he'd reached the foot of the bridge there had been quite an audience gathered. Several had been taking videos on their phones yet no one had been going near him.

'Has someone called the police?'

'An ambulance more like…'

'Yes, I called them—and an ambulance.'

There was a communal gasp as the man tottered.

Samuele swore and began to climb the bank towards the pedestrian path across the bridge.

'Keep back!' the guy yelled hoarsely.

Hell, he looked so young! What could lead someone with their whole life ahead of them to a place like this? 'Fine, I'm not coming nearer to you, but I'm afraid I can't hear very well, so I'm just going to climb a bit higher.' He put a hand up and vaulted onto the guard rail where the man stood, though still a good twenty feet away.

'I'm not going to come any closer… My name is Samuele…and yours is…?'

'Go away! I know what you're trying to do!'

Which is more, Samuele thought wryly, *than I do.* It wasn't really a matter of doing the right thing; it was more a matter of doing something. Something that hopefully didn't make a bad situation even worse…

The thing was, he really thought that he was talking the man down, or at the very least injecting some level of calm into the situation, but it was the sound of a police siren that did it. One moment he was listening to

Samuele tell him that he too had lost someone he loved very much and the next he had just launched himself off the bridge into the river below.

Samuele's response had been less down to finely honed logic and more to a split-second instinct. He'd jumped in after him.

'Sorry I left you in the lurch like that. Did you have my notes for the speech?' he asked Diego, stripping off his wet shirt and fighting his way into the clean one that had been provided.

'I did. But actually, your fiancée, she gave the whole speech herself.'

In the act of zipping himself into dry trousers Samuele froze and ground out a curse.

'Actually she—'

Samuele silenced him with a hand. 'No, it's all right.' Although it really wasn't. 'It's not your fault. I'll get this—'

'But—'

'It's fine, Diego, leave it to me.'

Maya had kicked off her shoes but she was still wearing the red dress and she was still raging high on her second wind of fatigue-defying fury when the door opened.

She knew exactly who was standing there but she didn't turn her head as she crammed the last item into the case and forced the lid closed before she straightened up.

'I am so, so sorry, *cara*.'

'Oh, well, then, that makes everything all right, doesn't it?'

She moved towards him with a sexy glide of red silk that sent a surge of heat through Samuele's body. 'I'm sure,' he rasped, 'that it's not as bad as you think. I'll phone around and do a bit of damage control.' He took in the significance of the cases and his expression altered, his eyes hardening. 'You're not going anywhere.'

'No, I'm not—you are.'

'What?'

'Don't look so worried, it's not as if you'll have to resort to sofa surfing, but the thing is I just didn't want to sleep in the same room as you!'

'*Dio*, Maya, I know it must have been bad tonight but—'

'You think I made a fool of myself, don't you?' she said. 'Well, it's always good to know what a wonderful opinion you have of me, but sorry, I don't require your efforts in damage limitation, because I smashed it—I was a success, brilliant.'

'That's fantastic! I knew you could do it—'

She folded her arms across her heaving chest and directed a narrow-eyed glare up at his face. 'Not two minutes ago, you didn't! You thought I'd fall flat on my face and you let me do it because you're a selfish bastard who really doesn't give a damn about me.'

'Look, I'm sorry but tonight—I shouldn't have left in the first place. I should have refused to jump through hoops for the sake of the statues.'

'Easy to be wise in hindsight,' she sneered. 'Tonight you did me a favour—it really brought a few thing into focus. I would walk away from you right now if it weren't for Mattio, but *he* needs me, so *I* won't abandon him. I will marry you, and I will do this sort of nonsense tonight, but I will *not* continue to share my bed with a man who cares more about a few lumps of old marble than he does about keeping p...promises he has m...made to people.' She scrunched her eyes closed and stood there, her hands clenched into fists. 'I will not cry over you.'

'Oh, *cara*...'

Her eyes flew open again, wide, dark and stormy. 'Don't *"cara"* me! I am making the rules now. I was a very good deal for you, Samuele, and you blew it!'

'My God, you're so gorgeous.' With a hunger approaching desperation, his eyes moved over the soft, delicate contours of her face.

'Do you really think that a few compliments will make me melt into your arms? Oh, yes,' she added, in full flow now, 'and I have decided I want to alter the terms of our *contract*. That open-marriage deal you suggested? I've started to think it's a damned great idea!'

It took a while for his brain to decipher the words she'd just spoken, but when it did he went pale and literally swayed where he stood.

'Open marriage?' His woman seeing another man? *His* Maya, his *wife*, being touched, made love to by someone else? The reaction to the images in his head rippled through him like an electrical charge and his body went rigid with rejection. He scowled fiercely. 'I don't think so.'

A sudden need to reach out to her made him take a step forward but then she snapped out, 'It was your idea to begin with, *remember*? And unlike most of your ideas, I think it's a good one. Very *civilised*!' she hissed.

'This is all just a misunderstanding,' he protested.

'No, it's not. Have you even heard a word I've said? I hate you!'

'Let me explain...' He stopped as his voice was drowned out by a loud wail.

'Now look what you've done!' she accused, pushing

open the door into the living room that separated the bedroom from the nursery wing.

Samuele, a step behind her, stopped short when they entered the nursery, where the wail was now almost deafening. Rosa was standing there with the crying baby in her arms.

She gave Maya a look of gratitude as the baby was transferred to her.

Samuele heaved a sigh of frustration. 'We'll speak again in the morning.'

The first thing Maya did the next morning, after she had applied the cold compresses to her eyes to help the puffiness that was the cost of crying herself to sleep, was scroll down her phone to see if she had been as much of a success as she had boasted to Samuele.

She typed in the word Agosti and waited for the results. The news of the gala was there but preceding it was the headline: *Italian Banker in Dramatic River Rescue!*

She swung her legs over the side of the bed and clicked the viral video attached to the headline.

The video was still playing when she ran into the sitting room where Samuele was sitting on one of the sofas, looking as though he hadn't slept a wink.

She looked wildly from the phone in her hand to him. 'Why didn't you tell me?'

'I was waiting for you to wake up.'

'You jumped off a bridge!' She was shaking the phone at him, the video still playing.

'There weren't many other options, *cara*.'

'Maybe *not* jumping off a bridge?' Her brain had been frozen with panic, but as it started working she felt dizzy with fright. *She could have lost him!* 'That's why you didn't arrive back on time, isn't it?' When she thought of all the things she'd said to him, she could have wept if she'd had any more tears left inside her. 'Why didn't you send me a message?'

'My phone was at the bottom of a river and it took me some time to convince the hospital staff that I wasn't suicidal myself.'

'Did he…the man…did he…?'

'The jumper survived.' One day he might be grateful he was alive, but not last night—a fact he'd managed to communicate to Samuele as he had dragged him onto the shore before collapsing himself.

The things she'd said last night, the emotions she'd revealed, would be impossible to backpedal from. The only real option that Maya could see going forward was to explain that she'd reacted that way because she was so very much in love with him. In fact, she thought almost numbly, it would be a kind of relief to have it out in the open at last.

It would also be the kiss of death to any sort of ongoing relationship other than as Mattio's parents. But that wouldn't change anything either, just speed up the inevitable, because there was no way she could hide her true feelings for him for very much longer anyway. It wasn't in her nature.

He had moved to stand beside her and she could already feel her resolve slipping as the warmth of him, the well-known scent of his body, reached out and enveloped her. She clenched her hands to hide the fact she was shaking and studied her bare feet.

'Were you on your way to get the statues or…?' She despised herself for delaying the moment of truth.

'I was on my way back, but I never actually got there,' he admitted huskily.

She looked up to see that he was right there and looking into his dark eyes made her tremble. 'I don't understand,' she whispered.

'I didn't get there because I thought you needed me. As it turned out I was wrong, and you were right—you did smash it. I am so proud of you.' He took her face between his hands. 'I am such a fool, *cara*. Even as I was turning the car around to come back to you, I wouldn't admit to myself why. I was too weak, too scared to admit that I loved you with all my heart.

'Last night when you said you wanted an open marriage I was devastated. After you sent me away I could see my whole empty *safe* life stretching out in front of me without you, and all of the things I worked so hard for, they would mean nothing if you are not in my life, by my side. I know that you wear my ring already, *cara*, but I never asked you to marry me, not really. So, Maya, will you please be my wife and I promise I will try every day of our lives together to be the husband you deserve? But only if you stop crying, *cara*, because it is killing me!' he groaned out. 'I need you to love me back, but if you can't I'll spend my life trying to persuade you!' he vowed fiercely.

Maya dashed away the tears that were running down her cheeks. 'Samuele, I love you so much it hurts—'

She didn't get any further than that because he was kissing her and she was kissing him back.

'I love you,' he murmured against her hair when they finally came up for air. 'Have I said that already?'

She pulled back and caught his hand, lifting it to her lips, loving the way his eyes immediately darkened. 'Some things can never be said too often. You have shadows under your eyes, my darling...'

'I spent a very long night realising what a fool I'd

been and it was only the fact that I knew you'd hardly had any sleep either that stopped me waking you up… How is Mattio? He sounded pretty upset last night.'

'I think it was just a touch of colic.'

'You're going to make a wonderful mother. Oh, God, Cristiano would have been such a great father. I don't know what I'm doing half the time.'

'You're a great father too, Samuele. There's nobody who will love Mattio more than you. Speaking of which, if I could love you more than I already do, I would,' she whispered huskily as she gazed at him with eyes shining with the strength of her feelings. 'If only Violetta—'

'I have already disposed of that problem—oh, not literally.' He laughed when he saw her face. 'Not that the idea is not tempting,' he added drily. 'But when she heard we were getting married and were applying for full custody, she knew she'd lost because she'd already abandoned Mattio once, so she settled for a final payment instead. Everyone, it turns out, has a price.'

'That must have cost you a lot of money.'

'Money is not important. What is the most important thing is that she has agreed to allow us to formally adopt Mattio so he will officially be our child, and he and our other children will inherit equally.'

'Are we going to have more children?'

'You like the idea?'

She nodded. 'And I will love them all equally,' she promised with damp eyes. 'If they grow up to be like their father, how could I not?'

EPILOGUE

Maya lay on her back on the day bed in the observatory and squirmed languidly, digging her bottom into the soft layer of sheepskins she lay on. 'I wondered what it would be like to make love under the stars.'

'And now you know,' Samuele said smugly. 'I arranged the meteor shower especially for you.'

'Do you think your grandfather ever did this?'

'What, make love under the stars the night before he got married?'

'Well, I quite like the idea of the continuity,' she teased.

'Then I can think of a more pleasant form of continuity. That we spend each of our anniversaries here under the stars making love, though I might not be able to pull off the meteor shower every time.'

She emerged from the long languid kiss with a smile on her lips. 'In six hours and twenty-four minutes, I will be your wife.'

Samuele had wanted it to happen immediately but Maya had insisted she wanted to get married with her family there, which had meant that they'd had to wait a few months until Beatrice's morning sickness had improved enough for her to travel. The timing was perfect: in a dual celebration that morning they had signed the final papers that made them Mattio's adoptive parents.

'Are you all right about it?' she asked.

'Having the woman I love more than life by my side for the rest of our lives? I am *very* all right, *cara*. Come here and I will show you how all right I really am.'

'You've only got six hours and twenty-three minutes left...'

He grinned. 'Six hours will do me just fine.'

* * * * *

COMING SOON!

We really hope you enjoyed reading this book.
If you're looking for more romance, be sure to
head to the shops when new books are
available on

Thursday 14th October

To see which titles are coming soon, please visit

millsandboon.co.uk/nextmonth

MILLS & BOON

THE HEART OF ROMANCE

A ROMANCE FOR EVERY READER

MODERN

Prepare to be swept off your feet by sophisticated, sexy and seductive heroes, in some of the world's most glamourous and romantic locations, where power and passion collide.

HISTORICAL

Escape with historical heroes from time gone by. Whether your passion is for wicked Regency Rakes, muscled Vikings or rugged Highlanders, awaken the romance of the past.

MEDICAL

Set your pulse racing with dedicated, delectable doctors in the high-pressure world of medicine, where emotions run high and passion, comfort and love are the best medicine.

True Love

Celebrate true love with tender stories of heartfelt romance, from the rush of falling in love to the joy a new baby can bring, and a focus on the emotional heart of a relationship.

Desire

Indulge in secrets and scandal, intense drama and plenty of sizzling hot action with powerful and passionate heroes who have it all: wealth, status, good looks…everything but the right woman.

HEROES

Experience all the excitement of a gripping thriller, with an intense romance at its heart. Resourceful, true-to-life women and strong, fearless men face danger and desire - a killer combination!

To see which titles are coming soon, please visit

millsandboon.co.uk/nextmonth

MILLS & BOON

Coming next month

UNWRAPPED BY HER ITALIAN BOSS
Michelle Smart

'I know how important this maiden voyage is, so I'll give it my best shot.'

What choice did Meredith have? Accept the last-minute secondment or lose her job. Those were the only choices. If she lost her job, what would happen to her? She'd be forced to return to England while she sought another job. Forced to live in the bleak, unhappy home of her childhood. All the joy and light she'd experienced these past three years would be gone and she'd return to grey.

'What role do you play in it all?' she asked into the silence.

He raised a thick black eyebrow.

'Are you part of Cannavaro Travel?' she queried. 'Sorry, my mind went blank when we were introduced.'

The other eyebrow rose.

A tiny dart of amusement at his expression—it was definitely the expression of someone outragedly thinking, *How can you not know who I am?*—cut through Merry's guilt and anguish. The guilt came from having spent two months praying for the forthcoming trip home to be cancelled. The anguish came from her having to be the one to do it, and with just two days' notice. The early Christmas dinner her sister-in-law had spent weeks and weeks planning had all been for nothing.

The only good thing she had to hold on to was that she hadn't clobbered an actual guest with the Christmas tree, although, judging by the cut of his suit, Cheekbones was on a huge salary, so must be high up in Cannavaro Travel, and all the signs were that he had an ego to match that salary.

She relaxed her chest with an exhale. 'Your role?' she asked again.

Dark blue eyes glittered. Tingles laced her spine and spread through her skin.

Cheekbones folded his hands together on the table. 'My role...? Think of me as the boss.'

His deep, musical accent set more tingles off in her. Crossing her legs, thankful that she'd come to her senses before mouthing off about being forced into a temporary job she'd rather eat fetid fruit than do, Merry made a mark in her notebook. 'I report to you?'

'*Si.*'

'Are you going on the train ride?'

Strong nostrils flared with distaste. 'It is no "train ride", lady.'

'You know what I mean.' She laughed. She couldn't help it. Something about his presence unnerved her. Greek god looks clashing with a glacial demeanour, warmed up again by the sexiest Italian accent she'd ever heard.

'I know what you mean and, *si*, I will be on the voyage.'

Unnerved further by the swoop of her belly at this, she made another nonsense mark in her book before looking back up at him and smiling ruefully. 'In that case, I should confess that I didn't catch your name. I'm Merry,' she added, so he wouldn't have any excuse to keep addressing her as 'lady'.

His fingers drummed on the table. 'I know your name, lady. *I* pay attention.'

For some unfathomable reason, this tickled her. 'Well done. Go to the top of the class. And your name?'

'Giovanni Cannavaro.'

All the blood in Merry's head pooled down to her feet in one strong gush.

Continue reading
UNWRAPPED BY HER ITALIAN BOSS
Michelle Smart

Available next month
www.millsandboon.co.uk

LET'S TALK

Romance

For exclusive extracts, competitions
and special offers, find us online:

 facebook.com/millsandboon

@MillsandBoon

@MillsandBoonUK

Get in touch on 01413 063232

MILLS & BOON

Desire

Indulge in secrets and scandal, intense drama and plenty of sizzling hot action with powerful and passionate heroes who have it all: wealth, status, good looks…everything but the right woman.

MILLS & BOON
MEDICAL
Pulse-Racing Passion

Set your pulse racing with dedicated, delectable doctors in the high-pressure world of medicine, where emotions run high and passion, comfort and love are the best medicine.